THE SATURDAY NIGHT SUPPER CLUB

Center Point
Large Print

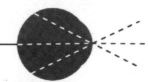

**This Large Print Book carries the
Seal of Approval of N.A.V.H.**

For Brandy and Evangeline,
my chosen sisters and fellow literary warriors.
I wouldn't have made it this far without you.

Acknowledgments

It's startling and humbling to know that a book isn't complete until it makes its way into the hands of readers. You fill in the blanks with your imagination and bring your own life story, making this book undeniably your own experience. Thank you for joining me in this story!

For those of you who have waited so patiently for this next book—I appreciate you! Your enthusiasm and encouragement is such a blessing to this writer. For those of you picking up one of my books for the first time, welcome. I apologize in advance for making you hungry. My characters cook their way through all my books, and for obvious reasons, this one is extra food-filled.

The process of getting the book to this state was certainly not a solo effort. Steve Laube, your guidance, wisdom, and practicality are more appreciated than I can express. I probably wouldn't be doing this without you. Jan Stob and Sarah Rische, thank you so much for believing in my vision. Your sharp eyes and gentle guidance helped make this book into something I can be proud of. To the rest of the team—Karen Watson, Sharon Leavitt, Mark Lane, Shaina Turner, Kristen Magnesen, Danika King, and the Tyndale sales force who work so hard to get this story into the hands of readers—it's a blessing to work with such a creative and enthusiastic group! Thank you for making me feel right at home at Tyndale.

To my friends and fellow writers-in-arms— Brandy Vallance, Evangeline Denmark, Elizabeth Younts, Laurie Tomlinson, Beth Vogt, Amber Lynn Perry, Candace Calvert, and Lori Twichell— thank you for your friendship, encouragement, and willingness to listen to endless plot points, realizations, and rants. It's a blessing to have people who really get what it's like to do this crazy job.

To my family—Rey, N, P, Mom, and Dad—I love you. I couldn't do this without all your support, both physical and emotional. You're the best.

Chapter One

Three hours into Saturday night dinner service and she was already running on fumes.

Rachel Bishop rubbed her forehead with the back of her sleeve and grabbed the newest round of tickets clattering through on the printer. Normally orders came in waves, enough time in between to take a deep breath, work the kinks out of her neck, and move on to the next pick. Tonight they had come fast and furious, one after another, tables filling as quickly as they were cleared. They were expecting two and a half turns of the dining room tonight, 205 covers.

It would be Paisley's biggest night in the six months since opening in January, and one they desperately needed. As part-owner of the restaurant, Rachel knew all too well how far away they still were from profitability. There were as many casual fine dining places in Denver as there were foodies, with new ones opening and closing every day, and she was determined that Paisley would be one of the ones that made it.

But that meant turning out every plate as perfectly as the last, no matter how slammed they were. She placed the new tickets on the board on the dining room side of the pass-through. "Ordering. Four-top. Two lobster, one spring roll, one dumpling. Followed by one roulade, two sea bass, one steak m.r."

"Yes, Chef," the staff answered in unison, setting timers, firing dishes. Over at *entremet*, Johnny had not stopped moving all night, preparing sides as fast as they came through on the duplicate printer. It was a station best suited to a young and ambitious cook, and tonight he was proving his worth.

"Johnny, how are we coming on the chard for table four?"

"Two minutes, Chef." Normally that could mean anything from one minute to five—it was an automatic response that meant *I'm working on it, so leave me alone*—but at exactly two minutes on the dot, he slid the pan of wilted and seasoned greens onto the pass in front of Rachel and got back to work in the same motion. She plated the last of table four's entrées as quickly as she could, called for service, surveyed the board.

A muffled oath from her left drew her attention. She looked up as her sauté cook, Gabrielle, dumped burnt bass straight into the trash can.

"Doing okay, Gabs?"

"Yes, Chef. Four minutes out on the bass for nineteen."

Rachel rubbed her forehead with the back of her sleeve again, rearranged some tickets, called for the grill to hold the steak. On slow nights, she liked to work the line while her sous-chef,

Andrew, practiced his plating, but tonight it was all she could do to expedite the orders and keep things running smoothly.

"Rachel."

She jerked her head up at the familiar male voice and found herself looking at Daniel Kearn, one of her two business partners. She wasn't a short woman, but he towered above even her. Her gut twisted, a niggling warning of trouble that had never steered her wrong.

"Hey, Dan," she said cautiously, her attention going straight back to her work. "What's up?"

"Can I talk to you for a minute?"

"Now's not a great time." Dan might be the rarest of breeds these days—a restaurateur who wasn't a chef—but considering he owned four other restaurants, he should be able to recognize when they were in the weeds. The energy level in the kitchen right now hovered somewhere between high tension and barely restrained panic.

"Carlton Espy is here."

Rachel dropped her spoon and bit her lip to prevent any unflattering words from slipping out. "Here? Now? Where is he?" She turned and squinted into the dim expanse of the dining room, looking for the familiar comb-over and self-satisfied smirk of the city's most hated food critic.

"No, he left. Stopped by my table before he went and told me to tell you, 'You're welcome.' Does that make any sense to you?"

"Not unless he considers questioning both my cooking and my professional ethics a favor." She looked back at the tickets and then called, "Picking up nine, fourteen!"

"You really need to issue a statement to the press."

She'd already forgotten Dan was there. One by one, pans made their way to the pass beneath the heat lamps and she began swiftly plating the orders for the pair of four-tops. "I'm not going to dignify that troll with a response."

"Rachel—"

"Can we talk about this later? I'm busy."

She barely noticed when he slipped out of the kitchen, concentrating on getting table nine to one of the back waiters, then table fourteen. For a few blissful moments, the printer was quiet and all the current tickets were several minutes out. She took a deep breath, the only sounds around her the clatter of pans, the hiss of cooking food, the ever-present hum of the vent hoods. After five hours in the heart of the house, they vibrated in her bones, through her blood, the bass notes to the kitchen's symphony.

Her peace was short-lived. Carlton Espy had been here, the troll. Of all the legitimate restaurant reviewers in Denver, a scale on which he could barely register, he was both the most controversial and the least likable. Most people called him the Howard Stern of food writing with his crass, but apparently entertaining, take on the food, the staff, and the diners. Rachel supposed she should be happy that he'd only questioned her James Beard Award rather than criticizing the looks and the sexual orientation of every member of her staff, as he'd done with another local restaurant last week.

The thing Dan didn't seem to understand was that slights and backhanded compliments from critics came with the territory. Some seemed surprised that a pretty woman could actually cook; others criticized her for being unfriendly because she didn't want to capitalize on her looks and her gender to promote her restaurant. She had never met a woman in this business who wanted to be identified as "the best female chef in the city." Either your food was worthy of note or it wasn't. The chromosomal makeup of the person putting it on the plate was irrelevant. End of story. Tell that to channel seven.

As the clock ticked past nine, the orders started to slow down and they finally dug themselves out of the hole they'd been in since seven o'clock. The post-theater crowds were coming in now, packing the bar on the far side of the room, a few groups on the main floor who ordered wine, appetizers, desserts. The last pick left the kitchen at a quarter past eleven, and Rachel let her head fall forward for a second before she looked out at her staff with a grin. "Good job, everyone. Shut it down."

Ovens, grills, and burners were switched off. Leftover *mise en place* was transferred to the walk-ins for tomorrow morning. Each station got scrubbed and disinfected with the careless precision of people who had done this every night of their adult lives, the last chore standing between them and freedom. She had no illusions about where they were headed next, exactly where she would have been headed as a young cook—out to the bars to drain the adrenaline from their systems, then home to catch precious little sleep before they showed up early for brunch service tomorrow. By contrast, Rachel's only plans were her soft bed, a cup of hot tea, and a rerun on Netflix until she fell into an exhausted stupor. At work, she might feel as energetic as she had as a nineteen-year-old line cook, but the minute she stumbled out of the restaurant, her years on the planet seemed to double.

Rachel changed out of her whites into jeans and a sweatshirt in her office, only to run into Gabrielle in the back corridor.

"Can I talk to you for a minute, Chef?"

Rachel's radar immediately picked up the nervousness beneath the woman's usual brusque demeanor. Changed out of her work clothes and into a soft blue T-shirt that made her red hair look even fierier, Gabby suddenly seemed very young and insecure, even though she was several years older than Rachel.

"Of course. Do you want to come in?" Rachel gestured to the open door of her office.

"No, um, that's okay. I wanted to let you know . . . before someone figures it out and tells you." Gabby took a deep breath and squared her shoulders. "I'm pregnant."

Rachel stared at the woman, sure her heart froze for a split second. "Pregnant?"

"Four months." Gabby hurried on, "I won't let it interfere with my work, I swear. But at some point . . ."

"You're going to need to take maternity leave." In an office setting, that was hard enough, but in a restaurant kitchen, where there were a limited number of cooks to fill in and new additions disrupted the flow they'd established, it was far more complicated.

Gabby nodded.

"We'll figure it out," Rachel said finally. "And congratulations. You're going to make a wonderful mother. I bet Luke is thrilled."

Gabby's words rushed out in relief. "He is."

"Now go get some sleep." Rachel's instincts said to give her a hug, congratulate her again, but that damaged the level of authority she needed to maintain, made it harder to demand the best from Gabby when she should probably be focusing more on her baby than her job. Instead, Rachel settled for a squeeze of her shoulder.

Andrew was the last to head for the back

hallway, leaving Rachel alone in the kitchen to survey her domain. Once again, it gleamed with stainless-steel sterility, silent without the drone of vents and whoosh of burners. It should probably bother her more that she had no one to go home to, no one waiting on the other side of the door. But Rachel had known what she was giving up when she set off down this career path, knew the choice was even starker for female chefs who had to decide between running their own kitchens and having a family. Most days, it was more than a fair trade. She'd promised herself long ago she wouldn't let any man stand between her and her dreams.

Camille, Paisley's front-of-house manager, slipped into the kitchen quietly, somehow looking as fresh and put together as she had at the beginning of the night. "Ana's waiting for you at the bar. I'm going to go now unless you need me."

"No, go ahead. Good work as always."

"Thanks, Chef. See you tomorrow."

Rachel pretended not to notice Camille slip out with Andrew, their arms going around each other the minute they hit the back door. The food service industry was incestuous, as it must be—civilians didn't tend to put up with the long hours, late nights, and always-on mentality. There had been plenty of hookups in her kitchen among waitstaff and cooks in various and constantly changing combinations, but they never involved Rachel. On some points at least, she was still a traditionalist—one-night stands and casual affairs held no appeal. Besides, she was an owner and the chef, the big boss. Getting involved with anyone on her staff would be the quickest way to compromise her authority.

Rachel pushed around the post to the dining room and crossed the empty space to the bar. A pretty Filipina sat there, nursing a drink and chatting with the bartender, Luis.

"Ana! What are you doing here? Did Dan call you?"

Ana greeted Rachel with a one-armed hug. "I worked late and thought I'd drop by to say hi. Luis said it was a good night."

"Very good night: 215."

Ana's eyebrows lifted. "That's great, Rachel. Way to go. I'm not going to say I told you so, but . . ."

"Yeah, yeah, you told me so." Rachel grinned at her longtime friend. Analyn Sanchez had been one of her staunchest supporters when she'd decided to open a restaurant with two Denver industry veterans, even though it meant leaving the lucrative, high-profile executive chef job that had won her a coveted James Beard Award. And she had to give part of the credit to the woman next to her, who had agreed to take on Paisley as a client of the publicity firm for which she worked, even though the restaurant was small potatoes compared to her usual clients.

Luis wiped down an already-clean bar top for the third time. "You want anything, Chef?"

"No, thank you. You can go. I'll see you on Tuesday."

"Thank you, Chef." Luis put away his rag, grabbed his cell phone from beneath the bar, and quickly slipped out from behind his station. Not before one last surreptitious look at Ana, Rachel noticed.

"Do I need to tell him to stop hitting on you?"

"Nah, he's harmless. So, Rachel . . ."

Once more that gut instinct fired away, flooding her with dread. "You're not here for a social visit."

Ana shook her head. "Have you seen the article yet?"

"The Carlton Espy review? Who hasn't? Can you believe the guy had the nerve to come in here tonight and say, 'You're welcome'? As if he'd done me some huge favor?"

Ana's expression flickered a degree before settling back into an unreadable mask.

Uh-oh.

"What is it? You're not talking about the review, are you?"

Ana reached into her leather tote and pulled out a tablet, then switched it on before passing it to Rachel.

Rachel blinked, confused by the header on the web page. "The *New Yorker*? What does this have to do with me?" The title of the piece, an essay by a man named Alexander Kanin, was "The Uncivil War."

"Just read it."

She began to skim the article, the growing knot in her stomach preventing her from enjoying what was actually a very well-written piece. The writer talked about how social media had destroyed civility and social graces, not only online but in person; how marketing and publicity had given an always-available impression of public figures, as if their mere existence gave consumers the right to full access to their lives. Essentially, nothing was sacred or private or off-limits. He started by citing the cruel remarks made on CNN about the mentally disabled child of an actress-activist, and then the story of a novelist who had committed suicide after being bullied relentlessly on Twitter. And then she got to the part that nearly made her heart stop.

> Nowhere is this inherent cruelty more apparent than with women succeeding in male-dominated worlds like auto racing and cooking. The recent review of an award-winning Denver chef suggesting that she had traded sexual favors in return for industry acclaim reveals that there

no longer needs to be any truth in the speculations, only a cutting sense of humor and an eager tribe of consumers waiting for their next target. When the mere act of cooking good food or giving birth to an "imperfect" child or daring to create controversial art becomes an invitation to character assassination, we have to accept that we have become a deeply flawed and morally bankrupt society. The new fascism does not come from the government, but from the self-policing nature of the mob—a mob that demands all conform or suffer the consequences.

Rachel set the tablet down carefully, her pounding pulse leaving a watery ocean sound in her ears and blurring her vision. "This is bad."

"He didn't mention you by name," Ana said. "And he *was* defending you. You have to appreciate a guy who would call Espy out on his disgusting sexism."

Rachel pressed a hand to her forehead, which now felt feverish. "Anyone with a couple of free minutes and a basic understanding of Google could figure out who he's talking about." A sick sense of certainty washed over her. "Espy knows it, too. Without this article, his review would have died a natural death. He should have been thanking *me*."

Cautiously, Ana took back her tablet. "I'm hoping people will overlook the details based on the message, but just in case, you should inform your staff to direct media requests to me."

"Media." Rachel covered her face with her hands, as if that could do something to stave off the flood that was to come.

"Take a deep breath," Ana said, her no-nonsense tone firmly in place. "This could be a good thing. You've told me about the difficulty women have in this business, the kind of harassment you've put up with to get here. Maybe this is your chance to speak out against it. You'd certainly get wider attention for the restaurant, not that it looks like you're having any trouble filling seats."

Rachel dropped her head into her folded arms. What Ana said was right. It would be publicity. But despite the old saying, it wasn't the right kind of publicity. She wanted attention for her food, not for her personal beliefs. To give this any kind of attention would be a distraction. And worst of all, it would make her a hypocrite. Playing the gender card for any reason—even a well-meaning one—went against everything she stood for.

"No," she said finally, lifting her head. "I won't. I'll turn down all the interviews with 'no comment' and get back to doing what I do best. Cooking."

"I thought you'd say that. I'll issue a statement

to that effect. Just be prepared. Reporters can be relentless when they smell an interesting story." Ana hopped off the stool. "I'm beat. Call me if you need me."

"I will." She hugged Ana and watched her friend stride out the door, five-inch heels clicking smartly on the dining room's polished concrete floors. Rachel didn't move from her perch at the bar, though she was glad that Luis was already gone for the night. He would take one look at her and pronounce her in desperate need of a drink. The last thing she needed to do was send herself down that unwitting spiral again.

Instead, she would head to her office in the back as she always did, look over the pars that Andrew had calculated for her that morning, and pay the stack of invoices waiting in her in-box. Work was always the medicine for what ailed her, even if she was hoping that for once, her gut feeling was wrong.

Because right now, her gut told her everything was about to go sideways.

Chapter Two

Morning came far too soon. Rachel sat in the driver's seat of her Toyota SUV, staring at the back door of her restaurant and summoning up the energy to climb out of the car.

She was getting old.

That was the only explanation for how she felt now, as sore and aching as if she'd been run over by a bus. Back in the day, she'd not only been able to work a fourteen-hour double shift, but she'd proceeded to party with the rest of the kitchen staff until the wee hours, catch a couple hours of sleep on someone's sofa or in her car, and do the whole thing again the next day.

Clearly, her body had gotten the memo that she'd just turned thirty and thrown the switch.

"Come on, Rachel. Woman up." At seven o'clock, she was already the last person in, the rest of the crew arriving early to prep for Sunday brunch, which started at ten thirty. Since they didn't take reservations on Sunday, the line would start forming outside the front door by nine and not stop until midafternoon.

If she were honest with herself, Sundays were the only part of her old life that she missed. Each Sunday until she turned eleven, she and her mom would dress up to attend service at their little white church in Hartford, munching donut holes from the bakery on the way and trying not to get powdered sugar on their clothes. She'd sit beside her mother in the pew and listen in rapt attention to the bearded pastor, wondering if that's what Jesus had looked like. Afterwards, they'd splurge on lunch and browse the expensive boutiques downtown, even if they couldn't afford to buy anything. It had truly been a day of rest, and those days together were virtually the only memories she still cherished of her childhood.

But those Sundays had ended long before she started cooking, and now a full day to herself felt like a distant dream. Rachel wrenched herself from her recollections and dragged her aching body from the car, then stumbled to the back door, where she could already hear sizzles and clatters coming from the hot line.

She shoved her sunglasses onto the top of her head and stopped first at the pastry section, where her baker and best friend, Melody Johansson, was hard at work.

"Morning," Rachel said quietly. "Everything good?"

Melody glanced up quickly from the sticky buns she was glazing, then did a double take. "You look awful."

"Thanks. I needed that."

Melody laughed. "Another hard night here?"

"Is there any other kind?" Rachel squeezed

Melody's shoulder before moving on to the prep cooks, who were already hard at work at the rear stations. She paused at the walk-ins, where Andrew was going over the stock with the clipboard. "Where's Gabby?"

Andrew looked up, his expression answering before his words. "She hasn't shown up."

"Call her and find out what's going on. And then meet me in my office."

He gave a respectful nod. "Yes, Chef."

She retraced her steps to the office, her haven and a monument to her type-A nature. In every kitchen she'd worked, the chef's space was a wreck, a jumble of papers and coats and books. Hers was almost sterile in its cleanliness, a collection of cookbooks and kitchen manuals lined up behind her on the wood shelves, the paperwork sorted neatly into a multitiered in-box, the labels on the containers in the drink cooler all facing the same way. The closet containing the staff's coats was neatly organized, each cook's garments lined up on rods between retail rack tags with their names, beside it a bin for dirty ones to be picked up by the uniform service. A little spot of orderliness in the chaos, yes, but it also set an example for her staff. She'd never be able to lecture a cook on working clean if her own space weren't pristine.

Rachel pulled a Gatorade from the mini-fridge by the door and twisted off the cap as she collapsed into the desk chair. Half a bottle later, she was feeling a bit more like herself. Definitely too old for these hours. She'd taken the lack of sleep and long days in stride when she hired on to her first fine-dining restaurant in New York, wore them as a badge of courage, even. Now, she wondered if she was just taking years off her life. And to think as a lowly line cook, she'd thought the executive chef had the cushiest job in the kitchen.

At least she had a couple of minutes to herself before the madness set in. Rachel fished a thick green journal from her bag and opened it to the frayed ribbon bookmark.

And sat, pen poised above the page, mind completely blank. It usually wasn't this difficult to think of something.

Finally, she scrawled beneath today's date: *Sunny mornings, even when I don't have long to enjoy them.*

Melody slipped through the door and set a cup in front of her. "Double Americano."

"Bless you." Rachel lifted the cup, ignoring the singe of hot liquid on her tongue, and enjoyed the warm trail it created down her throat and chest. Impulsively, she jotted *Strong coffee* on the next line, then snapped the book shut. "What's that?"

Melody set a plate in front of her. "Chocolate-almond brioche."

"New addition?"

"Experiment." Melody settled into a chair across from her as Rachel tackled the bun.

Like everything else the baker did, it was nothing short of amazing. Rather than being a cloying, overly sweet morning bun, the chocolate was subtle and bitter, laced with almond and a hint of espresso. Sophisticated. "It's excellent. How many do you have?"

"Six dozen."

"Okay, let's do it. The early birds get lucky today." Rachel dove back into the bun, tearing pieces off with her fingers and feeling a little better with every bite. While Melody technically reported to her, Rachel had given her carte blanche with the dessert menu and breakfast pastries, and she never disappointed. That was part of what made the brunch so popular at Paisley—the anticipation of what might be in the baked goods assortments placed at the center of each table. Rachel had done a *prix fixe* menu for that very reason—it limited the number of cooked-to-order items on the menu while allowing for some creativity, not to mention the fact it practically guaranteed a certain level of revenue for the week.

"Was Carlos in when you got here?" she asked when she finally felt coherent enough to talk.

"Yes. Already hard at work."

"Good. My Spanish must be getting better." Carlos was one of the prep cooks—a machine really, preternaturally fast with a knife—but he'd gotten a little lax on his start times. "I'm never sure if he's understanding me or not."

"I think Carlos chooses to understand what he wants to understand," Melody said. "Language barrier notwithstanding, he's probably the smartest guy in the kitchen."

No doubt. He worked the most hours, made the most money, and still had his evenings free to spend with his family, while the rest of them were toiling away in a stainless-steel box. "So, go ahead and ask. I know Ana texted you."

"Am I that transparent?" Melody laughed, then sobered. "What are you going to do? Are you going to give a statement?"

"I already told Dan I have nothing to say. Espy or this Kanin guy, it's the same response. Let someone else be the spokeswoman against sexism in the food service industry. I've got too much else to worry about."

Melody rose. "Okay. If that's how you want to play it, I'm behind you."

"You don't agree?"

"It doesn't matter if I agree or not. This is your restaurant. I just don't like the idea of someone else writing your narrative for you."

Rachel smiled. Melody did a good job of playing the laid-back bohemian baker, but every once in a while, she let her thorough and unconventional education slip out. "That's exactly why

I'm not responding. Because it's *my* narrative, and this is a story I refuse to be a part of. Let them criticize my food. The rest is none of their business."

Fortified by Melody's coffee and brioche, Rachel refocused on the specials menu, which was really two additional items derived from the leftover product in the walk-ins. A salmon-cake Benedict went on in addition to the standard crab cakes, and Tex-Mex steak breakfast tacos would use up the last of the New York strip. Done. She passed off the instructions to Andrew, who would be responsible for the specials prep; devised the limited cocktail menu, which would be handled by *garde manger* in the absence of a bartender; and changed into her whites for the day. Only then did she notice the flashing blue light on her cell phone that indicated a text message.

From Gabby. On the way to the hospital. Afraid I might be miscarrying again. Please pray.

The words hit her like a brick to the chest. *Again?* Gabby and her husband had been married for twelve years, and Rachel had assumed that they'd decided not to have children. But maybe it was more that they hadn't been able to have children. Rachel sent a prayer heavenward for Gabby's safety and that of her unborn child. That was all she had time for. It was now five minutes after ten, too late to call for a fill-in. She'd have to work the line after all. At least it would keep her from acknowledging the awful, shameful part of herself that hoped maybe she wasn't going to lose one of her best cooks as she'd thought.

Today was going to be a test of her experience, though, the combination of her work hangover and the caffeine stretching her nerves as thin as phyllo dough. Morning was different than dinner, where orders were expedited in courses. Brunch required everything to be cooked *à la minute* as it came in. Next to Andrew, who handled the eggs, Gabby had the hardest station for brunch, the rest of the protein.

Rachel put on her game face as she strode onto the hot line, rubbing her hands together. "All right, boys. Ready to get rolled?"

"Yes, Chef," came the chorus of answers, not without a ring of excitement. She shook her head in amusement, but even she felt the rush of adrenaline, the thrill of anticipation like a drug in her veins. She could complain all she wanted, but some part of her still lived for the brutal challenge of working the line.

One ticket followed another, the heat from the griddle blasting her like an Arabian desert and turning her skin hot and tight. The Benedicts went fast, followed by the steak tacos, so those were off her back, leaving the regular breakfast meats and the crab cakes to deal with. She took advantage of a brief lull while her bacon and ham were frying to grab another bottle of Gatorade from the lowboy and step away long enough to guzzle it in one gulp before she was back at her station.

And then it was over. When the last plate went out at three minutes after two, Rachel figured they had done almost as many covers as the night before. That would make it a record Sunday for receipts.

"I need you to supervise the close," she murmured to Andrew before she left the kitchen in favor of the cool quiet of her office.

Away from the line, the last dregs of adrenaline drained from her body, leaving only a bone-deep ache, that flu-coming-on feeling that had nothing to do with a virus. It was the natural result of pushing her body too long with too little sleep and nourishment. But she had no choice. She had the restaurant to think about, dozens of employees who depended on her, a steady clientele of hungry guests. Not to mention the fact that this was her dream. She'd sacrificed everything to get here, and this was part of how her debts were being called in.

She fished her cell phone from her pocket and checked the messages—none—before tapping out a reply to Gabby: Any news?

By the time she'd changed into her street clothes, there was a reply: Baby is ok for now. I think I'm going to be on bed rest. I'm so sorry. Call you when I have details.

Rachel swallowed down the twin swells of relief and terror. Bed rest meant that Gabby had a chance of having a healthy baby. It also meant she would not be coming back.

She squeezed her eyes shut against a prick of tears born of pure exhaustion, grabbed her tote bag, and headed straight from the restaurant without saying good-bye.

Directly into a microphone.

"Rachel Bishop? Would you care to make a statement?"

Rachel squinted into the sunshine and shoved on her sunglasses so she could make out the overly made-up features of a woman shoving a microphone the size of a bazooka in her face. She recognized her, vaguely. She was some field reporter for channel nine. Or was it twenty-four? Was there a channel twenty-four in Denver? Rachel was so wiped out she couldn't remember.

"Make a statement about what?"

"About the vicious attack on your integrity from Carlton Espy and the attention it received from the *New Yorker*. Did you know that Espy's review has now gotten over three hundred thousand hits?"

Three hundred thousand? How was that even possible? That was half the population of Denver. She blinked, momentarily stunned. She should simply tell the reporter that her publicist would issue a statement, but exhaustion had brought down her filter. "I don't even understand how this is news."

"You don't think the topic of sexism in the workplace is an important one to women?"

"I think people need to stop taking Internet trolls like Carlton Espy seriously. If I were a more litigious person, I would sue him for libel."

It was the wrong thing to say. The reporter perked up. "Are you going to sue him for libel?"

Rachel put her head down and headed for her car, hoping the reporter would take the hint. This time her only answer should be "no comment."

"Why do you think there are so few female chefs? Is it because women are ill-suited for the profession?"

Rachel whirled, her jaw dropping. "I don't know. I haven't interviewed every woman who has decided not to be a professional cook. Male or female, if they don't have the dedication and skills to succeed, they shouldn't be there. The guest doesn't care if it's a man or a woman cooking their food; they only care that it tastes good."

There. Let them air that little sound bite. Rachel unlocked her car door, plopped into the driver's seat, and backed into the alley as quickly as she could manage, only marginally concerned with not hitting the cameraman who was following her car's progress with his camera. Seriously, how was this even news? Was the media so low on shootings and natural disasters that they had to resort to talking to chefs about topics no one really cared about?

She drove home in an exhaustion-laced stupor, almost surprised that she managed it safely, then parked on the street in front of her house, a charming but run-down Victorian condo conversion in the Wyman Historic District. Routine took her up the paved walkway to the lower unit, where she let herself into the sparsely decorated space, walked straight to the bedroom, and fell asleep with her shoes on before her face even hit her pillow.

Chapter Three

There was nothing like hanging off the side of a sheer rock face in high winds to put life into perspective.

To be truthful, Alex Kanin's only perspective right now was on how much it would hurt if he fell. He surveyed the expanse of red rock above him, looking for the handhold he knew to be there, assuming he'd followed the proper route up the side. He forced himself to relax his grip and save the strength in his fingers and forearms for the next move, however contrary to instinct it was when facing one's own mortality.

"Enough with the histrionics," he muttered. He was clipped in to a bolt five feet below him. The worst the fall would do is give him a jolt through the climbing harness and some bruises as he banged into the rock. Assuming he didn't die of a heart attack first.

"You thinking about building a summer home up there?"

The shout drifted up to him from his friend and climbing instructor, Bryan Shaw, then dissipated on the wind. Easy for him to say. Bryan was one of the top-ranked technical climbers in the country, whereas Alex had only been climbing for three years. This little 5.10-rated route in

Colorado's Castlewood Canyon State Park might be easy for Bryan, but to Alex it might as well be Everest.

The taunting must have worked, though, because there was his next hold, a full foot out of his reach. A dyno. Alex gritted his teeth and coiled his muscles in preparation for the leap. For one sickening moment, he hung in midair, his hands and feet free of the rock face. And then his chalked fingers found the hold at the deadpoint, the zero-gravity pivot between jumping and falling. His hands, forearms, and biceps strained against the downward pull of his body weight while he felt for his foothold and secured himself on the rock.

Bryan whooped triumphantly from below, and Alex laughed aloud. Now it was clear climbing to the top. Energy flooded his body as he scrambled up the last ten feet and levered himself over the edge. He clipped in to the top anchor and then flipped himself into a sitting position, swinging his legs over the forty-foot drop below.

"Yeah!" Bryan pumped his fist in the air, and Alex laughed at his friend's enthusiasm. "Now you have to get back down!"

"Shut up!" he yelled back. "Let me enjoy this for a minute!"

Alex flexed his hands and rolled the kinks free from his neck, the knots a sure sign he'd been climbing tense. Only then did he notice the raw patches on his fingertips. That would make typing difficult tomorrow, but it was worth it. This route was his hardest climb to date, something he'd been too chicken to try until Bryan forced his hand. And now he couldn't wait to do it again.

"All right. On belay?"

"Belay on."

"Climbing." He moved himself off the edge of the rock, ignoring the quiver of nerves as he got his hands and feet into position. He could have rappelled or walked back around, but Bryan insisted he be as comfortable with downclimbing as he was with the ascent. It was a slow process of finding his footholds and pausing to remove his quickdraws—the webbing-linked carabiners—from the permanent bolts.

When his feet finally hit the solid ground and he called off belay, Bryan greeted him with a hard, affectionate slap on the back. "Nicely done. I was sure you were going to bail for a second."

"I almost did. I thought I was looking for a crimp and started doubting my route."

"Now that you've led a 5.11d successfully, are you ready to try some easy multi-pitch climbs with me in California this fall?"

Alex laughed. That easy multi-pitch climb was a three-day ascent up Yosemite's Half Dome. "Not remotely. Wait, what do you mean 5.11d?"

"I might have understated the difficulty of this one," Bryan said. "But you were ready."

Alex shook his head at his friend. He'd known Bryan since their high school days, and back then he'd already been a world-class junior climber. It was only when Alex started feeling the toll the writing career took on his body that he took Bryan up on his offer of lessons. He should have known he'd be pushing him every step of the way.

"I blame the fact you made it look easy," Alex said. "I don't think I have one more in me today, though."

"I need to go anyway. I promised my parents I'd make an appearance at their thing tonight."

The "thing" was more than likely a fund-raiser or a party that rivaled the White House Correspondents' Dinner, but Bryan tended to regard the black-tie affairs like Alex would a potluck. The side effect of being the black sheep of a wealthy family, he guessed, or maybe his friend's way of showing his gratitude that his father hadn't disowned him when he became a professional climber rather than following in the family's real estate business.

"Who are you bringing?" Alex began to remove the chalk bag and quickdraws that hung from his climbing harness.

"Kirsten."

"Which one is she? The blonde?"

"They're all blonde. She's the yoga instructor. I fully expect her to ask my mom if she's ever tried a juice cleanse before the night is up."

Alex chuckled. So maybe Bryan didn't toe the line completely. "Ah, the vegan health nut. Think your mom will go for it?"

"I think there's more chance of my mom getting Kirsten to eat meat than doing anything remotely like a cleanse." He shrugged. "It makes for good entertainment on a boring night. Don't suppose you'd like to drop by?"

"Not with that kind of resounding endorsement. Besides, they didn't invite me."

"You know you're like family. You don't need an invitation."

That was true. Maybe he'd dust off the tuxedo and drop in. The evening might be slow, but the food would no doubt be amazing. He'd been to more than one of those events in high school, during the long periods he'd lived in one of the Shaws' spare rooms while his professor parents were off at a conference or doing a research sabbatical in Europe. Bryan's dad and mom had never balked at Alex's presence. They'd simply put another plate at the table, signed his permission slips, and bought him new school clothes when he'd outgrown his own but run out of the money his parents left in his account.

"If I don't show up, tell your dad I'm in for the fall gala."

"I will." They hoisted their gear and started up the far gentler ascent toward the parking lot where they'd left their cars. With every step,

Alex's rubbery legs complained even more. He'd be feeling this climb for days. He'd thought he was in pretty good condition, but he was going to have to add another weight day into his workout schedule. Bryan seemed determined to make a respectable traditional climber out of him, even though Alex had barely graduated from artificial terrain at the gym.

The clouds were beginning to mound overhead when they reached the parking lot, and the first big drops of rain spattered down around them, raising the musty smell of damp concrete. In the distance, thunder rumbled.

"Tuesday at Red Rocks?" Bryan asked.

"I'll be there. We're running the steps first?"

"You know it." They heaved their gear into the back of their cars, then slammed the trunks. Alex slipped into the driver's seat as the clouds let loose.

Rain drummed on the roof of the car and poured down the window. They were out of the flash flood range now, but had they been a few minutes later, Alex would have been stranded on the slab while Bryan bolted for safety. The gullies and ravines that made up the park's climbing areas could turn into deadly rivers in mere minutes.

With visibility so bad, he had no choice but to wait it out. He reached for the cell phone he'd left in his cup holder and saw the blinking green light that indicated messages.

The first one was from his literary agent, Christine. "Alex, have you been on Twitter? Call me as soon as you get this."

The next three were from Christine as well, various permutations of the first. What exactly had happened to cause the usually sanguine agent to turn so twitchy?

He tried to open his Twitter app, but the state park was located in a sketchy cell zone south of Denver, so all he got were connection-error messages. Might as well hear it directly from Christine then. He dialed her number, and after a couple of seconds of deciding whether to connect or not, the call rang through.

"Christine?"

"Where have you been? I've been calling you all morning!"

Alex blinked. She was nothing if not brusque and businesslike; this note of excitement in her voice was completely foreign. "I was climbing. I left my phone in the car."

She didn't even acknowledge the comment. "Have you seen Twitter?"

"I don't have data out here."

"It went viral."

"What went viral?" By the sound of her voice, he was thinking a contagious disease.

"Your new essay for the *New Yorker*. It went up online last night and it's already been shared thousands of times."

"What?" Alex leaned back against the seat of the car. This particular piece had been written as exclusive online content, not even to be printed in the magazine. He'd figured no one would bother reading it.

"It hit a nerve. People are sharing it everywhere, talking about what's wrong with our social media society. I've got to tell you, Alex, I thought you were procrastinating, but you really played this one right."

"I didn't—" He broke off. There was no point in arguing the issue. He hadn't set out to write a viral post—as if one could even predict what would make a piece take off. In fact, it had been little more than a veiled rant, coming off some unkind, if rather ironic, reviews of his book, *Mis-Connected*, a volume of essays about his traditional upbringing in the digital age. "What does this mean?"

"Well, for one, it means that the e-book is trending at number thirty right now. You're outselling David Sedaris in memoir at the moment." Christine paused. "We have to capitalize on this, Alex. Your publisher is being flooded with interview requests. You need to do as many as you can. This is your chance."

To salvage his career as an essayist, she meant. Interviews meant more exposure, which meant more book sales. He knew how this went. Milk the publicity for all it was worth, use that to get another book deal while the publisher was still excited about him.

Show up all the critics who had used him and his absurdly large advance as an example of what was wrong with legacy publishing today.

"Okay. I'll call Stephen this afternoon and see what they have for me."

"Good. Good. And I'll want a new proposal as soon as you can have it done. Don't let this one slip away, Alex."

"I'll keep you posted." Alex clicked off the line and sat there for a moment, stunned. He'd pretty much written off *Mis-Connected* as a failed experiment, and as recently as this morning, he'd been sure the book he was supposed to be writing a proposal for would never see the light of day. He made a pretty good living as a freelancer, so that had seemed like a smarter way to spend his time. Until now.

The rain passed almost as quickly as it had come, decreasing to a halfhearted spatter, so he put his car into gear and made the slow, winding drive out of the park onto the rural highway. As soon as he neared the town of Parker, the little icon indicating a data connection blinked to life on his phone's status bar, and he pulled into the first gas station he saw. He had to resist the urge to check his book's online sales rankings, instead opening Twitter to see his mentions.

Tweet after tweet with comments like:

This!

Couldn't have said it better myself.

Finally, a guy who gets it.

Why isn't this guy married? He's totally hot.

Okay, so that last one made him smile a little wider.

And then some unexpected ones:

Anyone know who this chef is?

Has to be Rachel Bishop.

Why hasn't anyone called out @CarltonEspy?

Some of them linked back to the restaurant review that had helped spur this article in the first place, a few of them linking to Rachel Bishop's restaurant or her page on the James Beard Award website.

The first hint of disquiet rippled over Alex's skin. He'd tried to be judicious about the details he'd used, not wanting to send more people to read the disgusting reviews that Espy churned out. But he'd underestimated the cross section of readers who would have seen that review and read the *New Yorker*, or who at least spent too much time on Twitter. Still, it had to be a good thing, right? It called attention to the unfairly harsh criticism leveled at people in creative careers, specifically women. This was the kind of article you wanted to go viral, compared to, say, a photo essay on Kim Kardashian's butt.

He let out a long breath while he processed the news, then tossed the phone onto the seat next to him and stepped out of his car, headed for the gas station's mini-mart. He'd call Stephen, the publicist who had handled *Mis-Connected* and who incidentally had stopped taking his calls nearly three months ago. But first, coffee. He had a feeling he was going to need it.

Thirty minutes later, reviewing the notes spread across his desk, Alex knew he would need more than coffee to get through the coming weeks. The promotion schedule Stephen had set up for him would require a continuous caffeine IV. Print, radio, maybe even some television. The in-house publicist had apparently been instructed to go big while the buzz was still strong enough to catch the attention of segment producers.

He should be excited. He was getting a second chance that few writers did—but those were the books that went on to hit bestseller lists, and his publisher knew it. Christine had to be very specific that he was to do everything and anything they asked of him while she began talking to his editors about a second book.

So why did he feel like he'd done something terrible?

It was because he'd inadvertently given those trolls a national stage, which was exactly what they wanted. And he was profiting from it. The whole thing made him feel like an ambulance chaser.

He made his decision before he realized he

was even considering it, his fingers closing on the plastic-shrouded hanger that held his tuxedo. Mitchell Shaw might be his best friend's father, but he'd also been something like a mentor. In the time Alex had known the family, Mitchell's company had gone from a modest commercial developer to a major player in Denver's urbanization movement, all without losing the guiding principles and morals that had made him a success. If anyone could help him put his uneasiness to rest, it would be Mitchell Shaw.

Alex showered and shaved and then pulled on his formal wear, praying it still fit. He spent most of his time in sweatpants and T-shirts these days; ever since he and Victoria had broken up, there was little need for a tux. To his relief, it fit well enough to wear, even if the trousers' waist was a little loose and the jacket a bit snug across the shoulders, a result of his expanded climbing routine.

Bryan hadn't mentioned what time the event started, but seven was a safe bet, so Alex timed it to pull into the driveway of the Shaws' Capitol Hill mansion a few minutes past. He'd once been intimidated by this hulking 1920s brick edifice, so far removed from his family's modest bungalow in its equally modest east side neighborhood. The Shaws might as well have been the Waynes of Gotham to his thirteen-year-old self. Only later did he learn Mitchell and Kathy had rescued the historic home from demolition during the new wave of conservationism in Denver.

Alex turned over his Subaru to one of the uniformed valets on the large circular driveway, straightened his tuxedo jacket, and strode up the brick steps of the home into the paneled front foyer, which glittered with light from the crystal chandeliers and buzzed with conversation. Dozens of guests milled around with glasses of champagne or cocktails in hand, the men garbed in tuxedos and the women in opera-worthy evening gowns.

He moved into the main parlor and then the dining room, looking for Mitchell or Kathy among the crush of guests. He finally found them in the library toward the back of the house, speaking with a distinguished-looking older couple. Alex took a flute of champagne so he had something to do besides stand awkwardly at the edge of the room and wait to be acknowledged. Finally, Mitchell looked his direction, his eyebrows rising for a moment before he lifted a hand and waved him over.

"What a surprise!" Mitchell held out his hand, which Alex shook enthusiastically. Kathy greeted him with a hug and a kiss on the cheek.

"I'm so glad you came," she said. "Do you know Roberto and Carol Veracruz?"

Alex shifted so he could shake the hands of the couple to whom they'd been talking, as Kathy went on. "Alex is a close friend of our son, Bryan. He's a critically acclaimed essayist and writes for the *New Yorker*, among other publications."

Carol's eyebrows lifted. "How interesting," she said, and did legitimately seem interested. "I'll have to look you up."

Alex smiled politely and exchanged a couple words of small talk before the Veracruzes wandered off to chat with someone else. Now that they were alone in the conversation, Kathy put her hand on his arm. "I saw your post. Beautifully written, Alex. It was something that needed to be said."

"Thank you." Somehow the praise made him feel guiltier. "I was hoping I could grab a few minutes of your time to talk about that, Mr. Shaw."

Mitchell glanced at his watch and considered. "I have a few minutes until dinner. Kathy, do you mind?"

"Of course not." Kathy smiled at the both of them. "I'll go check on the caterers and see when we'll be ready to begin seating."

Mitchell gestured with his head for Alex to follow, and they wound their way through the crowd toward the front staircase, Mitchell pausing long enough to greet friends and acquaintances as he went. Alex climbed the stairs to the second floor behind him, feeling vaguely uncomfortable about taking him away from his own party.

"I'm sorry to crash the benefit," he said. "What exactly are you raising money for?"

"The university arts program," Mitchell said. "You knew Kathy studied music there, didn't you?"

"Yes, I remember her mentioning that." Mitchell had been an engineering major and his wife had studied . . . flute, maybe? However comfortable Mitchell might seem with the high-society set, he'd always enjoyed the construction side of things more. An opposites-attract situation if ever there was one. And it seemed to work, considering they had been married for forty-two years.

Mitchell led him past the first two doors in the hallway, but Alex couldn't help but pause and peer into the second one as they went. That had been his space for nearly his entire senior year of high school. It looked exactly as it had when he'd lived there—four-poster bed, heavy antique furniture, Oriental rug. No matter how many times they had told him he could decorate it to his taste, he hadn't been able to bring himself to change a thing. It wasn't his home, not really, and to settle in like it was would have felt like a betrayal. And yet when he needed advice, it was Mitchell Shaw he went to, not his own parents.

He hurried to catch up and followed Mitchell into a modest but period-appropriate study at the end of the hall. Alex took the chair that was offered him opposite the desk while Mitchell settled on the other side.

"I take it your parents aren't back yet," Mitchell said by way of opening.

Alex frowned. "Back?"

"Maybe I'm mistaken. I thought they were out of town for a conference this week. We'd invited them to the benefit, since it's their university, but they sent their regrets."

"Right, of course." He hadn't spoken with his mom and dad for almost two weeks; naturally they wouldn't have thought to mention their upcoming trip. Ever since he had abandoned academia in favor of commercial writing, they seemed to think that made him a traitor to the cause.

"What's on your mind, son?"

Alex poured out his concerns without hesitation, telling him how he felt like he was somehow morally culpable for bringing such filth to the attention of the wider masses and profiting off it. Mitchell sat and listened, his expression quietly considering.

"Let me ask you this: what obligation do you have to your publisher to help promote your book?"

"Contractually? It's not really written in."

"Maybe not legally, but there's the expectation that you help promote it, right?"

Alex nodded.

Mitchell leaned back thoughtfully. "And refusing to do it will hurt the sales of the book?"

"Most likely."

"Then you have a quandary. They paid you a great deal of money with the expectation you would do everything you could to make the book a success. If that now conflicts with your personal convictions, you need to decide which is more important to you—those, or keeping your word to someone who has invested in you."

Somehow Alex had thought that Mitchell would help him come to an answer, not give him more to think about. "You think I'm being oversensitive, don't you?"

Mitchell smiled. "If there's one thing I know about you, it's that you think deeply on everything. It's what makes you a good writer. But let me ask you one more thing—have you prayed about it?"

Alex shifted uncomfortably in his seat. He'd known it would eventually come around to this, just as he knew he was going to have to answer no. It still wasn't second nature to him to seek God's guidance on daily matters. He'd been raised in the Russian Orthodox Church, which focused far more on traditionalist doctrine than personal spiritual experience. By that definition, Mitchell and Kathy, with their nondenominational Protestant beliefs, didn't even qualify as true Christians. Besides the night he announced he was quitting his PhD program, the moment he told his parents he was leaving the Orthodox Church was the most disappointed he'd ever seen them.

And yet times like now, he realized how much he still reached for some sort of rule book for answers.

Mitchell smiled as if he understood his conflict. "Think about it. Pray about it. The fact that you're concerned about doing the right thing means you're halfway there. Just remember, you're not responsible for everyone else's actions. Only your own. So whatever decision you make, be sure you're doing it because it's what God would have you do, not simply because it's most comfortable."

Alex stood and held out his hand to shake Mitchell's. "Thank you."

"You know I'm always here if you want to talk. Are you going to join us for dinner?"

"I shouldn't. I didn't realize you were having a plated meal. Thank you, though."

Mitchell ushered him out of the office. When Alex set foot on the bottom floor, instead of turning toward the dining room with the rest of the guests, he headed for the front door. He would do what Mitchell suggested. He'd weigh his responsibilities and ask God for guidance. He hoped that today God felt like answering back.

Chapter Four

Rachel's head pounded so hard she swore she could hear the physical thud outside of her skull. Her face was mashed into the sweaty spot in her pillow where she'd fallen the night before and where she still lay, now with the addition of a drool spot that wet the flowered pillowcase. At times like this, she was glad she lived alone: there was no one to witness her shame.

She lifted her head, hoping to find a leftover water bottle on her nightstand, anything to get rid of the dry taste in her mouth. She must have crashed the minute she got home. Which would make it, what, midnight?

She squinted at the red numbers on her alarm. Only eight? She'd be willing to swear she'd slept longer than a few hours. Only then did she realize that the light streaming in from her window wasn't the golden glow of sunset but the obnoxious flood of full sunshine.

Eight a.m. She'd slept almost eighteen hours. In the same position. No wonder she felt like something that had been dragged behind a semi on the freeway.

Rachel pushed herself up on the bed and half-stood, half-fell from the end. Her phone vibrated from her back pocket. She pulled it out and saw that she'd had four missed calls before this one, all from Ana.

"Mrph," she answered, trying unsuccessfully to untangle her tongue from the roof of her mouth.

"I've been knocking at your front door for ten minutes. And I called you four times. I was about to call the police!"

Only then did Rachel realize that the pounding hadn't been coming from her head. She stumbled to her front door, where Ana's indistinct silhouette waited on the other side of the stained glass panel, unlatched the deadbolt, and pulled the door open, the phone still pressed stupidly to her ear.

Ana lowered her own phone, her expression turning to one of sympathy. "Ah, hon, you look terrible."

"Mmm-hmm." Rachel backed up, leaving Ana to let herself in, and stumbled toward the kitchen. "Coffee?"

"Please."

Rachel made their coffee automatically, grinding beans, boiling water, pouring it into the French press without conscious thought. The smell of fresh coffee penetrated the fog enough for her to form coherent words. "What are you doing here?"

"You wouldn't answer your phone. I thought you were avoiding me. Wait, did you sleep in your clothes?" The side-eye Ana gave her wrinkled jeans and sweatshirt would have made Rachel laugh, were she physically capable of it. Even at eight in the morning, Ana was perfectly turned out for work in an ivory silk blouse, a black pencil skirt, and a gorgeous pair of patent snakeskin pumps that made Rachel's feet hurt just looking at them. She must have stopped on her way into the office.

Rachel avoided the remark about her wardrobe and instead focused on the first part of the statement. "Why would I be avoiding you?"

"Coffee first. This is definitely a discussion you need to be caffeinated for."

The jittery feeling that had been dogging her since Ana's unannounced visit to the restaurant came back with a vengeance. Ana wasn't here simply to make sure Rachel was alive. Given events of late, that couldn't be good.

Rachel pushed aside those concerns in favor of the immediate one, pulling out two plain china mugs from the many-times-painted cabinets and finding a pint of half-and-half in the refrigerator. Not that it was hard to find, considering there were only a handful of items in the avocado antique. It, like the rest of the kitchen, dated back to an ill-conceived 1970s update, something that Ana and Melody teased her about relentlessly— an award-winning chef with a kitchen that was barely functional. But if Rachel wanted breakfast, she made it at the restaurant. If she wanted dinner, she picked it up on the way home. Her microwave was her most-used appliance.

When the coffee had finished brewing and Rachel had fixed them both a cup the way they liked it—hers with cream, no sugar; Ana's with a healthy dose of both—she settled into a chair at the battered table beside her friend. "So. Lay it on me."

Ana heaved a sigh. "I thought you weren't going to respond to the media. I issued a statement to that effect."

"Ah." The reporter yesterday. "I know I should have blown her off, but I didn't do much more than explain why I wasn't going to comment."

"That's not what it looks like." Ana grimaced and pulled out her tablet—the Tablet of Doom, Rachel had begun to think of it—then opened a video. There she was, looking only slightly better than she probably looked now, exhausted and irritated at the questioning of the reporter. Then the voice-over: *"Rachel Bishop is one of the few female chefs making a successful career in the kitchen, but she seems to believe that she is the only exception."* Rachel flashed onto the screen saying in what now sounded like an arrogant tone, *"They don't have the dedication and skills to succeed. They shouldn't be there."*

Ana pressed pause, her expression conflicted.

"That's not what I said! Or at least they took it completely out of context. I said that regardless

56

of whether a cook was a man or woman, if they didn't have the skills and the dedication, they shouldn't be there. And then I said that the food was the thing that was important and I couldn't speak to the wider ranks of women in the workplace because I hadn't interviewed every one of them who chose not to work in this industry."

Ana relaxed visibly, though her brow was still furrowed. "I don't understand why, if you were going to talk to anyone, you would talk to Squawker. Their entire business model is based on sensationalism."

"Squawker? But I thought . . ." Clearly, in her post-service fog, she hadn't recognized the reporter as she thought she had. Squawker was known for trying to trap celebrities in embarrassing statements and out-of-context situations. Never mind the fact that three days ago, no one had known who she was.

Rachel nibbled a thumbnail reflexively. "What should we do?"

"That depends on you. It's still not too late to give an interview. Discredit whatever this site might write about you. Most people will dismiss this for what it is, a trumped-up rant on Squawker's part. But there are a few who will take it seriously. Expect angry e-mails. Disable posts on your Facebook page so no one can post there for a while."

"I don't even have my password to Paisley's Facebook page."

Ana gave her an indulgent look. "I wrote it down for you."

"And I put it somewhere safe. I just have no idea where that is now."

"I assume that means you still want to remain quiet?"

Rachel gave an emphatic nod. "I won't dignify these sorts of things with a comment."

"You kind of already did." But Ana seemed resigned now. "The first thing we should do is tell your staff—and *you*—not to talk to any more press. As for the rest, we lie low. Had some random writer not decided to draw attention to Espy's review, we wouldn't be having this discussion."

"If you had to guess, what's going to happen here?" Rachel asked.

"I never predict, Rachel. If you won't let me get in front of this, we're going to have to let it play out and see what happens. I still don't get why you're so anti-publicity, though. You barely did any interviews after the Beard."

"Because all anyone wanted to talk about was what it was like to be a woman in the kitchen. What kind of discrimination did I face? How do I manage to have a social life? What do men think about the fact that I do this kind of job? What will happen once I get married and have kids?

Can you imagine asking a male chef that sort of thing?"

"That's why you should speak up, Rachel. Obviously there are still a lot of people who need to be set straight."

"But the people asking are part of the problem, and as you can see, things rarely get portrayed in the way they're meant. I'm not like you, Ana. I'm not great with words. I'm not good on camera. That's why I went into the kitchen in the first place."

Ana nodded sympathetically, but Rachel could tell she still didn't understand. "In any case, I need to get going. I'll call you if there's any news."

"Stay a couple of minutes. I'll make you something to eat."

Ana wavered between duty and food, and in the end, food won out. She slid back onto the chair while Rachel began pulling ingredients out of the sparsely stocked refrigerator and much-better-stocked cabinets. With a knife in hand, she could relax a little. Publicity might be foreign to her, but this she knew. The sharp blade cutting through shallots was a more effective calming measure than meditation.

"How's Rob?" she asked.

"Rob is . . . gone." Ana rolled her eyes. "Big surprise. You predicted he wouldn't last."

"I did, but I'm still sorry. What was it this time?"

"He found out I made more money than him."

"Good riddance, then. You'd think he'd be happy you could pay for your own stuff if you wanted."

"Yeah, but with that, plus the fact I know half the chefs in town thanks to you, he could never impress me with dinners out." Ana smiled, but there was something fragile beneath it. Unlike Rachel, Ana really did want to find someone special. A high-powered career woman had difficulties finding a secure man as it was; her family's expectation that she marry a traditional-minded man, quit work, and have lots of babies couldn't help matters either.

Rachel transferred the shallots to a small pan with diced ham while she started mixing savory crepe batter. "You need to find a man who isn't threatened by your connections."

"Easier said than done." Ana smiled. "What about you? Anyone interesting come along lately?"

Rachel shot her a look and Ana laughed. "Right, the only people you know are cooks. And you'd never date one."

"Not if he works for me," she said. "Are you still coming over for dinner tonight? Melody said she's in."

"Of course I am. I might be late, though."

"No worries. I don't go in until ten tomorrow." Of course, Rachel didn't tell Ana that she would be dropping by the restaurant later today to check on things and look over the prep lists that morning crew would use first thing tomorrow. A day off only meant a day off from customers; it didn't mean there weren't things to be done.

Ana drank her coffee at the table and watched while Rachel cooked, telling her the outrageous client stories from that week, many centering around Denver's professional athletes and politicians. Even as ridiculous as they were, it was somehow comfortingly normal, the life of a friend who had a nine-to-five job. Well, more like nine-to-nine. Rachel assembled the crepes, cheese melting over the ham filling, and set one plate in front of Ana. She watched expectantly as Ana took her first bite and rolled her eyes back into her head in ecstasy.

"Seriously, Rach, this is amazing. Can I move in with you?"

Rachel laughed and picked up her own plate. "I think our hours would clash, but otherwise, yes."

"Come on, sit. You can't stand and eat. It makes me nervous."

Rachel hesitated, then refreshed their coffee and took the chair next to Ana. For a moment at least, sharing a simple breakfast with one of her dearest friends, she could believe that all was right with her world.

As soon as Ana left the condo, now an hour late for work due to her "breakfast meeting," Rachel straightened up the trail of belongings she'd left on her way in yesterday, then jumped in the shower to wash off the grease and grime of the day before. That sense of wrongness came back full force while she drove to the restaurant. When she pulled up to the lot behind the building, she understood why.

Two cars sat there already, a gleaming black Range Rover and a silver Mercedes. The back door of the restaurant was cracked open, a sure sign someone was inside.

Dan sometimes dropped by during service to eat; Maurice, the other owner and a chef friend of Rachel's, came in at the beginning of prep when he wouldn't be disturbing anything. Neither of them ever visited on a Monday when Paisley was closed, even though it was no secret that Rachel would be there.

Her heart squeezed in a fist of dread, clenching tighter with each step toward the back door.

Slowly, she entered the restaurant and made her way toward the low voices in the front. Dan and Maurice sat together at the bar, both staring at the screen of a laptop. They looked up when she entered, Dan's expression tight. But it was Maurice's vaguely guilty look that made her stomach toss.

"We tried to call you," he said in his faint French accent. "You didn't pick up your phone."

She reached for her back jeans pocket and

found it empty. "I must have left it at home."

"Sit down, Rachel," Dan said.

His tone immediately raised her hackles—that of a father about to scold a wayward daughter, not a business partner about to discuss some matter of business. Still, she swallowed down her annoyance and slid onto the stool. "What's this about?"

He swiveled the computer to her, the browser open to Twitter, and her breath caught.

Ana had set up Twitter accounts for both Rachel and the restaurant when Paisley opened, but Rachel rarely checked them unless her app told her she had direct messages or she wanted to advertise a new seasonal menu to her couple thousand followers. That meant there were rarely any tweets involving the @PaisleyDenver account.

Now, there were page after page of them. Rachel reached for the laptop and began to read them, wide-eyed.

Apparently a woman's place is everywhere but the kitchen. So my place will be everywhere but @PaisleyDenver.

@ChefRachelB breaks the glass ceiling, sets feminism back 40 years. Well done.

If @ChefRachelB doesn't want other women in her kitchen, we won't eat in her dining room either. #BoycottPaisley

And those were the nice ones.

"I thought you weren't going to talk to the media," Dan said, his tone tight.

"I wasn't planning on it. I was blindsided."

"How difficult is it to say, 'No comment'?" A vein throbbed at Dan's temple, and Maurice nudged him in warning.

Rachel looked between Dan and Maurice. "You both know me. You know what I think about this subject. It's pretty clear that this was a hatchet job. Pure sensationalism."

Maurice leaned forward, his tone and his expression sympathetic. "Why didn't you issue a statement after the article came out and then leave it at that?"

"Ana did issue a statement, and we were hoping since Denver isn't exactly a major market, the whole thing would stay quiet."

"I think we can safely say that it didn't stay quiet." Dan took the laptop back from her and clicked over to a different tab, then turned it her direction.

"The Huffington Post picked it up?" Rachel said, dazed. "How could this happen? People pay publicists huge amounts of money to get something to go viral, and instead we can't keep one little thing quiet?"

"That would be a question for Ana, wouldn't it? I told you I had reservations about hiring her to handle the restaurant's publicity, but you felt so strongly about her . . ."

Rachel shook her head. "This isn't Ana's fault, and you know it. I asked her to handle this in a low-key fashion because I didn't want to be onstage. I had no idea it was going to get out of control like this." She pressed her fingertips to her eyes. "I think I'm going to be sick."

Maurice finally jumped in. "Listen, Rachel, you are an incredible chef. But your reputation—"

"My reputation is impeccable," she said.

"With diners," Maurice said. "Not in the industry. Ever since you walked out on that panel discussion at Johnson & Wales last year, you have a reputation for being a diva."

"I didn't want to be associated with the direction that panel took," Rachel said. "That's part of why I've stayed out of the public eye. They basically wanted a bunch of female chefs to get up there and bash our male colleagues, and I refused to do it. Some of the best cooks I've ever worked with have been men, and while there are some wonderful women, there aren't that many of us. It would be a slap in the face to the chefs who gave me my start."

Dan was shaking his head now, maybe from shock at her naiveté. Even as the words came from her mouth, she understood how her actions could be misinterpreted. But really, what did that matter? It was the customers who came back for the food who made Paisley successful. What the other chefs in the city thought of her was largely irrelevant. She said as much, but Dan continued shaking his head.

"It may not matter to you, Rachel, but it matters to me. This is considered part of my restaurant group, even if you are the majority owner by 1 percent. Your behavior—and this social-media frenzy—reflects on all my properties. My other chefs are getting requests to comment from the media, and that's not the kind of attention we want for them."

Rachel pushed her hands into her hair and let out a long sigh. She'd been so painfully naive to think this was going to go away on its own. The public liked nothing better than scandal, even if it had to be bootstrapped. "Then we go into damage control mode. I'll issue a statement in person. I'll do a press conference, whatever. I'm sure once I explain—"

"Rachel, it's a bit too late for that. We all agreed when we started that we would do what was best for the restaurant. You've become a liability."

"I've . . . what?" The truth came flooding into her with horrifying clarity. "You're cutting me out?"

"Rachel—" Maurice began.

"You can't cut me out. I have 34 percent ownership."

"And together we have 66," Dan said. "Maurice and I have discussed it, and we'd be willing to allow you to buy us out." He named a figure—almost double what they'd invested in Paisley—that had her eyes widening.

"I can't do that," she said. "You know very well I don't have that kind of money."

Dan withdrew a check from his pocket and slid it across the polished bar to her.

She looked at it in stupefied dismay. There were a lot of digits there. Her investment into the business plus another 30 percent. "What is this?"

Maurice cleared his throat uncomfortably. "We can't discount that this restaurant wouldn't have done this well without you. We still believe it can be profitable, and it didn't seem fair to give you back your investment without acknowledging the potential long-term value of your contribution."

She understood then. Dan had wanted to cut her out without throwing her a bone, but as a chef himself, Maurice understood there was so much more to making a restaurant successful than pouring money into it. It was her menu, her culture, her staff, her design decisions. She *was* Paisley. If they were going to kick her out, he was going to make sure that she walked away with something to show for it.

"There's nothing I'm going to say to change your mind?"

Dan shook his head. "Our contract is pretty clear. You and I will make the announcement to your staff in the morning."

Her staff. He couldn't even take ownership of

them. Slowly, she folded the check in half and slipped it into her pocket, then slid off the stool. "You are welcome to do whatever you want with *your* staff. Assuming they still want to be your staff. But don't expect me to gracefully pass the baton."

She went to her office and pulled several boxes from the closet, then began to pile her personal items into them. One box held her coats and her knives. The rest she filled up with the cookbooks she'd brought from home and the composition books that contained all her recipe notes and ideas for future dishes. One by one, she began to carry the boxes out to her car. Maurice appeared briefly to help, but she glared at him until he backed off. He could try to pretend that he'd been pushed into it—and maybe he had—but he could have just as easily sided with her against Dan. She would expect to be betrayed by the money man, but not by a fellow chef.

Once she had all her things loaded in the back of her vehicle, she climbed behind the wheel and sat there in disbelief. Everything she had worked for, all gone in a mere three days. That might be a world record for the shattering of a dream.

A curious sort of numbness enveloped her on the drive home, stayed with her through the multiple trips into her house with her boxes. She texted Melody and Ana and then sat down with her phone on the sofa, watching the tweets stack up, some vicious and some just plain stupid. Surely people would get tired of this at some point. Wouldn't they?

By the time Melody and Ana arrived, it was clear that it wasn't going to end at a few comments. Rachel watched as the tweets and Facebook posts and Instagram photos took on a life of their own. Somewhere between Rachel finishing a half-dozen cookies herself and ordering delivery pizza, someone came up with the hashtag *#WeBelong* and women began posting photos of themselves holding signs in places they were in the minority: not only restaurants, but laboratories, research universities, construction sites.

By midnight it was clear that one innocent comment had spawned a movement. She might have been proud of it had it not been for all the posts that called her out in opposition.

Show @ChefRachelB #WeBelong.

@ChefRachelB, you may not think #WeBelong, but 2.2 million nurses feel differently.

Rachel huddled in the corner of her sofa with a blanket, too stunned and pained to do anything but stare at the messages scrolling down her phone. It kept getting worse. Until the last nail in the coffin.

Alice Mears, the chef under whom she'd gotten her first shot as a sous-chef, posted a photo from her own kitchen, clearly in the middle of service. We don't let anyone tell us where #WeBelong.

Hot tears slipped down Rachel's face as she curled into a ball and, for the first time since she was fifteen years old, cried until she could cry no more.

Chapter Five

"So do you blame social media for the lack of civility in today's society?"

Alex reeled his thoughts back from where they had wandered and settled them on the question. This radio interview had only gone on for about ten minutes, but it felt like longer considering the host was more interested in pontificating than asking Alex questions. He shifted his phone to the other ear while he considered. "I think social media is a great thing in many ways. It allows us to stay connected over long distances in a way that letters or even e-mail couldn't accomplish. But the anonymity definitely causes people to do things they would never dream of doing in person. We've seen the mob mentality play out in history, and we're now seeing the same thing on the Internet."

"It's the Wild West out there, you're saying," the host said with a laugh.

No, that wasn't what he was saying, but he couldn't contradict the host without looking like a jerk. "It's definitely lagging behind real life in terms of monitoring and mores, yes."

"Clearly this is a subject you feel strongly about, given the definitive tone of your piece for the *New Yorker*. How, then, do you feel about the fact that it's spurred a movement that has taken on quite the opposite effect?"

Alex's thoughts stopped short and tumbled on top of one another. "Excuse me?"

"I take it you haven't seen Twitter today? The *WeBelong* hashtag?"

He still wasn't following. "No?"

"Well, for your benefit and that of our audience, apparently Chef Rachel Bishop of Paisley restaurant in Denver—" in case there was any question of how to track her down and bully her more, Alex thought—"made an offhand remark to a reporter in response to your article, which has spawned . . . oh, looks like in excess of ten thousand posts under the hashtag *#WeBelong*, defending women's rights to work in traditionally male-dominated fields."

Alex felt like he had entered the Twilight Zone, where everything looked and sounded familiar but nothing actually added up. "That's precisely what I meant to defend in my piece."

"And once more, it seems that social media has unintended consequences," the interviewer said smugly. "That's all we have time for today. For more observations on the trials and tribulations of life in the digital age, look up Alexander Kanin's *Mis-Connected*, available wherever books and e-books are sold."

Alex hung up, a hard kernel of cold forming in his stomach. After prayer and consideration, he'd decided the damage had already been done and he had an obligation to his publisher to promote the book the best he could. At the very least, it would give him the opportunity to reiterate the point he'd been trying to make in the first place. So what was this movement to which the host had referred?

He slid his laptop toward him on his desk and flipped up the lid, then opened Twitter to search for the hashtag in question.

His heart fell a little further with every post. Some of them were little more than shows of female solidarity in difficult professions—EMTs, military personnel, scientists—but others were downright vicious, taking personal stabs at Rachel Bishop. He couldn't figure out what had started the attack until he followed a link to a video of the exhausted-looking chef throwing a few words over her shoulder before she climbed into her car.

"They don't have the dedication and skills to succeed. They shouldn't be there," she said. The next shot showed her slamming the car door.

Her cadence made it clear they had edited bits from a longer sentence. This was what passed for reporting? True, Squawker was yellow journalism at best, but it only served to emphasize the way sensationalism had overtaken any sense of responsibility.

And how one small video could somehow go

viral, spawn its own hashtag, and turn into an international movement overnight.

No, this was because of a sexist, crass review that would have gone unnoticed had he not dredged it up and spit it out onto a national stage.

This was his fault.

Alex dropped his head back and stared helplessly at the ceiling. It didn't matter that he hadn't meant for this to happen; it was still a direct consequence of his actions. The irony of an anti-bullying article beginning a particularly vicious round of bullying was not lost on him.

The worst part was, he knew what it felt like to be targeted—one only had to go online and read the comments on his work by those who said he'd misappropriated his Russian heritage for a buck, that he was perpetuating harmful stereotypes even though his gently satirical stories about his family had been approved by that same family before publication.

Right when it seemed like his publishing career was dead, someone else's controversy had brought it back to life, and now he was benefiting from it. But what else could he do? Viral was exactly that—the story was already far beyond his control.

"Whatever decision you make, be sure you're doing it because it's what God would have you do."

He'd already determined that he had an ethical

obligation to his publishers to promote this book, but now the nudge to his spirit was too strong to ignore. He had to talk to Rachel Bishop. He had to ask her forgiveness.

She would probably run him over with her car, though, if he tried to catch her outside the restaurant, and she wouldn't thank him for interrupting in the middle of dinner rush. He'd have to catch her before.

He pulled up a reservation app on his cell phone and found Paisley. Booked solid for the next week. Clearly, the controversy hadn't hurt reservations.

The listing showed they opened for dinner at five thirty on Tuesdays. He'd have to arrive early and hope she'd be willing to talk to him.

Decision made, he shuffled his notes in front of him, trying to focus on the next interview and the preapproved questions they would be asking him. Instead his mind kept straying back to that weary woman trying to get away from a shark with a microphone. His apology might not count for much, but he still had to try.

Alex arrived at the restaurant a few minutes after five. He parked in an absurdly expensive lot and strode down the sidewalk toward the narrow, glass-windowed space, wedged between a trendy boutique and another restaurant. High-rent area, he thought, suited to the upscale dining concept that defined Larimer Square. Lots of pressure to succeed.

The front door opened and closed with a subtle whoosh, sealing off the street noise and leading him into a small reception area. The restaurant was bigger than he thought from the outside, stretching back toward the open kitchen, which was still shy of its full complement of cooks. The ones who were there were clearly men. No one who could be the executive chef.

"May I help you, sir?" A stylish young woman spotted him from across the room and glided across the polished concrete floors to meet him.

"I'm looking for Rachel Bishop," he said. "Is she available?"

Her expression shuttered, and something akin to outright suspicion registered on her face. "Are you press?"

Technically, he could probably claim the title. He shook his head. "No."

"I'm afraid that Chef Bishop—"

"I'll take this one," a feminine voice said, and the hostess practically crumpled in relief. She backed away while the pale, freckled blonde moved toward him with every bit as much suspicion as the first woman. Apparently, Rachel's staff was protective of her privacy. Somehow that made him feel better, knowing that she had people watching her back.

"How can I help you, sir?"

"I'd like to speak with Chef Bishop if she's available."

The woman studied him for a minute. She looked like kitchen staff—her long-sleeved black shirt was rolled up to the elbows and dusted with smudges of flour, as was her pin-striped apron. But there was something proprietary about the way she narrowed her eyes, as if his inquiry were a personal affront.

"Why do you need her?"

He cleared his throat. "I'm Alexander Kanin. I feel like . . . I owe her an apology."

Emotions flickered across the woman's face, finally settling on something like disdain. "I would say you owe her a lot more than that. Rachel Bishop is no longer associated with Paisley."

He blinked. "I'm sorry?"

"She left. Sold out to her partners yesterday."

He wiped a hand over the lower half of his face, not sure what to make of this. Had she quit because of the scrutiny? Or had she been forced out?

"You're a friend of hers?" he asked quietly.

The woman gave a single nod.

"Then I want you to know this was never my intention. The opposite, in fact. Do you know where I could find her so I can tell her in person?"

She laughed, a tinge of bitterness laced through the sound. "Trust me. You don't want to talk to her right now. You'd be taking your life into your own hands."

"As I well deserve. What if I'm feeling particularly suicidal?"

She stared at him stonily.

He sighed again. "Listen. I understand that she's angry. I'd understand if she spit in my face. But I was raised to take responsibility for my actions, whether she's willing to forgive me or not. If you don't help me, I'll find her some other way."

The first crack appeared in the woman's facade, and she seemed to be considering. "Fine. Tomorrow. Six o'clock at the food truck pod in RiNo. You know it?"

"I know it well. Thank you . . ." He trailed off, arching an eyebrow.

"Melody."

"Thank you, Melody. And if you wouldn't mind not tipping her off—"

"Oh, trust me. I'm not telling her anything. And I'd appreciate you not saying I'm the one who set this up. She'd never forgive me."

"Agreed. Your involvement will never come up. I appreciate it."

"Mmm-hmm." She turned and walked away, seeming to have an angry conversation with herself as she left. He felt a bit of disquiet at her earlier words. So Rachel was a bit of a spitfire, was she? Well, he shouldn't be surprised. The kind of drive that motivated a woman to own her own restaurant at thirty was usually associated with a strong and determined personality.

Hopefully Rachel Bishop would hear him out, give him a chance to explain. She didn't have to forgive him. He didn't really expect her to. But he wouldn't be able to rest until he somehow made amends.

Chapter Six

She was wallowing.

Rachel knew she was wallowing, but she couldn't help herself. For the first time in almost fifteen years, she had woken up with nowhere to go. Her day had no structure. She watched the clock tick up and thought about what she should be doing at the restaurant: looking over the inventory, concocting the day's specials, checking in with all her cooks.

Her cooks. She'd hired them, mentored them, pulled a few from prep positions at other restaurants because she recognized their potential. Her departure would most likely mean a promotion for Andrew, at least temporarily. She had been thinking he needed another year, maybe two, before he was ready to run his own kitchen. This was an accelerated promotion she wasn't entirely sure he was ready for.

As much as she would like to believe the rest of the staff would walk out in protest, she knew the truth. They needed the jobs, and in the end, they were more loyal to their careers and their wallets than to any one person. She didn't blame them. But now, pacing her condo with the shades down, she'd have given nearly anything to go back in time and reconsider the decisions that had led her to this point. It was fine to stick to her ideals as a chef when it didn't cost her anything; now those ideals were all she had left.

Tired of her own angst, Rachel finally collapsed on the sofa in front of the TV with a pint of ice cream and watched competitive cooking shows, a particularly masochistic way of passing the time. All the while she ignored the flashing light on her cell phone that indicated messages. As if the Twitter harassment hadn't been enough, the phone calls had started coming in from reporters and talk show hosts before the sun even came up. All wanting a statement, all wanting to perform an autopsy on her career before their voracious audiences.

How painfully ironic that her attempt to keep the focus on her food had turned into a glaring personal spotlight. She couldn't even muster the self-righteous zeal to defend herself. Not when deep down, she wondered how much truth was contained in those horrible accusations. She had been foolish to think she could make this work. Foolish to believe that in the end, she would be anything more than a failure.

No. She pressed Stop on that recording before it could begin playing as an endless loop in her brain. She wasn't a failure. The check, now lying on the coffee table, crumpled from its place in her pocket, proved that. She'd made a profit, a healthy return on her investment. Maurice might think he'd been doing her a favor, but she'd earned that money. She'd laid all the groundwork to make the restaurant a success, and it would continue to be, assuming that Dan could keep it together. If it started going to seed, would Maurice step in? Despite kowtowing to Dan's will, he was a good guy and an excellent chef, but he was from a different era: a true veteran of the French brigade kitchen, with its hazing and grunt work and military-like mind-set. Whereas Rachel had been trying to build a different sort of atmosphere in which her cooks could grow and advance, and hopefully leave to open their own restaurants someday. She had tried to be a mentor as well as a boss, if never their friend.

A little past seven o'clock, a knock at her condo door jerked her out of the light sleep she'd fallen into. She opened the door and nearly melted into tears again when she saw Ana and Melody standing at the door. Ana was holding a familiar bag from her favorite Thai restaurant, Melody a pink bakery box tied with string.

"We thought you might need pad Thai, followed by cupcake therapy," Melody said.

Ana pushed past Rachel to the kitchen, where she plunked the bag on the counter. "You haven't been moping around here all day, have you?"

Rachel closed the door behind them and looked down at her T-shirt and sweatpants. "I'm decompressing."

"You're feeling sorry for yourself." Ana was soundly in tough love mode, something Rachel was not nearly ready for. Melody seemed to understand that, because she pinched Ana's arm and whispered something furiously in her ear.

"Sorry," Ana said immediately. "I'm not used to you like this. You're usually the one telling us to pull it together."

"I went from co-owner of a restaurant to unemployed in less than twenty-four hours," Rachel said. "I need time to process."

Melody was pulling bowls from her shelves while Ana opened boxes. Together they transferred the noodles to dishes, found lacquered chopsticks in a drawer, and brought the food out to the living room. Melody set down the bowl on the coffee table, then lifted the check. Her eyes widened. "You didn't tell us they paid you out this much. This is almost enough to open another restaurant!"

"It's barely enough for a food truck," Rachel said. "It took three times that to open Paisley."

"And if I recall, you weren't thrilled with the Larimer space," Melody said. "You wanted to open in Platt Park or River North, do something edgier, hipper."

"I like the way Paisley turned out," Rachel said. "It was still my vision. Still my menu. At three times the price, of course, but that clientele expects it."

Melody didn't say anything, just levered pad Thai into her mouth with chopsticks.

"Wait. You think I sold out. You think I caved on my vision for the restaurant because of Dan and Maurice's input."

"No," Melody said. "Not sold out. You were forced to compromise."

"Compromise is the same thing as selling out."

"Compromise is how the world works," Ana said from across the room. "No one gets everything they want. Not in their career. Definitely not in love."

"Ooh," Rachel said. "You had another date. How did it go?"

"You're changing the subject."

"So are you. What was wrong with this guy?"

Ana shrugged. "Nothing. We're going out again this weekend."

"Wait, someone actually made it through the first-date gauntlet?" Melody said. "Why aren't you more excited?"

"I don't know. He's a nice guy. There's nothing *wrong* with him. At least I couldn't find a reason to not go back out with him. But it's just—"

"There's no spark?" Melody suggested.

"Yeah. No spark. But sometimes that comes later, right? All the guys I've dated because I was instantly attracted to them turned out to be total jerks in the end. My radar is seriously broken."

"I don't know. It sounds like settling to me," Melody said.

Rachel maneuvered pad Thai around her bowl. "Maybe that's better. At least you can keep your common sense intact. It's only when people fall madly in love that they suddenly lose their minds."

"Yeah, yeah, marriage is a trap." Melody rolled her eyes, but they'd had this discussion too many times for there to be any heat behind the words. "Doesn't mean you can't go out, have some fun, see what's out there."

"Yeah, 'cause the bar scene is teeming with decent guys *not* looking for a hookup," Ana muttered.

For reasons Rachel couldn't fathom, Melody elbowed her and gave her a sharp look. Ana blinked and then added, "But then again, it's an alternative to Internet dating, which as we know hasn't worked out so well for me either."

Rachel looked between the two of them, her eyes narrowing. They were plotting something. They'd never showed much interest in her love life before. Were they thinking that she would somehow get over her grief at losing her restaurant if she had a man in her life? If so, they didn't know her at all. Men only complicated matters. They never made them better.

Melody clapped her hands together. "Okay, this is what we'll do. You get one more day to mope.

And then you're going to get it together, take a shower, put on something cute, and go out with us. We'll pick you up tomorrow at five thirty, so make sure you get in all your feeling-sorry-for-yourself before then."

"On a Wednesday night? Aren't you working?"

"No. I quit."

Ana stared at her. "And you're just now telling us that?"

Melody shrugged. "I hadn't planned on quitting right away. I figured Rachel could use a spy on the inside. But Dan started trying to tell me how to do my job. I told him this was the way I always did it, and you were fine with it. He said things were going to change now that he was in charge, and I told him they could change without me."

Rachel's jaw dropped open. "I can't believe you did that. Mel, you didn't have to quit for me."

"I didn't quit for you. I quit for me. The only reason I took the pastry chef job at Paisley was to work with you. Dan wasn't satisfied with having me do the baking in the morning and leaving the plating to my assistant during service. And I'm not working fourteen hours a day simply because he's a micromanager. So I quit."

"I'm sorry," Rachel said, even though she was secretly pleased that Melody had walked out. "What did everyone else do?"

"Andrew, predictably, was given charge of the kitchen. You could tell he was uncomfortable, but he wasn't going to walk away from the chance to prove himself. Everyone else seems to be hanging in there to see how it goes. Except Carlos. He totally lost it."

Rachel blinked. "What?"

"Yeah, he started shouting at Dan in Spanish, and the only words I understood were the bad ones. He packed up his knives and left. From what the other guys translated for me, he said they betrayed you and they could find another prep cook."

"Wow." Rachel fell back against the sofa cushions, both shocked and warmed. Who knew? She had been pretty sure Carlos merely tolerated her. Secretly, in the uncharitable part of herself, she was glad to know they'd struggle without him. They'd have to hire two people to make up his productivity.

"It's going to be okay, Rach," Melody said softly. "Just take some time before deciding on the next thing. You've earned a break."

And then she was back in the mud with the twin washes of sadness and terror. She'd been cooking her whole independent life. It was the only thing she'd ever been good at, the only thing that had ever felt like home.

And if she were to be completely honest with herself, she had absolutely no idea what to do without it.

Chapter Seven

Rachel took her friends at their word. She allowed herself one more day to wallow—though she finally turned off the cooking channels and instead binge-watched sitcoms on Netflix— staying in the same sweatpants and T-shirt she had worn for the last two days. Then she pried herself up off the sofa, where she was beginning to leave a permanent imprint, shoved herself in the shower, and went about making herself look halfway presentable.

There wasn't much to be done about her ghostly pallor, given the fact she had lived her life in the kitchen under fluorescent lights, but she applied enough makeup and bronzer to make a fair approximation of a day-dweller. For the first time in years, she blew her long, dark hair dry around a fat roller brush, making it look bouncy and shiny, curling over her shoulders like a Miss America contestant's. When she was done applying mascara and lip gloss, she stepped back and blinked at herself, almost unable to recognize the woman staring back in her mirror.

This girl looked like she knew how to go out and have fun. This girl wouldn't spend her days locked in her condo feeling sorry for herself.

Well, like people always said—fake it 'til you make it. From the way she felt, she was going to be doing a lot of faking.

She dug in her drawer for a clean T-shirt and tugged it over her head, then pulled on a pair of faded jeans as the knock came at her front door. She pulled it open and blinked at her friends standing in the hallway. "I thought we were going to dinner."

"We are," Ana said. She was dressed in a flowing black jumpsuit and platform heels that added a couple of inches to her petite frame, while Melody was wearing a bohemian-looking sundress that could have been brand new or a vintage find from one of her thrift stores.

"Your hair and makeup look great, Rachel." Melody linked her arm with Rachel's amid the clink of bangle bracelets. "Let's go pick out your clothes."

"What's wrong with what I'm wearing?"

Melody cast an exasperated look over her shoulder at Ana and dragged Rachel into the bedroom, then made a beeline straight to her closet. She slid hangers aside. "You have practically nothing in here."

"You mean for the one day a week I'm not in uniform?"

Melody grimaced. "Right. Oh, hey! You have flares? These are great!" She pulled out a pair of dark denim jeans and waved them triumphantly.

"You bought them and then decided they looked better on me, remember?"

"Rachel, these still have the tags on them!"

Melody looked slightly hurt, so Rachel sighed and held out her hand. Melody brightened and tossed them to her, then shuffled more hangers. "This is cute." She pulled out a dark-blue, layered tank top, also still bearing its original tags. "What did you buy this for?"

Rachel shrugged. "I liked it. Just haven't had a chance to wear it."

"There's hope for you yet. Get dressed."

Rachel stripped off her clothes and shimmied into the jeans and the flowing tank top while Melody selected accessories. It wasn't that she didn't know how to dress herself or look pretty; she was simply in such a habit of downplaying her looks that she rarely had occasion to put those skills into practice. Why they were insisting on getting her dolled up on a Wednesday night, she couldn't begin to fathom. Unless . . .

"You didn't set me up on a date, did you?"

"No, nothing like that." Melody held up a copper pendant necklace that someone had given Rachel for Christmas. "Wear this one and those brown motorcycle boots and you'll be perfect."

Rachel did as she directed. Of the three of them, Melody possessed the creative eye, great taste, and an instinctive read on people. She always joked that if the baking career didn't work out, she could make a living as a personal stylist or interior designer. The only reason Rachel's apartment had any style at all was completely due to Melody's touch. She draped the necklace around her neck, thanking the flowing top for hiding the softness around her middle that came from the constant tasting of rich food, gave her hair a shake, and grabbed a real handbag. At Melody's prompting, she did a slow spin.

"Perfect. Now we're going to go out and have a good time and remember that we're three independent women with fantastic lives."

"Think you might be trying a bit too hard there, Melody?"

"I've got a job interview tomorrow. This might be my last night of freedom."

Before Rachel could ask about the job, Melody was off again to join Ana, who let out a low whistle when Rachel entered the room. "You clean up nice, Chef."

Rachel rolled her eyes, but her friends' enthusiasm did warm her a bit. "Come on, before I decide to go back to wallowing."

"Point taken." Ana led them out the condo and down the steps to where her black Mercedes SUV sat at the curb. Rachel climbed into the shotgun seat while Melody slid into the back. As Ana navigated her way into evening traffic, Rachel tried to push down the nagging feeling she was supposed to be somewhere else. They passed

91

restaurants that were just beginning to fill with corporate workers ending their days, and she knew that in the back of the house, the kitchen staff were beginning the greater part of theirs.

"This is killing you, isn't it?" Ana asked.

"A fifteen-year habit is hard to break. Telling me to go out and have fun on a work night is like telling you to stop giving tough love advice or Melody to stop being so cheerful."

"I'm not sure whether to be flattered or insulted," Melody said from the back.

"Flattered," Ana said. "Definitely."

"Where are we going anyway?"

"Come on, you have to ask me that? Where else do we take you when you need cheering up?"

Rachel gasped. "Rhino Crash?"

"Yep." Ana laughed at her ecstatic expression.

Now Rachel's spirits lifted. It was ridiculous, she knew. Rhino Crash—the name a play on its RiNo location—was an outdoor cantina with a food truck pod, featuring several regulars and a couple of rotating slots that changed at consistent intervals. But not just any food trucks—some of the best food one could find outside of Denver's hottest restaurants, including that of several friends. Her hours were such that she never had a chance to see them, let alone sample their cooking.

When Ana found parking down the street, Rachel could see crowds already forming inside. She was the first out of the car, waiting impatiently on the curb for her friends. They moved up the street, drawn by the heavy beat of the music playing inside the patio enclosure.

The vibe was as funky as the River North neighborhood in which it was located, the brick-enclosed bar blurring the line between indoors and outdoors. A few rare suited corporate types mingled with hipsters and college students, clustered together on folding chairs at metal tables beyond the garishly painted fences. The overall mood was relaxed and jovial, one reason Rachel loved it. They were all there for the food, the drink, and the ambience, even as everyone devoured plates as disparate as Korean *bibimbap* and French *vichyssoise*.

"I'm going over there." Ana pointed to a midnight-blue food truck that was known for having the best *bao*, steamed Vietnamese buns, in Denver. Which, given the popularity of the southeast Asian cuisine in the city lately, was more of an accomplishment than it might have seemed.

"What about you?" Rachel asked Melody.

"I'm having what you're having. You never steer me wrong."

"Then A Parisian in Denver is the way to go. Come on. I want to say hello to Lilia."

They found their way to the end of the line in front of a food truck painted in red, blue, and white, and Rachel craned her neck to get a better look at the chalkboard that proclaimed the day's specials. There was French street food like crepes and merguez sausages alongside trendy favorites like duck confit *pommes frites*. When Lilia had started the mobile business, she'd been afraid Denver wouldn't embrace her blend of French and American, but it had been so popular, it had earned a permanent spot at Rhino Crash and a faithful following throughout the city.

When Rachel and Melody finally got up to the window to order, the petite blonde with an order pad let out a squeal. "Rachel! You're here!" She dropped everything and raced to the front of the truck, then tumbled down the steps toward Rachel. She gave her the expected air-kiss on both cheeks and then threw her arms around her. Whoever said that the French were reserved and aloof had never met Lilia.

"What are you doing here?"

"I suddenly have a lot of time on my hands," Rachel said with a wry twist of her mouth.

"No! Because of all this—" she waved a hand looking for the proper English term, then gave up—"*désordre*?"

"This mess, yes. That's a good way to put it. But I've been craving your pommes frites for months, so it's not all bad."

"Pommes frites right away." Lilia grabbed both

Rachel's hands and squeezed. "We must catch up. When I have a lull."

"Of course," Rachel said, even though she knew Lilia would be absorbed with customers until they ran out of food, sometime toward ten o'clock tonight. And she wasn't sure what she was going to say anyway. Lilia would understand, be sympathetic—after all, she'd ditched her line cook job to open a food truck—but this sort of thing was like the flu. Everyone sent their regrets from a distance, afraid that her misfortune might be catching.

"And what would you like, Melody?" Lilia asked, displaying her impressive memory, considering that the two women had only been introduced once, and that years ago.

"Whatever Rachel's having," she said.

"Excellent." She inclined her head toward the growing line of customers, most of them looking a little impatient at the interruption. "It's on me."

"Lilia—"

"Your money is no good here, Rachel. Now I need to get back."

"We understand. Your adoring public awaits."

Lilia flashed an apologetic smile and scampered back into her truck, where she continued to charm her customers with her French accent and adorably chic ways and then dazzle them with her food. If there were anyone made to be the spokesperson for a business, it was her. If only the spotlight came so easily to Rachel.

Ana sidled up beside them, her food already in hand, a trio of folded steamed buns brimming with different fillings. "Should I get a table for us?"

Melody surreptitiously checked her watch. "We'll be right there."

There was definitely something going on. If they hadn't already dragged her out of her apartment, Rachel would think they'd staged an intervention. Except Melody and Ana were the only ones who really cared what happened to her. She might think of her kitchen staff as her family, but they were more like countrymen—a shared citizenship, outsiders among the larger mainstream community, bonded by their weird hours and neuroses and gallows humor. They were probably sad to see her go, but they wouldn't think of her much beyond what her departure meant to them during work hours.

Melody nudged her. "You okay?"

Rachel sucked it up, straightened her shoulders, and pushed away the beginnings of self-pity. "I'm fine. Just hungry."

Their food came up next—enormous helpings of thick-cut fries topped with shredded duck, piled incongruously in red-and-white-checked paper boats. They took their food and wound their way back through the ever-increasing crowd to where Ana had managed to snag one half of a table in the back corner. Melody slid in beside Ana, and Rachel squeezed into the small space between the fence and the table.

"I've been craving these for weeks." Rachel took a fry from her basket and bit into it with a sigh. They were perfect—crisp on the outside with a creamy interior, at once both salty and sweet from a double bath in boiling duck fat. Not exactly the healthiest of choices, but oh, was it worth it.

"So . . ."

Ana's tone immediately pegged Rachel's intervention meter. Rachel put her entire attention on her food. "So what?"

"What are you going to do now?"

Rachel put down her French fry before she could even finish it. No sense letting the conversation sour her enjoyment of such deliciousness. "Do I really have to have a plan?"

"You know I understand the need to mourn. But I also know that you're going to go crazy if you're not working. You need something to occupy your time."

"Why not something like this?" Melody gestured toward the coaches. "You've got enough seed money to buy a truck and outfit it."

Rachel shook her head.

"Why not?"

How did she explain without seeming like a

snob? It wasn't that she believed a food truck was beneath her. She thought it was a great opportunity for chefs to express themselves without the constraints of P&L and overhead and worrying about turns of the dining room. It was almost complete culinary freedom, and the public themselves determined who succeeded or failed, not the accountants. And yet . . .

"Food is only one part of what I do," Rachel said finally. "It's all about the experience. Hospitality. When I had my own place, it was like inviting people into my home. I trained the front of the house to a certain standard, to make sure that every person who walked in felt like a welcomed guest, not just a customer. Here—" she waved a hand—"there is no house. Not in the same sense. The only element I'm in charge of is the food, and that feels incomplete."

"Has anyone ever told you that you're a control freak?" Ana asked with a little smile.

Melody snorted. "That's hilarious, coming from you."

"Hey!" Ana said.

"I don't know what I want to do yet," Rachel said. "It feels like you're telling me to start dating before the ink is even dry on the divorce papers."

"We really need to get you a boyfriend," Ana said.

"I'm not interested in a boyfriend." She avoided

their knowing gazes, scanning the patio behind them, and felt her muscles freeze.

She might not want a boyfriend, but that didn't mean she was immune to the specimen of pure male beauty walking toward them. She'd had plenty of experience with Tall, Dark, and Handsome, especially in the manscaped streets of Manhattan, but the guy walking toward them could have stepped straight out of a Colorado outdoors magazine. Tall but not too tall with mussed brown hair, light eyes that looked either green or blue from this distance, and a chiseled jaw shaded with just the right amount of stubble. He wore jeans and a light canvas jacket over a T-shirt tight enough to hint at toned muscle beneath.

And he was looking right at her.

She was suddenly finding it hard to breathe, and the unaccustomed bloom of heat in her cheeks meant nothing good. "Holy . . . ," she murmured beneath her breath.

"What?" Melody asked.

"Don't look!" she hissed, but it was too late. Both Melody and Ana were swiveling toward the guy, who hadn't wavered from his trajectory toward their table.

"You know, I think we need to go get drinks." Melody rose abruptly. Too abruptly. "Do you want anything?"

"Other than to sink into the concrete? Fine. Something nonalcoholic. Surprise me."

They were off faster than she'd ever seen them move, a few seconds before the man arrived at her table. She steeled herself against her inevitable, involuntary reaction and still felt a little tremor. Hazel. His eyes were hazel, and a dimple flirted at the corner of his uncertain smile.

Uncertain?

She composed herself and looked up at him again, waiting for the introduction. Or more likely, an inquiry about the time because his girlfriend was late. A man like that had to have a girlfriend. Or a wife.

Instead, he shoved his hands in his pockets and asked, "Rachel Bishop?"

A bucket of cold water doused the lovely glow she was feeling. "Who are you? Press? I have nothing to say." She began to gather their meals together, until he thrust a hand out.

"Wait. I'm not press. Not really. My name is Alex Kanin."

Kanin. She stared at him for a moment, wondering why that sounded familiar, sure that she would have remembered him if she'd met him before. No matter how busy, she wouldn't have forgotten that face. Then it dawned on her. The article in the *New Yorker*. Alexander Kanin. She straightened and sent her best glare his direction, the one that made her cooks cower in apprehension. "I have nothing to say to you."

"Please." He seemed to be gathering himself,

his expression pained. "You don't have to say anything. Just listen." When she still didn't relent, he pleaded, "I'll only take a couple of minutes. I promise."

Rachel looked for her friends in the crowd, but they were still standing at the outdoor bar, waiting for their drinks. The crowds had piled in even thicker now, and if she gave up their table, there was no telling when they might nab another one. She clenched her jaw while she considered. "Fine." She pulled her phone out of her pocket, set the timer, and plunked it on the table between them. "You have exactly two minutes. Go."

Alex looked startled, but he lowered himself onto the bench opposite and leaned forward over his folded hands. "I owe you an apology. I never thought when I wrote the article that anyone would make the connection to you, least of all that it would turn into this. You have to believe me. . . . Denver isn't exactly New York. Who would have thought anyone would take such an interest in a review written by a third-tier journalist like Espy?"

Rachel stared at him. He had sought her out to apologize, but that didn't change what he had done, what his actions had set in motion. Never mind the fact that he was even better-looking up close, that she got a delicious waft of a clean-smelling cologne when the breeze briefly changed directions.

"I think the way that everyone has taken after you is unfair and uncalled for, and a five-year-old could tell that you were set up on that interview. I feel completely responsible for this, even if I had no idea it would turn out this way."

Why did he have to seem so sincere? It was much easier to hate him when he was a callous, anonymous opportunist only interested in the advancement of his own career. She pressed her lips together to keep from responding. This was his two minutes. She'd promised to hear him out.

"I'm here to ask for your forgiveness and let you know this was never my intent. If there's anything I can do, I'll do it. Just tell me what it is."

"You may be sorry, but that doesn't change the fact that my career as a chef may well be over now. I've had to close all my social media accounts to stop the harassment. I don't want anything from you—"

The timer beeped, and she reached to turn it off. But he swooped it out of her grasp, his thumbs flying across the virtual keyboard. Then he set it back down between them.

"In case you change your mind." He rose from the table as Ana and Melody returned, holding three tall glasses between them, then gave them each a nod. He paused before he turned away. "For what it's worth, Rachel, I'm really sorry.

If I could go back and do it differently, I would."

Her friends took their seats again, even though they craned their necks to watch him walk away. "What did he say?" Melody asked, sliding a glass of soda across the table.

"He—wait. Shouldn't you be asking who that was?" Rachel narrowed her eyes. "Unless you already knew . . . You did. You set this up!"

Melody looked sheepish. "He came into the restaurant looking for you, and he looked so pathetic I told him we'd be here tonight. He apologized, didn't he?"

"Yes, he apologized, but somehow I don't think him looking pathetic was what swayed you." Despite herself, she scanned the crowd to catch a parting look. Then she shook herself sternly. "It's not like he can do anything about what happened."

"But he writes for the *New Yorker* and, from what I can tell, a bunch of other places too. He probably has connections."

"And you think I should play on his guilt? That's not how I work."

"Why not?" Ana asked. "It's the least he could do."

Rachel shoved her phone toward them. "He put his number in my phone."

Ana and Melody exchanged a look.

"What? He said if there's anything he could do, he'd do it."

"That sounds like volunteering his connections to me," Melody said.

"To do what? I'm two days past losing my restaurant. Even if I knew what I wanted to do next, who's going to invest in a project with me after all this?"

"If there's one thing I've learned working in publicity," Ana said, "it's that everything blows over eventually. Especially when it comes to something like this. We need to work some damage control, repair your reputation. You know very well most of your guests don't care about this stuff. It's the industry and the pundits and the social media trolls. And they'll lose interest in you as soon as someone else does something stupid."

"Thanks," Rachel said.

"You know I didn't mean it like that."

"The problem is, I have no idea how I would win over anyone. What am I going to do, invite every influential person in Denver over for dinner and show them that I'm really not a terrible person?"

Melody and Ana exchanged that look again, the one that made her feel like she'd been the subject of conversation. "What?"

Ana pulled out her tablet from her oversize bag and tapped in a few letters on the keyboard. Then she swiveled it around. "Read this."

It was an article from some magazine talking

about the rise of nontraditional venues and vehicles for gourmet food. Seriously, how did Ana have time to keep up with this stuff? The woman was a walking encyclopedia of pop culture. Rachel flicked the screen with her finger, skimming the text. Food trucks, which she'd already ruled out. Upscale food courts, a trend that Denver had already embraced and presented the same problem for Rachel as the coaches— lack of control of the overall guest experience. Then she came to the last paragraph and stopped.

"Pop-up restaurants?"

Ana took the tablet back, practically vibrating with excitement. "Once a month, even once a week. Fixed menu, unusual locations. Heavy emphasis on experience and hospitality."

"I know what they are." They'd been popular in Europe for many years now. Some of them were spectacular productions closer to a circus, like Gingerline in London. Others were immersive experiences in the same place using rotating themes. A few farm-to-table chefs in Colorado already hosted pop-ups at their farms for a select guest list. Tickets were as coveted in the food world as white truffles and twice as hard to acquire.

"Think about it." Melody's voice held the same sort of anticipation. "You would have complete control of every aspect, from menu to location to decor. It would be an opportunity to really show what you can do to a handpicked group of influencers."

"Like a supper club," Rachel murmured to herself. "An alternative to the usual weekend dining experience."

"Good food, good conversation. And exclusivity would pretty much guarantee that it was the most talked-about event in town, especially since you're notorious at the moment."

Rachel cracked a bare smile. She would have never thought she would do anything to make herself notorious, but maybe it could be put to good use. And so far Denver had very few options of this sort. Given the right spin, it could be wildly successful.

It came to her in a flash. "The Saturday Night Supper Club." They stared at each other, a hush falling over the table, a cocoon of silence amid the pounding beat of music and the laughter of other diners. "We've got something, haven't we?"

Melody nodded slowly, and even Ana looked a little stunned. "Oh yeah, we've got something."

Rachel looked between her two friends and for the first time in days, a feeling that was not terror or grief built in her. "So. Where do we begin?"

Chapter Eight

That could have gone better.

Of course, it could have gone much, much worse, and Alex had been steeling himself for reactions ranging from a drink in his face to a full-on screaming match.

Instead, Rachel Bishop had looked at him with this closed-off, hurt expression and set her cell phone timer for two minutes. Two minutes in which he had poured out his regrets about his part in the situation and then been summarily dismissed.

He wound his way from the food truck court toward his dark-blue Subaru parked down the street. Fine. Perfect, actually. He'd done what he'd come to do, apologize and offer his assistance, and she'd refused. He was off the hook.

Except he was still thinking about her. That was about as far from off the hook as he could get.

He opened his car door with his key fob and threw himself into the front seat. He'd made an error coming here tonight. He'd prepared himself for all the possible ways she might react and how he would handle it. He'd just been thinking of her in terms of a wronged chef whose career had been damaged.

It hadn't even occurred to him that she might be an extremely attractive woman.

He'd looked her up online, of course. Her only photos on her restaurant's website and her Facebook page had been the run-of-the-mill head-shot variety: hair in a knot, white chef's jacket, arms crossed over her chest while she gazed seriously at the camera. If she'd been wearing makeup, it was the kind devised to make her look natural and no-nonsense.

He hadn't expected a dark-haired beauty with a killer figure and long, wavy hair that begged a man to bury his fingers in it. So no, he might not have given his apology the full attention it deserved.

He really was a jerk. Wasn't that the very thing he'd been trying to call Espy on, the tendency to judge a woman who had done extraordinary things solely on her looks and sex appeal? Of course, he wasn't actually judging her on her looks; they were an unexpected bonus.

That was some hard-core justification if he'd ever heard any.

Alex pulled away from the curb into the waning evening traffic and made his way southeast through the city to his condo in Cheesman Park. Denver's neighborhoods ebbed and flowed into each other much more smoothly than a city map might suggest, pockets of distinct architecture separated by commercial space of every vintage and dotted with contemporary homes that had sprung up in place of historic ones that were too old to be saved—or where the demand was too high to justify leaving an 800-square-foot foursquare intact.

His building was a 1970s high-rise, built on the site of a former 1930s mansion, long since torn down to accommodate the city's population growth. It had been updated several times over the decades, the last time while he was living there. He'd written his first—and possibly only—book in the middle of a construction zone, the hammering and sawing so relentless that it had invaded his dreams. Now, however, he found himself with prime Denver real estate, equity in the bank, and a rental unit next door that brought in enough income to keep him there.

It was the one truly good thing he'd gotten out of his last relationship. There were advantages to dating a real estate agent, after all.

Alex turned onto his street as one of his neighbors pulled out of a spot, and he navigated the wagon into the empty space. He grabbed the plastic bag holding his food—from the amazing French truck at Rhino Crash—and made his way into the lobby and up the elevator. Silently, the metal box slid upward to one of four penthouses on the top floor. Yes, he'd gotten lucky for sure. Thirty-one-year-old self-employed writers typically didn't get penthouse apartments in the city.

The new lock turned smoothly and he pushed through to his loft space, dropping his keys on the table by the front door and striding through to the open renovated kitchen. Good for resale, Victoria had said, picking out high-end appliances and finishes that made it the perfect bachelor pad for the man who liked to entertain.

He'd never even turned on the oven.

Instead, he found a chilled bottle of pop in the refrigerator, pulled out some utensils, and took his takeout to the drafting table in his bedroom. He could eat while he worked on his proposal. Now that he'd dispatched his duty to Rachel Bishop, the block he'd had against putting words on the page should evaporate and he could get both his agent and his publisher off his back.

But the blinking cursor on the screen didn't move, even as the pile of duck-fat fries and shredded confit shrank to nothing more than a smudge at the bottom of the paper container.

He had nothing to say.

"That can't be true." Alex tipped his chair back on two legs. He always had something to say about everything—according to Victoria, it was one of his greatest faults. A teenager walking through the botanic gardens with his eyes on his cell phone rather than the beauty around him would spawn an incisive essay on how technology had at once heightened society's focus and damaged its ability to see the bigger picture. Fitness enthusiasts running the stairs at the Red Rocks Amphitheatre in their designer exercise duds with perfectly coiffed hair might spark musings on the commercial intersection of fitness and beauty. The world around him was filled with details that other people missed. It was his job to draw attention to those things.

And yet the only detail on which he could focus was the slightly uncomfortable way Rachel had sat at that table, looking lost and out of her depth. What was she doing right now? What was she going to do next? Was she like all the people who left corporate America—or prison—and realized that no matter how bad it was on the inside, it was better than a world of free choice?

There was an essay there, all right, but unless he wanted to make matters worse, Rachel Bishop could never be the topic of his writing.

Alex shoved back from the desk with a frustrated sigh and took his empty paper bowl to the trash can beneath the sink. He wasn't going to get anywhere on the proposal tonight. He picked up his phone and texted a quick message to Bryan: **Going to the gym. Meet me there if you're free.** Outdoor climbing was always his first choice to settle his thoughts, but desperate times called for desperate measures.

Bryan texted back immediately. Be there in 30.

At least Alex felt better about one thing: at the moment, Bryan had no more of a social life than he did.

The gym wasn't exactly packed, but it still took Alex a few minutes to find Bryan in the expansive, warehouse-like space. This wasn't a typical gym; it catered to Denver's extreme-sports enthusiasts. It wasn't unusual to see men and a few women training for things like *American Ninja Warrior*, taking advantage of all the unusual obstacles meant to build the skills necessary to hang from, vault over, and flip off the sides of cliffs and buildings. Every time he felt good about his level of fitness, all he had to do was show up and watch someone running the parkour course like it was a child's inflatable obstacle bouncer. He was still recovering from his last attempt at the salmon ladder.

When he finally located his friend, Bryan was climbing the twenty-foot bouldering wall, scaling the side with such rapidity that a couple members had stopped to watch him. Alex waited until he reached the top, then called up, "Are you done showing off?"

"Not quite," Bryan called without looking behind him, then began downclimbing with as much fluidity as he'd shown on the way up.

"You can't help yourself, can you?" Alex said when Bryan came back over to him.

"What?"

Alex followed his friend's gaze and saw a pretty blonde give him a shy smile before she went back to talking to her friend. "You going to go talk to her?"

Bryan shrugged. "I see her around here sometimes. Respectable climber, though she's got some bad habits."

"Somehow I don't think you were showing off for her because you're interested in her climbing habits."

"How did the conversation with the chef go?"

Alex shook his head with a wry smile. "Nice subject change." He might have a good reason to be gun-shy about jumping into a relationship again after Victoria, but Bryan should have no such qualms. Women practically fell at his feet, including nice ones that he could take home to his mother. Yet even if one did catch his attention long enough to date, she didn't last past the first month.

"I take it the fact you're here means it didn't go well?" Bryan started toward the room in the back where the parkour course was located, along with some separate apparatuses set up specifically for climbers.

"She gave me two minutes and then basically told me to get lost."

113

"Then you're off the hook."

"Yeah."

Bryan looked at him sideways. "Wow. She was that hot?"

Alex blinked. "What? Who said anything about her looks?"

"You're a good guy, Alex, but even you don't feel that guilty over a stranger unless you've got some personal interest in her. So what gives?"

He almost felt embarrassed to voice it aloud. "She's clearly not the type to skate by on her looks, but she could if she wanted to. No question."

Bryan whistled. "And she can cook? Marry her."

"She won't even talk to me. I thought she was going to slap me when I put my number in her phone."

"Nice one. I didn't think you had it in you."

"To help her out professionally."

"Sure. Keep telling yourself that."

Alex rolled his eyes and approached the ledge on the far side of the room. "Can we get to it here? I'm afraid you're going to spring a 5.13 on me next time you call me out for an easy climb."

"Fine." Bryan shrugged. "But you know you suck at multitasking. As long as she's out there and she hates you, you're not going to write a single word. You remember our senior year? You were going to fail AP Lit until I forced you to ask out Belinda Ashton. As soon as you had the date set up, you wrote your entire term paper in an evening."

"I wrote my entire term paper in an evening because I was afraid of not graduating."

"Right. So you're welcome."

Alex climbed the steps to take his position at the slanted concrete wall, wishing his friend didn't know him and his strange work habits so well. It was easier to tell himself that he didn't have a problem when Bryan didn't needle him about it. Instead, he chalked his hands and then reached up for the narrow ridge of smooth concrete. The wall sloped away toward the floor so there was no way to get a foothold and help support his body weight; it was hand and forearm strength all the way across. To make it harder, the ledge undulated up and down, changing the balance and grip. Lack of concentration or strength meant an eight-foot drop to an only slightly padded floor below.

He took his position and inched his way across, his feet swinging while the muscles and tendons in his hands and forearms strained.

"Ninety degrees!" Bryan called, and Alex pulled himself up to put the stress on his biceps and not his elbow joints. This was the perfect metaphor for his life. Hanging on by the tips of his fingers, a fall beneath him if he made one wrong move. No matter what Bryan said, he needed to pull himself together, write the proposal, and get to the other side. This was the time to power through and keep his mind on the task before him.

Not on a beautiful chef and the mess he had inadvertently made of her life.

Chapter Nine

First thing the next morning, even before Rachel had finished her coffee, she drove to the bank and deposited the check in the ATM.

Such a small thing, but cashing it was her first acknowledgment that her season at Paisley was over. Her investment had come back to her with interest, which technically made the restaurant a success, however much it felt like she had failed. She needed to move on.

She took her second cup of coffee and her notebooks out to the front porch of her bottom-floor condo, letting the morning stillness wash over her. The sun had begun its ascent into the sky, the light changing from morning blue to bright cheery yellow, the birds striking up an enthusiastic serenade in the trees beyond her chair. This was something that she always loved but never got to enjoy. She got in late, crashed hard, woke up with barely enough time to shower, change, and head back to the restaurant. The most leisurely her mornings had been in years was when she got into her office extra early and enjoyed a cup while she put together the evening's specials.

She started with her green journal first, tapping her pen on the page while she considered her entry. *Money in the bank*, she finally decided, then turned to her fresh composition notebook. On the cover, she wrote in large block letters: THE SATURDAY NIGHT SUPPER CLUB.

On the first page, she began a list of things that still needed to be decided:

1) Venue
2) Calendar/frequency
3) Guests
4) Promotion/publicity (if any)
5) Menus/themes

Basically, the only thing that had been decided was the name. And while Ana enthusiastically insisted that she could sell the concept on the name alone, Rachel knew it would take much more than a clever idea to make her new venture a success.

Those five lines glared at her, demanding exploration but defying any ideas she had to further define them. She needed help. A plan. Someone's coattails to ride while she figured out how to get herself back into the public's good graces.

She had a phone full of such contacts, some of whom had stayed conspicuously quiet on the #WeBelong situation. She could only hope that some of them would still take her calls.

Instead her phone woke to the last contact added to her list.

Alex.

"Just 'Alex,' huh?" Was he so sure he was the only Alex in her life that he could just go by his first name? Not that he was in her life. In fact, if she had her way, he would immediately be *out* of it. He'd already done enough, thank you very much, and she wasn't about to give him another opportunity to send what was left of her career down the toilet.

She scrolled through the contact list until she came to the name Caleb Sutter. Might as well shoot high. She pressed Call and waited while the phone dialed.

A man answered on the third ring, his low voice muted by the sound of activity in the background. "Rachel. I was wondering if I'd hear from you."

Just hearing his familiar voice relaxed her. Caleb was one of her few chef friends she hadn't actually worked with. He'd opened his own place around the time she'd come to Colorado for the exec job at Brick & Berry and quickly worked himself to the top of the fine-dining food chain. They'd hit it off at Denver's annual food and wine festival, two young chefs trying to make names for themselves.

"Am I that predictable?" Rachel asked. "I thought you'd expect me to hold out until at least the end of the week."

"I know you. You get bored. You can't stand to not work. But you do have good timing. I have an opening for a floater in my kitchen right now."

Rachel flushed with embarrassment. The floater position was usually a training ground for a sous-chef, staffed by a strong all-around cook who could step in on any station when someone was sick or demands were particularly high.

It was a long, hard step down for someone like her.

The fact that he would even have her in his restaurant was encouraging, though. Maybe not everyone believed the worst about her. "I appreciate that, Caleb. And I'll keep it in mind. But I think I want to stay out on my own."

"Equity is doing well, but not that well. I don't have the money to invest in another venture. I'm completely sunk into this one."

"It's not that. I'm looking for an endorsement."

Silence on the other end of the line. She plowed ahead and told him about the supper club, how she was hoping someone might partner with her on the venture, another chef who had an excellent reputation and the right connections to pull it off.

The silence stretched, and when Caleb finally spoke, his voice held a mix of admiration and regret. "I think this is a great idea, Rachel. But I'm afraid I'm not the one you're looking for. I wish I could help."

"I'm not willing to hitch my future to yours" was what he was really saying. And she couldn't

blame him. Not when the public had turned so quickly and violently on her. "I wish you could too. But I understand."

"Really, though, if you need a place, my door is always open."

"Thanks, Caleb. I appreciate that. Keep in touch?"

"Absolutely. You too. Come by the restaurant anytime."

Rachel hung up, knowing that the only way she was going to see or hear from him was if she made a reservation. There were plenty more people to call, however.

The next two didn't answer their phones. Either they were already in the throes of prep for the day or they were ignoring her.

The fourth person answered and made her wish she hadn't. Melina De Soto gave a snort in place of a hello. "Well, you've got a brass pair, I'll give you that."

"Hello to you too, Melina. Did I miss something?"

"The feminist movement, apparently."

Rachel sighed and fell back against her chair. "You know as well as I do that I was taken out of context."

"I would have been willing to give you the benefit of the doubt were it not for your little temper tantrum at Johnson & Wales."

Would that never cease to haunt her? "I left

because I didn't like the way Nina and Toni were talking about our male colleagues. You're well aware that you wouldn't be where you are if it weren't for all the male chefs you worked with. It's a poor way to repay them by bad-mouthing them for their gender."

"Maybe that's true. But we women have to stick together. Which is the reason I haven't spoken out on social media about you. You might have dug yourself a hole, but I'm not going to fill it full of water while you're down there."

Typical Melina with her overblown metaphors. She was a crazy-good chef—a Beard nominee the year Rachel won, in fact—but she was the circle-the-wagons type. Rachel wouldn't be finding any help from that quarter. "You know what? Never mind. It was a long shot anyway."

She hung up, not really caring if she burned any more bridges. The one between her and Melina was already smoldering and had been since Rachel proved she had a mind of her own.

And that was it, she realized. Four people she could call on in her time of need. There were others who would support her, no doubt, but they weren't in a position to help in the way she needed.

She scrolled past Alex's entry again.

No, that was a ridiculous thought. There was nothing he could do for her. He was a writer, not a chef. And he might be a big deal in New York, but that didn't necessarily translate halfway across the country to Denver, where people still tended to be less impressed by the goings-on at the coasts.

He was just trying to displace his own guilt. He certainly didn't have anything to offer, nor did he really expect her to take him up on it.

Which didn't explain why her fingers brought up an online bookseller and tapped in his name.

A single book came up, titled *Mis-Connected*. The blurbs were impressive: big names in journalism, humor, and satire, all raving about his take on America through the eyes of a Russian immigrant family; his satirical view of the cultural differences that separated him from his well-educated Russian parents; the clash of a generation that valued privacy and modesty with an American culture that demanded transparency. She bypassed the urge to read the sample—after all, she already knew he could write—and instead scrolled down to the reviews. For every three raves, there seemed to be one infuriated reader. Some felt that Alex was judging them as Americans, even though he had been born in Colorado. Russian expats accused him of co-opting their cultural narrative for commercial means. One said he was a two-bit essayist whose work wasn't worth the paper it was printed on.

Yikes. No wonder he'd been so worked up over

public criticism. If this was what he dealt with all day, she could hardly blame him. It was exactly why she had wanted to hide in her kitchen, expose as little of herself to the public as she could. At least then the worst they could do was criticize her food.

Somehow, her finger took on a life of its own and clicked the sample button, beaming the first chapters directly to her phone.

Just getting to know her adversary. That was all.

Her coffee grew cold and her pen fell to the cement of the porch as she read. He was a gifted writer. She might not be a great judge of literature, but even she could see how he managed to walk the line between criticism and compassion as he related scenes from his Russian-American upbringing: stories of his strict, intellectual parents; the expectations that he would follow their footsteps into teaching; his eventual abandonment of academia to write what his parents termed "little stories." Page after page painted a picture of the frustrated intellectual, too conservative to be avant-garde, yet too independent for his traditionalist family—the outsider who could see all too clearly the foibles of both camps. In an odd way, Rachel understood exactly how he felt. Still, when she was done with the sample, she could scarcely believe the direction of her thoughts.

Maybe Alex really could help her with the supper club.

She put down her phone and kicked her feet up on the porch railing. That was insane. He was the reason she was having to do the supper club in the first place. He was a public figure of some note, and from what she could tell from a quick Google search, he was capitalizing on her misfortune by doing interview after interview on the topic.

But her gut told her his apology, his insistence that hc hadn't intended this outcome, was sincere.

Where did that leave her?

Before she could second-guess herself, she tapped out a message to him: This is Rachel. I'll bite. What did you have in mind?

Almost as if he were waiting for her text—she prayed she wasn't that transparent—his message came back immediately. Let's discuss over dinner tonight. Six? You pick the place.

She narrowed her eyes at the screen. He wasn't taking her seriously. Or maybe he was thinking of this as a date, which it most certainly was not. The closest this got was a potential business arrangement. Or an olive branch.

Well, if he was going to let her pick, she was going to meet him on her turf. Or the closest she had right now. Caleb had invited her, so she would take him up on it. Equity Bar and Grill? I'll get us reservations.

He didn't respond. Humph. Maybe he wasn't willing to shell out for the kind of prices Equity commanded. Apparently, apologies were cheap. She dropped her feet to the ground, gathered her pen and notebook, and walked into the house, annoyed that she'd so quickly let herself be suckered.

She was rummaging through the refrigerator for lunch ideas when her back pocket buzzed. She fumbled for her phone.

You're on.

Her heart leapt with traitorous enthusiasm and just as quickly fell somewhere in the vicinity of her knees. She frantically tapped out a group text to Ana and Melody: Somehow I ended up agreeing to dinner at Equity with Alex tonight. What do I do?

Melody responded first. You go shopping with me! I'll be right over.

Wait, shopping? No. I'm not dressing up for him.

Ana finally chimed in. Oh, you're dressing up, Rach. You're not going out in public to a restaurant owned by the second-most-visible chef in Denver and not dressing to kill.

Rachel nibbled her thumbnail, that somer-saulting heart of hers now plummeting to the ground floor. What stupid impulse had made her come up with this idea in the first place? She really hadn't thought it would go this far. No, she hadn't thought at all. She'd been overcome with misplaced affection over some good—and clearly manipulative—writing and made a deal with the devil.

A devil with hazel eyes and a dimple she couldn't stop thinking about.

"You've got to be kidding me, right?" Rachel held up the black spandex thing that looked like what would happen if you crossed an old-fashioned swimsuit with a rubber band. Sized for a two-year-old. "You don't really think I'm going to fit all of *this* into this?"

Melody pulled the Spanx out of her hand. "Look, it's stretchy. It's supposed to be tight to hold all *that* in the right place. Not that you have that much to rearrange. Seriously, girl, how is it possible that you stay so skinny?"

"Are you kidding me? I'm shaped like a drumstick. Chicken legs on the bottom, meat in the middle."

Melody threw back her head and laughed. "It's always food-related with you. Now stop whining and put it on."

"Fine, fine." Rachel snatched the elastic shapewear out of her friend's hand and marched to the bathroom. Once behind the closed door, she stripped down to her bra and underwear and gave a dubious look to the *thing*. Here went nothing. She shoved her legs into the girdle-panties and tugged upward. They slid up to her knees and stopped.

"Melody? I think I'm stuck."

"You need to kind of, you know, shimmy it up."

"Like a sausage?"

"Exactly like a sausage."

"Great. I'm a human sausage." After five minutes of tugging and squeezing and rearranging, she was encased in an elastic tube that came up to the lower edge of her bra. "How am I supposed to eat in this?"

Melody suppressed her laughter when Rachel toddled out into the bedroom, stiff-armed and -legged. "You might try walking more naturally."

"No, *you* might try walking more naturally. I've lived in what essentially amounts to professional pajamas for fifteen years. This is . . ."

Melody held up the body-skimming jersey dress. "Drop-dead sexy. Now stop whining and put it on."

Rachel slid the garment over her head, letting it flow over her now-smoothed-out curves. From the front room, she heard the door open and close, the telltale click of impossibly high heels making their way across her wood floor.

Ana appeared in the door of her bedroom. "Wow. Rachel, you look . . ."

"Like a sausage draped in cheesecloth?"

"Absolutely gorgeous. Are you trying to give the guy a heart attack?"

Rachel rolled her eyes, though inwardly her heart gave a little lift. It wasn't wrong to look amazing, was it? Especially since he was so . . . so . . .

Irritating. That was the word she was going for.

"Okay, enough. Let's get this show on the road. Is my hair okay?" She patted her hair, suddenly doubting the unaccustomed style. "I feel like a little girl playing dress-up. Why did I let you talk me into this? This is so not me. I'm a jeans and—"

"Right, but it won't kill you." Ana picked up the little handbag that Melody had brought over and shoved it into her hands while Melody guided Rachel's feet into wedge-heeled pumps. "Now, you're going to be late. Get moving. We don't want him to think you stood him up after you went to all this trouble."

Melody grabbed Rachel's elbow and dragged her from her bedroom out the front door. "Let us know how it goes. We'll lock up behind ourselves. And we'll text you in about an hour in case you need a quick exit."

"This isn't a date, you know," she said. "I can excuse myself if I need to."

"Mmm-hmm. Watch for the text in case you need a rescue."

Rachel strode toward her aging SUV at the curb, then quickly realized she would not be striding anywhere in these pumps. She felt like a geisha, taking mincing steps so she didn't fall off the heels, her body wrapped so tightly in fabric that she couldn't breathe. How did women do this all the time? She'd be lucky if she made it through dinner without having a Victorian-style fainting spell.

She climbed behind the wheel, kicked off the wedges so she could work both the gas and clutch without destroying them, started the car, and pulled away from the curb, the waistline of the super-girdle cutting into her stomach the whole time.

Whatever Alex had in mind, it had better be worth it.

Chapter Ten

Alex checked his watch for the third time in as many minutes, plagued by the sinking feeling that Rachel wasn't coming. Maybe she hadn't forgiven him. Maybe this was an elaborate way of exacting revenge.

But no, that was a childish thing to do, and if there was one thing that Rachel wasn't, it was childish. He understood that much about her at least.

He shifted restlessly in his chair beneath the hem of the white tablecloth and fiddled with his tie. He had overdressed a little, even for this modern, high-end steakhouse. Denver wasn't a fancy, dress-up sort of place—Coloradans expected world-class food that they could eat while wearing jeans and cowboy boots, and this place was no different. But he wanted her to know he took this meeting seriously. That he took her seriously. That he could help her.

Even if he still had no idea how he was going to do that.

At a quarter after six, he was about to give up and order, when the hostess led a tall, dark-haired woman toward his table. He blinked, his nerve endings snapping to attention as she neared. It was Rachel all right, wrapped in a patterned dress with a skirt like an upside-down tulip and high-heeled shoes that showed off the long line of her legs. He swallowed and rose, his mouth suddenly dry. This *was* supposed to be a business meeting, wasn't it?

"I'm sorry I'm late," she said.

He faltered, not sure whether he was supposed to greet her with a kiss on the cheek as a date might or simply a nod. She took care of that confusion by holding out her hand. He shook it, noticed how hard she gripped his hand.

A business meeting, then.

He realized he hadn't responded to her apology. He cleared his throat. "No problem. I haven't been here long."

The hostess pulled out Rachel's chair and she sat, immediately taking up the single-sheet menu. He watched her throat work and realized that she was nervous.

Well, that was a surprise. Nothing about her had indicated she was capable of nerves.

"I have a feeling you know the menu better than I do," he said. "What do you recommend?"

"I don't think you can go wrong with anything here. Caleb is one of the most inventive chefs in Denver."

"Besides you?"

Her eyes flicked up to his, holding surprise and amusement. "Besides me, yes."

"I'm going to let you order for me, then."

"That's very secure of you."

"Don't worry, I don't stake my manhood on knowing what to order off an unfamiliar menu. Especially not when I'm out with an award-winning chef."

"I'm getting the feeling you're trying to flatter me."

"It's not flattery if it's true, and yes, I absolutely am." He leaned back and grinned at her, rewarded when she smiled back.

Their server, Aubrey, arrived to take their drink orders.

"Sparkling water with lemon for me, please," Rachel said.

"I'll have the same." When Aubrey left, he asked, "No wine?"

She shook her head. "I have to admit, Alex, I'm not really sure why I asked you here. I know you volunteered—"

"I know why. You're practical and you're ambitious, and you would kick yourself if you didn't look at every avenue offered to you."

Rachel folded her arms on the edge of the table and leaned forward. "And exactly what avenue are you offering me?"

Aubrey was back with their drinks, lightning-fast service if he'd ever seen it. He suspected that the manager or the chef knew Rachel was in the house and had impressed on their server that they were to get VIP service. Rachel gestured for

Aubrey to come close and engaged her in rapid conversation about the menu, ordering so quietly he didn't catch the selections. Then she focused her attention back on him, clearly expecting an answer to her question.

"What am I offering you? I guess that all depends on what it is you want."

Her eyes narrowed as she studied him. Her words came out with a hint of challenge. "I want my own restaurant again. And for that I need an investor. A *silent* investor."

"As you have probably guessed, I have a few connections who might be interested in something like that. But you also have probably guessed that you're not a great risk right now."

"Thanks to you."

"*Partly* thanks to me." He ignored the sting of her words as they struck. "But the Beard means something. You don't get two nominations and a win by not being the best."

She held his eyes for a long moment. "You're saying I need a way to prove myself. I've already thought of that." She reached into her purse and pulled out a composition notebook.

He turned it to face him. On the cover, printed in neat block writing, were the words *The Saturday Night Supper Club*. "A supper club?"

"Part pop-up restaurant, part dinner party. Exclusive. An opportunity to show what I can do."

Alex nodded slowly. "And you think I can help how?"

A flush rose to her cheeks and she took the notebook back. "I knew this was a bad idea."

"I wasn't trying to be difficult. I really want to know. It seems like you have it all figured out."

Rachel swallowed hard, seemed to be chewing on her words. "I had a good reputation among the dining public, at least until recently. But in the industry . . ." She raised her eyes to his, and he caught that same hint of vulnerability that had pulled him in the night before. "I've cashed in all my chips. I don't have any more credit left to spend here."

"So you need a patron?" His wheels began to turn. The idea was a fascinating one. A salon of sorts, the old-fashioned type where people gathered for good food and drink and stimulating conversation.

"Not a patron. A cohost." She hesitated for a long moment. "I read part of your book."

He sat back in his chair. Now he understood. Not only had he proved he was on her side; she figured his friends might not be as swayed by media opinion as the general public.

Sure, he had the connections—both his own through his work as a writer and from his association with Bryan's family—but her confidence in him was more than a little unnerving.

"How do you see this working? Am I hosting and having you cater? Are we supposed to be friends? Is this a business venture?"

She was chewing her thumbnail, an unexpected sign of insecurity. "I hadn't worked out all the details. I thought I'd be responsible for the food, and you'd take care of the guest list, preferably influential types that would post about it on social media. Eventually we'd sell tickets, but Ana thinks we should build some buzz first. Sort of like how businesses host friends-and-family or press nights before they open."

"Sounds like you've already thought of all the angles. I'm assuming you need a venue."

"That would be the first step, yes."

The answer was clear, but he wasn't sure she would go for it. A back waiter appeared with their first course, tiny plates holding translucent slices of something he was almost certain was raw fish.

"What's wrong, Alex?" Her words held a hint of a challenge. "You don't like octopus?"

In response, he forked a slice into his mouth.

It was disgusting. However, he gave it a couple of manful chews and neither gagged nor reached for his water glass.

He could see by her expression she wasn't fooled.

"It's okay," she said, attacking her own plate with enthusiasm. "It's an acquired taste."

No point in trying to pretend. "I don't mind sashimi. But it's the texture of the octopus, not the taste."

"More for me." She gave him a sly little smile. "Don't worry. I was more conservative with the rest of my choices."

By conservative, though, she didn't mean light-handed. Course after course came out, and he couldn't deny each was more delicious than the last. The octopus was followed by a small charcuterie plate, then an heirloom bean salad. He was half-expecting some elaborate plated entrée that looked like modern art, but instead Aubrey set before him a beautifully cooked rib eye smothered in blue cheese butter.

Rachel flashed him a little smile. "So maybe I hedged my bets on that one."

He sliced into it and took a bite. "This might be the best steak I've ever eaten."

"No argument here." Rachel turned to her fish—an Asian-style barramundi—but he saw a little glimmer of mischief again. If he wasn't mistaken, this might also be the most expensive steak he'd ever eaten.

So perhaps she wasn't above a little payback.

He could hardly count this as suffering, though. When dessert came out—a flight of sorbets—he exhaled in relief. He felt about ready to burst.

Aubrey brought the check, and to his surprise, Rachel reached for it. Alex slid it out of her grasp.

"I told you to pick the place, so this is mine." He managed not to let his eyes widen at the figure on the ticket when he slid his credit card into the folder. He waited for Aubrey to take it before he voiced the idea that had been rattling around his head all night.

"We should hold the supper club at my place."

Rachel's eyes narrowed. "Your place?"

"Don't sound so suspicious. You should see it before you make up your mind."

"I can't imagine why I would be suspicious."

"I'm not sure which hurts more: the aspersions to my character or the lack of confidence in my creativity. Seems a little cliché, doesn't it?"

"You're not helping your case."

He shrugged. "Bring your friends along if you're worried about my intentions. But you need a venue, and I have one." She still looked like she couldn't decide, so he took her notebook and scrawled his address on the last page. "Check it out. Call me in the morning if you want to take a look. And if you like the idea, we can talk further."

Rachel still looked doubtful, but she shoved the notebook in her handbag and pushed away from the table. "Thank you for dinner."

"Thank you for introducing me to an excellent restaurant. I enjoyed it. Even the octopus. A little."

"Liar." The corner of her mouth lifted into a

slight smile. "I'll call you tomorrow and let you know if I'm coming."

"I hope the answer is yes."

She gave him a little nod, then turned and left the restaurant. He sank back into his chair and let out a breath. Rachel at his place. She was right to be suspicious. Because after less than two hours in her company, he wasn't sure that guilt or business were anywhere present in his thoughts.

Chapter Eleven

Rachel tapped the piece of notebook paper repeatedly on the edge of the table, earning a glare from the older couple next to her. She set it down and folded her hands in her lap. Where were Ana and Melody? She'd sent out the SOS first thing this morning after a sleepless night, knowing that Ana would probably be at the gym and Melody would be finishing up her shift at her new job. The bakery had taken one look at her qualifications and hired her on the spot.

She sipped her Americano and shoved down her impatience. At last, she caught a glimpse of a tousled blonde head coming in through the front door, turning every which way to catch a glimpse of Rachel. She half stood and waved Melody her direction.

Her friend wove her way through the tables at the retro breakfast joint in Denver's Ballpark neighborhood, revealing an off-the-shoulder eighties-style sweatshirt over a pair of leggings. When she slid into the booth, Rachel noticed there was still flour in her hair. "Sorry I'm late. Ana hasn't arrived yet?"

"I just got a text from her. She got called into a meeting, but she'll be over as soon as she can get free."

Melody looked at her closely. "This isn't a morning-after walk-of-shame breakfast, is it?"

Rachel gasped. "Of course not. You know me better than that. Last night was strictly professional."

"Pity," Melody said. "The professional part, I mean, not the walk-of-shame thing. I was hoping one of us had a little romance in her life. Heaven knows there isn't a man present anywhere in mine."

"You mean it's hard to find a guy who puts up with your schedule? I can't imagine what that's like."

Their young male server approached, his eyes lingering a little too long on Melody's bared collarbone and shoulder. Rachel suppressed a smile. Melody's nonexistent love life certainly wasn't because of lack of interest. She was simply as married to her job as Rachel was. As Rachel *had been*.

Melody ordered a pot of decaf and then began fiddling with the paper sugar packets in front of her. "So what's this about? Something must have happened to make you convene an emergency waffle meeting."

"I'll tell you as soon as Ana gets here." On cue, Rachel glimpsed the dark head of her other best friend through the front window. Ana caught sight of them immediately and marched through the restaurant, an imposing figure in her designer business suit.

"I've got less than an hour," Ana said. "I have a conference call at nine, and I lied about an off-site meeting so I could skip staff meeting."

"It wasn't a lie," Melody said. "Rachel has important news."

Ana flagged down a passing server—not theirs—and asked for an espresso, and then focused her attention on Rachel. "So it wasn't a waste of a good dress?"

"I don't know about that, but at least it wasn't a waste of time. Alex says he's in. And he thinks he has a venue for me." Rachel paused. "He offered his place."

Immediately, both Ana's and Melody's expressions shifted to alarm.

"Rachel," Ana began.

"I know. I thought the same thing. And then I looked up the address." She brought up the listing on her phone and swiveled it around to face them. "This is the building in Cheesman Park. Obviously not his apartment, because this one is up for sale."

Melody blinked. "I don't understand."

"It's a fifteen-story building. His apartment is on the fifteenth floor. According to his neighbor's listing, there are four penthouse units, and each has access to a private roof deck overlooking the city."

"How exactly does a writer afford that kind of place?" Ana asked. "That sounds suspicious."

"Even so, it's probably worth checking out, right? He invited me to take a look today. Said to bring you two if I was worried about his intentions."

"I don't like the idea of you going over there yourself, but I can barely keep my eyes open," Melody said. "And Ana sounds booked today."

"You were the one who set up the meeting at Rhino Crash!" Rachel exclaimed. "And now you think he's a serial killer?"

"They never *look* like serial killers," Ana said. "Haven't you seen those crime shows? All the neighbors say what nice, normal men they were. 'We never would have known he had bodies of women buried in his basement.' "

"You two are a lot of help. I'm going. I was hoping one of you might be able to come with me, but . . ."

Ana reached across the table for the notebook paper. "Is this the address?" She snapped a photo of it with her phone. "Let us know when you get there. If I don't hear back from you in two hours, I'll call the police."

"You're serious."

"Dead serious." Ana grimaced. "Poor choice of words. Listen, he's probably a nice guy. Just be careful. Go with your gut."

That was the first good advice she had heard. Her gut rarely steered her wrong, and now it was telling her that Alex was her best shot at getting her life back. Rachel pulled out her phone and tapped out a message to him. I'd like to take a look at your venue if the offer is still open. Hopefully that didn't sound too much like innuendo. Hopefully he really had been serious about using his place for the supper club.

Was she crazy for trusting a complete stranger, who happened to be the man who had gotten her into this situation in the first place?

Yes. She was. But she was out of options. It was clear from the fact her other contacts hadn't returned her phone calls that she was persona non grata in the industry right now. No one was willing to jump into the cross fire.

They ordered their breakfasts and turned the conversation to another topic, but the whole time Rachel was aware of the black rectangle of her phone screen on the table beside her. Maybe Alex had rethought his offer and decided he didn't want to risk his reputation? Or maybe he hadn't had the courage to tell her in person that he wasn't serious about the offer of help.

Then, just as the server brought the bill, the screen lit up.

Come over anytime. I'll be here.

"I guess we're on," she said. "Wish me luck."

"Good luck," Ana said. "And be careful."

"We'll want all the details tonight," Melody added.

Ana picked up the tab, and then they were off

their separate ways. And Rachel began praying she wasn't making a huge mistake.

Alex's building was a 1970s contemporary from the outside, all brownstone and glass with the boxy shape that characterized that area of the city. Rachel mercifully found parking down the street, from which she could study the place unobserved. If she hadn't found the real estate listing and seen what one of the other penthouses looked like, she might doubt that he was being honest about its suitability as a venue.

"Stop procrastinating," she told herself. She climbed out of her car and locked the door behind her, then made her way slowly into the lobby of the building.

Unlike the outside, the lobby was sleek and modern, with concrete floors and marble wall tiles leading to two elevators positioned at the exact center of the building. Her stomach quivered as she walked to them and punched the up button.

Silently, the elevator glided down to the ground floor and the doors slid open. She stepped in and pressed the button. Sure enough, the elevator only went up to floor fifteen.

"There's no reason to be nervous," she told herself, even though she wasn't sure if she was nervous about going alone to a strange man's apartment or seeing Alex again. Maybe both.

She should have waited until Melody or Ana could come with her.

The elevator delivered her into a wide, square landing on the top floor, only four doors marking the hallway. As she'd read, four penthouse units. She found 1504 and rapped sharply on it. Almost immediately the door swung open.

"You came," Alex said with a hint of surprise. "I'm glad. Come on in."

He opened the door wider and stepped aside for her to enter. Clearly, he wasn't trying to impress her; what man invited a woman over and then answered the door in bare feet, wearing paint-spattered sweatpants and a plain gray T-shirt?

A man who knows how good he looks in everything, her brain answered. Hard to tell whether it was a warning or a note of appreciation.

"So as you can see, it's mostly a loft." He extended a hand and walked forward as if he were a real estate agent giving her a tour. "Completely open floor plan, except for the bedroom, which is of course closed off, so you don't need to see that. I have the dining area set up for eight right now, but the table has a leaf that we could extend for twelve. You weren't thinking of more than that, were you?"

"No," she murmured, turning in a circle. "Twelve would be fine."

It was stunning. Even trying to find a reason this wouldn't work, her imagination was dazzled by the possibilities. Big, open spaces with gleaming, acid-stained concrete floors. Floor-to-ceiling windows on one side of the living area, opening up a gorgeous view over the city. Contemporary decor that managed to be at once industrial and inviting, a mix of steel, glass, wood, and acrylic. Either he had an eye for interiors along with his writing talent or he had paid a pretty penny for a designer to fix it up.

"It's lovely," she said, understating the obvious. "You could hold a party three times the size here."

"Would you like to check out the kitchen? Make sure it works for you?"

Rachel turned toward the adjacent kitchen. It was as modern as the rest of the place, with long expanses of counter space and a combination of sleek cabinetry and open shelving. A massive stainless-steel refrigerator was set into the wall on one side, and a semicommercial range took pride of place in the island.

She trailed a finger along the stainless steel of the wall ovens. "This is very nice. You cook?"

"No. I renovated it with an eye for resale, for someone who did cook."

"You have excellent taste, then."

He looked a little embarrassed. "I can't take the credit. It was my ex who made all the design decisions."

"Ex-wife?"

"Ex-girlfriend." Amusement sparked in his

hazel eyes. "She's the reason I have this apartment in the first place. It was a pocket listing for her, an investor who had bought up the top floor of this building when it was converted from apartments to condos. He needed out fast, I had the money to invest . . . so I took half the floor. Oversaw the renovations, leased the other unit to pay for this one." He shrugged. "It's a little flashy, I admit, but the way real estate is going these days, it's a good investment."

It was more explanation than she needed, and that was telling. "The kitchen is more than adequate for my needs," she said finally. "Especially considering I once catered a fraternity ball with a two-burner camp stove and a pressure cooker. Don't ask."

He chuckled, lighting his eyes with humor and firing that ridiculously engaging dimple again. "I won't. But I bet it's a pretty good story."

"It is, actually." She looked around and threw her hands up in defeat. "I honestly can't find anything wrong with this place. It's perfect."

"Oh, but you haven't seen it all yet. Come with me." He gestured toward a spiral steel staircase at the far end of the room, in a nook beside what she assumed was his bedroom. Just as she reached the stairs, she stumbled into the railing. A fat orange tabby wove between her feet and then jumped up onto the back of the sofa.

"Sorry. Should have warned you about

Sunshine. Didn't think he'd make a run for it."

Rachel looked from the cat to Alex, not sure which ridiculous statement to address first. "You have a male cat named Sunshine?"

"Technically, my sister has a male cat named Sunshine. One of her roommates turned out to be allergic and she talked me into taking him until she gets her own place." Alex's mouth twisted into a wry smile. "Which was three years ago, so I'm beginning to think we're stuck with each other. Even if Dina is the only human he actually likes."

Rachel cast another look at Sunshine and followed Alex up the spiral staircase. Somehow, the fact he was sharing this modern space with a slothlike feline commended him more than anything he could have said. Not that serial killers couldn't be animal lovers, but the bemused resignation on his face would be hard to fake.

He led her through a narrow steel door at the top of the stairs, and she stopped short, a gasp leaving her lips. As spectacular as the condo had been, the rooftop deck was even more beautiful. Brick half-walls enclosed it and gave it some privacy from the other patios; potted plants and trees around the outside edges made it a garden wonderland. A long metal table dominated the center of the wood-decked space, with smaller conversation areas set up among the plants. He had even strung lights up above.

And the view: she could see all the way south

to the edge of the city. At night, there would be no better place to be.

"It's gorgeous," she said. "I love your garden. Your ex's doing as well?"

He smiled. "Now that, I can take credit for. My mother always kept a garden and I was cheap labor. Came in handy up here." He moved to a potted lemon, twisted a bright-yellow fruit off a stem, and handed it to her. "It's nice to be able to grab fruit right off the tree. Of course I bring the citrus inside during the winter."

Rachel stood at the railing, the sun beating down on her skin and a refreshing breeze ruffling her hair. It really was beautiful. Romantic, even. How many women had he brought up here?

And why did it matter to her in the first place?

"So what do you think?" he asked. "Is it okay?"

"It's perfect." She turned to him, found him watching her a little nervously from by the door. What did he have to be nervous about? "I think I'd do cocktails and dinner downstairs, and then digestifs above afterwards. Because it's summer, it could be timed for sunset. It would be spectacular."

"So we're on? Partners?"

Faced with the final decision, the practical, suspicious side of her psyche reared its head. "Alex, tell me the truth. What do you get out of it?"

He pressed his lips together for a second, as if he were thinking. Her heart beat a little faster. "Honestly?"

"No, lie to me. Yes, honestly."

He cracked a smile. "For one, I get to stop feeling like a world-class jerk for what I did to your career. For another, I get to show off for my friends and family by throwing a couple of really spectacular dinner parties. Most of them think I sit around in my sweatpants and stare at the wall all day." He looked down at himself and then held up a finger, his dimple surfacing again. "Don't say it. And third, I get to spend time with you."

Her lungs stopped working as she stared at him, all sorts of unhelpful things floating through her head. And then he grinned.

She let out a sigh of relief. "You almost had me there."

"What? I'm being completely serious!"

"Yeah, sure you are." She looked around her. "Are you sure you really want to do this? It's going to be a lot of work, and you barely know me."

"I've got nothing but time."

Rachel took a deep breath, part of her unable to believe she was about to embark on such a huge venture with a complete stranger. But she had no choice. This was her best chance to get her life back.

"Okay then. Let's do this."

Chapter Twelve

Rachel pulled a sheet pan from the oven and inhaled deeply. Her Parmesan crisps had come out lacy and golden brown, like cheesy little snowflakes. She set them aside and picked up her knife, turning to the handful of basil that waited on her cutting board. "He's in."

"I know he's in," Ana said. "He's been in since the day he showed up at the restaurant looking for you. But the question is, are you?"

Rachel paused, surprised by the question. "Do I have any choice?"

"Of course you have a choice," Melody said from her place beside Ana at the table. "Didn't you say that Caleb offered you a job?"

"Floater. It's a step down. Several, in fact."

"But it's a paycheck," Melody replied. "You don't think I'm baking at a tiny little café because it's good for my ego, do you?"

A pang of guilt nagged at Rachel. Melody needed the job, and regardless of what she said, she'd only left Paisley as a show of solidarity. Rachel threw a look over her shoulder at her friend. "That's exactly why I'm doing this. It's a means to an end. A way to get my own restaurant again, where you will once more be my brilliant pastry chef. You'll be back to terrifying interns in no time at all."

"I do not terrify interns," Melody said. "I very nicely tell them that if they touch my dough, I will break their fingers."

Rachel grinned, knowing that neither scenario was the full truth. Melody was sweet but tough; never said a harsh word to anyone, but she always got the job done. She was practically the perfect kitchen staffer, and her way with pastry bordered on wizardry in Rachel's eyes.

"In any case, he seems like he has the connections, and you should see his place. It's like something out of *Architectural Digest*."

"Sure he's not the typical rich guy looking for a pretty wife who can cook?" Ana asked darkly.

"I very much doubt it. Besides, I don't get the impression that he's so much rich as he made a good investment. Besides, you guys were the ones who set me up in the first place. Now you're going to be all suspicious?"

"I was just giving him the opportunity to apologize," Melody said. "I figured it would help you move on. I didn't expect you two to become partners."

"I don't know exactly what we are. But we're meeting tomorrow to go over some ideas." Rachel peeled the crisps from the baking sheet onto a plate, piped an artful swirl of mousse atop each, and then garnished them with the basil chiffonade. She placed the plate in front of her friends. "Now. Try this and let me know what you think."

Melody lifted a crisp and took a bite. Her eyebrows flew up. "That's amazing."

Rachel waited for Ana, who took a bite and nodded vigorously. "I can taste the asparagus and the leeks in the mousse, but it's not too strong. I love it."

"Good. This can be the *amuse-bouche*." Rachel looked at Melody with a sly smile. "I don't suppose you'd like to invent something for the dessert course, would you?"

"I don't know, let me think." Melody rolled her eyes. "Of course."

"Once you get this going, I bet I could convince a couple of my clients that this is the place to be," Ana said. "Have Alex Instagram a picture with some cryptic caption and my hipster foodie clients will be frothing at the mouth."

Rachel was back at the counter, putting finishing touches on her second trial dish, a wild boar *ragù* which would be served over some sort of shaped pasta. She hadn't decided on what yet. "If you dislike your job so much, why do you keep doing it?"

Ana sighed. "It's not that I dislike it. I've been doing this for ten years and it's begun feeling a little . . ."

"Fake?" Melody suggested.

"Contrived," Ana said. "You know Laura James?"

Rachel thought for a moment. "The health and fitness guru? The one who's all about clean eating and vegetarianism?"

"Yep. She has her staff pick her up barbecue and then smuggle it into her house in a Whole Foods bag."

"Are you kidding? What's so bad about barbecue?"

"Exactly." Ana shook her head. "Do you know how many women would buy her videos and read her books if she came clean? 'You can eat the things you love and still look like me, as long as you're not insane about it.' I've been telling her to drop the act and be authentic for years now, but she can't let go of the image."

"And you wonder why I hide in the kitchen," Rachel said. "You can't fake food. Either it's good or it isn't."

"Except everyone fakes something, and you know as well as I do that you didn't lose your job because of your cooking."

"You still think I should have done the interviews?" Rachel asked.

"Honestly, I don't think it would've made a difference. It would have been damage control, yes, but it would have only delayed the inevitable. The big problem was that you *were* Paisley and no one knew it. So it wasn't a big deal to get rid of you."

"I thought the same thing," Rachel admitted,

shifting the pan to the back burner as she began to plate their dinner.

"Then let's not make the same mistake twice. Sure, Alex is hosting this thing, but it's your supper club. You need to make sure everyone knows that. Otherwise, it's no different from any other gathering: Alex gets a pat on the back for finding a great chef and no one has any obligation to you."

Rachel hated interpersonal politics. The need to work an angle. Shouldn't good food be good food and the credit automatically flow to the one responsible?

Ana laughed when she said as much. "This is why I love you, Rachel. That idealism. I wish I didn't know how truly egocentric people are."

There it was again, that hint of longing and regret in Ana's voice, buried beneath her self-deprecating humor. But Ana would deny it if pressed, so instead Rachel finished up their food and brought the plates carefully to the table.

After they oohed and aahed over the boar, Rachel mentally noting what she would change in the seasoning for next time, Melody set her fork down. "Admit it, though, Rachel. This whole experience is more fun considering the eye candy involved."

Rachel ignored the words. But the thought had already crossed her mind. And that was exactly what worried her.

. . .

Alex was surprised at how easy Rachel had been to convince. True, his condo with its roof-deck views was pretty impressive. But more likely her quick agreement was due to her own desperation rather than any inherent trust of him.

He knew how she felt. Every day, there was a call or an e-mail from Christine "checking in" on his progress, each message growing more concerned and urgent. The publishing world was fickle. All it would take was a single catastrophe to take the attention off social issues like the ones he'd been writing about and completely divert the direction of nonfiction acquisitions. He needed to get a placeholder into next year's fall catalog before they decided to give his spot to a newer and trendier author.

"Okay. Time to do this." His conscience was light. He was doing what he felt God was telling him to do: make it up to Rachel even though this whole debacle had been a complete accident. He was going to give her access to people who *might* be interested in investing in her future restaurant, give her an opportunity to show that she wasn't the heartless cook the media was portraying her to be. In fact, in the short time he'd been in her company, that was the last thing he would call her. Guarded, tough-minded, determined, yes. Heartless, no.

Or maybe that was just him thinking like a man rather than a writer.

Enough of that. Alex put on a fresh pot of coffee and booted up his laptop in his bedroom, gazing out on the panoramic views of the sun-drenched city. Seven hundred thousand people, a small population by most standards, all going about their business. All with their unique perspectives, prejudices, habits. Surely there was something out there that could serve as his inspiration. He went back into the kitchen, poured himself a mug of coffee, then meandered back to his desk, where he set it on an electric warmer. Squared the notepads and his pens to one another and to the edge of his desk. Opened up his proposal, sank into his chair, and placed his fingers on the keyboard.

The cursor blinked at him, a challenge. A dare. An accusation.

He clicked over to another document and typed across the top: *The Saturday Night Supper Club*. Below it, he typed: *Guest List*.

Bryan's father was the ideal investor for Rachel's restaurant, but Alex would wait to invite him until the kinks were worked out. He'd start with a couple of journalists he knew, one who worked the city desk at the *Denver Post*, another who wrote features for *Westword*, a well-regarded if highly alternative weekly. His neighbor Robert, across the hall, who was a political strategist and had connections both across the state and in Washington, DC. His parents' academic acquaintances, one of whom he knew had an extensive wine collection. A couple of fellow CU alumni with whom he'd kept in touch through the professional mixers that the university occasionally hosted. Different ages, different professions, different religions, but they shared the most important demographic criteria for this experiment: they had moderate amounts of money and very good taste. Most importantly, they held some influence within their wider circles.

He opened a new message in his e-mail client and began to compose a letter, making it as casual and no-pressure as he could manage. *Putting together a supper club at my place with a talented local chef friend. What's your availability for July?* He cut and pasted into individual e-mails so it wouldn't look like he was mass e-mailing everyone he knew, then flipped back over to his proposal, where, shockingly, no words had magically appeared at the blinking cursor.

He drummed his fingers on top of the desk. *Get started. Just write.* It didn't have to be good. Maybe begin with marketing copy, which everyone knew would never resemble the finished product anyway. It didn't have to be precise, just appealing.

A ding alerted him to a response in his e-mail in-box. Already?

It was Margot Lee, an artist friend he'd met through Bryan. *Sounds fantastic. I'm in if I can bring my fiancé. But the only Saturday night I have free is two weeks from now.*

He flagged the message to reply once he'd had a few other responses.

Slowly, for the rest of the afternoon, replies trickled in. Alex started a scrawled, four-column list showing the different Saturday dates and the various invitees' availability. Only two begged off with requests to be kept in mind once the summer was over.

It was looking like the Saturday after next, the one following the Fourth of July, was the clear winner.

The only problem was, most of the invitees written under that Saturday were very serious. If he wasn't careful, they would lack the levity and good humor necessary to not only make the party come off without a hitch, but to put people in a good enough mood to tweet and Instagram and Facebook their experience.

Too bad his sister wasn't living in Denver right now. She had always been great at these sorts of gatherings, winning over even their parents' stuffiest friends. But she was all the way on the left coast, doing her best to make it as an actress.

It had been a while since she'd been home.

Alex picked up his cell phone and dialed Dina, trying not to feel guilty about the little notation that told him it had been over six weeks since he'd used the number. And he was the one in his family who spoke to her the most.

"D-Rex!" he said when she picked up. "What's shakin', little sis?"

"Ugh," she groaned. "Do you have to call me that?"

"Yes. I'm your big brother and I do have to call you that." It was a variation on what he'd called her when she was a little girl, "Dinasaur," and had morphed into all sorts of variations on the theme. If you couldn't hold a younger sister's prehistoric creature phase against her, what good was having one?

"So what's up, big bro? Did Mom and Dad put you up to calling me to make sure I'm not doing *those movies?*"

Alex stifled his laugh with a cough. She did such a perfect imitation of their mother, with her Russian accent and her hushed tone when she talked about something the least bit racy, he couldn't understand how Dina hadn't picked up a job based on her impression skills alone. "No. Last time I saw them, I told them you had gotten some good roles and were doing fine."

"So you lied," she said. "Not that I don't appreciate it."

"Say nothing of it. Seriously. I was wondering if you might like a trip home for a visit in a couple of weeks. Think you can swing it?"

"Let me guess. You're introducing a girl to

161

Mom and Dad and you need me to take the heat off you."

He smothered another laugh. Despite the ten-year gap between them, he'd always loved his sister's brutal sense of humor. He'd forgotten how much he missed her. "Actually, I have a dinner party coming up and all my guests have a bit of a serious nature. I thought maybe I'd throw you in the mix and have you lighten them up a bit."

"That sounds like fun. But I can't. I try to pull doubles on the weekend so I have weekdays free for auditions. If I miss a few days, I won't be able to make rent."

He paused. He'd been under the impression that she really was doing fine, and the few walk-on roles and commercials she'd booked were holding her over through the lean times. "Do you need money, Dina?"

"Not if I keep showing up for work."

There was something in her voice that bothered him, but he couldn't quite pinpoint what. Now he really did want her to come home, so he could make sure she was okay. "What if you were coming out here for a job?"

"What kind of job?"

"Well, my chef friend is going to have her hands full cooking, and we could use a food runner."

"*Her?* You didn't say anything about a *her*. Who is she? Is she pretty? Are you dating?"

Alex chuckled. No sense in lying, because she'd

know for herself soon enough. "Her name is Rachel. She is very pretty. And no, we are not dating."

"Wait. Not Rachel Bishop? That chef you completely wrecked?"

"How do you know about that?"

"*Everyone* knows about that. Besides, I follow you on Twitter. Only you would be able to pick up a girl whose life you'd ruined."

Alex leaned back in his seat and propped his feet up on his desk. "I did not pick her up, and this supper club is my way of trying to make amends. Introduce her to some people who can speak well of her, rebuild her reputation, find her an investor."

"Gotcha. You're fixing things again."

"I do not—"

"Yes, you do. You've been trying to fix things with me and Mom and Dad for over three years now. If I come out there to play waitress for a day, you're going to talk me into going over to Sunday dinner at their house and hope that we're going to miraculously get along. You do this every single time, Alex. You need to learn that some things you can't fix."

The words sent an unreasonable current of fear through him, even though she was talking about her damaged relationship with their parents. She was right. So far he had failed at mending the rift between them and Dina, something he would always regret, given his part in it. Surely he wouldn't fail Rachel, too.

"So you'll come, then?"

She seemed to be considering. "You'll pay for the ticket?"

"I'll pay for the ticket."

"And you won't make me go to Mom and Dad's?"

"Cross my heart."

Dina sighed. "Okay. I'm in. Book me a late flight from LAX on that Friday and I'll be there."

"If I can't pick you up for some reason, I'll send a car."

"Yeah, yeah, big-time writer doesn't have time to get his sister from the airport. I get it." But her tone seemed a little brighter than it had earlier, and he knew now that he was doing the right thing. There was definitely something going on with his sister.

"I'm booking your flight now. Love you, Dinasaur."

"Love you too, idiot."

Alex laughed and clicked off the phone. He would no doubt be able to convince her to work the party before and after with her trademark charm, lighten up the mood. Now he just had to let Rachel know that he'd picked the date and taken care of the server situation.

Despite the fact that he was only thirty words further along on his proposal, it felt like a good day's work.

Chapter Thirteen

Rachel had been staring at the boxes she'd brought from Paisley for nearly a week, as if by leaving them unopened, the whole situation might prove to be a bad dream. Like she might magically stumble upon a restaurant lacking a chef and move the boxes straight into her new office as if she had planned it that way.

That wasn't going to happen.

She lifted the lid on the first, found the cookbooks that she had dragged around with her since she'd first moved to New York. They were battered and stained, older than her, considering she had found some of them in a secondhand bookshop in Greenwich Village. *Larousse Gastronomique*, the encyclopedia of French cooking, an early edition. Jacques Pépin's *Complete Techniques. The Escoffier Cookbook*, an abridged English version of Georges Auguste Escoffier's *Le Guide Culinaire*. Basically, the books that had helped her through her first jobs in fine dining—culinary school for those who couldn't afford culinary school.

She went to the white-painted built-ins in her living room, shoved over a handful of other books, and slid them onto the shelf.

One by one, she withdrew the composition

notebooks that she bought in bulk. Each one had a date written on the front in thick black Sharpie, the day she started a new one. Twelve years' worth. The early books had notes from the first New York kitchens in which she had worked, some of which were barely decipherable now. The later ones were more relevant, containing ideas for new dishes, flavor pairings, ingredients to try out and the best place from which to buy them. If she lined them up in chronological order, she'd see her growth, her progression from kitchen assistant to line cook to chef. Looking at how far she had come, there was no reason to believe she couldn't pull off a menu that would dazzle everyone.

She found the last two, dated earlier this year, and brought them with a pen over to her dining room table. Surely there was something in here she could use for the supper club.

Rachel flipped through the pages slowly. Some were cryptic: *fennel, acid, add crunch.* Others were extremely specific, full recipes that she could make right now. They were written to be specials or menu items, with notes on ordering. Not that she couldn't scale it down to a meal for twelve, but there were some things—shaved truffles, for example—that weren't practical when the food costs were coming out of her own pocket.

Focus. Flipping through these books wasn't

getting her anywhere. She'd told Alex she would have some ideas written up in a few days. Right now all she had were columns that said, *Amuse-bouche, soup, salad, seafood, meat, dessert, cocktails.* She needed to get it together, or she'd be serving them pieces of notebook paper and calling it performance art.

Her phone, left on silent to filter the trickle of calls she was still receiving from the media, lit up. She saw Alex's name flash on the lock screen with his text message: Can you meet for coffee tomorrow morning?

She picked up the phone, happy for the distraction from her current predicament. Going to farmers' market in the a.m. Meet me at The English Department before?

I can be there at 6:30.

A smile spread across her face. Sure you'll be able to get yourself properly dressed by 6:30? It's not the sort of place that likes sweatpants.

Are you flirting with me, Chef? It sounds like you're flirting.

A laugh slipped from her lips. You wish.

You're right, I do.

Her breath gave a hitch as she stared at those four words on her screen. Then a follow-up came through. Okay, you win. 6:30. I'll be the one looking caffeine-deprived but wearing grown-up clothes.

Deal. She set down her phone and exhaled. She

was imagining things. Alex was a jokester; she'd seen that from the beginning. Liked to show off how clever he was, which no doubt translated into women thinking he was flirting with them. There was probably no shortage of disappointed hearts when they realized he was like that with every woman. Unless, of course, he took advantage of the admiring glances he got from half the population.

Probably not the thing to be thinking about a man who was essentially a business partner, or at least a comrade-in-arms in her mission to rebuild her career. There was no reason the same rules shouldn't apply to him as they did to the restaurant staff with whom she'd worked over the years.

Alex Kanin, for more reasons than one, should be completely off-limits.

When Rachel woke to her alarm the next morning, a knot of nervousness immediately formed in her stomach. It took her a moment to remember she was meeting Alex at her favorite LoDo restaurant in an hour, and she still had absolutely nothing to show him. For all her reading and brainstorming and flailing about, she had made very little progress.

Unless, of course, she defined progress as making a "refrigerator soup" of all the leftovers sitting in her vegetable crisper. An excellent use of things that would otherwise go to waste, but perhaps not the best use of her time considering she was no closer to a completed menu than her initial list of courses.

She dragged herself out of bed and stumbled into the kitchen to put on a pot of coffee. By the time she had downed her first cup, she felt slightly more coherent. She had too much time on her hands—that was the problem. She was used to putting together a specials menu in thirty minutes based on the week's leftovers. Entire days to plan were completely foreign to her process.

Rachel pulled out the notebook and began another list.

Amuse-bouche—asparagus mousse on
   homemade crisp
Vegetable—braised fennel with apples
Soup—cold corn gazpacho
Seafood—pan-seared scallops on summer
   greens salad
Meat/Game—duck three ways with
   something brilliant on the side
Dessert—whatever amazing thing
   Melody comes up with

Okay, so it barely qualified as a menu, but it was respectable and she wouldn't embarrass herself by having absolutely nothing. It wasn't like she was married to it. She still had weeks to go through her notebooks, come up with some great ideas, and put together a menu that would wow the guests.

And then do it however many more times it took to land an investor.

Rachel groaned and scrubbed her fingers through her messy hair. This should be simple for her. What was with the sudden mental block?

She glanced at the clock, realized it was already five past six, and darted for her bedroom. She threw on a pair of jean cutoffs, pulled a bright-green tank over her head, and thrust her feet into shoes that were part ballet flat and part sport shoe. No time to deal with her unruly mop, so she twisted it on top of her head, stuck a pair of chopsticks through the bun, and grabbed her market tote from the closet. At the last minute, she remembered her wallet and her keys, somewhat important if she was to drive anywhere or buy anything today. If Alex thought that she'd accepted his help for any reason other than desperation, her appearance today would put that to rest.

Denver's Saturday morning traffic was blissfully light, with more cyclists on the road than cars. Rachel found metered parking down the street from Union Station in front of a row of still-shuttered storefronts. As she made her way to the historic building, the pleasant breeze and dawn-blue light put a spring in her step. Later the temperatures would soar into the nineties, the sun shining with enough fury to crisp the skin on her shoulders when she stepped out to water her herb garden, but for now, it was the perfect farmers' market morning.

Union Station's facade—Romanesque revival, she'd read somewhere—was all white stone and filigreed arches, topped with an iconic vintage neon sign that she found unaccountably charming. It barely even functioned as a train station these days, with only a few Amtrak trains and a light-rail line coming through each day. Instead, it had been renovated into one of Lower Downtown's premier shopping and dining spots.

Rachel pushed through the double doors into the expansive, gleaming-white hall, then made a sharp turn down the corridor toward The English Department. Hands down it was her favorite morning spot in the city. Common as the design scheme might be, she still loved its marble and vintage tile and weathered wood, not to mention the way it morphed from casual breakfast and lunch to elegant fine dining in the evening. It was a concept that had always secretly appealed to her—part coffee shop, part restaurant, part general store. But this was the chef-owner's second location, his first award-winning restaurant giving him the clout and name recognition to make the concept a success. It only worked because he'd already risen to the top of the fine-dining heap and could count on his reputation to back the concept, two things she couldn't say about herself.

Yet.

She got in line at the wood counter and ordered herself a black cold-brew coffee over ice. At the last moment, she added one of the gorgeous golden-brown empanadas in the glass display case. That was something she hadn't considered as a menu option: empanadas. Or some sort of hand pie . . .

"That will be $6.05," the cashier prompted her, his tone saying this wasn't the first time he'd tried to get Rachel to pay.

"Right. Sorry." Rachel pulled out a ten-dollar bill, waited for her change, and then tucked a buck into the tip jar.

She was picking up her order when a low voice said in her ear, "You made it. I thought you had changed your mind."

A shiver ran down her back, and she inhaled the clean scent of soap and freshly laundered cotton before she realized she was doing it. She turned. "Just running late."

Her gaze met familiar hazel eyes, tinged green this morning from the light and their surroundings. She involuntarily looked Alex up and down, taking him in—crisp white T-shirt, khaki cargo shorts, clean running shoes—and felt her breath hitch again. What was wrong with her? It was practically the city's Saturday morning uniform; every guy in the entire place was dressed like that. And yet . . .

"I saved us a table outside on the patio. Let me take your food while you grab your flatware." He took her drink and plate from her hand and headed back outside, leaving her to stare after him like an idiot.

By the time Rachel grabbed a fork and a knife and a stack of napkins, she had herself together. She slid into the wrought-iron bistro seat across from him and set her cutlery neatly beside her plate. She had to look at this objectively. He was obviously attractive. The looks that the women around them kept casting their way said that clearly enough, as did the way their gazes lingered on her. No doubt they were wondering how someone like her, puffy-eyed and looking like she'd just rolled out of bed, landed someone like him. She felt like telling them to give it a rest since she had no interest in him besides the contents of his virtual Rolodex.

He unhooked his sunglasses from the collar of his shirt and slipped them on, giving her a glimpse of defined biceps and proving she was a big fat liar.

"Eat." He nudged her plate toward her. "We can

talk business when you're done. I'm enjoying the sunshine before it gets too hot."

Already too hot for my taste. She stifled a grin. At least she was maintaining a sense of humor about the whole thing.

Rachel cut into the empanada with her knife and fork and took a bite. "The spinach one is my favorite."

"You should try the chorizo. It's inspired. Although I've probably had all of them a dozen times."

Here she thought she was setting the meeting on her own home turf and it turned out to be his as well. "You come here often?"

"At least once a week since it opened." He swept a hand toward the plaza and the sidewalk beyond. "It's one of my favorite places to people-watch."

"I'm surprised I haven't run into you. Melody, Ana, and I meet here almost as often. Ana works up the street."

Alex sat back in his chair. "The three of you have known each other a long time?"

"Six years. Or rather, I've known them for six years. Melody was a pastry assistant at my first restaurant here in Denver, but she and Ana have known each other for longer."

"A formidable trio, I'd say."

Rachel smiled. "Something like that. We complement each other's strengths and weaknesses. Despite our crazy jobs, we manage to get together a couple times a week. More now that I'm not chained to the restaurant."

"Is that how it felt? Chained?"

"Are you psychoanalyzing me, Alex?"

He chuckled, having the grace to look embarrassed. "Sorry. Bad habit. I'm always curious about the words people use. Especially interesting people."

She skimmed right over the implied compliment. "What about you? What do you do when you're not writing?"

"That's a double-edged question. I'm either writing all the time or not writing at all. And when I'm not writing, I'm doing anything I can to keep myself busy."

"Ah, so that's the reason for the early-morning invitation." Rachel polished off the empanada and leaned back in her chair too, cradling her glass in her hands.

"Actually, I have news. I took a quick poll of the first guest list, and it looks like the inaugural event for the supper club will be two weeks from today."

Rachel coughed as her iced coffee went down the wrong way and spluttered until she could regain the power of speech. "What? Two weeks? No, I can't possibly . . ."

"You're going to have to. It's the only weekend we'll get a decent turnout until the end of July.

You're telling me that you can't come up with a menu in two weeks?"

"Of course I can come up with a menu in two weeks. It's all the other things. First we have to settle on a theme. Order the food. Figure out the decor and the plating to match the theme. Then I'll need waitstaff to help—"

"I've already got the last one under control. My sister is going to be in town, and she's volunteered to help. She's a struggling actress in LA, so she has a lot of experience as a server."

He'd been that sure she would agree? She supposed she'd never had a choice, anyway, since their schedule was dictated by their guests, but somehow she'd thought she'd have more time to prepare.

"What exactly are you afraid of here, Rachel?"

"I'm not afraid." She narrowed her eyes. "You're analyzing me again. What are you, a shrink?"

"Yes."

"Very funny." She sipped her coffee, then realized he wasn't smiling. "Wait, you're serious?"

"I got all the way through a master's degree in psychology before I realized I had no interest in clinical practice. I guess I should be happy I figured it out before I got too far into my PhD."

"Must be nice to be able to walk away from an

176

education like that." Too late, she realized how accusatory it sounded.

"Trust me, my parents were furious. They're academics, so naturally they figured I'd either choose counseling or teaching. When I said I was going to be a freelance writer, I thought they were going to try to have me committed." He cracked another smile, that irresistible dimple peeking out. "That's a shrink joke, by the way."

As if she hadn't had enough reasons to be wary of him, now she knew he could probably read her like a book. "So have you been analyzing me all this time?"

"Of course not. At least not really. I only use my powers for good." He leaned forward. "Relax, Rachel. Just because I'm trained in psychology doesn't mean I'm going to start telling you that you've got control issues. Anyone who spends time with you could tell that, psych degree or not."

Rachel's mouth dropped open in shock until she realized he was joking. She threw her crumpled-up napkin at him. "You're such a jerk."

"I know. My mad psychology skills make me incredibly self-aware." He grinned broadly. "So, are we going to go or what? We don't want to miss first pick of the vendors."

"You're going with me?"

"Of course I am. You don't think I'm going to oversee my investment?"

"What investment? Your reputation, you mean?"

"Oh no. These are my friends, not paying guests; therefore I pick up the tab. Not for your experimentation, of course, since you could consider that the cost of doing business, but I'll expect an itemized invoice the night of the dinner."

She stared at him. "I can't figure you out, Alex."

"I'm flattered that you'd try. Now we better go. I'll even let you drive."

Chapter Fourteen

Rachel was taking his pushiness remarkably well. Alex had been pretty certain that she was going to refuse his company and tell him she didn't need his input. Instead, she finished her coffee and stood, sending him a pointed look. "Well? Are you coming?"

"Yes, Chef." He rose and tucked his newspaper under his arm.

"I wish you wouldn't do that."

She had slipped on her sunglasses, so he couldn't tell if she was serious or not. He fell into step beside her as they headed across the plaza to the crosswalk. "Do what?"

"Say, 'Yes, Chef.' You're not my employee, and in any case, you don't really mean it."

"What makes you think I don't mean it?"

She lowered her glasses and pegged him with a direct stare. "What do you get out of this? Really? I know what you said before . . ."

"But you don't believe I would go through this elaborate setup to have the pleasure of your company?"

She nodded.

"You're right. If I only wanted the pleasure of your company, I would have asked you out instead of offering my place as a supper club.

Which I considered, because it's much less trouble."

It was all truth, but once more phrased in a way that she could easily brush off. Why she had such a hard time accepting that a man might find her attractive and want to spend time with her, he didn't know. Or maybe she got that too often and it was *all* they wanted out of her. That seemed more likely.

Rachel had stopped in front of a battered Toyota SUV, so he climbed into the passenger seat and waited until she got behind the wheel before he gave her a serious answer.

"I pride myself on doing the right thing. I might not always manage it, and God knows that I do the wrong thing plenty, but I couldn't live with myself knowing that I had helped kill your career without trying to do something about it. And if there's one thing I've found about my creative muse, it's that it doesn't do well with guilt."

She finally focused on him. "That's the first time you've told me the truth."

"The others were the truth too; this is just the entire truth."

"So basically you can't work until I do?"

He nodded.

"And both of our careers hinge on the success of the supper club?" She threw him a mischievous grin, the first indication that they might be finding an equal footing. "That seems fair."

"You're kind of mean; do you know that?"

Now she grinned widely as she pulled onto the street. "That's the second true thing you've said to me this morning."

He grinned too. Who knew that telling her the truth—the one that he thought would make her run as far away from him as possible—would be the thing that cut all the tension between them? Clearly she couldn't believe he would do something for her out of the sheer goodness of his heart, and he supposed he couldn't blame her. His initial offer had been altruistic, but even that had come out of his need to work.

"Are you listening to this?" He reached for the radio, but she slapped his hand before he could touch the buttons.

"Driver chooses the station. You should have thought of that before you let me drive."

"Yes . . . ma'am."

"I liked it better when you called me *chef*," she said. "You mean *ma'am* even less."

"I guess I'm going to have to suffer through this hipster music you young folk like."

"It's classic rock. I'd hardly call it hipster."

"Tomato, tomahto." He sat back in his seat, enjoying the frustrated smirk she sent his way, and stifled his laughter. He was really beginning to like this woman, and not because of the picture she made beside him, the streak of sunshine giving her dark hair a golden halo and warming her skin so it gave off a faint, undeniably feminine aura of jasmine.

Okay, not *just* because.

"So where are we going?" he asked. "There are farmers' markets all over Denver."

"Cherry Creek. The Highlands one is usually better, but it's tomorrow."

She navigated the Denver streets with the surety of a native, something that always made him wish he was on foot or bike with all the one-way streets, two-way stops, and never-ending road construction. This probably felt like nothing to her, coming from New York.

"Why did you come to Denver?" he asked.

"A job offer." She glanced at him briefly before returning her eyes to the road in front of her. "One of my old bosses, Aaron Collins, is a Colorado native, and he moved back here to open a new restaurant. It did well and he wanted to open a second location, so he called me in to run it. I was working as a sous in a Michelin three-star restaurant in Manhattan, so it wasn't an easy decision, but it felt like the right move."

"So this was a step down?"

"Not exactly. Running your own kitchen is what most of us work for. I'd never been to Denver, so I didn't know what to expect. There isn't even a Michelin guide for the city. But I trusted Aaron, so I took the job, packed up my life, and came here."

"That's a high level of trust."

"That's the kind of man he is. Cooking isn't like the corporate world. The best chefs are teachers. Their hope is to train you well and send you off to learn from someone else. If my performance reflected well on him with other chefs, they'd send their protégés to him, and so on. It's kind of expected that you're going to move on once you've come up through a good kitchen. So I trusted that if he was telling me it was a step up, it was a step up."

It was a foreign concept to him. Universities had tenure, and corporate cultures were all about employee retention. Purposely turning over your best staff to a competitor? Anywhere else it would sound mad. Executives fretted over that sort of thing all the time.

"And that's where you won the Beard award?"

"He gave me full control over the menu. I stayed true to his concept, but the actual vision was mine. When I got to Denver and realized the whole seasonal cooking approach that had recently become popular in New York was gathering steam here, I wanted to do something new and exciting with it. First we were nominated for best new restaurant, but we didn't win. I got nominated for best new chef. And didn't win. And then two years later, I actually won. Believe me, it was completely unexpected. I was pretty sure it was going to be a case of 'always the bridesmaid.' "

"So when did you decide to go out on your own?"

"When my sous was ready to take over, I felt like it was time to move on. I found investors, the location, worked up a business plan, and Paisley was born." Pink rose to her cheeks. "I'm talking too much."

"No, I like it. This is new to me. I kind of thought someone went to culinary school and came out being called *chef*."

"Maybe that's the way it works now, but I went the old-school route. Worked my way up from the bottom . . . Oh look, a parking spot!" She cut herself off as she whipped into a curbside parking place. "We're going to have to walk. I hope you don't mind."

She climbed out and waited for him to do the same, then locked the car behind them. They fell into step together and no one spoke, but for the first time it was a comfortable silence.

"So, do you have a goal for this trip?" Alex asked finally.

"Now that you've sprung a two-week deadline on me, I need to get my head together and settle on a menu."

He could understand the need for inspiration. This trip was certainly serving that purpose for him, though the ideas it was inspiring were probably not ones that were fit to be put down on paper.

They turned the corner and the market appeared, row after row of vinyl awnings set up in the parking lot of the mall in the center of town, throngs of people already crowding the aisles at this early hour. Rachel dove into the madness like a farmers' market veteran, bypassing some stalls in favor of others, though he couldn't distinguish any difference between them.

"Ooh," she exclaimed, weaving her way close to a particular one with bushels stacked on risers, French market style. "Look at this. Have you seen anything so gorgeous?"

"What is that?" The vegetable looked like a mutant celery, with fernlike fronds sticking out at crazy angles.

She stared at him. "It's fennel. You know, fennel? It tastes like anise."

"And I should know what anise tastes like because . . ."

She thrust it in his face. "Take a whiff."

"Licorice?"

"Yeah, kind of." She buried her nose in the fronds, then held it up to the stand's proprietor before shoving it into one of her mesh bags.

"Well, now that you've molested it, of course you have to buy it. What on earth are you going to do with it?"

"It's not that unusual. It would be great with a mixed greens salad, diced up to flavor a vinaigrette and the fronds used as a garnish. Or braised with shallots and served as a side to fish or a really good sausage. Or maybe shredded with apples and kohlrabi for an interesting slaw . . ."

He could practically see the wheels turning in her mind, her face brightening and her eyes lighting with excitement. It started a warm feeling in him that he didn't care to explain. He waited until she paid and then let her steer him back into the flow of pedestrians while they looked for the next find.

It came two stands later, when she declared a bunch of beets "absolutely gorgeous" the way most women would talk about a Cartier diamond. "These are Chioggia. It's an Italian heirloom variety, and they have these wonderful red and white stripes. I'd probably thinly slice these and serve them raw. But these golden ones . . . Can you believe the color? I wouldn't expect to find these beautiful small ones this late in the season." Those went into the string bag too, a growing collection of fragrant, leafy vegetables that burst from the wide-open mesh of her carrier.

"What about these?" He reached around her for a bunch of tricolor carrots, the typical orange bundled with purple and yellow. "I've never seen purple carrots before."

Someone bumped into him from behind, jolting him up against her. His arm automatically closed around her waist to keep her stable, pressing their bodies together from shoulder to knee. He swore he felt a sharp intake of breath, a softening against him, before she moved away. Or maybe that was just her getting the wind knocked out of her from the impact.

"Sorry," he murmured.

"It's getting crowded." Rachel took the bunch of carrots from him and examined them a little too carefully.

No, he had been right the first time. The unflappable chef was flustered by him.

That probably wasn't a great thing for him to know.

"Where now?" he asked. "You're running out of room."

She pulled out two more string bags exactly like the first. "I come prepared. But I've got enough to begin now. If I can't come up with something amazing with this beautiful produce, I should just throw in the towel."

"So you're done?"

"I think so."

"Good. My turn." He grabbed her by the elbow, not missing her flinch as his fingers touched her bare skin—he prayed it wasn't from repulsion— and tugged her down the aisle to *his* favorite attraction at the market.

"Funnel cakes?"

"Yes, funnel cakes. Why are you looking at me like that? They're delicious!"

She lifted an eyebrow. "I didn't think you were the type."

"And what type is that, exactly?"

"Just . . ." She waved a hand up and down. "I figured you subsisted on protein bars and plain chicken breasts."

"I'm flattered. I think. But yes, I like real food. And I like things that don't qualify as real food, like funnel cakes."

Alex stepped up to the window of the truck, the scent of hot oil and frying dough and cinnamon sugar enveloping him. "Two please?"

"Just one," Rachel put in behind him. "I'll take a little bite of yours."

"You really aren't putting an adequate amount of trust in me."

"Hey, I put churros on the menu at Paisley for summer."

"But you probably did some fancy French thing with it."

She actually looked embarrassed. "I made them from *pâte à choux* and rolled them in sugar and *garam masala.*"

"I rest my case." He handed over a bill, received a massive tangle of fried and sugared dough in return, and drew her aside. "Now. Taste."

Rachel moved in close enough to rip off a small piece and put it delicately in her mouth. She tried to hide her smile as she chewed, but it was useless. "That's really good."

"I told you." He took his own piece and sighed with happiness. "Really, what's there not to like?"

"Maybe we should have gotten two." She ripped off a bigger piece this time and munched it while they walked back toward the end of the market where they had parked. He had to resist the urge to offer to take care of the sprinkling of sugar that lingered on her full bottom lip. Definitely not a good idea.

"So tell me—" he changed the subject as quickly as he dared—"what inspiring dishes have you come up with from this trip?"

"I don't know yet. I've got plenty of ideas for dishes, but they all need to work together as a whole. I'm tempted to do a golden beet borscht—what?"

"I'm Russian, so I'm fine with the idea. But I'm not sure anyone else is going to go for borscht."

"That's because they haven't tasted *my* borscht. Of course, it would be a shame not to use any of the heirloom tomatoes. Maybe a baked tian with some sort of crunchy topping . . ." She sighed happily. "You'll practically be able to taste summer."

He watched her from the corner of his eye as they walked back to her car. She radiated contentment with her string bag of vegetables and sugary fingers. He didn't believe it was because of his presence. Had the supper club given her a sense of purpose? She seemed so far from the guarded, suspicious woman he'd confronted at the food truck pod, he had a hard time believing she was the same person.

"Thanks for letting me come along," he said when they reached their parking space. "That was fun. Got me out of my writing cave for a while."

"Thanks for the company. You make a good farmers' market wingman. Maybe I'll take you along next time."

"You know where to find me."

They fell into another comfortable silence on the way back to Union Station, one that this time he was loath to break with idle conversation until she pulled up behind his car in a paid corner lot.

"I'll call you when I have a menu. Maybe we should meet at the end of this week to talk about the decor and the service and all that?"

"Absolutely. Just let me know." He smiled at her and climbed out of the car with an odd sense of loss. "Friday morning maybe."

"You're on." Rachel gave him a little wave and watched until he reached his car, then backed her way out of the tight lot.

Alex shook himself. Rachel was the last person he should be interested in romantically right now. But the feeling of longing in his chest was suspiciously familiar as he drove to his empty condo, parked, rode the elevator up to the top level.

He sat down at his computer in front of the floor-to-ceiling windows and began to type. The writing that flowed out of him, however, was something that he could never publish.

For one thing, it didn't contain even a hint of cynicism. And for another, it revealed far too much of his interest in a beautiful stranger.

Chapter Fifteen

She had too much food.

Rachel scanned the contents of her countertop, taking stock of how long it would take her to eat this herself. A plateful of different amuse-bouche. Two versions of the scallop salad, each with minute but important changes that affected the perception of the overall dish. Two vats of flavored ices, swelled to gargantuan proportions by the constant tweaking and addition of ingredients. And now she was contemplating a tray of raw lamb chops and some quail, wondering how she could possibly justify cooking these when there weren't enough hours in the day to eat it all. It felt like a waste, of both time and money.

She'd already called Melody and Ana. An equipment emergency in the bakery had doubled Melody's shift while she tried to batch bread in and out of the single working oven. Ana was equally occupied with a publicity nightmare involving a married celebrity and some compromising photos, an all-hands-on-deck sort of call from the head of the firm even though it wasn't her client. So that left . . .

Alex.

She glanced at the clock in her kitchen, saw

that the hands were edging past four on a Friday afternoon. No doubt he would be getting ready to go out for the evening, as someone like him did. Though technically she didn't know him well enough to know what kind of someone he was. It was that uncertainty, and the conviction that she had misinterpreted the moments between them at the farmers' market last weekend, that had prevented her from calling and setting up the meeting they'd discussed.

But now, faced with the proposition of wasting all this food, her natural frugality won out. She dialed.

Alex picked up on the third ring. "Rachel, hello!"

He didn't *sound* like she was interrupting anything. And the fact she was trying to gauge that by his voice showed exactly how far back she'd moved toward high school crushes. Not that she had a particularly large body of experience in that quarter.

"I'm sitting here with a kitchen full of experiments and everyone's busy. I don't suppose you might be free, would you?"

"I don't know," he replied, a note of teasing in his voice. "Considering I seem to be the last resort."

Rachel flushed. "You know I didn't mean it like that. I just thought . . . I figured you'd have plans."

He chuckled, and she relaxed. He was going to let her off the hook. "As luck would have it, my plans for tonight got pushed back. I would be happy to come over and help rid you of the excess experiments, as sketchy as that sounds."

"I promise, they are all edible. Actually, they're all good. I could use some help deciding which ones should go on the menu."

"I'll be right over, then. If you're ready. Text me your address?"

That's right. She'd been to his place, but he didn't have any idea where she lived. "I'll do that right now." She texted Alex her address, then got to work on the lamb and quail, both of which would take time in the oven. By the time they worked their way through the other courses, the meat should be rested and ready to serve.

Then she looked down at herself.

Beneath her apron, her cutoffs and skimpy tank top, chosen because of the heat in her un–air-conditioned kitchen, probably sent the wrong message. She pulled the apron over her head and tossed it on the table, then hightailed it back to her bedroom to put on something more conservative. Unfortunately, conservative didn't necessarily mean nice: her wardrobe was decidedly circa-2005 with a strong concert tee vibe, ironic since she'd been too busy working to actually attend any of those concerts. She pulled on a pair of comfortably faded and worn jeans and a rumpled chambray button-down, the sleeves of which she automatically rolled back. Good enough. He was coming for the food and not for her anyway.

Even so, she ducked into the bathroom, brushed her hair, and put it up into a reasonably neat knot at the top of her head. It was far more relaxed than her usual restaurant chignon, which she sprayed and combed into submission. While she was at it, it couldn't hurt to put on a little face powder and mascara and lip gloss. Just enough to make it look like she hadn't been sweating over the stove all day, but not enough to make it look like she was dressing up for him.

Which, let's face it, she totally was.

She did a quick sweep of her house, making sure she hadn't left anything embarrassing out: straightened magazines on the end table, collected a half-filled mug of tea, picked up the pair of socks she'd pulled off when she'd slipped on her kitchen clogs. She might as well start brewing a pitcher of tea in case Alex wanted something stronger than water. She didn't drink soda, and besides her usual pot of coffee in the morning, she lived on the citrus-infused water that she stored in a jug in the refrigerator.

Rachel was beginning to think Alex wasn't coming when the doorbell rang. She strode to the door and yanked it open, her lips lifting into a smile. He stood there, far better dressed than the occasion called for, with a glass bottle in each hand and a third in the crook of his elbow. A set of keys dangled precariously from his fingers.

"There you are," she said. "You found it okay?"

"I vacillated between the wine choices too long," he said. "And then I decided to bring them both."

Rachel chuckled and took the one from his elbow. "A pinot gris. Perfect with the scallops. What's the other?"

"Sangiovese," he said, holding it up.

"You must have been peeking through my window. That will go well with the main courses."

"Courses, plural?"

"I told you I'm still deciding." She stepped aside and waved him in, then shut the door behind him. "What's the third?"

"Small-batch ginger beer. Nonalcoholic." At her surprised look, he shrugged. "You weren't drinking at Rhino Crash or Equity. I thought maybe you didn't."

"You thought right." She looked at him, marveling that he'd been so observant, then indicated he should follow her to the kitchen.

He lifted his face and sniffed appreciatively. "Everything smells good. Can't we serve it all?"

"If you like everything, we can save some for next time. We are planning more than one of these, aren't we?"

"That would be completely up to you." He looked around. "What can I do?"

She nudged him toward the shelf next to the sink. "Grab some wineglasses and open the white and the ginger beer. I'll start putting things on the table."

He did as she asked, seemingly unconcerned with the directive to poke around her kitchen. Which was one of the reasons she liked the open shelving. Not only did it mimic the flow of her commercial kitchen, but it let guests help themselves without feeling like they were snooping around her private spaces.

"Flatware?"

"Drawer on the other side of the sink."

"Done." He brushed by her on her way back from the refrigerator, his fingers trailing against her lower back as he squeezed by. The touch, even unintentional and absentminded, lit her up like a gas flame.

It might be a long night after all.

Rachel's place wasn't what Alex expected, but he should have. From the outside, it was another slightly dilapidated Victorian of the type that dominated the Cheesman and City Park neighborhoods, the ones that remained having been either restored or converted into multi-unit properties. It needed a new coat of paint, and the original porch was sagging too much to claim structural integrity, but from the minute she opened the door, it was like getting a glimpse into her psyche.

The interior was almost painfully orderly, decorated in an eclectic bohemian-industrial-vintage sort of vibe that he suspected was more out of utility than any desire to align with the current fads. From the front entry, he glimpsed a living room furnished with a dark-green velvet sofa set on a faded Persian rug. A stack of magazines had slumped against a glass lamp on a metal table that could have come from either West Elm or a local garage sale. Hard to tell.

The kitchen, he saw as he followed her into her domain, was immaculate. Not nearly as "professional" as he might have anticipated, but clearly as scrubbed and sterile as a hospital. A green vintage refrigerator occupied a space by the back door in contrast to a gleaming stainless-steel cooktop and hood. Battered wood shelving carried around the entire space, holding an eclectic collection of white restaurant-style dishes, pans in steel and copper, and a mismatched set of glasses and stemware. For someone who didn't drink, she had a remarkable variety of wineglasses.

All in all, it was exactly what he should have expected of her—functional, vaguely stylish, and entirely unfussy.

He collected glasses and silverware and opened

the bottle of white wine for himself, then sat at one side of a long, scarred table while Rachel took out plates and bowls and pots from the refrigerator. She then began plating the various salads with as much care as she might in her own restaurant.

He'd never thought that watching a chef at work would be sexy.

Of course most chefs weren't as effortlessly beautiful as this one, bent over the countertop as she dressed and garnished greens, tendrils of hair that had escaped from her bun falling against her neck. It made him want to trail a finger across that skin before tucking the hair into her knot.

And from what he knew of Rachel, she might break his finger if he tried it.

"All right, these are the options for the amuse-bouche. On the night of the actual event, I would bring one of these out first, one per person." She produced a platter upon which three different composed bites were placed, evenly spaced down to the millimeter. "There's crab with avocado and lemon *crème fraîche* on a sesame cracker. Chicken liver mousse with caramelized onions and apples. And Ana and Melody's favorite, asparagus and leek on a Parmesan crisp."

Alex tasted them one by one, clearing his palate with a glass of ice water between bites. They were stunning. That was the only way to put it. Little bursts of unexpected flavor on his tongue, just enough to make him wonder what else she had in store. That was the point, he knew—a sneak peek into the chef's world, something to build anticipation for what was to come.

"So . . . ?" Rachel hovered by the table, her arms crossed in front of her and one fist pressed to her lips.

He leaned back in his chair and considered the empty plate. "I don't know. They were all amazing."

"You don't have to be nice. I really want to know. This is your dinner party, remember?"

"No, I'm being serious. They're all different. If I had to narrow it down, I would say either the crab or the asparagus mousse. The Parmesan crisp is fantastic."

"Okay, that's three votes for the asparagus, then. Give me a couple of minutes on the salads." She swept away the platter and placed it in the sink, then put a pan on the cooktop and cranked up the flame while she took out a covered plate of scallops from the fridge.

He pushed back his chair and crept up behind her, not sure why he felt so curious. She carefully placed each of the scallops in the hot oil in the pan, sending up a hiss and a sizzle. He had to resist the urge to touch her again while she didn't know he was there, instead linking his hands behind his back.

"They cook quickly, so you have to watch

them," Rachel murmured, and he realized she had been aware of him the entire time. "You see how they go from translucent to opaque almost immediately?" She stared at the scallops as if she could determine the exact moment they cooked through—she probably could—then took them off the heat with a pair of tongs and placed them on the bed of dressed greens sitting on the plate beside the cooktop.

She picked up the plate and nodded toward the table, an indication he should sit down. But once more, she remained standing.

"Aren't you going to join me?"

She hesitated.

"It makes me uncomfortable to have you serving me if you won't join me." He nudged the chair across from him away from the table. "Please."

Slowly, she slid into the seat. He pushed the salad plate to the center of the table. "You need to share this with me. I'm never going to make it all the way through the courses if you make me eat it all myself."

"No one's forcing you," she said with a smile.

"I'm not willing to let food this good go to waste. So, come on. Get to it." Alex picked up his fork and knife and cut a piece of scallop, then forked it into his mouth with a stack of greens. The seafood was indeed perfectly cooked, tender and sweet and juicy, and the slight tang of the dressing complemented the mild flavors of the scallop.

"What's in the dressing?" he asked.

A crafty smile formed on her lips, a sparkle in her eye. "The dreaded fennel."

"That's fennel? I like it. It's not all that licorice-y."

"Not in these concentrations." Rachel took a bite, lifting her eyes to the ceiling as she considered. "I like this one. Simple. Tastes like summer to me. But it's too . . ."

"Common?"

"That's exactly it."

"I don't know. I like the scallops. They're perfect. Maybe with some sort of starch. Not as light."

Rachel took another bite. "Puree. Artichoke maybe, with wild mushrooms." She gave him a reluctant smile. "I knew I made the right decision in calling you."

"You agonized over that one, did you?"

"Not really. I didn't want to be too presumptuous."

Impulsively, he reached across the table and placed his hand over hers. "You do realize that we're in it together, don't you? Partners."

"Are we?" The edge to her voice could have either been amusement or challenge. "Because no matter what you say, you don't seem to have much at stake here."

"You're still questioning my motives."

She pulled her hand from beneath his. "I'm not so much questioning your motives as . . . Okay, so I'm still questioning your motives."

"Because we don't know each other." He folded his arms on the table in front of him. "Ask me anything."

"Why did you write that article? And don't tell me it was out of concern for me."

That was the last thing he'd expected her to ask. Once more, he'd underestimated her. "Truthfully? I was angry."

She simply looked at him and waited for him to elaborate.

Alex sat back in his chair. "When I started writing, I was determined. Obnoxiously so. I had given up a profession I'd already spent almost seven years studying, and I had to prove I was capable of doing this. I wrote nonstop, article after article on spec—that means before I got paid for it or even knew there was interest—until eventually I landed something at *Slate*. One thing led to another and I was writing for *Wired* and *Rolling Stone*. When I wrote a very popular essay for the *New Yorker*—which in itself is a Holy Grail sort of experience—a literary agent called me to see if I wanted to do a book. She said I was the next big thing, thought she could sell a book on the buzz alone.

"Of course I was flattered. Maybe a little cocky.

I figured there was nowhere to go but up. And for a while, it looked like I was right. There was a bidding war for the book, and it sold for a lot of money."

Rachel lifted a skeptical eyebrow. "I'm not getting the part where you should be angry."

It did sound pretty impressive from the outside. He'd been just as seduced by the big numbers. "Here's the thing about selling a book for six figures. It's a risk—for the publisher and for the author. You have to hit it big, and the pressure is immense. Even before the book was out, pundits were using the deal as an example of what was wrong with legacy publishing."

"And people begin to form opinions before they even read it."

"Exactly. When the book released, lines were already drawn. Half the reviewers loved it. Half of them hated it. Sales were what really mattered, though, and they weren't great. They weren't terrible, but it wasn't the instant *New York Times* bestseller everyone was banking on."

"I'm sorry," Rachel said. "I know that must have been frustrating."

"It was. But I'm a grown-up. I understand how these things work. Publishing is an educated guessing game. I just didn't expect the flat-out venom I got. People who didn't even know me, taking pleasure in being cruel. Assuming things that weren't true. It stung. It made me angry.

So when I saw Carlton Espy making all sorts of unfounded allegations in his review, it was the tipping point. I'd had enough."

"And ironically, the social media frenzy jump-started your career while it killed mine."

She said it matter-of-factly, but he still flinched. "Yes. So you see, I owe you."

Rachel's eyes locked with his for a moment, as if she was trying to read the truth. And then she pushed back her chair. "Time to choose a palate cleanser. I hope you like sorbet?"

So they were done with the personal. "If you make it, I'm sure I'll like it."

He did, though he preferred the cucumber-mint to the tomato and watermelon that she put in front of him. Both the lamb shank and the quail were great, but they agreed that lamb said spring more than summer and chose the quail. When Rachel cleared the last of the plates, Alex rose and nudged her away from the sink. "Let me do the dishes. It's the least I can do."

"Okay," she said with a nod. "That's why I have open shelves. So you know exactly where to put them."

Ever since he had told her about his professional problems, Rachel had seemed to relax. Was it because it proved he didn't consider himself above her? That she wasn't a charity case to him? When the dishes were cleaned and dried and put away, and Rachel had wiped down every last surface in the kitchen, she looked at him and asked, "Do you want a tour now? It will be a short one."

"Sure." This felt like an olive branch, an offering in honor of their newfound under-standing. He followed her from the kitchen into the nearby living room.

"This is it. One room, besides my bedroom and the bathroom, of course."

"It's nice," he said, and he meant it. "Did you bring this all from New York?"

"No. I bought a car in New Jersey as I left—because no one really needs to own a car in Manhattan—and came out here with my cooking supplies and one suitcase of clothes."

"Taking advantage of the flea market?"

Rachel grimaced. "I didn't actually decorate any of this myself. I used my moving boxes and crates as end tables and slept on a mattress on the floor for at least a year. Melody's the one who finally decorated the place." She shrugged. "I've worked long hours six days a week since I moved here, and on my day off, I don't want to do much but sleep and binge-watch Netflix."

He stared at her incredulously. "But you've, you know, done things. Right?"

"Like what?"

"Hiked? Gone to Garden of the Gods? The Museum of Nature and Science? Seen a concert at Red Rocks?"

206

She stared back at him blankly.

"You're seriously telling me that in six years, you've done nothing but work, eat out, and sleep."

"I don't think you understand what my job is like. I haven't had a weekend or a holiday off in twelve years. Until now, of course."

"So you've never seen a fireworks display for the Fourth of July."

"Not since I was a kid."

"Then you should come over for Independence Day festivities at my house next week. Starts at eight. Bring your friends if you like."

He didn't wait for a response, but instead continued to wander around the perimeter of the room, trailing a finger over the impeccably dusted surfaces and stopping to look at the few decorations that marked the walls and the mantel. Then he paused in front of the bookshelves that flanked the fireplace. They were crowded with books, few empty spots left on the floor-to-ceiling shelves.

"*Great Expectations*, *The Iliad* . . . most of these I haven't even thought about since college." There were culinary-school books, too, with boring-sounding titles like *The Professional Chef* and *Principles of French Cooking*. Clearly she had kept every text from every class she had ever taken. "I admire the fact you kept all your course materials. I couldn't wait to dump my psychology texts into the nearest recycling bin."

Rachel said nothing, and that alone was unusual enough to make him cast a look over his shoulder. She was studying the shelves with a strange expression.

"What?"

She cleared her throat. "I didn't go to college. Or culinary school. Or finish high school." Her voice had drifted low by the end, though he was pretty sure it wasn't shame he was hearing. Maybe regret. "I got my first restaurant job at fifteen, so I got my GED instead."

"Your parents were okay with that?" He'd thought his mother was going to have an aneurysm when he announced he was giving up his PhD candidacy.

"They didn't really have a choice," Rachel said. "You're looking at my informal education on those shelves. And of course all my kitchen jobs. Like I told you the other day, that's kind of how the industry works. Or it used to, before all the college kids decided not to use their expensive educations and go to culinary school instead."

There was definitely some resentment in those words, but he was pretty sure he was bordering on the limits of what she was willing to tell him. He tipped out a copy of *Ulysses*. "Then you have my utmost respect. Anyone who would tackle

James Joyce without being forced is a braver soul than I."

"I don't display my collection of CliffsNotes."

Alex let a vague smile flit across his lips as he replaced the book and went back to his perusal. She was so confident and well-spoken, he'd assumed she had a formal education, but she was obviously equally comfortable in the rough-edged kitchen environment. So far, Rachel was defying his efforts to categorize her.

He was about to turn away from the shelves when a small stack of books caught his eye. He lifted them, surprised to find that one was a tattered, leather-covered Bible. On top of it was a thick green journal with a pen clipped to the cover.

"I forgot those were there." Rachel swooped them out of his hands before he could ask about them, strode across the room to her closed bedroom door, and quickly deposited them inside.

"You don't need to be embarrassed," he said.

"I'm not." But her tone clearly forbade him to speak any further on the subject.

That was something more than unwillingness to let him see she had a Bible, and he'd be willing to bet it was about whatever was written inside that other book. But pushing merely to satisfy his curiosity would damage the tenuous understanding they'd established.

He flashed her a mischievous smile. "I don't get a peek at your bedroom?"

The guarded look vanished, and a twinkle lit her eyes. "Nope. And you never will."

"Ouch. And here I thought I'd proved that my intentions are honorable."

She sent him a look that practically dared him to say otherwise. He glanced at his watch. "As much as I'd like to stay here and convince you, I have to go. My mom is a stickler for punctuality."

"Your mom? You're seriously ditching me for your mom?"

"You're welcome to come with me. They're always telling me to bring a date."

"While I would love to take you up on that—" her tone held a hint of amusement—"I think that would send the entirely wrong message."

"To them or to me?"

"Both."

"Next time, then." He moved toward the door and paused with his hand on the knob. "The menu really is perfect."

"Thank you. And thank you for helping me eat it all."

"See you on the Fourth?"

"I'll think about it. Depends on whether Ana and Melody are available."

"Fair enough." He gave her a wink and a little wave as he left, but his good mood lasted only as long as it took to reach his car. He really did wish she'd decided to come. If he showed up with a woman, it would be one less part of his life laid bare to scrutiny.

On the other hand, he liked Rachel too much to subject her to that.

Crosstown traffic was light as he made his way through the city to Hale, a little neighborhood nestled in the quadrant of Colorado and Colfax near Rose Medical Center. He'd never quite understood why his parents had chosen to settle here, so far away from the Russian community on the southeastern edge of the city. Maybe it had felt like the quintessential American neighborhood to them—tree-lined streets, quaint 1920s bungalows, small-town feel. Even now, seeing how well-maintained his childhood block remained, he couldn't resist a wash of bittersweet nostalgia.

Nostalgia because he really had had a relatively good childhood here. Bittersweet because every time he came back, the visit ended in an argument. Somehow he didn't have much hope that today would be different.

He sat in his car, staring at the covered porch, and took deep breaths in and out. Now or never.

Alex strode up the long walkway to the front steps and pushed through the unlocked door without knocking. "Mom?"

"In here, Sasha!" came a lilting female voice from the kitchen.

He followed the familiar smell of cooking toward the back of the house, his heart lightening a degree. "What's going on? You never make *zharkoe* in the summer."

Veronika Kanin looked up from the stove, as slender and beautiful as ever, an apron covering her slacks and neatly pressed blouse. Too late, Alex realized she wasn't looking at him. He followed her gaze to the antique oak dinette behind him, and his stomach sank.

"Hello, Alex." Dr. Gregory Hirsch rose from where he sat with Alex's father, his hand extended.

Alex put on a smile to cover his dread and shook the man's hand with more enthusiasm than he felt. Dr. Hirsch was the chair of CU's psychology department and Alex's former dissertation adviser. Or he would have been, had Alex not abandoned his PhD studies after the first semester.

Clearly he'd been naive to think this invitation was his parents' way of making amends. It was simply another ploy to try to bring him around to their way of thinking.

Hirsch's smile faded, and Alex realized he was scowling. He released the professor's hand. "To what do we owe our good fortune tonight?"

"I had mentioned to Dr. Kanin that I hadn't had *zharkoe* since I was in Moscow years ago. She was kind enough to invite me to dinner tonight."

"How fortunate." Alex realized he was doing a poor job of hiding his feelings with his stilted formality, but he was waiting for the other shoe to drop—and clock him on the head in the process. No chance that Dr. Hirsch's presence was merely a coincidence.

Alex's father, Alexei—the other Dr. Kanin in the room—looked at him with sympathy from where he still sat at the table. Wordlessly, he poured Alex a glass of red wine and nudged it in his direction. So this was Mom's idea. He should have known.

He took the glass and moved uncomfortably to Veronika's side. "Can I help with anything?"

"There's a cheese platter in the refrigerator. Could you put it out while I finish here?"

Alex did as requested and found a wooden board with cheese, sliced meat, olives, and pickles, then set it on the table with a stack of small plates. Even though he was still stuffed from Rachel's food, he piled a plate high. With his mouth full, no one would expect him to make small talk.

Hirsch didn't seem to take the hint. "Your father was telling me about all the press you've been getting."

"Oh?"

"I read your piece and found your conclusions compelling. I'm beginning a study on social media behavior. I could use a research assistant. I thought it might be something you'd be interested in."

And there it was. His mother's attempts to get him to reconsider his PhD had failed, and now they were dangling a research position as a carrot to pull him back in.

The look his father shot him over Dr. Hirsch's shoulder made it clear Alex would not be rejecting out of hand what was obviously a favor. Alex answered cautiously, "It does sound interesting. Can you send me some information about the position and the study?"

His mother's shoulders relaxed almost imperceptibly. She'd expected him to turn it down flat. Maybe it would have been better if he had. At least then he wouldn't be giving her false hope about his openness to going back to his postgraduate studies.

Unbidden, Alex's mind drifted to Rachel. Her comment about college graduates abandoning their education showed some buried resentment and longing. What had happened to cause her to drop out of school and start working at fifteen? She said her parents didn't have any say in the matter. As much as Alex hated his parents' tendency to push and manipulate, they were still part of his life. He had the niggling feeling she couldn't say the same.

When the *zharkoe* was ready, they moved to the table, where they served themselves family style.

214

Dr. Hirsch, of course, raved about Veronika's cooking and ate two helpings, while Alex tried not to give away that he was so full he could burst. When the professor finally made his excuses—after dessert and one last drink—Alex heaved a sigh of relief.

"You've gotten a lot less subtle," Alex said as soon as they were alone. "What did you have to do to get him to offer the position?"

"Sasha!" Veronika's insulted look made him realize he'd crossed a line. He accepted the rebuke with a bowed head as she continued, "I only suggested he come to dinner to make you an offer in person."

"Forgive my skepticism, but I don't believe he's the one who has been sitting around thinking up ways to make me reconsider my career path." The fact he was a friend of the Kanins and a staunch Russophile probably played into his interest far more than Alex's academic promise.

"Sasha," his father said, more gently than Veronika, "you would have made an excellent clinician. You are intelligent and insightful, two qualities that make for an accomplished psychologist. Don't let all those years of study go to waste."

"They're not going to waste. Do you have any idea how rare it is for a writer to become so successful so fast? That's due at least as much to my psychology background as to any innate talent."

"But, Sasha, writing—"

"—is at least as worthy in its value to society as psychology. Besides, I was a terrible clinician."

"That's not true," Veronika protested.

"Then how come I've never been able to get through to you or Dina? She's been gone three years. Have you even talked to her once?"

His father's expression closed. "That's none of your business."

"She's my sister. You're my parents. Of course it's my business. What I want to know is, when I finally convince you that this writing career isn't a phase, are you going to cut me out the way you did to Dina?"

They stared at him, shocked. Good. They needed to be shocked. Sure, Dina was just as stubborn, but she was a twenty-year-old girl. They were the parents. They needed to bend before they lost their daughter forever.

"That's enough, Sasha," Alexei said, his expression pained. "You don't understand. Dina made her choice."

"Yes. Her choice. She was rejecting all your plans for her. She wasn't rejecting *you*. But you can't see that. I just don't understand what made her rebellion so much worse than mine." Alex rose. "I'll look over Dr. Hirsch's information as I said I would, but I intend to turn down the offer.

Hopefully I'm still welcome here when I do."

His mother jumped to her feet and grabbed his arm before he could leave. She took his face in her hands, her dark eyes imploring. "Sasha, you are always welcome here. And so is Dina. All she has to do is ask."

He stared at his mother. Veronika wasn't a bad person, even if he didn't agree with her priorities. His words came out softly. "*Mamushka*, sometimes it's okay not to win. You are allowed to change your mind."

Alex kissed her on the cheek, hugged his dad, and made his exit without further comment. He always hoped things might change with them, but they never did. His parents were set in their thinking, their expectations, their disappointment that their children hadn't turned out to be the people they wanted them to be.

It no longer made him angry. It simply made him sad.

Chapter Sixteen

After five different tries, Rachel had finally decided on a layout for the menu that would be used for the upcoming supper club and all the events thereafter. Elegant, but not stuffy; modern, but not too trendy. She momentarily considered the possibility that she was being too middle-of-the-road, and then dismissed it. This wasn't a restaurant, for one thing; it should be as elegant and accessible as her food, for another. A simple, modern sans serif font with a slight midcentury twist was enough to evoke the feel of Alex's throwback contemporary home and the classic nature of her food.

She printed out a copy on plain paper and started the process of choosing the stock from a samples folder she'd gotten from a local paper supplier. These were the types of decisions that no one knew a chef made, the little touches that made a difference to the overall guest experience.

A knock shuddered her front door, and she wandered to the window to peek through before she opened it. Melody stood on the front porch, holding a huge cardboard box loaded with smaller white pastry boxes and bags.

"What are you doing here?" Rachel took the

box from her friend and stood aside so she could enter.

"You can't finish your menu or your plating until we decide on some desserts, so I brought samples."

"Enough for the entire neighborhood?" She headed into the kitchen and set the box down on the table with a surprisingly solid thud.

"Lots of choices," Melody said. "I'll admit, some are day-olds I swiped from the bakery. They're my recipes, though, so I'm within my rights to bake them for you. With any variations you want." She began to unpack the boxes one by one, pointing out the contents. "These are simple custard fruit tarts. I know they're standard catering fare, but these are particularly good examples, if I do say so myself. These round ones right here are cinnamon-sugar donuts, which I can of course do with a variety of different flavors and sauces. Those would need to be prepared ahead of time and then deep-fried on site, so you would have to bring along a countertop fryer. I can lend you mine if you need it."

"Makes me wish I hadn't had breakfast," Rachel said.

"We can have second breakfast. You put on the coffee; I'll get the plates."

Rachel chuckled, but she did exactly that. "I take it the bakery thing is working out?"

"For now. I don't care for the hours, honestly,

but I knew going in it would be difficult to find a boss as flexible and generous as you. I'm still looking."

"Given your employment history, you shouldn't have trouble landing a high-profile restaurant." Rachel froze, her hand on the coffee grinder. "It's not because of your association with me, is it?"

"No, nothing like that. There just aren't many openings at restaurants, and all the artisanal bakeries are one-man operations or family-owned."

Rachel paused to grind the beans, then shook them into a French press. "Maybe you should open your own place."

"And you know as well as I do that I don't have that kind of money."

"Your mom wouldn't help?"

Melody shot her a reproving look.

Right. Her country music–star mother would love to swoop in and save the day with her checkbook and larger-than-life personality, but Melody had learned long ago that her mother's help always came with strings. She had almost as little contact with her parents as Rachel did with hers—which was to say, virtually none. Another thing they had in common.

Rachel changed the subject. "What's your schedule like for the Fourth of July?"

"It's a weekday. Why?"

"Alex asked me to come over for a celebration

at his place and said to invite you and Ana. But it's okay if you're busy. I was thinking I wouldn't go."

"What? Of course you're going. Are you crazy?"

"Mel, he's just an acquaintance. Maybe he'll become a friend at some point; I don't know. But we're working together, so—"

Melody put her hands on Rachel's shoulders. "Hon, I know you adhere to this 'no dating coworkers' rule like it's a religion, but seriously . . . in this case it's an excuse."

"How is it an excuse? We *are* working together. Besides, do you have any idea how it would look if we became . . . close? It would totally ruin his credibility. Best that we're barely acquaintances with a similar business interest. That way when he recommends me as a chef, there's no possibility anyone can call it favoritism."

"You're way overthinking this," Melody said. "Though I'm not sure how you can think at all when you're with him, considering."

Rachel's mind wandered toward all the things there were to be distracted by—the lovely, ever-changing hazel eyes, the way he always seemed to be looking for a reason to laugh, the taut muscles that dared her to reach out and touch, even if she had to pretend she didn't notice. Oh, there were plenty. And considering that was with barely an acquaintance, she didn't trust her common sense to overcome her attraction were they to become anything more. She'd seen firsthand how strong, capable women could become mere shells of themselves when they fell under a handsome man's spell.

"Can we get back on topic here?" Rachel pushed down the plunger on the French press, poured them each a cup of coffee, and opened the rest of the pastry boxes. "Where should we begin?"

Even taking only a few bites of each and drinking the strong black coffee in between, Rachel felt stuffed before they made their way through all the samples. In the end, they settled on a pistachio variation of Melody's almond *financier* cake, which Rachel would pair with homemade ice cream. It was simple and comforting without being rustic—exactly what the menu needed. With some careful plating and garnish, it could be every bit as elegant as a composed dessert.

"I'll have to leave early, but let Alex know that I'd be delighted to come to his Fourth of July party. And find out if we can bring anything. I hate showing up empty-handed."

Melody was really going to make her do this. "I'll ask Ana, then. Hopefully her clients can go one night without setting themselves on fire or posting something damaging to Instagram."

"On the Fourth of July, with the amount of

alcohol involved, I would put the possibility somewhere between slim and none." Melody began to split the remnants of the baked goods into two boxes, one obviously to leave with Rachel. Her taste buds thanked her, even if her waistline didn't. While she was thinking of it, Rachel grabbed her laptop to type in the final line where there was currently only a placeholder: *Dessert.* "How are we describing this?"

"How about 'pistachio *financier*, orange blossom ice cream.' "

"Perfect." Rachel tapped in the description, clicked Print, and retrieved the newly printed menu.

Melody looked it over for a long moment; then her eyes met Rachel's. "You're really doing this."

"I'm really doing this." And soon, she would know whether or not it would pay off.

Chapter Seventeen

The Fourth of July dawned with the kind of blinding, blue-sky heat that came to Colorado in waves, settling in for a few weeks at a time, unrelenting and untempered by even the usual afternoon thunderstorms. Rachel spent the day in the shade of her front porch, where at least she could catch a breeze, making list after list for the supper club that would be commencing in only a few days. The kind of planning that went into this sort of event wasn't unlike the kind she had to do in the restaurant. There was food to be purchased, with a certain overage for loss, mistakes, or extra guests. Some had to be precooked or parcooked and then reheated on site, which would make things much easier once she got there. Others would be prepared in Alex's impressive kitchen, and she needed to make sure that she had the tools to do it properly. He had e-mailed her to say that she didn't need to worry about decor or flatware, but she would need to bring her own plates if she had something specific in mind.

In short, this twelve-person supper club was almost as much work as preparing for a two-hundred-cover service, at least in terms of the items that needed to be checked off her to-do list.

And the whole time, her mind kept drifting back toward her closet.

She must have been possessed by some temporary insanity, but she had passed this perfect dress in a boutique's front window and been unable to resist. It was utterly unlike anything she owned, which was perhaps part of its appeal.

It hadn't occurred to her to wonder if Alex would like the way she looked in it. Of course not. Because that would be foolish.

Still, when the sun finally began to dip toward the horizon and Rachel wandered back to her bathroom to shower and primp and get ready for the party, she had to admit it wasn't her friends she was hoping to impress.

It was still hot, the humidity unusually high considering Denver's typically dry climate, so she braided her hair loosely and tossed the end over her shoulder, then put on the bare minimum of makeup: powder, bronzer, mascara, lip gloss. Nothing too elaborate, nothing that said she was hoping to be noticed. The crisp chambray of the loosely constructed shirtdress skimmed over her curves and floated above her skin, making it feel like the temperature had dropped ten degrees. She cinched the waist with the belt and then slid her feet into simple espadrilles that made her feel like she should be spending the evening on the beach. The effect was . . . not bad.

Let's face it, it still wasn't the most feminine example of a dress, though the cutout on the upper back was pretty dramatic. Her style was somewhere between utilitarian and tomboy, and there wasn't much that was going to change that. Maybe she shouldn't have made the effort after all. It was sad that even her attempts to look pretty ended in these sorts of results.

She opened her door to her friends and immediately said, "I know, I know, I'm going to change."

Melody darted inside to grab her arm. "Wait, why?"

"Because I look silly." Her friends highlighted how much she had to learn about "life on the outside," as she'd begun calling her post-restaurant existence. Melody looked like a beautiful gypsy tonight, a full, multicolored gauze skirt swishing around her ankles, an armful of bangles jingling with every movement. Ana was appropriately cool and preppy, in tailored navy shorts, a striped short-sleeved blouse, and pretty gold sandals that showed off both her tanned skin and her brilliant-blue pedicure.

"You do not look silly," Ana said firmly. "You look amazing. And Alex is not going to know what hit him."

"That's not why I dressed up."

"Sure it isn't," Melody said soothingly. "Now grab your purse and whatever you're bringing, and let's go. I can't wait to see this place of his. It has to be amazing if you were impressed."

Rachel was bringing a simple side dish—a watermelon, feta, and basil salad—that should go with any summery food Alex might be serving, so she grabbed the bowl from the refrigerator, took her tote from the hook by the front door, and moved with her friends to Ana's SUV parked out front. She felt nearly as jittery as she did at the start of a big night, a mix of anticipation and dread and determination to face whatever challenges dinner service would bring. Except tonight there was no reason to feel that way. Despite her love of solitude, she wasn't awkward in crowds. She could chat with strangers without any problem. And two of her best friends would be there. She could simply relax and enjoy herself.

Except the nervousness intensified when she thought about spending the entire evening with Alex.

Melody and Ana were already oohing and aahing when they entered the marble-lined lobby, even more impressed when she hit the button for the penthouse level. When they stepped off the elevator onto his floor and knocked at his door, it was already a few minutes past eight.

Alex opened the door immediately amid a rush of cold conditioned air. "Come on in."

He moved aside, favoring each of them with

227

a warm smile. "Nice to see you again, Ana, Melody. Everyone is upstairs on the deck."

Melody held up a bottle of sparkling lemonade. "Where should I put this?"

"There's a big bucket of ice upstairs with all the drinks. You can drop it in there to chill and we'll have it later. Plenty of food, too, so please help yourself. If you want to head up, I'll find a spoon for Rachel's salad and we'll join you in a minute."

Ana and Melody exchanged a look, obviously thinking that he wanted some time alone with her. They were wrong, of course. As soon as her friends headed for the spiral staircase, Alex went to a drawer in his kitchen and rummaged around for a serving spoon. Rachel pulled off the plastic wrap and stuck the spoon into the bowl. "Shall we?"

"After you." He fell in behind her and then said, "Wow."

"What?"

"The back of that dress is something else."

She felt a flush rise up her neck. "Thanks, I think?"

"That was definitely meant to be a compliment." When they reached the top, he gently placed a hand at the curve of her back and led her forward. She hadn't even realized that she was holding back, examining the scene first.

Big amber lights crisscrossed the deck overhead, giving a soft glow in the dark night. A

228

cloth-draped table held salads and chips and delicious-looking dips, while a muscular blond man worked a charcoal grill, cooking up burgers and hot dogs. There were perhaps a dozen people total, grouped in twos and threes, and Rachel immediately spotted Melody and Ana talking to a couple, already holding drinks.

"Let me introduce you to everyone." Alex took Rachel's bowl and set it with the other food, then slipped her arm through his as he brought her to the guy at the grill.

"Bryan, I want you to meet Rachel. She's the chef I was telling you about."

Bryan looked up from the grill, and his eyebrows lifted. Obviously she was not what he had expected. He held out a hand with a smile. "Nice to meet you, Rachel. What are you having? Hamburger or brat?"

"He grills a great burger," Alex said in her ear. His breath stirred a stray tendril near her ear and tickled her neck.

She swallowed and tried to catch her breath enough to speak. "Burger it is."

"One burger. What about you, bro?"

"I'll have a burger too." Alex tugged her away from the grill, saying, "I've known Bryan since I was a kid. He's also my climbing instructor. So when he wants me to have one of his burgers, I say yes."

"Smart move."

Alex pulled her toward a couple about their age, standing at the railing. "This is my old CU buddy Marcus and his wife, Lena. Guys, this is Rachel Bishop."

"Oh, right, the chef!" Lena's eyes lit up and she shook Rachel's hand enthusiastically. "Alex was telling us about your supper club."

"They were begging for spots, actually," Alex said with a grin. "I told him I wasn't sure where we were on the guest list for the next one. Do we still have spaces?"

It was a generous gesture, shifting the ownership of the event to her, even though the next one was still largely theoretical. "I'd have to check. You can always e-mail me or Alex if you want on the guest list."

"Do you have a business card?" Marcus asked.

She dug in her purse and brought one out, then handed it over. Fortunately she'd kept simple cards with her personal e-mail and phone number in addition to the restaurant's cards. They made it easier for people to track her down even if she moved jobs.

Alex guided her away, and when they were briefly out of earshot of the others, she asked, "Is that why you brought me here? To fill up the other supper club dates? Or to make sure that I could do the meet-and-greet thing without embarrassing myself?"

"You give me too much credit, and you give

230

yourself too little," he said. "I wanted to see you and I didn't want to wait until the weekend."

She waited for the joking words that would soften the meaning, the little twist of a smile that said he was tweaking her. But as she looked up at him, his expression seemed completely sincere. His eyes, dead serious.

Her heart did a triple step and stopped completely before it picked up its normal rhythm again. After that it was impossible to not be aware of the pressure of his hand on her lower back, the way her arm brushed against his body and released that cotton and soap scent she'd already come to associate with him. Only then did she recognize his gentle guidance and introduction to his friends not as an entrée to them, but a subtle claim on her. It should annoy her, and it didn't. Deep down, some part of her liked it.

That was what annoyed her.

Bryan brought them their burgers, and they went back to the table to dress them, then settled in two of the folding chairs that Alex had set up in a semicircle facing southwest. Rachel bit into her burger. Perfect. Alex's friend had a touch with the grill. She leaned forward until she caught Bryan's eye and gave him a thumbs-up. He held up his hands like he was basking in the applause of an audience.

She laughed. "Let me guess. The life of the party?"

Alex leaned forward to catch a glimpse and shook his head. "Something like that. He had plenty to choose from."

"Popular kid?"

"Rich kid." At her raised eyebrow, he hastily added, "That wasn't an insult. Just that there was always some sort of big event going on. His family are good people, do a lot of charity fund-raisers. I spent a lot of time at their house, and they never had a problem putting an extra plate at the table for me. In fact, I spent most of my senior year living with them."

"What happened?"

"My mother was offered a guest chair position at a university in Moscow, and it was the kind of offer you don't turn down." Alex shrugged, but from the way he didn't quite meet her eye, Rachel wondered if there might be some resentment behind the casual statement. She should be able to recognize it—she knew it well.

"I guess you should count yourself lucky that you had a suitable replacement." Now that had come out harsher than she'd expected it.

"You had a less-than-ideal childhood too?"

"I dropped out of high school at fifteen and crashed in the owner's apartment above the restaurant. You tell me."

Alex raised his bottle. "To early independence. It sucks."

"Yes, it does." She clinked her glass to his

bottle. In the far distance, she saw a colorful flash of light. "Were those fireworks?"

"Those were from the Aurora Reservoir, I think. The advantage to being so high, we can see everything in the city."

She leaned forward in her seat, straining to see the faint bursts of color in the distance. Then a firework went up nearby, the boom so loud that it shook her bones and made her jump halfway out of the chair. She snapped her head around to where the first flurry of fireworks went up to the north.

"That's the display at Mile High Stadium," he said, leaning over so she could hear him below the pops and the cracks. He pointed to another one farther out west. "And that's the one over Red Rocks Amphitheatre."

Rachel smiled and sat back again, propping her feet against the railing of the balcony. The cool breeze that came from the deepening night ruffled her hair and caressed her skin. She let out a contented sigh.

"So you really haven't seen a fireworks display since you were a kid?"

"Now that you mention it, I caught part of one a few years ago at Civic Center Park. The Fourth fell on a Monday, so the restaurant was closed."

"But . . ."

"I was so tired I fell asleep and missed most of it."

He laughed. "If you could sleep through fireworks, I'd say you needed the sleep more than the show. That's probably the only advantage to the current situation."

She nibbled her thumbnail. "Truth?"

"Of course."

"I don't like to sleep."

He quirked a look at her. "You've got insomnia?"

"Oh no, I sleep like a log, when I do sleep. I just don't like to. I stay up until I can't keep my eyes open, and then I sleep hard. It was easy when I worked in New York. We didn't close until midnight, and then there would be cleanup, and then the bars . . . I'd stumble home and catch a couple of hours and then get up and do the whole thing again the next day. It wasn't the healthiest lifestyle, I fully admit."

Alex was studying her with that searching look, the one that made her think she had given too much away. "Is that why you don't drink anymore?"

"No," she said carefully. "I don't drink anymore because it was so easy to drink too much. And I got too good at it."

"Hmm."

"See, you do that, and then I'm left here wondering what you're thinking. Was that *hmm* a shrink version of 'that's interesting'? Or is it that you're sorry you asked the question?"

He glanced at her, the pops of color and light alternately shading and illuminating his face. "I realized I was prying. And you don't like that."

"No, I don't." She heaved a sigh. "But I guess it's no big secret. My life has been various shades of stress, and it was too easy to look for escape in a bottle. I wasn't an alcoholic, but I could feel myself traveling down that road, and I'd already seen what was at the end of it."

"So you, what? Decided to stop drinking one day? What did you replace it with?"

Rachel went back to working her thumbnail with her teeth. "You promise you won't laugh?"

"Cross my heart."

"Bible study."

He laughed.

"I told you not to laugh!"

"I know, but I expected you to say yoga or meditation or chewing gum. I didn't expect Bible study!"

Rachel cracked a reluctant smile. "I know. Neither did I. So, this one dinner service was a total disaster. We were in the weeds from the time we opened—that means we couldn't keep up with the orders—and I had *way* too much to drink to unwind afterwards. I dragged myself out of bed early, still a little drunk, promising myself that I could grab a cup of coffee and a breakfast sandwich from the diner down the street, pull myself together before I showed up at the restaurant. I was already the *chef de cuisine*, so I was in charge, you know? I couldn't wander in looking like a hungover line cook.

"But when I got to the diner, it was packed. Not a single table open. I was taking my food to go, feeling pretty depressed about the whole thing since eating on the subway is not exactly my idea of a relaxing breakfast, when these ladies flagged me down. They offered me a spare seat."

"Ladies' Bible study?" he guessed.

"Exactly. Which in itself was crazy—a group of Baptist ladies holding a Bible study at 7 a.m. in a diner in Harlem. But it was a seat, and they seemed nice, and to be honest, they seemed to be having such a good time that I wanted to soak that up for a few minutes. So I sat down."

"Was this your 'Saul on the road to Damascus' moment?"

The question, though he meant it to be light, struck an inexplicable feeling of longing in her. "Not quite. I was actually raised in the church. For a long time, it felt safe. After my mom got remarried, we switched churches, and then it was all about being on my best behavior and making sure I kept up appearances. When I left home, I guess I left that behind too. It's not like I ever had the opportunity to go once I started working weekends. But when I sat down with those women, it felt kind of like I remembered, back when it was only my mom and me."

She smiled at the recollection. "I sat there and listened, and they invited me back the next week. I didn't think they meant it, but when I went in the following Wednesday, they were so excited to see me. After that, I dug up my old Bible from the bottom of a box and did the readings so I could join the discussion. It became a regular thing. I saw a few of them around the neighborhood from time to time and they asked me how it was going and how I was feeling, and I didn't want to admit I was hungover, so I quit drinking. And went to Bible study instead."

"That is the best story I've heard in a long time," Alex said. "I'd venture to say that more people need a Harlem Ladies' Bible Study in their life."

"Your turn. You sound like you had a church upbringing if you're throwing a Pauline conversion at me."

"Russian Orthodox." He craned his neck. "You can probably see our church from here if you look hard enough."

"Like, services in Russian, Russian Orthodox?"

"*Da.*"

"Everyone knows '*da.*' "

"*Da, ya govoryu po-russki.* Is that better?"

"I have no idea what you said, but yes. So, church. Russian Orthodox. Do you still go?"

"I still go to church, but not there. I've been

going with Bryan's family since I lived with them. It's in English and everything."

"That's kind of a big deal, isn't it? Leaving an Orthodox church? Don't you get excommunicated or something?"

"You can only excommunicate someone who is still a member. Being around Bryan's parents, I realized I was going through the motions, doing what was expected of me without really developing a faith of my own. Mitchell—Bryan's dad—made me see that if what you believe doesn't impact the way you live and the way you treat other people for the better, then maybe your faith isn't genuine. For me, that meant leaving the Orthodox church. I didn't mean it to be an indictment on everyone I left behind, but my parents took it that way. It tops their list of ways I've disappointed them."

Alex smiled, but she could hear the twinge of hurt in his voice, the sense of betrayal that his family hadn't understood his crisis of conscience. Rachel smiled back, pushing down an uncomfortable quiver inside her. It was the first time she'd opened up about matters of faith to anyone but Ana and Melody, mostly because she could barely articulate where she stood to herself, let alone to someone else. And yet she suspected Alex of all people might understand her ambivalence, were she to tell him the whole story.

But she barely knew him, so instead she turned forward to face the fireworks and pushed darker memories aside, if only for tonight. She watched the bursts of color with their staccato pops of sound, sipped her ginger ale, and allowed the pleasure of an unscheduled evening to wash over her. Only then did she realize she'd been talking with Alex for some time without any thought to her friends. She twisted and looked for their familiar silhouettes, momentarily wondering if they'd abandoned her. But no, there was Melody laughing with a group near the food. And Ana looked to be in an animated discussion with Bryan, who was hanging on her every word. Interesting.

"So what's his story?" Rachel asked, inclining her head toward Bryan.

Alex glanced at his friend. There was something guarded in his expression when he looked back at her. "What do you mean?"

"I mean, what does he do? Besides make excellent burgers."

"He's a professional rock climber."

Rachel started to laugh. "Way to go breaking type, Ana."

"Not into athletes?"

"Not unless you count making money as a sport. Don't get me wrong, that's not what she's after. She just doesn't like having to deal with guys' insecurity about not making as much as she does."

Alex relaxed visibly. "Well, Bryan could be a partner in the family business, but he doesn't care all that much for that sort of thing."

Rachel propped her feet against the railing, puzzled by Alex's flash mood swings. Was he that protective over his friend's reputation?

Then it dawned on her that he'd thought she was interested in Bryan herself. The idea that Alex might be jealous brought an irrational rush of pleasure. She stole a look at his profile, letting herself imagine for a moment that it was her right to lean over, run a hand through that artfully mussed hair and brush her lips against his. The mere thought made her catch her breath.

Alex heard it and turned toward her. "Problem?"

"No. No problem." Not as long as she kept her mind on the fireworks beyond this balcony and not the ones going off inside her. Best she keep her focus where it belonged: getting her career back on track and finding an investor for a new restaurant. This was a rare, brief reprieve from her real life, not a new start. Within six months, she would be as focused on her work as she had always been, and the steam and clatter of dinner service would replace warm nights on a rooftop deck.

Probably better not to get used to it.

Chapter Eighteen

"So tell me again how I got roped into doing this?" Bryan lifted one of the aluminum patio chairs and moved it in the direction Alex indicated, casting a smirk over his shoulder.

"I told Rachel I would have this ready before she gets here to prep for the supper club tomorrow, and she's already stressed enough. Not having it done might throw her over the edge."

"So what's the deal with her? You looked pretty cozy on the Fourth. You still trying to tell me this is a business arrangement?"

Alex thought back to the party and gave a sharp shake of his head. Rachel had opened up a little to him, but there was so much about her still to unpack: the real reason she left home so young, whatever bad experiences had led her to leave her faith behind. She was as protective of her personal beliefs as she was of the Bible she'd whisked out of sight, almost as if she were afraid they'd be used against her.

It was such a stark contrast to the capable, fearless demeanor that it only made him want to dig deeper. Learn her entire story. Get to know her in a way that was decidedly unbusinesslike.

"That's how she wants it," Alex answered finally.

"But not how you want it, obviously."

"Is this how we're going to play it?" Alex threw back. "Do you want all my innermost feelings now, or should we wait until we paint each other's toenails later?"

"Look who's deflecting now, Dr. Alex. You're usually the one prying."

"Then I'll pry. What's up with you and Rachel's friend Ana?"

Bryan made a face. "Absolutely nothing. And not for a lack of trying. I asked for her phone number; she said no. I offered my phone number; she said no. I told her if she wasn't interested in dinner, I'd be willing to skip straight to dessert, and for some reason she still said no."

"I can't imagine why she would have said that. Don't take it personally, though. I guess she's more into the banker type."

"She seemed plenty interested that night. And the feeling was mutual, believe me. Hot, smart, and doesn't take any garbage from anyone. I like it." Bryan carried the chair cushions and arranged them on their proper chairs, then added and removed outdoor pillows a few times. "What am I supposed to do with these? Fluff them or something?"

"I think you're supposed to karate chop them. You know, to put that divot in the top." Bryan looked at him like he'd lost his mind, so Alex walked over and demonstrated. "Like that."

"Dude, you shouldn't even know that."

"I watched HGTV last night hoping for some ideas," Alex admitted. "I might have oversold my ability to put this together myself."

"And you think Rachel won't figure that out? I'll bet you a hundred bucks she shows up on the night of with a bunch of extra stuff in tow, in case you screwed it up."

"I'm not dumb enough to take that bet. But I have a secret weapon. I have my sister." Alex looked at his watch. "In fact, I need to pick her up from the airport. Can you finish here without me?"

Bryan pegged him with a look that said he would pay for this later, hundred-dollar bet or not, but he didn't make tracks for the door, so Alex assumed that was a yes. The advantage to having friends who were more like family— they did stuff like this to store up credit for their next heinous favor. Making Bryan rearrange and redecorate his roof deck would most certainly come back to haunt him.

"Okay, I'll be back. I owe you one."

"Five," Bryan said, but he was laughing. Alex climbed back down to the main floor, grabbed his keys from the hook by the door, and headed for the airport.

Twenty minutes later, he was driving past the massive blue mustang statue that marked the entrance to Denver International Airport. Some

Denverites called it "Blucifer," which wasn't too far off the mark—it had become a local legend when a chunk of it fell off and killed the sculptor before installation. Those glowing red eyes gave even Alex the creeps.

He glanced quickly at the text message Dina had sent him five minutes ago—I'm at the fourth United sign at arrivals—and got in the proper lane for the United terminal. Three minutes later, he was pulling up at the curb on the arrivals deck, spotting Dina's hot-pink, owl-emblazoned luggage long before he saw her. He threw the car into park and jumped out to open the hatch for her things.

"You're on time!" she said. "I can't believe it!"

"So are you." He enfolded her in a hug and gave her hair a tug. "Purple this time?"

"I get bored." She handed over the luggage for him to load, picked up her handbag, and circled around to the passenger side. Alex slammed the hatch and gave himself a second to process. He expected the wild hair, even the undercut with the purple streaks, and it wouldn't surprise him if she'd gained another tattoo or piercing in the three months since he'd seen her. But he hadn't expected her to be so thin. Too thin.

But you did not talk about a woman's weight without good reason, even when it was your sister, so he climbed in the driver's seat and beamed a genuine smile her direction. "It's nice to see you, Dinasaur."

"Yeah, yeah. So, tell me about this girl."

Alex navigated his way back out into the through lanes toward the airport exit. "Didn't I tell you about her on the phone? Her name is Rachel. She's a big-time chef, James Beard Award and everything."

"So what does she need you for?"

"Finding investors," he said. "Like I said, I owe her."

"Mmm-hmm."

"What's that supposed to mean?"

"I looked her up online. She's pretty. Or she would be if she dressed herself up. She's like one of those plain girls in a teen movie, where you can see they're actually gorgeous, but they stick them in big glasses and overalls."

No point in lying when Dina would see for herself soon enough. "You're right; she is pretty."

"How long have you guys been going out?"

"Going out? We're not."

"You're going to all this trouble for a girl you're not even dating? Why?"

"It's called being a decent human being."

"No one is that decent of a human being. You're into her."

Alex sighed. He clearly wasn't going to convince his sister that his interest had nothing to do with wanting to date Rachel, probably because he didn't have a good argument against it. It was all he could do not to be jealous of the interest he saw in other guys' eyes, though Bryan clearly had locked in on Ana. A good thing, because the rush of jealousy Alex had felt when he thought Rachel was asking after his friend was neither pleasant nor welcome.

"So tell me about all the auditions you've been on since we talked last."

Dina waved a hand. "You know how it is. Cattle calls, a million girls for the same role. Ever since I changed my look, I'm getting more callbacks, but they're not all roles I would want to do, you know?"

Alex let out his breath carefully to conceal his relief. Dina had never been one to blend in, even if their parents managed to curb her edgier tendencies when she was still under their roof. She'd definitely developed her own sense of style since moving to LA, but Alex was always a little concerned that she would abandon their parents' conservative morals along with their dress code. He didn't want to see her make decisions that couldn't be undone.

"So what's next?"

"I've got a couple of auditions next week and a callback for a big commercial, so we'll see. All rebellious teenager roles, so I figure I've got at least one of them locked. Talk about typecasting."

"That sort of thing happens when you have purple hair and neck tattoos." Alex reached out and ruffled her hair, then laughed when she smacked his hand away. "Did you bring clothes to wear for tomorrow night?"

"Black pants, white button-down. I don't have an apron, though, so if she wants me to wear one, she'll have to bring it."

"I'm sure she's got that all figured out. I really appreciate you doing this."

"And I really appreciate you paying me five hundred dollars for it."

"What? The deal was three hundred plus your airfare, and that was to cover your lost tips for the weekend."

"You can't blame me for trying." She grinned at him and nudged his arm. "You know, your poor, struggling actress sister and all."

"Fine, five hundred." In truth, Alex had already planned on slipping an extra two hundred or so into her pay to help her out without hurting her pride.

"I knew you'd come through for me. You must be rolling in it. How's the book coming?"

"It's coming."

"Which means you haven't even started."

"Exactly." Unfortunately, Dina knew his process too well. He was either on or he was off, inspired or completely dead to his muse's nudging. There was no plugging along for him, which was why he had gone back to magazine writing. That, at least, he could produce on demand. An entire book of essays with a cohesive style and some sort of overall thematic arc? Not so much.

"So maybe we're both washed-up artistic failures."

A laugh barked out of him. "Thanks, Sis. I appreciate that."

"I call them like I see them. Can we stop and get something to eat?"

"Somehow I knew you'd say that. Food trucks?"

"Definitely."

Alex took the highway exit that would get them back to the north side and darted a surreptitious look at his sister. It was good to see Dina. They were so far apart in age—ten years—that they practically hadn't been raised together. At seven, she'd moved to Russia with his parents while he completed his senior year of high school. When they'd come back, he was already in college. He'd never lived at home again, and though he checked in frequently while he was living on campus, it wasn't the same.

When Alex pulled up several blocks away from the food truck pod, it would've been obvious the party was in full swing if only from the distinct lack of parking. Music pumped from the patio, long lines stretching from the trucks and the bar alike, good-natured laughter ringing out from the tables. Alex couldn't help himself—he looked for a familiar brunette even though he knew she would be home checking and rechecking her lists for tomorrow night. They fell into line in front of Dina's favorite truck—the barbecue one—and were soon taking heaping paper baskets of ribs and brisket and beans back to the tables beneath strings of twinkle lights. They finally nabbed a square foot of bench each at the end of a long table full of college students, leaning over the space between them to hear each other.

"Got a boyfriend back in LA?"

Dina choked on a bite of ribs. "Uh, not something I'm going to talk to my brother about."

"So that's a yes?"

"That's a 'not anymore.' I was seeing someone and it didn't work out. Word to the wise: don't date actors."

Alex didn't press, instead attending to what was very good Texas barbecue until Dina asked, "What did Mom and Dad say when you told them I was flying in?"

"I didn't tell them."

She stopped and put down her fork. "Why not?"

"You didn't want me to. I figured if you wanted to see them, you'd tell me."

"That's surprisingly hands-off for you."

"Listen, I don't know what was said when you left, but I know they miss you and you miss them. I also know you are all too stubborn for your own good. But I'm done playing mediator. You guys can work it out yourselves."

"Easy for you to say. When's the last time you even saw them?"

"Once-a-month dinners at the old house, remember? Mom gets to grill me on why I've abandoned my education, I get to hear about their latest research, and everyone ignores the fact that they want to talk about you but no one wants to be the one to break." He nudged her hand. "Gee, I can't imagine why I don't do it more often."

Dina gave him a reluctant smile and finished her food, then rose to throw away the empty container in a nearby trash can. "Should we go? I'm really tired. I just want to go to bed, especially since it's going to be a long night tomorrow."

There it was again: an underlying hint of unhappiness below her tough tone, enough to sound warning bells. But she wasn't going to tell him what was bothering her, so he rose. "Let's get you settled, then. The couch is already made up for you."

Dina was quiet on the short ride home, and all the way up the elevator to the apartment. Alex dropped her suitcase at the end of the sofa and nodded toward the bathroom. "You can use the shower first if you want."

"Thanks," she said.

"No problem."

"No, I mean, for flying me out here. It's good to be home."

"Thanks for helping me out."

"Well, it's the least I can do if I can finally help you nab a girlfriend. You're not doing so great by yourself."

Alex lunged for her and chased her around the sofa. "Take it back." He got her in a headlock and rubbed her head until she screamed.

"Never!" She broke free—he didn't try all that hard to keep her—and dove for the bathroom, slamming the door behind her. Alex laughed, out of breath, until the memory of his earlier suspicions sobered him. Something was going on with his sister, and he needed to find out what it was.

Chapter Nineteen

Product prep. Check.

Sauté pans, serving bowls, plating kit, and knives. Check.

Clean jacket, apron, and extra side towels. Check.

Rachel stood staring at the growing pile of equipment in plastic milk crates near her front door, crossing each item off her list as she came to it. She'd been up since dawn, cutting and chopping and slicing and parboiling, ensuring she had the minimum number of tasks to complete for tonight. She was all too aware that it wasn't only her food that would be under scrutiny, but her method, so she would do everything she could to make sure she worked as cleanly and professionally as possible. Someone might forgive a disorganized chef as long as the food tasted good, but they certainly wouldn't invest in her restaurant.

Of course, this level of organization in any other profession would be cause for clinical treatment.

Rachel glanced at the clock and saw the hour hand was already edging toward four. Enough time to shower, dress, put on a little makeup, and then get over to Alex's to set up ahead of the first guests.

She wasn't sure which made her more nervous: the inaugural meeting of the Saturday Night Supper Club or the prospect of seeing Alex again.

She'd kept her distance for the past several days, claiming preparations for tonight but really needing space from both him and her feelings toward him. That could, of course, be the wrong approach. It was just attraction, after all. Chemistry tended to wear off once you got to know a person and learned all their quirks and flaws. The fact she hadn't yet found any deal-breakers was simply proof that she hadn't spent much time with him.

A text message beeped through on her phone, as if he knew she was thinking about him. How's everything going? Need help with your supplies? Should I bring a paper bag for you to breathe into?

She texted back, I'll text you to help me carry everything up when I get there. Have paper bag standing by.

Immediately, his response: Yes, Chef.

Somehow, the fact that he was thinking about her and planning ahead took some of the nervousness from her stomach. He was taking this as seriously as she was, making sure she was okay, that everything was running smoothly. This should be a piece of cake anyway. She was an award-winning chef. Her problem was one of image, not talent or execution. The menu was excellent, creative but not too high-concept, both elegant and accessible. It was a good representation of what she had done at Paisley, what she was capable of executing on a larger scale. As long as she kept her head in the game, smiled and made polite small talk, and didn't burn anything, it would be fine.

She managed to convince herself of that through her shower and makeup. She selected a bright-blue, pleated jersey tank that no one would see under her jacket, simply because it was her favorite. Her hair got braided first and then twisted into a knot on the back of her neck, her typical no-nonsense kitchen style; though tonight she added a pair of big silver hoop earrings. She wavered on footwear before sliding her feet into her least orthopedic-looking pair of kitchen clogs. It was what she was used to, and standing on Alex's concrete floors for hours would wreak havoc on her back without them.

And then there was nothing left to do. Time to go.

She gave herself one last once-over in the mirror, took a deep breath, and grabbed her tote. Showtime.

When she arrived, Alex was waiting for her in the parking lot, obviously taking her at her word that she would be there at six sharp. He hopped off the low brick wall and strode toward her car, looking so casually handsome in his dress pants and relaxed button-down shirt that her breath caught in her throat for a moment. Thank goodness she had tinted windows or he would see her gaping at him. She'd thought the impact of those good looks would have worn off by now, that it was simply her memory constructing an improved picture of reality, but every time she saw him, she was taken aback all over again.

God had done good work when it came to him.

She stepped out of the car and put on a confident smile. "Door-to-door service. I'm impressed."

"I aim to please," he said, beaming that megawatt smile in her direction. "Everything's in the back?"

"Three crates," she said. "And the cooler."

He took the cooler and the heaviest of the crates, leaving the others for her, and they half-walked, half-waddled up the sidewalk into the lobby. "I hope you approve of the decor. My sister has been fussing over the details since she got up this morning and telling me I know nothing about design."

Rachel grinned. "I can't wait to meet her."

"And she can't wait to meet you. I apologize in advance for the questions you're going to get. Dina is nosy."

"That's okay. I'm used to it. I have the two nosiest friends in the universe."

Alex juggled his load and pressed the elevator

button with his elbow. "Do you need more than a half hour to set up? I put seven on the invitation, but one couple is perennially early."

"Nope. We're good. Everything's ready." She didn't tell him that she had a list of tasks, timed to the minute, stuffed in her pocket in case she got overwhelmed. It had been a long time since she needed a cheat sheet, but it had also been a long time since she worked with a new menu in someone else's space. Catering and private cheffing were far different than cooking in a commercial kitchen. She'd made sure to adjust for the residential cooktop and standard oven when she made her schedule.

The elevator leveled out at the top floor, and Alex leaned against the door to keep it open while she moved her boxes out. No sooner did his hand touch the condo's door handle than the door swung open to reveal a pretty young woman.

"There you are! Do you need any help?"

"Nope. This is it." Alex hustled his crates over to the kitchen, then returned for Rachel's. "Dina, this is Rachel Bishop. Rachel, my sister, Dina."

"Nice to meet you." Rachel shook the girl's hand, looking her over surreptitiously. She upgraded her initial impression from pretty to beautiful, no surprise considering her older brother, with pale skin and dyed-dark hair tied up into a bun on top of her head. Bright swaths of purple showed through the brown, several industrial piercings marked her ears, and the edge of a tattoo peeked around the side of her neck. Pretty much on par for every server Rachel had worked with. Unlike many of those, however, she was dressed professionally in conservative black slacks and a crisply pressed white shirt.

"Can I help with anything? I'm sitting on my hands until everyone gets here."

It wasn't an idle offer; she seemed to be really eager to help. Rachel nodded toward the crates. "You can help me unpack if you wouldn't mind. I need to get the fish from the cooler to the refrigerator."

"I'd love to." Dina hefted the cooler onto the countertop and began taking out the seafood, which had been cleaned and nestled in individual plastic bags of ice, while Rachel unpacked metal ninth pans filled with prepped ingredients.

"I appreciate the help tonight, Dina. Alex tells me you came all the way from LA for this. I hope it didn't ruin your weekend plans."

"No, I jumped at the chance. I wanted to see my brother. And this woman that he's going all out for." Dina stole a look at her. "No offense."

"None taken." She sent a wry look toward Alex where he was straightening the sofa cushions. "Your brother has an overdeveloped sense of honor, I think."

"He does. He's a good guy. Which is why I wondered why you two aren't dating yet. You are into guys, aren't you?"

Rachel gave her a bemused look. "Yes. I'm into guys. I just have a rule about dating people I work with. It never ends well, and this is kind of like working together."

"That makes you the smart one, then," Dina muttered. "I'll never make that mistake again."

"Sometimes we have to learn the hard way." Dina didn't seem to have a filter, but Rachel liked her all the same. She had a good-natured, if direct, way about her. No doubt she made good tips as a server. She wondered if this "hard way" was the reason Dina had come a thousand miles to help with a dinner party.

"Rachel, do you want to take a look at the roof deck before you get started?" Alex came over to the island, giving her a significant look.

"Good idea. Dina, can you finish unpacking these? I'll sort through them when I get back." Dina nodded, and Rachel followed Alex to the staircase and up to the roof.

"Sorry about that," he murmured over his shoulder. "She's been trying to drag details out of me since she flew in last night. Doesn't believe me that there are no details to tell."

"No problem." Rachel didn't want to acknowledge her disappointment that Alex was dismissing the possibility so thoroughly when she'd done the exact same thing a moment ago. They emerged into the bright afternoon sunlight and a delighted smile broke onto her face.

"This looks amazing." While the setting had been casual for the Fourth of July party, today he'd arranged the outdoor seating into groupings, creating little pockets of privacy with the potted plants. The Edison lights still crisscrossed overhead, waiting for dark to fall so they could light up like tethered fireflies. Combined with the breathtaking views, it would be the perfect way to end an evening.

"I can't take all the credit. Bryan and Dina helped. Well, Bryan mostly mocked me. Come to think of it, so did Dina."

"It's your place, so of course you get to take the credit. I won't tell anyone." Rachel glanced at her watch. Already a quarter past six. She needed to get going with her mise en place if she was to stay on time.

"I'm throwing you off schedule."

"No. Well, yes, but that's okay. Have I thanked you yet? I really appreciate this."

"Don't thank me until you wow them. Which you will." He nudged her arm, his smile giving her a warm glow inside and beginning the next round of butterflies.

"I hate this part. And I love it. Even in the restaurant, it was like waiting for the curtain to go up on opening night."

"You have nothing to worry about. They will be as impressed by you as I am."

If she could see her reflection, she'd find her cheeks had turned pink; she was sure of it. "I always avoided publicity because I tend to stick my foot in my mouth."

"Relax. You don't have to sell yourself. Your food will do that. Just have fun. Be yourself. They'll love you." He cocked his head. "Although . . ."

"Although what? You're making me nervous."

"You should lose the jacket."

She looked down at the crisp white garment. "Why? People are used to seeing chefs in jackets at events."

"Exactly. I don't want them to think you're the help. You're the cohost who happens to be cooking as well."

"Are you sure?"

"Sure. Now take it off." He gave her a wicked grin, to which she just narrowed her eyes. But she did as he asked, handing over her apron first and then unbuttoning the long placket.

"Much better." He shook out the apron and stepped forward to wrap it around her waist again. She dared not breathe while he had his arms around her, forced herself not to react at the barest brush of his hand against her skin while he wrapped and tied the strings in front of her. It was a thoughtless gesture that had suddenly become one of the most intimate things she'd ever experienced.

She couldn't hold her breath any longer and it came out in a shaky exhalation that gave away far more than she'd intended. His gaze moved to hers, and she saw the exact moment he caught her thoughts, his eyes darkening. So he felt it too. Maybe that shouldn't please her quite so much.

"I think you're right," she said finally. "Much better. However, I wait too much longer and we're not having dinner. Shall we?"

"After you."

She clambered down the stairs back to the main floor, taking the opportunity for a mental reset. Mind on the food, not on her cohost. Not on the fact she swore his gaze had dipped to her mouth for a split second when only inches had separated them. Not on the fact her heart was beating so hard that he could probably see it through the thin fabric of her shirt. Focus on the first task, and then the one after that. It wasn't Alex she needed to impress tonight.

By six thirty on the dot, everything was ready, glass bowls of prepped ingredients arranged neatly on the counter next to her cutting board, freshly sharpened knives laid out on a side towel. At six forty, the first knock came at the door.

Alex strode by the kitchen island on his way to the door and gave her a wink. "Showtime."

So it began. After the first knock, it didn't stop

for the next twenty minutes. Alex brought each group of guests to the kitchen to meet Rachel, introducing each with a summary of how he knew them and an interesting fact about them. Alex was a good host, skilled in striking up a conversation, though he quickly moved them away to mix drinks at the bar cart on the opposite side of the room. Soon, the room was pleasantly full, eleven guests plus Rachel, Alex, and Dina, the latter circulating through the room offering drink refills to the guests. Inevitably, a few guests wandered to the barstools at the kitchen island, where Rachel was working on the first course.

"You're the chef who got destroyed on Twitter," said one woman about her age—Margot, the art director, Rachel recalled—then clapped a hand over her mouth. "I'm sorry, I didn't mean it that way."

Rachel grimaced. "No, that's me. Note to self: verify press credentials before speaking to anyone with a camera."

Assured that she hadn't offended her, Margot leaned across the island with her drink. "What are the apples for?"

Rachel had had some experience doing demonstrations at food and wine festivals, so she'd purposely left herself some prep work that was both nonessential and allowed her some quick use of very sharp knives. "These are part of the second course. Fameuse variety. Have a taste." She pushed a piece of apple to the edge of her cutting board with the spine of her knife and waited as the woman nabbed it.

"Ooh, that's sweet. I can't wait."

"Local Colorado produce," Rachel said with a conspiratorial smile, then turned to Margot's companion. "So, Roger, Alex said you are a news producer? Sounds interesting."

"Not as interesting as what you do," he said. "But it pays the bills."

Handsomely if that ring on his fiancée's finger was any indication. She couldn't help wondering if he was one of the people Alex intended as a potential investor. "I'm going to send out the first course now. Do you want to grab the bread baskets and ask Alex to call everyone to the table?"

"Sure." Margot grabbed one of the baskets on the island, glad to be of help—another thing Rachel had learned from her demo experiences. It didn't matter what the guests did as long as they felt like part of the production.

Roger went upstairs to retrieve the guests who had gone to the roof deck with their drinks, while Rachel pulled the glass dish from the oven and began portioning the baked tomatoes onto pristine porcelain dishes Alex had on the shelf. For someone who didn't cook, he certainly had all the right equipment for it. The kitchen was set up as she would have done it herself, all things within easy reach, sensibly organized for maximum efficiency. She let herself think about cooking for him in this space for a bare minute before she ditched it and put her mind back on the work.

Guests began converging at the table, and Dina materialized gracefully to explain the amuse-bouche that had already been set at their places.

Alex caught Rachel's eye and gave her a nearly imperceptible nod. Even though she had printed out menus and placed them on each plate, she still needed to talk. She moved to the head of the table, reminding herself she'd done this sort of thing every day with her staff, and waited until the chatter died down. "For the first course tonight, we've got heirloom tomato tian with truffle-thyme breadcrumbs. With the exception of the seafood, everything we're eating tonight has been grown or raised on family farms in Colorado."

Murmurs of appreciation went around, and people picked up forks as their plates were set before them. Rachel returned to the kitchen and cleared the remnants of that first course, wiped down the countertops and cutting boards, reset her mise en place. Course number two. The whole time, she darted looks at the faces of the diners, noting whether their expressions were pleased, disgusted, or neutral. Some of the guests were difficult to read, but mostly she registered positive responses. The conversation picked back up again, laughter beginning, the tone noticeably brighter than it had been several minutes ago. That was the best indication that the food was good—the lightening of moods, the breaking down of inhibitions.

A cold dish was next, smoked trout with horseradish and apples; it plated up quickly and gave Rachel time to prepare for number three. The scallops, served over artichoke puree with sautéed wild oyster mushrooms, were a tricky proposition because they required a quick sear while she was getting down the puree so everything went out hot. She put down pans on two burners, cranked them up, then took hot plates from the warming drawer. The scallops went on in stages, giving her enough time to plate each pan and have Dina whisk them away to the table as they were finished. Total time to serve the entire table? Four minutes.

She'd found her groove at last, Dina's expert assistance letting her work like she would in her own restaurant, quietly calling her for pickup of the plates as she finished them. Meanwhile Alex presided over the table, opening the properly matched bottles of wine and passing them around, steering the conversation when it lulled. She was beginning to get used to the sound of his voice tickling at the edge of her awareness, a pleasant tenor that made her smile whenever it deepened in laughter. Now that she'd listened to him all night without being a participant in the conversation, she thought she could hear the bare edge of a Russian accent, so slight that no one who wasn't looking for it would ever pick it up.

"Rachel." Alex waved her over. Her heart jumped into her throat as she moved to the table.

Craig—a wine distributor, if she recalled correctly—looked up at her. "This ricotta cheesecake is magnificent. What is it that I taste? I pick up the raspberry in the compote, but I can't place the other flavor."

Rachel smiled conspiratorially and leaned down to reply, "It's fresh fig."

He brightened like she'd given him the secret to some unsolvable puzzle. "That's exactly what it is. Truly a surprise, young lady. Lovely food."

"Thank you." She looked around the rest of the table, unable to keep from beaming as the rest of them added their compliments.

The cucumber-mint sorbet came out next, more an intermezzo than a full course. Then dessert: Melody's elegant pistachio financiers. Rachel had topped the tiny French almond cakes with homemade orange blossom ice cream and garnished it with candied citrus peel and chopped pistachios. She could swear she heard a couple gasps of delight when Dina put the plates down in front of them.

And then, like that, it was over. Three hours

of focused work, being in the spotlight along with her food, and everyone was moving up to the roof deck for after-dinner drinks. She began to clean up, but Dina pushed her out of the way. "I'll do these. You go up and mingle. There were a lot of whispers about you between courses, so I think you should go be social."

"Thank you, Dina. You were absolutely perfect. I'd hire you in a second if you were available. And if I could actually offer you a job."

"I would take it. I think you made my brother even more popular than he was before."

Rachel removed her apron and folded it on the counter, then checked herself over to make sure her clothes were clean and her makeup intact. She climbed the stairs to the roof deck, where the party was still in full swing, people laughing with glasses in their hands and the lights glowing like stars overhead.

"Come meet your adoring public." Alex's voice in her ear was close enough to make her heart jump all over again. He pressed a glass in her hand with the whisper, "Lemonade," and then steered her toward a group with one hand on her lower back.

"Chef Rachel, the woman of the hour!" one man said. His name sailed straight out of Rachel's head in the face of his ebullient greeting. "Alex was just telling us about the difficulty with Paisley. What exactly happened there?"

"Just a nasty bit of politics and an unfortunate interview with a tabloid. We decided it was better that they buy me out of the restaurant while I worked on some new concepts." An abbreviated and whitewashed version of the truth if she'd ever given one.

"So what's the new concept, if I might ask?" Mystery Man's wife, Sophia, asked.

"I'm still working on the details while I look for the right partner. But I'd most likely continue along the lines of modern Continental with a farm-to-table ethic."

Alex whisked her away to another group, who simply wanted to compliment her food and take a selfie with her, to which she of course agreed. A few guests wanted to know her culinary background and were surprised she hadn't gone to school, then were impressed by the list of restaurants in which she'd worked in New York. It seemed that Manhattan's fine dining cred extended all the way to Denver, at least within certain circles. And then she and Alex were bidding the guests good-bye as joint hosts, giving her the weird sensation that they were a couple sending them away from their shared home.

As soon as the door closed on the last guest, Rachel swept the remaining dishes into the sink. She waved off Dina while she rinsed plates and transferred them to the dishwasher. "I'd say that was successful."

"More than successful. Look." Dina showed her phone screen. "You're trending."

"What? Who started the hashtag?"

Dina grinned. "Alex and I might have tweeted and Instagrammed each dish as it went down."

Rachel grabbed the phone. "Wait. You're kidding. You two have more than thirty thousand followers combined."

"The power of social used for good and not evil." Alex beamed, clearly delighted with himself. "Look at all the people who are asking how they get an invite to the next one."

Rachel leaned back against the counter, overwhelmed and overcome. "You guys . . ."

"No, we didn't do anything. *You* did this. Rachel, it was probably the best meal I've ever had. You really outdid yourself. Roger was asking what kind of investment you were looking for, even though I don't think he has the kind of money you'll need. But he knows people who do."

Rachel's attention fixed on Alex. Her vision was getting surprisingly blurry. "Thank you."

Dina pushed away from the island. "I think there are still some glasses upstairs. I'm going to go check."

Alex didn't seem to notice his sister's departure. "Hey, no tears allowed. This should be a celebration. Your food was amazing and you were magnetic. Everyone knew they got a glimpse of something special tonight."

"I have to admit, the meal was pretty impressive."

"The meal was nothing short of spectacular."

She threw her head back and laughed, her mood swinging back hard enough to give her whiplash. She impulsively threw her arms around his neck. "Thank you. I could practically kiss you right now."

"And I'd be perfectly okay with that." His voice turned husky as he pressed her a little closer.

She immediately pulled back. "Alex . . ."

He sighed, but he didn't move away. Instead, he reached up and began to remove the pins from her knot with agonizing slowness, until her braid unwound down her back. "We've been dancing around this since we met."

"But we work together—"

"I don't see either of us getting paid for this." He unraveled her braid, his fingers combing through the still-damp strands and sending shivers down her back. "I'm convinced that you can't think like a woman while you have chef hair."

She laughed, but the sound came out breathy and not at all with the derisive tone she had intended. "That's not a thing."

"It is most definitely a thing. Now. What does Rachel Bishop—not Chef Rachel—want to do?"

Rachel stared up into his face for a long moment. There was desire there, no mistake, but there was also amusement and endless patience. He was not at all what she had thought he was, not when she had first read his byline and not when he made his initial offer to help her. Even now, when the lightest touch in her hair had her trembling, he wasn't going to push his advantage.

She should do the sensible thing and walk away, keep this relationship strictly friendship, preserve her autonomy. And yet she was edging closer to him as if drawn by an irresistible magnetic force. "Things are just starting to go my way. What if we get involved and then the supper club suffers . . . ?"

"Don't overthink it, Rachel." His breath came warm on her cheek, so close his lips would be on her skin if she moved a millimeter toward him. The knowledge struck her with a wave of longing so strong it nearly took her off her feet, too strong to resist. She let it sweep her into him until their lips met. And then their arms were around each other, fingertips caressing, mouths exploring with delicious, torturous patience. All of her earlier objections melted away beneath his touch. She'd wanted this for longer than she cared to admit, and now that she was in his arms, she couldn't remember why she'd resisted it.

"Hmm," a teasing voice said behind them. "So much for the rules."

Rachel pulled away, already-heated cheeks

flushing deeper, but Alex kept his arm around her waist.

"You have rotten timing, Dina." Alex's teasing tone held a hint of annoyance. "You couldn't have pretended to pick up glasses for a few more minutes?"

"I should be going anyway." Rachel stepped back, and this time, he did let her go. She found her plating kit and knife bag, glad they were already packed—her trembling hands didn't lend themselves to handling sharp objects. She piled the cases on top of the clean dishes in the crate and hefted them. "Could you two grab the rest and help me out to the car?"

Keep it professional. It's bad enough that you initiated it, even worse that Dina walked in on you. You can at least act like it didn't matter.

But it did matter. She would be lying to herself to think otherwise. She had crossed a line with him from which there was no coming back.

"Dina needs to shut off all the lights upstairs." Alex gave his sister a pointed look and lifted the other crate and the ice chest. "Come on, Rachel. I'll walk you out."

They rode the elevator down in silence, Alex seeming perfectly comfortable with it even while she suffocated beneath its weight. "Alex—"

"No overthinking, remember?" He bent down to drop a quick, not-quite-chaste kiss on her lips, right before the elevator arrived at the ground

272

floor and the doors slid open. "We'll need to set a second date, you know."

"A—a what?"

"For the supper club. Now that your food blew up the Internet, I expect every last person I know to beg an invite. Do you think you could come up with another menu for two weeks from now?"

The change in topic stunned her. She shook off her post-kiss daze. "I expect I could. That puts us into late July, so I'll have different produce to work with. Let me see what I can do."

"And I'll start filtering the requests. You may want to think about what you'd charge for a prix fixe menu like this in your restaurant and I'll put it out."

"Wait, I thought—"

Alex grinned at her. "One more like this and I expect the Saturday Night Supper Club will be the hottest ticket in town. The more you charge for it, the more everyone will be dying to be a part of it. Trust me on this one. Now you're in business."

"Then that makes us partners."

"I'm hoping it makes us more than that." He bent down, but this time, his lips only grazed her cheek. "Good night, Rachel. Congratulations again."

"Good night, Alex." She climbed in her car, put it into gear, and pulled away from his building, slipping into the dark night. She tried to sort through the successes of the evening, think about the next steps, but every time her mind drifted back to Alex and that prematurely interrupted kiss.

Chapter Twenty

Alex rode the elevator back to his condo, unsure whether he should first thank Dina for her excellent work or give her a hard time for interrupting his moment with Rachel. Little by little, Rachel had begun to drop her guard around him, maybe even begun to trust him a little, but his sister's terrible timing had only succeeded in making her more skittish than before.

When he reentered the unit, Dina had cleaned up the remainder of the mess in the kitchen and was busy sweeping the crumbs from beneath his dining table. So thanks would have to come first. She'd done an amazing job tonight, far better than even he had expected. Apparently the last two years in LA had matured her and given her the work ethic their parents had accused her of not having when she dropped out of college. They might not see her skill at waiting tables as a positive, but she'd really come through for him tonight.

"You did a great job, Dina," Alex said, locking up behind him. "Thank you. This wouldn't have gone nearly as smoothly if you hadn't been here."

"You're welcome." She swept the debris into a dustpan and carried it to his trash can. "Are we going to pretend what I saw didn't happen?"

"If we were going to pretend, why couldn't you have pretended you didn't see us and gone back upstairs?"

"Just protecting your reputation, Brother. Or hers." Dina gave him a mischievous grin. "You were looking pretty hot and heavy there for a minute."

Alex rolled his eyes. "Not the conversation I want to be having right now."

"You started it. Not interested in each other, huh?"

"Knowing Rachel, that's her story and she'll still stick to it." But try as she might to argue otherwise, she'd been all-in with that kiss. Had they had more time, he might have attempted to define what that meant for their relationship. But after they'd gotten interrupted, he knew full well that she was going to try to explain it away, tell him why it shouldn't happen again. That was the last thing he wanted. He suspected that was the last thing she wanted, whether she admitted it or not. Rachel did nothing that wasn't calculated, so that meant in some part of her mind, she'd already anticipated this possibility and considered her response.

"If you don't mind, I'm going to go take a shower and get ready for bed," Dina said. "Despite how easy I made that seem, this evening was hard work."

Alex grinned. She might have matured some,

but his sister hadn't lost her sass one bit. If anything, it had only intensified. "Don't run out all the hot water."

"Yeah, yeah." Dina's voice drifted away as she shut the bathroom door behind her.

His sister would be a while, so Alex went to his bedroom and turned on his laptop, staring out onto the sparkling cityscape while it booted. This evening had been a success, not only because of the interest it had generated among their guests, but for the momentum Rachel seemed to be gaining online. The only advantage to the fickleness of the social media age was that it took very little time for disgrace to be forgotten if something newer and more interesting came along. The Saturday Night Supper Club was new and interesting.

He started with Instagram, where he'd posted each course as Dina put it down, which of course she had shared as well. The comments below the photo said it all:

Yum! How do I get in on this?

Why have I never heard of this supper club before? I need this in my life.

Recipe? Please?

Fortunately, he'd anticipated this response, though it was further-reaching than he or Dina had ever expected. He took out his phone and snapped a photo of the menu, then posted it with a comment: Tonight's menu. What will it be next time? #SatNightSupperClub #Foodie #NomNom #Foodstagram #Yummy #Dinner. He rather hated #NomNom, but hey, it was about getting the word out regardless of what it did to his personal pride and sense of masculinity.

Then he responded to each of the tweets that were directed to him. Most of them weren't serious about wanting to attend; the ones that held potential, he replied to with a direct message including his e-mail address. At some point they were going to need to add some regular paying guests, even though he was slightly weirded out by the idea of having complete strangers in his home. While influencers would fund Rachel's restaurant, members of the regular dining public were the ones who would help with her reputation issues.

The shower turned off next door, but when the door didn't immediately open, Alex shut down his web browser and instead opened the file containing his proposal. Two measly paragraphs. That's all he'd done in the three weeks since the whole situation went down with Rachel and Paisley. His agent had even given up on her daily check-ins, evidently figuring out it was doing nothing to motivate him and only wasting her time.

Alex leaned back in his chair and stared at the blinking cursor. His first book had started with a guiding essay, and the essay started with the identification of a problem. A humorous way to shed light on the foibles of modern life, especially considering the place he lived and the people with whom he interacted. And yet, as he thought back through all of the things he'd done in the past several weeks, he couldn't find it within him to complain.

He was enjoying himself.

He was enjoying the interaction with Rachel, the amazing food she cooked, the preparation for the supper club. He was enjoying the anticipation of the next one, and the challenge of helping her rebuild her career when he had always been mostly focused on his own.

He was starting to care for her. Not simply because he was attracted to her or because he felt guilty about what he had done to her career. But because she was smart and funny and determined. Because she only cared about what other people thought as far as it affected her ability to live up to her own expectations. Pretty much the exact opposite of every woman he'd dated.

He smiled when he thought of how nervous she'd been about the supper club and how she had completely taken control. He'd never thought he'd find extreme capability in a woman sexy, but she was blowing plenty of his preconceptions out of the water.

A tickle in the back of his mind made him open a new file. He put his fingers to the keyboard, not expecting anything to come, but to his surprise, words poured onto the screen. Not just a paragraph, but page after page. When he finally looked up at his clock, it was nearly one in the morning; he'd spent over two hours typing without pause.

Alex saved the file and shut his laptop down without reviewing the document. He would look it over tomorrow and see if there was anything usable there or merely sentimental ramblings after having indulged in an incredible meal made by an incredible woman.

He rose from the chair and poked his head out into the living room. The lights were already off, though the flickering screen of the television projected colors onto the sleeping form of his sister. She was curled on the sofa beneath a light blanket with Sunshine, who had apparently emerged from hiding. She'd be flying home early tomorrow morning, ready to get back to her real life. Bad timing or not, he liked having Dina here. He'd missed a good chunk of her life because he'd been busy with his own, and now that she could use a big brother on her side, she was a thousand miles away.

Nothing could be done about that now. She was living her dream in LA and he would support her in that, even if their parents wouldn't. But if he paid her well enough, she might consent to returning in two weeks.

Two weeks. He had his work cut out for him if he was going to maintain the buzz and momentum until the second supper club. Tomorrow he would go over his list of potential guests and select the ones who were Rachel's next best bet for spreading the word. Knowing her, she'd have a provisional menu established by the end of the day and be testing recipes first thing Monday morning, something for which he fully intended to be on hand.

Rachel couldn't sleep. She tossed and turned in her bed, the streetlight throwing a yellow glow across her bedroom. It was the excitement of the evening, of course, the impulse to relive every course and analyze what went right and what went wrong. To sift through the guests' reactions, feedback they hadn't known they were giving her. The vegetable, fish, and scallop were flawless, as was the savory ricotta cheesecake, but judging from the amount of gnocchi left on the plates, the wild boar ragù hadn't quite gone over as well as she'd hoped. Probably not the taste, given that it was partially eaten, but rather that it was a bit heavy after the first three courses. She hadn't wanted anyone to go away hungry, so she'd erred on the side of generosity. Next time she would go with typical tasting portions, enough to satisfy but not enough to weigh them down.

She might also be doing everything she could not to think about Alex, which was proving near impossible. For one thing, he'd presided over the night with admirable aplomb, a born entertainer. He'd known who to introduce to whom and how to steer the conversation when it strayed into dangerous territory. He'd guided their impressions of the dishes when they were still deciding what they thought about them. And he'd brought his sister in, who had arguably made as much of a contribution to the night's success as Rachel and Alex had.

There was also his kissing prowess, which was not inconsequential. Even now, the memory of his lips on hers and his hands in her hair made her heart beat wildly. Sent her mind spinning off into the girlish fantasies she'd banished by necessity a long time ago.

"Forget it," she whispered to herself. She needed Alex for his access to potential investors, not as a boyfriend. She hadn't gotten this far in her career by letting herself be distracted by a pretty face and a knee-weakening kiss. There was only room in her life for one love, and that was cooking. She knew better than to succumb to whispered promises of a happily ever after that would likely never come.

No. Better to play it safe and keep things professional. The next time she saw him she would apologize for letting things get so out of hand. He would understand, given how excited she'd been about the evening's success.

Anyway, it wasn't like she had any time to think about getting personal. She had only two weeks to come up with a different seasonal theme and a new menu, and source all the food for the next supper club. She knew full well that Alex had intended this as a trial run to make sure she could pull off the concept and build her confidence. Next time the stakes would be higher. Her investor could very well be in that group. She needed to keep her head down and her mind focused, away from distractions.

And whatever else he might be, Alex was an enormous distraction.

Chapter Twenty-One

Alex had vowed to let Rachel make the next move and contact him.

He made it exactly two days.

It wasn't for lack of trying. Other than fielding the flood of responses to the surprisingly successful Instagram barrage, he had nothing to do but write. Now that he'd completed the first phase of relaunching Rachel's career, he should be able to focus. The words should be flowing onto the page.

And yet the only thing that was flowing was a river of panic. Every last bit of talent or inspiration he'd ever possessed was apparently gone.

Almost as if he were sending out an emergency beacon, his cell phone lit up, flashing Christine's number on the screen. Cautiously, he answered.

"There you are!" she said by way of hello. "I was beginning to think you were avoiding me."

"Not avoiding. Procrastinating."

"Yes, your time-honored method of creativity. Does that mean you're finally writing?" Christine's tone was patient, or maybe it was resigned to the hopelessly uncooperative nature of his creative process.

Alex hesitated. He still had no idea where

the book was going. Or if it was a book. Or publishable. "Sort of."

"How do you 'sort of' write?"

"Currently it's a random handful of essays and ramblings that may or may not have a cohesive theme. I don't know yet."

"And here I thought my fiction writers were eccentric. I tell you what. Send me what you have. I'll be the one to tell you if it's any good and if it's saleable."

"Soon. Not quite yet."

"You're killing me, Alex. You're literally throwing away the chance at a six-figure contract because of . . . what? Writer's block? Insecurity?"

"I told you when I wrote the first book, I would only write another when I had something worthwhile to communicate. I don't believe in putting work out into the world simply to have another publication to my name. And I'm still not sure if what I have to say will even be worth the paper it's printed on."

"Then we push the delivery date. But give me something to work with so we can at least get a contract in motion."

Christine was right. If he delayed much longer, this window of opportunity would close. And she might be a little pushy, but that's why he'd hired her in the first place—to have the killer instinct that he somehow lacked when it came to publishing. "I'll do my best. That's all I can promise."

"Then it's going to have to do. Just don't mess this one up, Alex. You're a gifted writer, but even gifted writers can sabotage their careers out of existence."

"I'll get you something in a couple of weeks and you can tell me if you can sell it. Deal?"

"Good enough. I'll talk to you soon."

Alex clicked off the line and set the phone beside his laptop, fiddling with it until it was perfectly parallel to the keyboard. Maybe Christine was right. Maybe he was sabotaging himself because he was afraid to have another bomb. His magazine writing was high-profile, but he didn't carry the weight of sales on his name alone. If an article didn't resonate, readers moved on to another one in the publication that did. But the thought of all those hardbound volumes languishing in a warehouse somewhere, unwanted by the reading public, was enough to give anyone writer's block.

So maybe his writer's block had nothing to do with Rachel in the first place.

And yet his eyes continually went to his cell phone, as if he could will it to ring.

He sighed, picked it up, and dialed Rachel's number.

She answered after half a dozen rings, sounding breathless. "Hey!"

"Hey yourself. Am I interrupting something?"

"Not really. Just testing some recipes for next

week and I couldn't find the phone. What are you doing?"

Alex smiled. "Trying to work on a proposal and getting distracted by you."

"Oh, really?" She gave what sounded like a nervous laugh, punctuated by the sound of sizzling in the background. Naturally she'd be multitasking. Rachel had an ability to focus that right now he envied.

She wasn't giving him anything to work with, though. Bryan would mock him for his total lack of game, but women didn't usually make him this tongue-tied.

"I was hoping you'd let me take you out sometime this week." There. That wasn't so bad . . . if he were a middle-schooler asking a girl to the movies. Nicely done.

"Like on a date?"

"Exactly like a date. With dinner and conversation and, if I play my cards right, a kiss that does not end with my sister barging into the room."

Rachel laughed, and this time there was no question she sounded nervous. "Okay. Friday."

"You're going to make me wait all week to see you?"

"I'm busy until then. Besides, I have a feeling you're used to getting your way. It won't kill you to exercise some patience."

"You promise?"

"If you die, you can absolutely say you told me so."

Now it was his turn to laugh. "Okay, fine. Let's say . . . seven on Friday? I'll pick you up."

"It's a plan."

"If I took you to coffee tomorrow morning, that wouldn't count as a date."

"Nice try." He could hear the smile in her voice. "I'm busy tomorrow."

"All right, all right. Friday. I'll try to be patient. But if you need someone to give an objective opinion on the menu—"

"Good-bye, Alex."

He laughed again and hung up the phone. He liked this woman. Her sense of humor, the fact she never let anything undermine her focus. True, he would have liked it a lot better if she'd agreed to see him every day this week, but the care she was putting into this menu should teach him a lesson in diligence.

Yes. His proposal. He could at least write something, if only to get Christine off his back. Surely he could find something to be ironic and irritated about. He'd made a career off his natural contrariness.

Except when he put his fingers to the keyboard, the only thing he could think of was the way Rachel had thrown her arms around his neck, the taste of her lips, the feel of her body against his. Maybe the stuff of poetry, which he didn't write, or sappy love songs, which he didn't write either, but not a book of essays. There had to be some universal meaning to his work, something to which all readers could relate.

And then the idea sparked, just a bare filament of thought. He followed it, not sure where it would lead, until his fingers were tapping across the keyboard and the screen filled with line after line of words.

Before he knew it, he'd written a complete essay he hadn't known he had in him.

He saved it and shut down the file. At least that was progress. He might not leave Christine and his publisher hanging indefinitely, though a single essay hardly qualified as a full proposal.

In the meantime, though, he had a date to plan. One he hoped would finally prove to Rachel that the only thing he wanted out of this arrangement was her trust.

Rachel set down the phone and turned her attention back to the fish she was searing in the hot pan.

Alex had asked her out on a proper date.

And for reasons she didn't quite understand, she had said yes.

Why had she said yes? Since Saturday night, she'd convinced herself that she needed to keep this relationship friendly and businesslike. It was safer that way. Less messy. The fact Alex hadn't made any kind of contact made it easy to believe he'd dismissed that kiss as a mistake, just as she had.

Rachel nibbled her nail. It had been a mistake, hadn't it? Yes, she'd enjoyed it. But she'd also been relieved Dina had interrupted them before she needed to put a stop to it. There were things Alex wouldn't understand. He'd take them personally. Wasn't that why she'd given up dating before she'd ever really begun?

The acrid smell of burning oil jolted her out of her reverie, and she snapped her mind back to the fish with dismay. A perfectly good piece of halibut, ruined. She twisted off the burner with a savage motion and dumped the fish directly into the trash can. She was wiping out the pan to start anew when she finally gave up. She was too distracted to cook fish, and halibut was a stupid idea anyway.

So she did what any sensible single woman in her situation did: she texted her friends and asked them to bring ice cream.

Two hours later, Ana and Melody arrived together, the first bearing a bag of whole-bean coffee, the second a half gallon of rocky road ice cream.

"What happened?" Ana asked immediately. "Is it the supper club? Alex? He didn't do something jerky, did he?"

Rachel stepped aside. "No, nothing like that.

I had an emergency ice cream craving and I realized I haven't even gotten to tell you about the supper club yet."

Melody took the coffee from Ana and moved past Rachel to the kitchen. "We saw on Instagram. The food looked beautiful. Have you searched the hashtag? It was trending."

Rachel flushed, remembering her reaction to that very fact. "I saw. By the way, there are strawberries and fresh whipped cream in the fridge."

Melody helped herself to bowls while Ana found the grinder and the French press. Rachel leaned in the doorway, smiling. They'd known each other long enough for her friends to treat this like their own place, something she secretly loved. Seven minutes later, Ana was serving up hot cups of coffee, while Melody had made them big bowls of ice cream, artistically garnished with strawberries and whipped cream.

Melody practically dragged Rachel to the living room sofa and tucked her feet up under her long skirt. "Now spill, and make it quick, because I have to be at work in an hour. I don't believe for a minute this is about needing an ice cream fix."

Rachel dug into the sundae with her spoon and licked off the creamy, chocolaty deliciousness. God bless Melody. This was no supermarket ice cream. This was some serious artisanal, organic, small-batch, hand-churned heaven.

"So that's how you're going to play it?" Ana arched an eyebrow. "Just use us for coffee and ice cream?"

Rachel set down her spoon. "I kissed Alex."

"What?" they asked in unison. Ana managed, "When?"

"On Saturday after everyone left the supper club."

"Wait a second, you kissed him three days ago and you're only now telling us?"

Rachel grimaced. "I know. I'm sorry. I was going to tell you sooner, but I wasn't sure how I felt about it."

Ana looked at Melody. "She kissed the most unreasonably hot guy in the state of Colorado and she doesn't know how to feel about it."

Rachel rolled her eyes. "You know why."

"Hon, I know you're nervous, understandably so." Melody put her hand over Rachel's. "But if you felt nothing in that man's presence, I'd have to recommend professional help."

"You guys are already Team Alex, and you don't know anything about him."

"I know he's the first guy to tempt you from your nun-like state, and therefore I like him," Ana said.

"If you're not interested," Melody said, "I'll take his number."

"Hey now!" Rachel protested. Ana and Melody started laughing.

"Anyway," Melody said, "I want to know how the kiss was."

Rachel took a bite of ice cream so she didn't have to answer, but she couldn't stop the heat that bloomed in her cheeks.

"That good, huh?" Melody rubbed her hands together.

Good enough to send a quiver of anticipation through her at the thought of being in his arms again. If she was honest, though, it wasn't just the kiss. It was the guy. There was something about him that had pulled her in against her will, made her want to get closer, reject the notion that they should be merely friends and business partners.

"Am I crazy?" Rachel asked, spoon poised above her bowl.

"Yes," Melody said immediately, "but not because of this."

Ana jumped in with her take-charge, utterly reasonable tone. "Let's look at this objectively. He's good-looking. He works. He's super nice." She ticked off each trait on her fingers and looked to Melody for help.

"Obviously has a conscience considering how hard he's trying to make things up to you," Melody said.

"Conscience, check. Know anything about personal beliefs?"

"Used to be Russian Orthodox, now just

unaffiliated Christian, I guess. Sounds like it was a big deal to his family."

"You've already had the family and religion talk?" Melody's eyebrows went up. "That's usually a third date sort of topic for me."

"That's why you end up with jerks," Ana said. "No offense."

"None taken. But for the record, the religion question does not necessarily screen for jerks. Some of them talk a good game."

Rachel looked between the two of them, some of her angst subsiding in the wake of the runaway conversation. "Not to be self-involved here, but we're talking about whether I'm crazy to be interested in Alex."

"Let's see," Ana said. "Good-looking, employed, super nice, and Christian? I'd say you're crazy not to be. If he were interested in me, yeah, I'd give him a second look."

"You know, Bryan is interested. And he seems to tick all those boxes."

Ana shrugged. "He's got to make an effort. He seems like the type to get by on his looks and his money, and as you know, I haven't done so well with those lately."

"How do you know he has money?" Was Ana's radar really that keen?

Ana gave Rachel a patient look. "Honey, there is not a single person in this city—except for maybe you—who doesn't know who Bryan Shaw is."

"I didn't," Melody said.

"That's because you're like Rachel. If he's not Jacques Pépin, you're not impressed."

"True," Melody said. "But you spent the entire Fourth of July evening with Bryan. You must have had some interest in him."

"When did this turn into a discussion of my love life? This is about Rachel locking lips with a hot writer." Ana swiveled toward Rachel again. "So what are you going to do?"

"He's taking me out on Friday."

"On a date?" Melody and Ana asked simultaneously.

"Yes, on a date. I don't even know why I said yes."

"Because he's beautiful and kind and obviously you feel safe with him, or you wouldn't have made it this far. From the look on your face, you're looking forward to this."

She was. No sense in denying it. "I probably need to buy something to wear, don't I?"

"Of course," Ana said. "I think it might require a special trip. And a new dress."

"Let's not go crazy." Inwardly, though, the prospect didn't sound half bad. She'd spent most of her life downplaying the fact she was a woman. Now she wanted to feel pretty and feminine, like she had on the Fourth of July.

For once, she might actually feel safe enough to be herself.

Chapter Twenty-Two

The week barreled toward the weekend, and Rachel had enough to do that she managed not to think about her upcoming date with Alex. Almost. In between trying recipes for the following week's supper club, she found herself replaying the kiss and trying not to obsess over what would have happened if Dina hadn't been there. By the time he called on Friday morning, she had a full menu and enough unresolved tension to play her own nerves like a violin.

"Ready for tonight?" Alex asked as soon as she picked up her cell phone.

She took the pan she'd been heating off the burner and moved it to a cool spot on the stove. This definitely would require her full attention. She hadn't forgotten that he'd made her burn her fish the last time they'd talked. "That depends. You still haven't told me what to wear. You realize that women like to plan ahead for these things, don't you?"

A long pause on the other end suggested surprise. "I'm sorry. I only finalized the plans this morning. Something like what you wore for the Fourth of July is fine."

"Okay. Still on for seven?"

"Absolutely. I'm looking forward to it."

"We're not hiking or anything, are we?"

"No, we're not hiking. I'm not that clueless. You can wear pretty shoes and everything if you want."

Very well then. She was definitely going to need to go shopping. "Okay. I'll see you tonight."

"I'm looking forward to it." His voice dipped low. "This has been a very long week."

Rachel bit her lip, unaccountably pleased to know he'd done as much thinking about her as she'd done about him. "I made good use of my time. I have a menu for you to look over."

"I would expect nothing less. See you at seven."

Rachel hung up the phone and allowed herself a dreamy, stupid sigh. Yeah, she was losing it. Over a guy.

Worse yet, she was enjoying it.

This called for reinforcements. She texted Ana and Melody immediately: Help. I'm second-guessing my ability to pick out my own clothes. Are you free? I've only got nine hours to figure it out.

Ana came back immediately: I can't believe you put it off this long! I'm going into a client meeting, but I could do a quick lunch break. Noon at Cherry Creek mall?

Done. Meet you at the Starbucks in the middle. Not that her already-stretched nerves needed caffeination, but the landmark was a good jumping-off point for every wing of the upscale shopping mall.

Testing the last recipe would have to wait. It was ten o'clock now. She had just enough time to get a pedicure—something else she never did—before meeting Ana to pick something appropriately pretty for her first real date with Alex.

Two hours later, her toes were ready to see the light of day, primped and softened and sporting a neutral pink polish—the pedicurist's suggestion, given that she hadn't yet picked an outfit.

When she arrived, her friend was already waiting with a cup of coffee in hand, dressed in a stylish black business suit with sky-high patent leather heels. She rose when she saw Rachel.

"Melody couldn't come?"

"No, I'm here. I just needed to get tea." Melody appeared behind Rachel, holding a paper cup. "Commence Operation Date Night."

"Look. My toes are pretty." Rachel wiggled her feet in her flip-flops, earning a grin from Melody and an arm around the shoulder from Ana.

"I'm so proud. All of our teaching has paid off, Mel." Ana hiked her handbag over her shoulder, back to no-nonsense field marshal. "Now. I have exactly an hour before I have to get back to the office, but we're going to find you something to wear if we have to look at every last store in the mall."

It wasn't far off. Rachel stopped counting stores at eight, and it was several more after that when they found something appropriately mystery-date-night-ish. She really needed to overhaul her wardrobe if she was going to stay on the "outside" much longer. Having to drag her friends shopping every time there was an event was going to get old quickly. She would let them dress her and buy everything they suggested—if Rachel picked it off the rack, it looked awful on her. If Melody or Ana picked it, it looked great. Thank goodness she hadn't decided to go it alone.

"All right, hon," Ana said, giving her a tight squeeze. "I have to run. I want all the details when you get home tonight."

"Promise." Rachel looked at Melody. "You have to go too?"

"Yeah, I've got a job interview. This place is killing me. They really need two bakers, but it's cheaper for them to demand overtime from me."

A pang of guilt struck Rachel. She'd been so focused on Alex that she'd forgotten why she was doing the supper club in the first place. "Melody, you know the minute I have my own place again and can hire you back—"

"I know." Melody gave her a quick hug. "But I also know that takes time and I have to pay rent. So I need to find a place that pays well without these crushing hours."

"Good luck. Call me if they need a reference."

"I will." But they both knew she wouldn't. Before, possibly. But an Instagram success didn't erase Rachel's bad press.

"Don't start feeling guilty now," Ana murmured. "She knows what she's doing. She'll be fine."

Ana was right, but it still didn't erase Rachel's feeling of guilt as she drove home. It had been so easy to forget why she was doing this whole thing. Not only for herself, but for all the people depending on her. Yes, most of them still had a job, but she had brought them to Paisley from secure positions at established restaurants, promising them good pay, long-term stability, a different environment than the punishing kitchens in which they'd been working. It never occurred to her that she might not be able to offer what she didn't have herself.

To be honest, she hadn't thought about Paisley in a while. The menu development had staved off the anxiety she often felt outside of work. It no longer hurt to drive by her colleagues' restaurants during the supper rush.

What did that mean, exactly?

Rachel puttered around her house, putting things in order while she waited for the clock's hands to crawl around its face toward date time. Finally, at four thirty, she drew herself a bath, sprinkled in some fragrant salts that had been a Christmas gift from Melody, and let herself enjoy the luxury of free time. She lingered until the water got cold and then climbed out and began the process of hair and makeup that she usually abhorred. For someone who had gone nearly a decade without ever dressing up for a guy, it hadn't taken her long to abandon those ideals.

She primped and painted and curled until she looked suitably ready for anything he might have prepared. The dress had ended up being Melody's choice, a pretty blue chiffon that gathered at the neck, then tied at the waist before flowing to her sandaled feet. Not too dressy, not too casual. She'd left her hair loose and curled in big waves over her bare shoulders and put a couple of metallic bangles on her right wrist. At the last minute, she changed her mind about the coral lipstick and instead put on a nude color dabbed with lip gloss. Perfect. She didn't look like she was trying too hard. She still felt like herself, but this was the Rachel who went out on romantic dates with handsome men, a Rachel with whom she was not yet acquainted.

The doorbell rang promptly at seven, and Rachel took a deep breath to calm herself before she opened the door. "Hi."

"Hi." Alex stood there, as impeccably put together as usual in the casual Colorado date uniform she'd seen over and over in the restaurant: jeans, dark T-shirt, dark sport coat. Somehow on him, it looked natural and

301

handsome. He leaned forward, making her heart jump into her throat, but his lips just lightly brushed her cheek. She inhaled his scent, amazed that it had so quickly become familiar, oddly comforting. Then he straightened and looked at her for a long moment.

She shifted under the gaze. "What?"

"You look beautiful."

"You don't look half bad yourself." Which was understating it by at least half. "Ready to go?"

He moved toward her again, but this time he simply reached for her hand and entwined his fingers through hers, which jolted her heart as abruptly as a kiss would have. "Yes. But first, do you trust me?"

Chapter Twenty-Three

For a split second, a flicker of dismay shot through Rachel when she recognized Alex's neighborhood and he pulled into his parking lot. "Are we stopping here first?"

"No, this is our final destination. You said you trusted me. Does that still count? I can take you home if not. Or we can go do something else."

Alex looked so uncertain that her doubts of moments before vanished. "No. I'm curious what you have planned."

He turned the ignition off and then jumped out so he could open the door for her. He held out his arm and she took it, letting him escort her into the building.

"I feel a little guilty," he admitted. "You're gorgeous. It seems unfair for me to keep you all to myself."

She licked her lips and decided to answer honestly. "I dressed for you, not for them."

He trailed a finger down her bare arm, once more making her think he was going to kiss her. But at that moment, the elevator arrived at the lobby level with a ding, and the doors slid open to reveal an elderly lady. She scowled at them as if reading their minds.

Alex cleared his throat. "Good evening, Mrs. Tajikian."

"Humph," she said, looking between the two of them suspiciously. They moved past her onto the elevator and the doors closed before they both started laughing.

"Let me guess. She doesn't approve of gentlemen having lady visitors?"

"She doesn't approve of anything that I can tell." Alex punched the button and the elevator moved silently upward, delivering them to the penthouse level. Alex fumbled for his keys and opened the door, then stepped aside for her to enter.

Rachel inhaled deeply. Enticing aromas wafted through the space, both familiar and foreign. From the stereo in the corner, the soft strains of traditional-sounding European music greeted them. She had to listen for a moment before she realized the lyrics were in Russian.

"What is this?"

He turned to her, once more looking uncertain. "I'm making dinner for you. Food I grew up with."

Something caught in her chest. "Really?"

"I know it's not anything fancy, but I thought . . . well, you always cook for everyone else, don't you? I thought you might like someone to do the same for you."

Tears pricked Rachel's eyes. "It's perfect. Really. No one ever cooks for me because they think I'll critique the food."

"I'm counting on you not being an expert on Baltic cuisine. And if you are, these are family recipes, so you're not allowed to criticize."

"I wouldn't dream of it. This is a treat." She slid onto one of the barstools and folded her hands while she waited for him to take his place on the other side of the island.

Alex took off his jacket and tossed it onto one of the dining chairs, then found a plain gray apron and tied it on. "This won't be a coursed meal or anything. I'm not good enough to time it all, and my mother used to serve everything at once anyway."

"You do realize that I don't eat like I'm at a restaurant when I'm home, right?"

"I'm surprised you cook for yourself at home at all."

"I usually don't. Unless it's a huge batch of soup that I can eat all week at two in the morning."

Alex lifted a lid on a pot that already sat on the cooktop. She caught a glimpse of bright-red liquid as the steam escaped the pot. "Borscht?"

"Naturally. Now I need to get the dumplings on and make the sauce for the pork. It won't take that long. I hope."

Rachel watched as he moved about the kitchen.

"You look pretty comfortable over there for someone who says he never cooks."

"Well, I helped make these things with my mother dozens of times when I was younger. They'd have friends from the university over, and they'd eat and drink vodka until the wee hours of the night. I'll admit, I had to call my mom for the recipes, but at least I remember what they're supposed to look and taste like."

Rachel leaned forward. "What was it like to grow up Russian in America?"

"I wouldn't say that I did. I'd say I grew up American in a Russian household." Alex paused for a second, wooden spoon poised in his hand while he thought. "My parents are . . . I don't even know how to classify them. They are all about the opportunities in America and taking part in them, and at the same time, they're very protective of their own traditions. Yet they were the furthest from traditionalists when they were back in the old country—exactly why they left in the first place."

"That must have been some sort of tug of war on you."

"I guess so," Alex said. "More so for Dina. But she was closer to them than I was. They encouraged my independence from the start. With Dina, they were always overprotective, maybe because she was an unexpected late-life baby. I don't know. We grew up speaking

Russian at home, but it was to be English only outside. They talked about how bad things had been in the Soviet days, but everything had to be 'the Russian way.' "

"It sounds like they were mourning a way of life there that *should* have been," Rachel said.

Alex looked at her thoughtfully. "You're probably right. Maybe that's why they went back when they got the opportunity. They wanted it all, and in the end, they did the best they could to merge both together. I can't help but think the blend was always lacking to them."

"When you miss something that much, all you can think about is how it should have been and how you can get it back. Or something like it."

"What was it that you missed?" Alex must have sensed her ambivalence, because he went back to cutting mushrooms so he wasn't looking her straight in the eye.

She traced the countertop's patterned stone with her fingertip. "A real family, I guess. My dad left my mom when I was young and we never had a ton of money. Hartford, Connecticut, isn't an affluent area to begin with, and my mom had to commute hours to work. I always had this fantasy that one day I would come home and it would all be different, that we would be like one of those TV families that sat down to dinner together every night."

"Is that why you started cooking?"

"Partly." That was a portion of it, but not nearly the whole story. "But then my mom got remarried and I realized the fantasy of a family I'd always had was just that—fantasy. I regretted that I didn't appreciate the life my mom made for the two of us, frozen pizza and all. In any case, I moved out when I was fifteen and started working and then the kitchen staff became like my family. They even call the staff dinner 'family meal.' "

"That's what I ruined for you," Alex said softly.

Rachel started. Somewhere along the line, she'd stopped blaming him. He wasn't the vindictive, careless person she'd thought he was. "The thing is, when you work enough places, you start to realize that all industry folk are like family. You've got a shared history, a shared language. We understand the crazy that most people don't see. You hang around in one city long enough, and eventually everyone has worked for and with everyone else."

"The stories of crazy chefs become like stories of Crazy Aunt Irma?"

Rachel laughed. "Exactly. You become like veterans sitting around and telling war stories. They might get embellished over the years, but everyone recognizes the parts that ring true."

"And you miss that. The camaraderie."

She looked him directly in the eye. "I do. And I miss the routine. The sense of purpose.

The adrenaline rush. The way that, when you're under the gun, everything else goes away. When you have a good team, when it's all flowing, it's magic."

Alex set down his knife. "Then that's what we're getting back for you."

"We?"

"We. Wasn't that the whole idea of doing the supper club in the first place?"

She smiled, but it was a knowing sort of smile. "I thought you said it was an excuse to spend time with me. And to rid yourself of writer's block."

"Oh, it was. At least on my end."

"Did it work?"

He smiled back. "You're here, aren't you?"

"I mean, did it fix your writer's block?"

Alex didn't look at her while he cranked up the burner beneath his pan. It was going to be too hot for the butter, which he would find out in a minute, but she didn't say anything. She wasn't here as a chef, and she certainly wasn't going to give him cooking pointers. Sure enough, the butter was already starting to brown when he dumped in the mushrooms. He hissed out his displeasure and turned the heat back down.

"In a manner of speaking." He added sour cream to the mushroom sauce, making something similar to Stroganoff. Despite the overbrowned butter, it smelled delicious. He wasn't a bad cook at all. "I'm writing, but I don't know if anything's going to come of it. I don't know if I can make a book out of it."

"Can I read it?"

He barked out a laugh. "Right now? No."

"Why not? I could tell you if it's any good."

He gave her a look. She chose to call it fond and not condescending. "I'm going to let my agent make that call. You're not unbiased."

"Why not?"

He winked at her. "Because you're into me. You'd be so overcome by my ability as a wordsmith that you'd say, 'Is there anything Alex can't do? He writes and cooks and climbs and looks good in an apron too?' "

Now it was Rachel's turn to laugh. "Don't forget to add your awesome humility and self-awareness."

"Oh, don't worry. I won't." He set aside the pan on the stove and then retrieved a covered casserole dish from the oven. "Braised pork loin."

"Smells great. One of my favorite ways to cook that cut."

He lifted the lid and transferred the meat to a cutting board, then looked dismayed. "I should have rested it while I was making the sauce."

Rachel smiled at his discomfiture. The timing was the hardest part of cooking, and right now he looked like a crestfallen little boy. "You're good. Just put the sauce over the simmer burner as low as it will go and stir it every once in a while. There's enough fat in the sour cream that it shouldn't curdle."

"In the meantime, I can plate up the borscht and the dumplings." He went back for a stack of plates and two soup bowls. Rachel resisted the urge to help. This was his show, and all things considered, he was running it pretty smoothly. He ladled the borscht into bowls and topped each with a dollop of sour cream and a sprig of fresh dill—very attractive, Rachel thought, both the presentation and the look of concentration on his ridiculously handsome face.

That thought made her struggle to hold back her smile as he brought the bowls to the table. The meat had been arranged on the platter in an elegant swoop of mushroom sauce with more drizzled over the top. He'd gone to some trouble to think it through and make it restaurant-worthy. The fact he'd given it so much effort only put more weight behind her smile.

He swept his hand toward the table and pulled her chair out for her. "Shall we eat then?"

"This looks amazing." She was rewarded with a pleased smile from him.

It was amazing, actually, especially considering he claimed he didn't cook. The borscht held just the right amount of sweetness, the beets tender but still fresh and bright, finely diced pork giving it further flavor. The dumplings, colored green from the spinach in the dough, were tender with a delicious cheese filling. When she complimented him on the texture, he made a face.

"I can't take credit for that. I bought them from the Russian deli. I ran out of time to make the dumplings."

"My compliments to the deli, then." Rachel moved on to the pork, which was tasty despite the ever-so-slightly separated mushroom sauce. "This is all good. You know, it really captures that traditional feeling. I can almost imagine your parents eating this back home."

"Almost?" Alex looked at her quizzically. "Of course they did. These are family recipes."

Rachel grimaced. She should have been more careful with her wording. "I'm sure they are. They must be very old or very new family recipes, though."

"Why do you say that?"

"Because these are definitely not Soviet-era dishes. Some of these ingredients wouldn't have been available. The borscht is probably the same, though I doubt there would have been meat in it. But fresh sour cream and mushrooms . . . it was probably more like mayonnaise and whatever she grew in her kitchen garden."

Alex stared at her.

"I'm sorry. I shouldn't have said anything. There was this deli in Brighton Beach I liked and the owner used to tell me stories." She was babbling now, desperate to cover her faux pas when he had gone to such lengths to give her a nice meal, to impress her.

Alex started to laugh.

"What? I don't . . . What?"

He rubbed a hand over his face. "That is exactly like my mother. Isn't that what we were talking about? How she felt the need to invent a rosier past for herself? Of course she would be cooking her grandmother's recipes in America. Or taking things from new cookbooks and passing them off as family tradition."

"So I didn't offend you?"

"Offend me? No. Inadvertently made me understand my mother for the first time in my life, maybe."

"I take it you aren't close?"

Alex set down his fork. "My relationship with my parents is complicated."

"Is that why you studied psychology?"

"You're the one who should have been the psychologist. You have an uncanny way of reading people."

Rachel flushed. "Sorry. I guess I tend to study people too. Usually they only show you the side they want you to see. I don't like being fooled." She snapped her mouth shut, feeling like she'd already said too much.

But Alex simply considered her like he could

see straight through her eyes into her thoughts. Then he looked down at the empty plates. "Are you ready for dessert yet?"

"I'm stuffed," Rachel said. "I couldn't possibly."

"Then how about I make some tea and we go up on the roof deck?"

"Tea would be nice." She helped him gather the plates and brought them back to the kitchen, where he quickly rinsed them and put them in the dishwasher. Then he went to the corner of the countertop and plugged in a cord coming from what looked like a metal urn.

Rachel followed and peered around him. "You have a samovar?"

"Christmas present from my mom. Which is funny, because even she uses an electric kettle." He found a glass jar of tea leaves and put some in the samovar's strainer pot, then filled both vessels with water and turned it on.

"How long will it take?"

"A while," he said. "The water has to heat in the bottom and then the steam heats the tea at the top."

"Then let's go up. It would be a shame to miss the sunset."

Alex held out his hand. She placed her own in it without hesitation and let him lead her to the spiral staircase. Up they climbed, and then they stepped out onto the roof deck.

"It's beautiful tonight." The sky looked like a rainbow, deep reds and oranges near the horizon, coloring wisps of clouds with watercolor hues against a fading blue sky. The sunsets were one thing that had struck her when she first came to Colorado, and they still hadn't lost their impact.

"I call these Broncos sunsets," he said. "God is clearly a football fan."

"Maybe He is, but He roots for the Patriots."

Alex's mouth dropped open. "I can't believe you would say something so hurtful and untrue."

Rachel laughed. "Honestly, unless you're a college team playing UConn, I don't really care."

"That's almost as bad." Alex gestured to the cushioned outdoor sofa, now piled with pillows and draped with a blanket. Rachel lowered herself to the edge of the bench and tucked one leg up beneath her.

He sat beside her and gave an exaggerated yawn before stretching one arm around her shoulders.

She arched an eyebrow at him. "Smooth move, Romeo."

Alex laughed. "That move killed with the high school girls by senior year."

"I bet you didn't need those moves to kill with the girls." That dimple alone probably got him anything he wanted.

"Contrary to what you may think, I was a bit of a nerd. Fortunately, there were enough nerdy girls in my high school that I managed to get dates for all the big events."

"So while you were going to prom in a powder-blue tux, I was cooking for prom-goers like you."

His expression turned serious. He combed his fingers through the ends of her hair and laid a thick wave across her shoulder. "Do you have any regrets about how you went about everything? Starting work so early?"

It might have been the first time anyone besides Ana and Melody had asked her that question. "I don't believe in regrets. I did what I had to do at the time. I missed out on a lot, but I also accomplished more than I would have had I taken a conventional route."

"How do you do that?" Alex asked softly, searching her eyes. "Accept everything? No second-guessing. No regrets."

She sensed there was more to the question than curiosity. "Practice. At not wanting any more than I can have."

The moment stretched, broken only by the soft sound of their breathing. His gaze lowered to her mouth, and her breath hitched in her chest with sudden yearning for all those things she said she had rejected. When his fingertips slid through the hair at the nape of her neck and his lips lowered to brush hers, she rose to meet him. She let herself sink into the kiss, let it swallow her up, envelop her senses. No other sensations but his taste, his smell, the warmth of his skin against hers. When he pulled her a little closer, she went willingly, stretching her arms around his neck, tunneling her fingers into his hair.

She'd avoided men because she'd been afraid of this, what happened after the instant flash fire of attraction, the desire that went deeper than the physical, the kind of madness that turned strong women into compliant, fragile shells of their former selves. And yet when she was with Alex, she didn't feel weak or bullied or afraid. This yearning felt natural. Uncomplicated.

When they parted and she laid her palm flat against his chest to feel the steady, hard beat of his heart, she knew. From the look in his eyes, he did too.

She'd fallen. And there was no coming back.

Chapter Twenty-Four

Alex had never thought a single kiss could shift the world on its axis, but he was fairly certain the ground had moved beneath him when he finally returned to the kitchen to get their tea. He'd wanted to do something special for Rachel, something she couldn't associate with work, and instead he'd been the one to have his breath taken away.

He found two ceramic mugs and filled them halfway with strong tea, which he diluted with water. Then he added sugar and transferred the cups to a wooden tray. Thanks to Victoria, he had all the proper entertaining accoutrements, even if he rarely needed to use them. He sliced the *muravejnik*—an odd little cake from the Russian deli that had been one of his childhood favorites—added the dessert dishes to the tray, and then climbed back to the roof deck.

Just in those few minutes, the sunset colors had slid over the mountains, bathing the city in blue twilight and overtaking the sky in a soft blue-gray glow. The city lights winked on around them, cars sliding by on the streets below in the dilute glow of their headlights. Rachel had her feet propped up on the glass outdoor coffee table, the blanket draped over her legs against the chilly night breeze. Her eyes flicked to him, and a smile lifted the corners of her mouth.

"Miss me?" He set the tray on the table at her feet and then handed her the mug, followed by the cake.

She patted the cushion beside her and sampled the tea and cake while he settled back onto the sofa. "So I've been sitting here wondering. What happened with your girlfriend?"

That was the last thing he expected her to ask. "What do you want to know?"

"You must have been pretty serious if she decorated your place. Seems like she assumed it would be hers someday. What went wrong?"

"I don't know. I think she had the wrong idea about what life with me would be like. When we met, I had just signed a book contract for an absurd amount of money and I was getting a lot of attention. I think she was sure I was going to be famous someday."

"But that didn't pan out?"

Alex shrugged. "Like I said before, the book bombed. My publisher suddenly stopped taking my calls. Interest dried up. I was still writing for major outlets, but there wasn't the same level of . . ."

"Glamour?"

"Something like that. Victoria wanted me to jump back in and write another book. You see, she was a high-end real estate agent. She was all

319

about the hustle. If you lose one deal, you go out and close two more. She hated the fact I was only taking on a handful of assignments, living off my rental income, climbing with Bryan while she was working. To her, that meant I lacked drive and vision, which was apparently a deal-breaker to her."

"Why didn't you? Jump in and write another book, I mean. Isn't that what you're doing now?"

The question stopped him short. Why hadn't he?

"I don't know," he said finally. "I guess I didn't want to do it on demand. I wouldn't have been writing because I had something to say or the book filled a need; it would have been only to keep me from looking like a washed-up has-been in other people's eyes." In fact, it would have been easier to keep the books coming, prove to his parents and Victoria that he hadn't made the wrong decision in leaving psychology behind. He'd striven beneath the weight of those expectations for far too long: go to church, finish his degree, keep up appearances. Get a steady job, win the respect of his peers.

"I guess I look at this career change, my quick success, as something of a miracle. All I can do is trust that God put me on this path for a reason. All the hustle in the world won't get me anywhere if it's not His will."

Rachel put aside her dessert plate and picked

up her mug. "You wouldn't like me very much when I'm running a restaurant. I'm all about the hustle."

"But you had other people's money riding on your success. Employees to take care of. Running a business can be all-consuming. You were doing what you needed to do to fulfill your obligations. Not to mention it's something you love."

"I think you might be giving me too much credit," Rachel said. "It's true that most of us—professional cooks—are in it because we love it. It's a mental and physical challenge, and most of us do embrace the service aspect of the job. But after a while, we cook because we're cooks. We've done it for so long that we don't know what else to do. Some of us get addicted to the adrenaline rush, and some just like knowing where we'll be every night. It's easier to be at work where you can simply do as you're told and not make your own life decisions. Eventually it does become your real life." Rachel shot him a wry grin. "My best line cooks were always the ones who had done time in prison or the military. They knew how to take orders."

Alex slid his arm around her shoulders and tugged her to him. After a moment, she relaxed and nestled into his side as if she belonged there.

"So what's your story, then?" he asked. "Which one are you?"

"All of them. When I left home, I didn't really

321

know how to take care of myself. At work, there was always someone to tell me what to do, teach me what I needed to know, give me advice."

Her voice held a mixture of pain and fondness. Maybe that was the very definition of nostalgia, the same feeling he got every time he went home.

Rachel laughed suddenly. "This big Samoan line cook named Tito took me to get my driver's license on my sixteenth birthday. I ran over a cone, but they passed me anyway. You don't say no to Tito."

Alex smiled and pressed his lips to Rachel's temple. The more he learned about her, the more fascinated he felt. There was still so much she wasn't telling him, but he could picture her as a fifteen-year-old girl, all but run away from home to find a surrogate family in some small kitchen in Hartford.

"I wish I could have seen you back then, before you became this big, intimidating chef."

"I'm not intimidating!"

"Yes, you are. But lucky for me, I'm not easily scared. For the record, I'm very certain I would have liked you even when you were running the restaurant. There's something sexy about a woman in charge."

He edged closer, and she turned into him. "Oh yeah?"

He tipped her chin upward and kissed her again, her response immediately igniting desire in him. It didn't take a mind reader to know she'd avoided men in the past, so her openness with him was an undeniable stroke to his ego. When she pulled away and whispered, "Maybe you should take me home now," it took several seconds to grasp her true meaning and not the racier alternative that sprang to mind.

"Are you sure?" His lips found her neck for the briefest, most tempting moment. "It's such a pretty night for stargazing."

"Liar." Her voice came out breathless. "You're not paying attention to the sky anyway."

He nipped her earlobe with his teeth, and her hands fisted his shirt in response, giving him another jolt of serious want. "Maybe you're right. Much longer and I'm not going to want you to leave."

"Much longer and I'm not going to want to leave." She muttered the words to herself like a warning as she put aside the blanket and got to her feet.

"Hey." He tugged her back into his arms and pressed a barely-there kiss to her lips. "I want you to know I wasn't trying to pressure you into anything. You can trust me."

Her eyes searched his face as if she were trying to read the truth of his words. Then she gave him a little enigmatic smile. "Drive me home now?"

"Of course." He picked up their dishes and carried them downstairs. He watched the unsteady, uncertain way she gathered her things, simultaneously puzzled and fascinated. This might be the first time he'd ever really seen her unsure of herself. Even after their first kiss, she'd taken back her control immediately, the capable chef firmly back in place. The tentative way she took his hand now screamed vulnerability.

He wasn't sure what to do with that.

They rode down the elevator in companionable silence, then slipped into his car. He reached for something to say and realized he'd been too distracted to let her in on the news. "I talked to a potential investor today. Mitchell Shaw, Bryan's dad."

Rachel straightened, her attention riveted on him. "And?"

"He's leaving town for a few weeks, but he's interested in meeting you before he goes. I invited him for Saturday."

"Wait. *This* Saturday? As in, eight days to prepare?"

"You've been preparing all week. Besides, I figured sooner was better than later."

"Yes, I suppose it is. He doesn't have any dietary restrictions, does he?"

"Not that I know of, and I've eaten with him hundreds of times."

Rachel nodded, but she didn't seem to notice him anymore. He suddenly wished he'd called her tomorrow with the news, but he'd only found out this afternoon and she would kill him if he didn't give her every hour's notice possible. He reached for her hand again, aware it was a needy thing to do and yet not able to stop himself.

When they parked in front of her house, he walked her to the door. "When can I see you again? Dinner this week? Tuesday, maybe?"

"I don't know, Alex. I need as much time to prepare as possible, and when I get really involved in something . . ."

"I understand. I don't like it, but I understand."

She moved into him and pressed an all-too-brief kiss to his lips. "It's only this week. And then I'll be free."

"Fine. But you're coming with me to pick up Dina on Friday. Deal?"

"Deal." She turned to the door, her key in her hand. "I'll give you progress reports in the meantime."

"I'm counting on it." He waited on the step until she went inside and locked the door behind her, then returned to his car. He didn't immediately twist the key in the ignition, instead sitting alone with his musings in the dark.

Rachel was holding back. There was no denying their chemistry—he'd felt it since that dinner at Equity, and it had only grown since then. She'd been all-in every time they'd kissed, responding with the passion he suspected drove her determined nature. And yet she seemed hesitant to trust him. To trust whatever this was developing between them.

Maybe she simply didn't want to admit there hadn't been many guys before him—it didn't take a genius to read between the lines. Or maybe she thought things were moving too fast.

On the elevator ride up to his apartment, another, more worrisome option occurred to him. Maybe her talk about her life as a chef had been meant as a warning. She wanted to have a restaurant again, missed the job fiercely, had devoted herself completely to it.

That didn't sound like a life that had room for him.

Briefly, selfishly, he reconsidered his invitation to Mitchell, and just as quickly tossed out that impulse. He wasn't going to go back on his promise. It sounded like Rachel had had plenty of that already. He wouldn't be another person who failed her.

Even if the prospect of letting her go felt like being sentenced to a life of bread and water moments after he had been given a taste of an exotic banquet.

"Man up, Kanin." He cleaned up the remaining dishes, switched the dishwasher on, wiped down the countertops. Then he moved to his bedroom and booted up his laptop. He surely wouldn't be sleeping soon, so he might as well get some words on the page.

For someone who was hopelessly blocked, he seemed to gather plenty of inspiration from Rachel. Words poured onto the screen, tapped out on his keyboard like the falling of raindrops, until he had several pages of another completed essay.

He sat back in his chair and read the three pieces he had so far.

"Not bad." A cohesive theme was beginning to emerge, unexpected as it might be, and it was compelling. Burning with new enthusiasm, he opened the empty proposal and pasted in the three essays, then began filling in the marketing and positioning sections.

Well after three o'clock, it was complete. Alex gave it one last once-over, attached it to an e-mail, and pressed Send.

Now that his proposal was done and no longer hanging over his head, he could turn all his attention to his new and thoroughly unexpected muse . . . for as long as he still had her.

Chapter Twenty-Five

Ana and Melody had demanded that Rachel call them once she was home from her date, but when Alex left her at her front door, she was too conflicted to do anything but analyze and decompress. Instead, she tapped in a message saying she had a great time and inviting the girls over for breakfast at her house, where she would no doubt be peppered with questions. At least that would give her time to formulate answers.

Normally, she'd go straight to the kitchen and cook something to let her percolating thoughts straighten themselves into some semblance of order, but she'd meant it when she said she was stuffed. Alex was actually a good cook—the food had been hearty, filling, and well prepared, even by her standards. Ana would probably dismiss the dinner as his way of getting off the hook for coming up with an elaborate date, but Rachel had to believe that Alex had known exactly what would be meaningful to her.

She turned on the electric kettle and then retreated to her bedroom to change from her filmy dress into a pair of lounge pants and a T-shirt. After she poured herself a cup of herbal tea—no point making it any more difficult to sleep than it already would be—she climbed into bed and turned on a late-night TV show she knew full well she wouldn't watch.

She'd never met anyone like Alex Kanin. Driven, yet grounded and playful. Principled, even moral, but with a wicked sense of humor. Rather than being scared off by a woman in charge, he seemed to appreciate her strength. Found it appealing, even.

Impulsively, she flicked on her reading lamp and reached for the journal that sat on top of her Bible on her nightstand. She'd continued with her daily readings, but she hadn't been able to write more than a few words in the journal since leaving Paisley. Not because she was still mourning that loss—even though she was—but because somewhere inside her, she was afraid naming those happy moments in her day would cause them to flee as quickly as they'd come.

Slowly, she opened the journal and wrote today's date, her heart thudding dully in her throat. It took her several moments to get the courage to write the word.

Alex.

Rachel snapped the book shut and pressed the top edge to her lips, trying to push down the flutter of panic that welled up inside her. Silly, maybe. No, definitely. But putting him in the journal was like acknowledging he'd earned a permanent place in her life.

The thought was simultaneously more thrilling and more terrifying than she'd expected.

Her phone screen lit up on her bedside table, and she snatched it up, hoping it might be a message from Alex. Instead it was Melody's reply: I'm there. I want details!

Almost immediately, Ana responded: Me too! See you tomorrow.

Rachel put the phone back down, cursing the renewed surge of adrenaline coursing through her system. She'd never get to sleep at this rate. Instead she picked up the composition book on her nightstand and looked over the menu she'd set for the following weekend.

She'd been so sure about it before, but now it seemed simplistic. Appropriate for an impromptu gathering with friends, but not an accurate example of the kind of food she'd want to cook in her new restaurant. She needed to up her game. Show Mitchell Shaw that she could match any of the big-name chefs in New York or London.

All of whom had worse reputations for being prickly than she did.

Rachel pushed away the flash of irritation at the double standard, flipped to a clean page, and began making notes until she had line after line of different dishes. She tossed aside the notebook and strode into the living room to her bookshelf. She filled her arms with cookbooks thick and thin, cuisine and home cooking, then struggled back to her bed with them.

Hours later, multiple books lying open around her, she thought she'd found her new menu. It was perfect. Elegant and balanced, light enough to account for the heat but still satisfying. She had sketched plating ideas on the following pages, using the blooming plants on Alex's patio for inspiration. It would require some careful thought to tie each dish together, but she could do it. As she looked at the page, her chest filled with a determination she hadn't felt since the day she walked out of Paisley. She would have her own place again, and this was the menu that would do it for her.

"Okay, spill. You've been tight-lipped since we walked in."

Rachel threw a look at Melody over her shoulder. "I'm busy. I'm cooking. You should know better than to ask me to answer questions when I'm cooking." She pulled open the oven to check on the cheese-and-bacon scones currently baking in the oven and then closed it quickly. Two more minutes, maybe three. Saturday breakfast had turned out to be more of a brunch anyway. Melody liked to grab a couple of hours' sleep when she got off at six, so the clock was already edging toward noon.

Ana, on the other hand, had probably been up

since sunrise, hitting the gym first thing before her day got started. If Rachel had her discipline when it came to exercise, the waistband of her jeans wouldn't be digging into her stomach quite so much right now.

"I think she's avoiding the question," Melody said to Ana.

"I'd say she's definitely avoiding the question." Ana reached for her coffee and took a sip.

"I'm not avoiding, I promise. I will answer any and all of your questions as soon as we sit down to eat." Rachel wrapped a towel around the handle of the cast-iron pan that held their veggie frittata and transferred it to the table, then put the lightly dressed salad next to it. She pulled the tray of scones from the oven, now turned a lovely golden color. Those went onto a plate along with a small bowl of bacon gravy. "I think that's it. Did I forget anything?"

"Maybe a dolly to wheel us out of here when we're done?" Ana stared wide-eyed at the spread. "Seriously, Rach, you made enough food for ten people."

"Then take it home and have it for breakfast tomorrow." Rachel slid into her chair. "Besides, how long have you known me? I cook."

"Especially when you have something on your mind." Ana waggled her eyebrows at Rachel. "Or is it a *someone*?"

Heat rose to her cheeks. "Whatever. Does someone want to say grace?"

Melody jumped in to say the blessing as eloquently as ever, and then the only sound was that of serving spoons against platters and forks and knives against plates.

"These scones are amazing," Melody said.

"They should be. It's your scone recipe. I just added the bacon, cheese, and chives to make them more savory."

"Really good," Ana mumbled, covering her half-filled mouth with her hand. "Worth the extra four thousand sit-ups I'm going to have to do later."

Rachel laughed and turned back to her own food. When she'd been working, they managed to do this sort of thing once a month, if they were lucky. She'd probably seen her friends more the past few weeks than she had all year. "I've missed you guys."

"We saw you yesterday," Melody said. "Stop stalling. Tell us about this date of yours."

Rachel smiled, trying to keep it a notch below a Cheshire cat grin, and sketched the outlines of the evening for them. "You know, he's a pretty good cook. I was surprised. I was fully preparing myself to lie."

"Rachel lying about food?" Ana said. "Must be serious."

Melody looked impressed. "He made you his

family recipes? That takes some guts on multiple levels. I like this guy already."

"Me too," Rachel said.

They stared at her.

"What?"

"You . . . no." Ana cocked her head. "Maybe?"

Rachel frowned. "What are we talking about?"

"You and Alex. What exactly is it that you like about him?"

The smile came back, unbidden. "He's a good guy. Principled, more down-to-earth than I would have expected considering the press and the fancy condo. The unreasonably hot part aside, it's easy to be around him." She caught her bottom lip between her teeth at the jitter of pleasure that came along with the thought. "It feels good to be with him."

Melody gasped. "You are! You're in love with him!"

She couldn't even deny it. "What do I do?"

"What do you mean?" Ana asked. "Seems pretty clear to me."

All the pleasure she'd felt, all the nervous excitement, seemed to drain out of her, leaving only a cold knot of dread. "I didn't mean for this to happen. I don't want a relationship. Besides, it's not like he feels the same way. This is temporary. He knows it. He wouldn't have hustled me out of his place so quickly if he didn't."

They continued to stare at her. Rachel sighed and recounted the intense moments on his roof deck, leaving out the part where thoughts of staying for more than dessert had flitted through her mind.

"Does he have a brother exactly like him?" Ana asked. "Usually on a first date I have to explain why I'm not going to sleep with the guy, and suddenly I'm frigid."

"What Ana's trying to say is that Alex obviously respects you. Or has some personal convictions of his own. Or both. That's not the kind of thing a guy does when you're just temporary. Trust me. He doesn't want to do anything to ruin this."

Rachel looked between her friends, trying to ignore the way their words buoyed her heart. "Maybe he doesn't, but I'm not willing to sacrifice everything I've accomplished for a man. My mother did that, and look where it got her."

"Alex is not Dale," Melody said. "Has he ever once said anything to make you think he'd want to change you?"

"No," Rachel said. "But my stepfather never gave us any hint he wanted to change us either. He seemed perfect . . . right up until he wasn't. And by the time we got a look at his true nature, it was too late."

Ana and Melody exchanged a look, clearly not swayed. Melody took her hand. "At some point you're going to have to take a leap of faith. Rachel, in all the years I've known you, I've never seen you light up like this. You're passionate about your cooking, yes. But you attack that like a challenge to be conquered."

Ana smiled. "You're happy. That's not something you run away from."

Rachel looked between them, conflicted. "So what? I just . . . keep seeing him? Hope I don't find any deal-breakers? Or better yet, hope that I find them before I invest too much time in the relationship?"

"That's pretty much what dating is," Melody said with a smile. "Just don't . . . you know . . . get carried away. You think you've got those borders drawn pretty well until things get serious. Trust me, the whole 'saving it for marriage' thing sounds a lot easier than it is, especially when you're kind of inexperienced and the guy is hot." She sighed. "If I could go back and have this conversation with past me, I'd save myself some idiotic mistakes."

Rachel flashed Melody a sympathetic smile. Deep down, she was a trusting soul who wanted to see the best in everyone; unfortunately, she'd run into some men who viewed that tender heart as something to exploit, who said all the right things to bypass her best intentions.

"Don't worry," Ana said. "You'll find out fast whether Alex's convictions are real when he's not getting any." Ana threw up her hands at Rachel's look. "What? I call them like I see them. Maybe I should just take a break from dating for a while. I've got plenty going for me without a man. If God really has the perfect guy, I'll run into him at the grocery store or something, right?"

"I hope so," Melody said with a sigh. "I'm too tired to put any effort into looking for one."

"I really hate to bring this up," Ana said, "but does Alex understand what your life is like when you're working? Right now you have all this time on your hands, but eventually you'll open another restaurant. Is he ready for that?"

"I don't know," Rachel said. "It's not like we've talked about it. But if he really cares about me, he'll understand. Right?"

"That's the hope," Melody said.

Ana shook her head. "I can't believe it. Our little girl is growing up. Next thing you know, we'll be walking you down the aisle."

"Stop." Rachel threw her napkin at Ana and they all dissolved into laughter. "Anyway, it's not like I have any time to think about it. This next supper club might be the one. Alex has an investor coming."

"What do you know about him?" Ana sipped her coffee and turned back to her plate.

Apparently, the interrogation about Alex was over. Rachel relaxed. "Only that it's Bryan's dad. He's a real estate developer."

Ana choked on her food, and Melody had to pat her on the back until she stopped coughing. "Mitchell Shaw? Please tell me you actually know who that is."

"Should I? I barely know Bryan."

"Ever hear of the Shaw Building?"

Rachel's eyes widened. Everyone knew about the new development in Lower Downtown, near Union Station. It had been getting press ever since the foundation was laid. "Wait, he's *that* Shaw?"

Ana nodded. "He's a millionaire, maybe a billionaire for all I know. Developer, philanthropist, activist. Last I heard, they're naming the new arts center at CU Boulder after him. He must have given a chunk of change to the program."

Rachel's stomach gave a brutal twist. She hadn't put it together, but even she knew about the huge dinner parties and benefits and concerts that the Shaws put on multiple times a year for Denver's elite businessmen and intellectuals. "I wish you hadn't told me that."

"Relax," Ana said. "He's probably eaten at one of your restaurants already. All you have to do is give him a vision for your new place, and he either likes it or he doesn't. Hopefully he'll like it. Because with the backing of Mitchell Shaw, your PR problems instantly go away."

"He still has retail spaces open in his building,"

Melody said. "You land him, you could potentially land a prime LoDo location."

Rachel threw Melody an exasperated look. "You too? You're supposed to be the one telling me that everything happens for a reason, and if it's meant to be, it will be."

"Oh, I still believe all that. But I also believe he can open doors for you that other investors couldn't. Assuming you want to walk through them."

Rachel took a deep breath and blew it back out. She had this. She was confident in her menu. It was well-balanced in flavor, texture, and theme; complex without being fussy; technique-dependent but not too showy. Anyone who knew food would know the effort it took to make it look effortless and be suitably impressed. Assuming she pulled it off like she knew she could.

No, no reason to borrow trouble. She may not know what to do about her relationship with Alex, but she knew how to cook. It was the one thing she'd always been good at, the one thing that never let her down. She could do this.

"Yes, you can," Melody said, squeezing her hand across the table. Apparently Rachel had said that last part out loud. "Are you sure you don't need help?"

"Alex's sister is running food for me. She's amazing, so no worries there."

No, Dina was the least of Rachel's concerns.

Usually her brunch meetings with her friends made her feel better, but now the stakes for her future felt ten times higher.

With Mitchell Shaw. And with Alex.

Chapter Twenty-Six

As long as Rachel didn't think about what was at stake, she was fine. She had plenty to keep her busy. The entirely new menu needed to be tested and tweaked and tested again. Lists were made, orders for specific ingredients placed. Everything she needed to pull off the most important meal of her life, listed in precise, minute-by-minute detail.

And yet if she wasn't careful, she found herself daydreaming about Alex when she should be concentrating on her work. It didn't help that he'd been peppering her with flirty texts since Saturday afternoon, making her feel like a giddy teenager.

She was in the middle of cleaning a tray full of fresh trout when a message popped up on her lock screen.

What are you wearing right now? Please tell me it's those sexy kitchen clogs . . .

Rachel snorted a laugh. She cleaned her hands so she could pick up her phone, angled the camera so he could see not only her messy-haired, aproned self, but the fish guts in all their slimy glory. She sent it back with the message: Living the life. How about you?

A couple minutes later, his response came:

Questioning my choice of careers. She tapped the attached photo to enlarge it and laughed so loud she was glad she was alone. Alex was sitting at his laptop in a T-shirt and sweatpants, his hair sticking up in all directions like he'd just rolled out of bed, wearing a hangdog grimace as he pointed to his laptop screen.

Without considering her response, she tapped out: Not fair. Even with bed head you are about the hottest guy on the planet.

And then the message sat there. Dread crept into her. That had been a stupid thing to say, hadn't it? She was terrible at dating, this flirty text thing. What did she know about men? She could be one of the guys at work, sure, but dating? She was a total—

His message came through. Liar. But you just wrecked my concentration. Now all I can think about is how much I'd rather be with you. Sure I can't see you before Friday?

Rachel sucked in a breath, her chest tightening and her heart lodging in her throat. It had gone from flirty to serious in one text message. Was it possible he felt the same way about her that she did about him?

She stared at the screen until the backlight shut off. She should respond. But what did a girl say to that? She finally managed an answer: No, but it will be worth the wait.

It always is.

She flushed. I meant the food.

I didn't.

Rachel let herself smile at the exchange for a minute, then put her phone aside and went back to the decidedly unglamorous fish-cleaning job. Now she wished Alex were here with her, even if it were to simply lean against the counter beside her and ask questions. Her heart squeezed in her chest so hard it made her momentarily breathless.

How had he so rapidly become such a big part of her life? How had she gone from a woman perfectly content with her career and her own company to one who felt Alex's absence like physical pain? It was as if acknowledging to her friends that she'd fallen for him had flipped a switch, no matter how hard she tried to maintain some emotional distance.

The week couldn't pass quickly enough.

When Alex knocked at Rachel's door at ten after three on Friday afternoon, she was ready. She had blown out her hair and put on a smidge of makeup. Melody's flares had made a reappearance with a drapey T-shirt she'd picked up on a whim last night. For a long moment, she doubted her choices, hand on the knob. Was she trying too hard? After all, this wasn't a date.

The concerns flew from her mind when she opened the door and saw Alex standing there, hands in the pockets of his jeans, a faded T-shirt straining across the muscles in his chest and shoulders. His hair still looked wet from the shower, a guess confirmed by the fresh waft of his soap.

Her insides gave a twist at being in his presence again. And from the way he was looking at her now, she didn't regret the extra effort a single bit.

"Sorry I'm late. I got caught up at the gym."

Time well spent, she thought. She stepped aside for him. "It's fine. I had things to finish up anyway."

He stepped over the threshold and closed the door behind him. "You look pretty."

"Just pretty?" she teased. "You're a writer and that's the best you can come up with?"

"You're right. Especially after you called me the hottest guy on the planet this week." He crossed his arms over his chest, giving her a front-row view of impressively muscled forearms and proving that assertion completely plausible. "You are 'a thing divine, for nothing natural I ever saw so noble.' "

Rachel's lips quivered. "You cheated. That's Shakespeare."

"You recognized it! I'm impressed!"

"I saw *The Tempest* at Shakespeare in the Park years ago, and that line stuck with me."

"You'll have to forgive my stealing, because when I'm around you, I'm stunned speechless."

Rachel's smile broke free. "Okay, that was pretty good. That earns you a kiss."

Alex didn't say anything. Instead he pulled her gently toward him, one hand at the small of her back, the other sliding up to tangle in her hair. She forgot everything else the minute his lips were on hers, gentle and sure, the hard beat of her own heart an ancient pulse that made her fears feel distant, irrelevant. This was dangerous—the way he made her feel, his ability to make her forget everything but him. She knew it and yet didn't have it in her to stop.

Somewhere in her house, the antique clock chimed the quarter hour, reminding her of the day's agenda. She pulled away enough to talk. "We need to get Dina."

"Dina can wait." Alex dipped his head to kiss her again.

She ducked out of his embrace, feeling a little shaky. "No, she can't. Did you tell her I was coming?"

"She threatened to disown me if I didn't bring you. I'm beginning to think she's doing a little matchmaking." He opened the door for her as she grabbed her purse, then waited while she locked up behind them. "Actually, I was hoping you might be able to help me."

"How so?"

Alex walked her to the car and held the passenger door open. Only when he was seated in the driver's side did he finally answer. "I've been worried about Dina, and she's dodging my questions. I was hoping that since she admires you, you might be able to get more out of her than I can."

"What's going on, exactly? She seemed perfectly fine when I met her, but of course I don't have a frame of reference."

"I don't know. She hasn't seemed happy lately, but she denies that anything is wrong. I think the whole acting thing is taking a toll on her."

"Acting is a rough gig. Everyone goes through moments of doubting their calling. Look at me."

"Which is exactly why I thought you might get through to her. If anyone understands what it's like to fight for your dream, it's you."

The raw admiration in his voice took her off guard. "I'm just doing what I know how to do, Alex. I'm no hero."

"Tell that to my sister. I think she's got herself a bit of a girl crush."

"She does, huh? And what about you?"

He shot her a wicked smile. "I have an entirely different sort of crush."

Rachel fought a smile as she sat back and watched the city slide by her window. Fortunately, they had gotten a jump on the afternoon traffic, so the route to the eastern edge of the city was clear and fast. They were pulling into the airport return loop when his cell phone beeped.

Alex handed it to Rachel. "Can you see if that's her?"

Hesitantly, she took the phone. He wanted her to check his messages? That was a very committed-relationship thing to do. A guy didn't hand over his phone unless he had absolutely nothing to hide.

She swiped the lock screen. It was indeed Dina. "She's already here. Waiting for us outside door 509."

"Great timing." Alex switched lanes to go to the arrivals level and fell into the slow-moving queue, while Rachel kept an eye out for his sister.

"There she is!"

Alex whipped into a spot at the curb being vacated by a badly parked taxi a few feet away from a sweatshirt-clad girl with a bright-pink owl suitcase.

Rachel immediately opened the passenger door, intending to get into the back seat, but Alex shook his head at her and popped the trunk. This was apparently a well-rehearsed procedure. Dina threw the roller bag in the open hatch, slammed the door, then slid into the back seat.

"Hey, Bro." She winked at Alex before turning her attention to Rachel. "I was hoping you might come along."

"Thanks for the invitation," Rachel said immediately. "I never turn down a trip to the food truck pod."

Dina put on her seat belt, the signal for Alex to pull back out into the lane. "You're better company than my brother, for sure."

"Hey," Alex said.

"Sorry." Dina smirked at him and went back to Rachel. "So you ready for tomorrow? Alex tells me that Mr. Shaw is going to be there."

"You know him?"

"Sure. Alex practically lived over at their house when he was a kid. Well, he *actually* lived there his senior year of high school. So they're somewhere between friends of the family and second family." Dina lowered her voice to a mock whisper. "I had a mad crush on Bryan when I was in high school. I know, how cliché of me, right?"

Rachel threw an amused glance at Alex before twisting around to face Dina. "I really appreciate you coming back to help out. You did such an amazing job last time, putting everyone at ease. Though I'm sorry to pull you away from your regular job. I imagine as good a server as you are, you probably live off your weekend tips."

Might as well get started on the info-gathering mission.

Dina stared out the window. "I quit."

Alex glanced in the rearview mirror, his sudden tension evident in his posture. "What happened? Everything was going so well."

"It's okay. It was time to move on anyway." Once more, Dina's expression shuttered. Maybe Alex was right. There was definitely more to this than just losing her job.

Chapter Twenty-Seven

Alex silently called himself names while he drove. Just when Rachel was getting somewhere with Dina, he had to go and push. Just like his parents. No wonder Dina wouldn't talk to him.

Rachel reached over and squeezed his hand before she changed the subject. "If you don't mind, Dina, I could use your help setting up the patio. It's getting late in the summer and things aren't in bloom anymore, so it's going to need to be laid out a little differently. I want an elegant, intimate sort of feel for dinner on the roof deck. I've been thinking I'd love to find a restaurant with a similar roof space, so this will be a good way to show the kind of ambience I have in mind."

"What kind of food would you serve?" Dina seemed grateful to be able to move on to a different topic.

"Modern Continental, local and organic. That's where the trends seem to be staying, the food court and truck craze aside."

"You *should* do a food truck," Dina said. "Rachel's Roach Coach."

Rachel groaned. "Yeah, that's exactly what I would call it."

"No, really! You could get a red double-decker

bus and put little tables on the top if you want roof deck seating."

"You know," Alex said, nudging Rachel's arm, "that's not such a bad idea." She shot him an incredulous look, and he joined his sister in her laughter.

Dina started talking about some of the food trucks she frequented in LA, and she pulled out her phone to show Rachel her favorites on Twitter. Rachel took the phone from her and scrolled down with a laugh. "I know this guy!"

"Really?" Dina looked suddenly interested.

"Yeah, he worked for a restaurant in Berkeley where I staged for several months. Great cook, but he always chafed a little at the thought of fine dining. Said that high-quality food should be accessible to all, not just the people who could fork over two or three hundred bucks on a dinner. I hadn't realized he'd started a food truck. It's a good fit for him."

"But that never interested you?" Alex glanced at Rachel, gauging her response. All this effort to find an investor for her restaurant, when she could probably buy and outfit a truck and have it under way immediately.

"Fine dining is what I do best," she said with a shrug. "Besides, there's a season for food trucks in Denver, so it can make for some lean winters if you're not careful."

"I think there would be a year-round demand

for Rachel's Mobile Kebab Shack," Dina said.

Despite the Friday afternoon traffic, they got to the truck pod in record time, before their favorites had even arrived. Most of the trucks didn't arrive until five on Fridays, where they would remain into the wee hours of the morning for the last-call bar patrons and club-goers; they'd be back late morning the next day to start all over again.

"What do you want to do?" Rachel asked. "We can wait for the others to show up, or we can take it as divine instruction to eat bao for dinner today."

"Bao's fine," Dina said. "Woman can't live on duck-fat fries alone, can she?"

"She can try," Alex and Rachel said simultaneously, and then shared a grin. Either they were rubbing off on each other, or this was just more proof of how ridiculously compatible they were. Or maybe he was looking for signs now that he realized how unprepared he was to let her go.

They were the first in line at the steamed bun truck when it opened its windows, and soon they had claimed one of the many empty seats on the garishly painted patio. Rachel took the seat directly across from Dina while Alex sat beside her. He dug into his bao, savoring the pillowy texture of the bun. When they'd made a dent in their food, he asked casually, "So how did all the callbacks go?"

Dina hung her head over her food and didn't answer.

Alex nudged her arm. "Dina?"

When Dina raised her head, there were tears in her eyes. She looked at him, the shame clear on her face. "I lied."

He frowned, then quickly put away the expression when Rachel shot him a warning look. "Lied about what?"

"There weren't any callbacks. There haven't been for a while. The job I booked in February was for a girl's princess birthday party. I played Jasmine." Dina dipped her head again, letting her tears drip into her food. "I couldn't tell you."

"Why not? You know I support you no matter what. It's a rough business. I get that."

"Yeah, well, I didn't. I never expected it to be this hard. But you were so enthusiastic about me following my dreams, and after you stood up to Mom and Dad for me, I couldn't tell you the truth." Dina swiped her eyes dry. "That's why I quit the restaurant. One of my roommates moved out, and even with tips, I couldn't make rent. I got a job in a call center in Van Nuys. I've been working there since I got back."

Alex sat back, simultaneously stunned and guilty. She'd been hiding the truth so she didn't disappoint him? That was the last thing he'd intended when he encouraged her to go to Los Angeles against their parents' wishes. That was the same thing his parents had done to him, causing him to stay in psychology long after he began to suspect the field wasn't for him.

"Dina, I'm sorry. I never meant—"

"It's not your fault. I was desperate to get away from all Mom and Dad's plans, and I'd always been good at acting, you know? I got a lot of practice at home 'living up to my full potential.' When you jumped in to back me up, I thought, why not?"

Alex saw Rachel watching them with puzzlement. "Dina is a genius."

She still looked confused, so Dina said, "He doesn't mean that metaphorically. They tested me. Off the charts in math. MIT offered me a full ride before I finished my junior year of high school."

Rachel blinked. "Wow. And you didn't want to go?"

"There's a difference between being good at something and wanting to do it for a living. Alex convinced me that counting cards in Vegas wasn't my best career move, and the last thing I wanted to do was spend the rest of my life locked in a lab with a bunch of nerds."

Alex gauged Rachel's reaction and saw she didn't quite believe what she was hearing. But they'd had that exact conversation after Dina got caught playing poker in an illegal home game with a fake ID—the hazard of having a brilliant sister with dark leanings and a rebellious streak the size of Colorado.

"So what are you going to do next?" Alex asked.

354

"I don't know." She peered up at him. "I can't let Mom and Dad know I failed. It was bad enough that I crushed their dreams. Even worse that I did it for nothing." Dina looked to Rachel, wide-eyed. "What do you think I should do?"

Rachel shook her head. "This is purely your decision."

"But I value your opinion. What do you think?"

Alex watched Rachel wrestle with words for several moments. "I think you're giving up far too easily."

It was the last thing either Alex or Dina expected from her. "W-what?" Dina stammered.

Rachel leaned across the table, her voice tight. "Here's the thing about dreams. Everyone thinks that if something is meant to be, it's going to come easy. Life isn't easy. It isn't supposed to be. Doing something worthwhile takes sacrifice. Do you think I've loved every minute I've spent at work? I've spent years being miserable. But I've given up everything to get to where I am, and I'm not going to let one little setback get in my way. I'm going to prove them wrong. No matter what. That's what it takes sometimes: sheer stubborn will."

Alex looked between his sister and Rachel, a stirring of disquiet in his stomach. Somewhere in that speech, she'd stopped talking about Dina and started talking about herself. He glanced at his sister and saw from her stricken, tear-filled expression that she thought it was directed toward her.

He covered his sister's hand with his own. "Dina, has acting ever really been your dream?"

Dina swallowed, the first tears sliding down her cheeks. She shook her head.

"Then come home."

"I—I can't." A sob lingered in her voice. "Rachel is right. If I come home and tell Mom and Dad I've failed . . ."

"Forget Mom and Dad. This is about you and what you want to do. Dina, I spent way too long doing things because I was afraid of disappointing them. I should have quit school years earlier than I did."

"But if I come home now, it's like all those years were wasted."

Alex shook his head with a gentle smile. "Nothing's wasted. Not with God. Even those supposedly useless psychology degrees come in handy now, and I'm betting what you've learned as a struggling actress won't go to waste either. Sometimes you just need to have faith that He's got what's next."

Dina's posture straightened a degree. "All my stuff is still in LA."

"We can drive back and get it if that's what you want to do. You can stay with me until you figure it all out. I'll support you in whatever decision you make."

Dina's glance flicked to Rachel, then back to him. "You'd do that for me?"

"Of course I would. I'm your brother. I've got your back."

Slowly, she nodded. "Okay."

"I'll go throw these away." Rachel began to gather their containers, her voice hoarse.

"Is she okay?" Dina asked in a small voice as soon as Rachel left the table. "It's not that I don't appreciate her advice—"

"Don't worry about it," Alex said, but that unsettled feeling was back. Far more had just happened than a pep talk gone awry. When Rachel returned, they went back to his car, the mood muted.

"You can drop me on your way home," Rachel said.

"Actually," Dina said, "since it's still early, I'm going to go hang out with a friend. You can take me to the DU dorms. I'll get a ride home later."

"Are you sure?" Alex asked. "Who is this friend? Do I know him?"

"*She* is Marcella Trujillo. You remember her, right?"

"Sorry, no."

"Yes, you do. She was the one who asked you to her senior prom."

Beside him, Rachel cracked a vague smile.

"I remember that. Excuse me if I don't walk you in."

"I was hoping you'd say that," Dina shot back. Hard to believe this was the girl who had been crying forty-five minutes ago. Now she seemed light, unencumbered. He wasn't sure which was stronger: his relief that she'd finally come clean or his guilt over making her feel like she had to lie in the first place.

He dropped her in front of campus housing for the University of Denver, where Marcella was apparently a business major. Then he looked to Rachel. "Home now?"

"Probably best. It's a long day tomorrow." Rachel paused. "I'm sorry. I didn't mean to come on so strong with Dina back there."

Alex chose his words carefully. "I think we both know that had nothing to do with Dina."

Rachel didn't speak, just stared out the window. Alex tried a different tack. "What happens if Mitchell doesn't want to invest in your restaurant?"

Rachel whipped her head toward him. "Do you think he's going to turn me down?"

"No, I think he's going to beg you to let him invest in your next venture. But what if he doesn't? What if no one does?"

"That's not an option. I can't fail now. Not after coming this far. I won't."

"You've really never considered doing anything but cooking."

"Not once."

A quick glance confirmed what he expected: she was dead serious.

"What else would I do, Alex? I don't have a college education. I barely have a GED. My high school grades were a disaster. But everything clicks when I'm in the kitchen. It's who I am. Without it, I'm nothing."

"That is absolutely untrue. You are so much more than just a chef."

Rachel let out a harsh laugh, one that sounded suspiciously teary. "Really. Tell me one thing that you like about me besides my cooking."

"Well, for one thing, you're gorgeous." The words slipped out before he could consider them, and he knew they were wrong the moment they passed his lips.

She snorted derisively. "It figures."

"Rachel—"

"No, don't 'Rachel' me. That right there is exactly why I'm so single-minded about cooking. Given the choice to be known for my abilities or my looks, which do you think I'd prefer?"

"Rachel, you know I didn't mean it that way. There is far more to you than your cooking or your looks. You're stubborn and determined—"

"Both of which came from my years in the kitchen," Rachel said flatly.

Alex took a steadying breath, feeling the conversation slipping away from him. He was nearing Rachel's house, so he took a moment to pull up to the curb and put the car in park. "All I'm saying is, that's a lot of pressure to put on yourself. If there's one thing I've learned from publishing, it's that most of it is completely out of my control. Don't you think there might come a point where this is all too much? Where you might want something else?"

"Tell me, Alex. If your career completely tanked and you married a woman who made a lot of money, would you quit writing? Would you lounge around and let her pay the bills?"

"Of course not. I would feel—" He broke off when he realized what she was getting at.

Rachel smiled at him, but the expression held no humor. "I have to go. It's getting late and I've got a lot of work to do before tomorrow." She pushed open the passenger door and stepped out.

"Rachel, wait." Alex jumped from the driver's seat and caught her on the sidewalk. "We need to talk about this."

"Alex, really, there's nothing to talk about. I'm just rambling. I'm tired—"

"No. You're not." He took her elbow. "Don't shut me out. I'm just trying to understand you. That's what you do when you care about someone."

She stared at him for a long moment and then gave him a single nod. He took that as an invitation and uncertainly followed her up the path to her front door.

Chapter Twenty-Eight

Rachel didn't slam the door in his face, so Alex must have guessed correctly about her intentions. She walked through her house ahead of him, flipping on lights, until she reached the kitchen.

"Coffee?"

"Uh, sure. Thanks."

She scooped beans into the grinder and began the process of making their coffee. "You should have met my mom. She was one of the strongest, most determined women I've ever known."

"Was? Did she pass away?"

A pained expression crossed Rachel's face. "In a manner of speaking, I suppose. She used to be a nurse. After my dad left us, she worked crazy hours to support us. But somehow she still managed to get most Sundays off to spend time with me. She talked about getting her degree as a nurse-practitioner so she could work normal hours in a clinic instead of in the hospital."

Alex pulled out a chair and seated himself, careful not to disrupt the flow of words. Right now, it felt like she was talking to herself as much as to him.

"I had no idea how good I had it. I was really young when my dad left, so I don't remember the times he was drunk and unemployed, how often my mom picked up extra shifts to pay the bills and the babysitter when he was incapable of watching me. I only knew that all my friends had dads and I didn't." She grimaced. "I thought I deserved one. So I started praying every night that God would bring me a father. The faith of a kid, you know?"

"You did deserve a father," Alex said. "But sometimes we don't exactly get the ones we hoped for."

"You have no idea how true that is." She poured coffee from the French press into two mugs. "Cream or sugar?"

"Both, please."

She mixed their coffees, then brought them to the table before picking up where she had left off. "I was eleven when Mom met Dale. He was perfect, at least to me. He had a good job; he wanted kids with his ex-wife but they weren't able to have them; he was a Christian. Immediately, I thought he was the answer to my prayers. I don't know if my mom had doubts and ignored them because I liked him so much or if he had her fooled too. But it didn't last long. We saw the truth pretty soon after the wedding."

Alex flinched inwardly, already anticipating where the story was going. But he only nodded and sipped his coffee.

"That warm, loving man disappeared and was replaced by a critical, harsh dictator. The house was too messy. My mom didn't cook enough. She worked too much, which obviously meant her priorities were out of order. Our church was far too liberal—because girls could wear pants and they allowed secular movies and music. Gradually, he managed to change everything about us. We left our church for his. My mom cut back on her hours at work and eventually quit. I started picking up the cooking duties, something he actually appreciated because it meant I would 'make a good wife someday.' " Rachel enclosed the last part in air quotes. "My wardrobe had to be approved by him every morning. If my skirts and tops were too tight, he'd call me a slut. If I wore shapeless, baggy things, he'd tell me I needed to try harder to look feminine or no guy would ever be interested in me. One time he said I didn't wear makeup because I was a lesbian and an abomination before the Lord. I cried for hours, and when I finally apologized—for what, I have no idea—he blamed me for making him feel bad."

Alex listened to the litany with revulsion. He'd come across domestic abuse situations like this while in his grad program, but knowing Rachel had lived through it made him physically ill. "How did you and your mom deal with that?"

"Mom completely changed. She turned from this strong, capable woman into someone who only existed to serve him. I don't know if she went along with it because she truly loved him or if she just was doing her Christian duty to obey him. But I could see the change in her. It was like a light got dimmer each day. She begged me to do what he said, defended his behavior as work stress. I think he blamed her when I didn't do what he wanted because I was her daughter.

"For a while, I toed the line, but I figured out fast that even if I did everything right, he'd invent reasons to punish me. So I rebelled. I cut class. Dyed my hair. Smoked in the woods behind the school. I figured if I'd be punished, it might as well be for something I actually did."

"And that didn't go over well, I imagine."

She gave a humorless laugh. "Not at all. Finally, when I was fifteen and the school had called to say I was absent for the third time that month, he confronted me. Said if I wouldn't follow his rules, I couldn't stay under his roof. I figured I'd call his bluff, thought my mom would step in. But she didn't. She helped me pack my bag."

Rachel's voice broke on the last word. Alex reached for her hand, but she pulled it away. "Before you say it, I know all about Battered Woman Syndrome and PTSD. And I know she was doing the only thing she could to get me out of there. But that's when I realized the person I'd known was dead. And I swore that I would never let a man do that to me. I would never let someone erase who I really was."

And there it was, whether Rachel realized it or not: the whole root of her reluctance with him, her workaholism, even the neat-freak perfectionism she probably didn't realize she possessed. The psychologist in him strained to point it out; his sense of self-preservation stopped him in time. Instead he asked, "Where did you go?"

Another smile, but at least this one held some humor. "Where any fifteen-year-old leaving home goes, of course. To see her stepfather's ex-wife."

"Ouch. I'm sure that was a surprise."

"Oddly enough, Louise knew who I was. She wasn't even that hard to track down; she owned a little Italian restaurant in Hartford. Anyway, before I even got out my full name, she took one look at me and knew. She asked if I needed a place to stay, and that was that."

"Your mom and Dale were okay with that?"

"Apparently. She went away and made a phone call. When she came back, she was furious, but she said there would be emancipation paperwork coming in the mail. This woman didn't even know me, but she took me in. A bond of shared trauma, I guess."

"So that's how you got your start in the kitchen."

Rachel nodded. "She gave me the choice of going back to school or getting my GED and going to work in the restaurant. I chose the latter. I worked as a food runner until I turned sixteen, which was when I was legally allowed to do kitchen work. It was like I was made to do it. I picked up everything they taught me, easily. The staff became like family and Louise became my mentor. By the time I was eighteen, I was running the kitchen. True, it was a hole-in-the-wall in Hartford, but it was mine and I loved it.

"And then one day, Louise handed me a bus ticket to Manhattan and a list of restaurants. 'Start at the top and work your way down until you find someone to take you on,' she said. I didn't realize until later that the list was copied straight out of the new Michelin Guide. It started with Alain Ducasse at the Essex House and ended with Café Boulud."

Alex smiled. He might not be a foodie, but he understood the significance of the two restaurants she'd just mentioned, how that list had expressed Louise's hopes for her.

"It was hard. You have no idea how hard it was. I was sure that Louise had made a mistake sending me there. I thought about quitting so many times."

"So why didn't you?" Alex asked softly.

Rachel rose from the table and returned with

the green journal in hand. Slowly, she pushed it across the table to him.

He took the notebook gingerly and flipped open the cover, not knowing what was inside but understanding what a gesture of trust this was. "What is this?"

"It was my mom's once. Her 'book of gratefuls,' she called it. She had a series of them over the years, always carried one in her purse. And every time something good happened, whether it was finding a parking meter with time left on it or a sunny day in January, she'd write it down. She said whenever things looked bleak and she was tempted to think God had abandoned her, she could look back and see all the blessings He had given her.

"It was years before I could even open it. I hadn't known she'd kept going after she married Dale, so this felt like a relic of the mom I'd lost. But when I was about to leave for New York, I forced myself to look. And I saw this."

She flipped past the first few pages and pointed to an entry toward the bottom. He would have instantly recognized that the writing didn't belong to Rachel, even if the date didn't read fifteen years ago, nearly to the day.

July 18. Rachel is leaving this house. If she leaves now, she will never make the same mistakes I did.

Alex jerked his gaze up in time to see Rachel wiping her eyes. "It took a long time for me to get up the courage to write my own, but seeing that I was doing what my mom wanted for me kept me going through a lot of hard years. I was determined to make it on my own, determined to be independent enough that I never found myself trapped like she did. I got the reading lists for NYU freshmen and read along. I bought used culinary texts from CIA graduates. It wasn't until I got the opportunity here in Denver that I realized I actually had a lot to be grateful for."

"After the Harlem Ladies' Bible Study?" he guessed.

She smiled. "Exactly."

He skimmed the entries that began on the next page in Rachel's now-familiar handwriting. They weren't all ebullient messages of thankfulness— he could clearly see times when she struggled to find anything to be grateful for, even as recently as last month. And then he got to the final entry, which nearly made his heart stop.

Alex.

He stared at his name for a long moment, the word taking his breath like a full-body slam. Before he could think of what to say, she yanked the book from his hand and snapped it shut.

"You wanted to know about me. There it is."

"Rachel—"

"Kind of sad, actually. My life is about food and whatever I can think to write about in this book."

"Rachel, stop." He captured her hand beneath his on the table. "Thank you for showing this to me. And telling me about everything."

She stood and retrieved the coffee press from the kitchen, refilled their mugs with what was left. "You're welcome. It's not a big deal. I'm sorry if I made you think it was this huge revelation."

"It's a big deal to you or you wouldn't keep it secret. I know that isn't easy for you."

She shrugged and tried to move away, but he caught her by the waist and turned her so they were face-to-face. "I need to tell you something."

"Nothing good ever begins with that statement."

"Has anyone ever told you that you can be a pessimist?"

"Not a pessimist. A realist."

"Okay, then let's get real." He waited until she met his eyes. "I would never ask you to give up your dreams for me."

"Alex—"

"I'm not kidding. Your stepfather felt threatened by your mother's independence and manipulated and isolated her until she could only depend on him. That's not a marriage. That's abuse." He

369

smiled wryly. "Trust me. I'm a psychologist. I know these things."

She stopped trying to pull away from him. A smile formed on her lips.

"I love your independence and your toughness. I love the fact that you throw yourself into your endeavors like they're life or death. I even kind of enjoy your bossiness. But, Rachel, believe me when I say you are all of those things even if you never step foot in a kitchen again. You may be a wonderful, talented chef, but it's not all you are." He took her face in his hands. "You are not the sum of your accomplishments or your failures. You have absolutely nothing to prove—not to me, not to your critics, and certainly not to your stepfather. If God had wanted you to be anything other than who and what you are, He would have made you that way."

She stared up at him for several moments. "For the record, I think you would have made a really good psychologist."

"I wasn't trying to get into your head, Rachel. I only—"

She stretched up on tiptoes and brushed her lips against his, stilling the rest of his words and his breath. "You don't need to explain. I trust you."

A proposal would have been less surprising than those words. He pulled her close and kissed her again, determined that he would live up to her faith in him, no matter what.

370

Chapter Twenty-Nine

Rachel slept in far later than she intended on Saturday morning. Apparently, last night had been more emotionally taxing than she'd thought. She hadn't intended to spill her whole history to Alex, but now that she had, she felt lighter, relieved of a weight she hadn't known she was carrying. They'd sat up late in her living room, talking and kissing until her sense of responsibility got the better of her. It would be a big day. The biggest of her career, even. She needed to be well-rested.

Fortunately, her diligence during the week meant she had only the usual prep work, the rest of her supplies and dry goods having been packed in milk crates. She finished in plenty of time to shower and put on makeup before dressing in a conservative button-down and slacks. Only when she picked up her cell phone to leave did she see the three missed text messages.

Morning, beautiful. You ready? Today's the day.

Getting ready? Let me know if I can help.

Okay, you're cruel. I am so making you pay when I see you.

Rachel laughed at the last one, warmed by his concern and his thoughtfulness . . . and looking forward to seeing what form his payback would take.

She texted Alex when she arrived in the parking lot for his building, and barely a minute passed before she saw a familiar figure stride out the lobby doors toward her car. He must have been waiting for her text. She suppressed a smile and leaned against the bumper of her SUV as he approached.

"Hey there," she called as soon as he was within earshot.

He smiled at her, but instead of replying, he took her into his arms and kissed her. Thoroughly. Rachel let herself get swept away for a moment before she pulled back and braced her hands against his chest. "That was some greeting. Or was that my punishment?"

"Neither. Can't a guy miss his girlfriend?"

A smile spread across her face. "Is that what I am?"

"I hope so." He leaned down to steal another kiss. "But if not, better tell me now so I can change my Facebook status from 'in a relationship' to 'it's complicated.' "

"It's always complicated. But no need to get crazy and give all your rabid female fans false hope. I'm not intending on letting you get away that easily."

"I like that." He winked at her and let her go. "What am I carrying?"

She led him to the back of her car and pulled

out a plastic milk crate filled with food in foil and plastic containers. "Grab the other crate and the ice chest if you can." She balanced her load while she grabbed her knife bag and then nudged the SUV's back door shut with her hip. They crossed the lot under the awkward loads, Rachel casting doubtful looks at the sky until they made it to the lobby. "Rain in the forecast?"

"Supposed to blow through in time to hail on the Eastern Plains," Alex said. "I checked the weather a couple of hours ago."

"Good." Part of the meal was the ambience, and she wanted everything to be perfect. "How's the deck looking?"

"Tropical. Dina and I went out and took advantage of the end-of-summer sales at the nursery and bought some of the last flowering plants they had. She insisted we needed color. She's been arranging and rearranging all afternoon."

"How's she doing?" Rachel balanced the crate on her knee and punched the floor number. The elevator doors slid silently shut, encasing them in quiet.

"Good. I think a weight's been lifted now that she confessed."

"I still feel bad about how I acted with her last night. Has she made a decision about what to do?"

"I'm not sure she knows. So far she's made decisions based on what she doesn't want to do and how to best annoy our parents. Sometimes I think she has it harder because she has more options than the average person."

"It's definitely easier when you only have one talent. When are you leaving?"

"Tomorrow. I'll be back in plenty of time for the next supper club. I can send out invitations while I'm gone."

"I'm not worried. I don't feel like you're bailing on me. Besides, after I impress your investor friend tonight, I expect to be very busy writing up a business plan."

Alex grinned. "That's why I love you. That confidence."

Rachel stared at him, but he didn't seem to notice, or maybe he didn't realize what he'd said. The doors slid open and they stepped off the elevator, the moment evaporating.

Had he really said he loved her? And what had he meant by it?

She couldn't think about that now. Her career hinged on this single night, and she couldn't let anything—not even what Alex may or may not feel for her—distract her from that.

As soon as they stepped through the door, Dina was in high gear. She snapped to attention when she saw Rachel. "Before you get started, come up and take a look at the deck, let me know if you want anything changed."

Rachel put down her things, shot a glance

over her shoulder at Alex, and followed Dina up the spiral staircase to the roof deck. The sun would usually be glaring down on them on a late July afternoon, but the mounded storm clouds overhead provided a respite from the week's heat wave. There was a coolness to the breeze that ruffled their hair and sent the tablecloths rippling like the surface of the ocean.

"What do you think?" Dina asked, a tinge of nervousness in her voice.

"I think . . ." Rachel turned in a slow circle. "I think it's beautiful."

The long patio dining table had been covered with white linen, contrasting napkins tied with twine, and overflowing pots of live flowers alternating with candles in pebble-filled hurricane lanterns. The plates and the tableware would be set out later, of course—anything left outside in Colorado instantly accumulated a fine layer of dust—but already she could see that Dina had an eye for design.

"There are a couple of conversation areas over here." Dina led her to the alcoves created with Alex's existing potted plants and furniture, also to be lit by more hurricane lamps.

"This is incredible. Are you sure your brother doesn't want to give up his place so we can use it as a restaurant?"

"I think he'd probably do anything you asked," Dina said with a grin.

Don't think about that. Focus on tonight. Then worry about what that means for your future with Alex.

"Let's quickly go over the tasting menu," Rachel said. "We're going to put out fresh bread and start with salmon *crudo*, which should already be on the table when they sit down. Then I'll have you bring out the roasted kale salad, followed by the *carpaccio*, the trout, and the *burrata*. We'll want to pace these carefully, because my quail's going to need time in the oven. We'll finish with dessert and coffee, and then I'll come up to the deck to mingle over cocktails."

"Perfect." Dina had pulled out a notepad and scrawled down each course as Rachel spoke. "Do you want to give me some more details so I can introduce the dishes?"

"I think the menus should do that. They're downstairs. Arrange them however looks best once the guests arrive."

"Gotcha. Alex has the wine, but he said he was doing the pairings again."

"Yes. You should check with him on the glasses for each course." Rachel stopped suddenly. "Wait. All the tableware and linens are new. Where did this all come from?"

Dina shifted her gaze.

"Dina . . ."

"We might have gone to more than the nursery this morning. Alex insisted."

"Of course he did." Rachel didn't know what to think about that. It was enough that he was hosting, inviting his contacts, and now paying for the wine and decor. She'd have to pay him back later. Maybe it had been okay for him to take on the responsibility when she felt like he owed her something, but their relationship had changed. She didn't want to be on anything but equal footing.

"I know you have to get to work," Dina said. "I can take care of the rest up here."

Rachel stopped Dina with a hand on her arm before she could move. "I wanted to apologize for last night. I put a lot of pressure on you when that was the last thing you needed."

Dina shifted uncomfortably. "It's okay. I know you were trying to help."

"I was, but I was wrong. You should do whatever it is that you want to do. Regardless of what I or your brother or your parents think. Don't let fear keep you from taking chances."

Dina's expression relaxed into a smile, and she hugged Rachel. "That means a lot to me. Thank you."

"You're welcome. Let's go see what your brother's doing. I don't trust him left to his own devices."

Dina laughed and followed her toward the stairs. "You're good for him, you know. He worked and worried too much before. He seems happy now."

Rachel smiled, even though the words started a quiver in her middle. A good quiver. The kind that made her wonder if she hadn't overthought his feelings for her after all, if maybe he loved her back. Loved her.

That was an odd thought.

When they came back down, Alex had a spray bottle of glass cleaner in hand and was wiping down the wall of windows.

Rachel whistled. "Right there is the sexiest thing a woman can see—a man cleaning."

"Very funny." He winked at her over his shoulder. "If I took off my shirt while cleaning, *that* would be the sexiest thing a woman could see."

"At least you don't let humility get in the way of your delusions."

Dina looked between them with a grin. "I'm going to go back up and finish the arrangements on the roof, let you two sort this argument out." She turned tail and pounded up the metal steps in a symphony of creaks and rattles.

Alex gave the window one last swipe, stood back to appreciate his work, then turned to Rachel. "What can I do?"

"Keep me company while I get started?" Rachel began to unpack the crates one by one, laying out all the product she'd need to make tonight's dinner.

"What's on the menu?"

Rachel pushed one of the printed sheets of cardstock to him. He scanned it quickly. "I'm hungry already. You can do all this in my kitchen?"

"It's going to be tricky because three of the first five courses require the oven, and you only have two. But as long as we don't rush the salad and the carpaccio, we'll be fine."

"I think Mitchell will be impressed," Alex said. "Did I tell you he ate a few times at Paisley?"

Instantly, Rachel's heart rate skyrocketed. "No. What did he say?"

"He enjoyed it. Seemed surprised to hear that you were no longer at the restaurant."

Again, her fault. Had she done all the publicity that she'd been urged to do, raised her profile as a chef and not just promoted the menu and the restaurant, they wouldn't have been able to push her out so easily.

Then again, she might not have met Alex. Strange how that seemed like the greater tragedy now, when she would have mocked herself for daring to think it a couple of months ago. How would things change when they no longer had the supper club as an excuse to see each other? Right now they spent a couple of evenings a week together, but that would change when she had a restaurant again and was consumed with making it a success. Would he be content to wait around for her? Would he go back to his own alleged workaholic ways?

"Where'd you go?"

Rachel realized she was staring into space. She laughed it off. "Sorry. Just thinking."

"About what?"

She carefully rearranged her ingredients around the cutting board and opened her knife case, anxious for something to do other than look him in the eye. "Us, actually."

"Oh yeah? I like the sound of that."

She suppressed a smile. "What happens to us once I'm working again and we're not doing the supper club anymore?"

Alex folded his hands on the countertop. "Depends on whether you're letting me down easy."

"What? No. That's not what I meant at all."

He shrugged. "I'm a writer. I can write in the evenings while you're at the restaurant and spend mornings with you before you go in to work. Or you can hire me as a server."

Rachel laughed. "Be serious."

"I am. About everything but the server part. I waited tables for about two weeks in college until I got fired. I'm terrible at it." He caught her eye. "But you do what you have to when it's someone you care about."

Rachel exhaled. "You do."

"Now get to it. We've got investors to impress."

Rachel selected a knife, gave it a quick pass over a sharpening stone, and got to work. Alex kept up a light stream of conversation while she methodically prepped the final ingredients for each course, telling her about the projects he was currently working on and the climbs that Bryan had organized for them, including a trip to Yosemite later this year.

"I've never been to Yosemite," she said.

"Then maybe you should come with us."

"I know better than to interfere with a guys' trip. Besides, by then I'll definitely have a job." For the first time the thought came with a sense of loss, which she immediately dismissed. Goals required sacrifice. She should know that better than anyone.

Rachel kept a close eye on the clock, began preheating the oven, and started to assemble the amuse-bouche and the first course. At exactly seven o'clock, the first knock came at the door.

Followed immediately by a deafening crash of thunder.

Chapter Thirty

Despite the dramatic warning, the rain seemed determined to hold off and the temperature remained warm, so they decided to risk the roof deck. Even with the cloudy skies, the view was too spectacular and Dina's work too elegant to not take advantage.

The first to arrive were a couple of Alex's university friends, Nadine and her husband, John, both of whom were professors at CU Denver. Nadine plopped herself down on a stool across from Rachel as soon as she walked in.

"That smells great," Nadine said, leaning over the pan. "What all's in there?"

"It's tomato confit. Simply cherry tomatoes with a little salt and pepper and a pinch of saffron."

"Nice. You know, we ate at Paisley right after it opened and thought it was fantastic. It's a real treat to get an invite, especially after everything we've seen on social media."

"Oh?" Rachel belatedly realized that she'd forgotten to check her Twitter account for the past week. That could be a good thing or a bad thing, depending on what Nadine was about to say.

"Yeah, everyone was raving about the food

at the last supper club, and then it got out you weren't the chef at Paisley anymore. John and I were there ourselves a week or two ago, and the food was okay, but the service was so slow."

That should make Rachel happy, but it was painful to hear her menu called *okay*. She'd left a well-trained staff, so there was no excuse, unless Dan's mismanagement had left everyone so demoralized they were no longer executing at the same level of precision.

"I hope you enjoy tonight's menu," Rachel said finally. "And service can't be too slow since it's only seven of you."

Nadine laughed. "I'm sure it will be amazing."

The next to arrive was Bryan with a pretty blonde in tow. He introduced her as his "friend" Lydia, which left her looking disgruntled and him completely oblivious to her annoyance. Rachel turned away. Maybe it was good he hadn't pursued Ana. Bryan seemed to shy away from serious relationships, and Lord knew Ana didn't need any more men wasting her time.

"Just waiting for Mitchell and Kathy," Alex murmured as he passed by.

Then came the knock she had been waiting for, and it sent her jitters into high gear. She practically held her breath while Alex opened the door to an older couple, giving each of them a warm hug. He immediately led them in Rachel's direction.

"Rachel, this is Mitchell and Kathy Shaw. I spent so much time in their house, they thought they'd accidentally adopted me. Mitchell, Rachel is the chef I've been telling you about."

Rachel shook hands with the Shaws, taken aback. They were not at all what she'd expected of a wealthy real estate developer and his wife. Had she not known better, she would have pegged them as someone's middle-class parents, he in khakis and a plaid button-down, she in slacks and a simple white blouse. Even Kathy's jewelry was understated and modest.

"I've looked you up, Ms. Bishop," Mitchell said. "You have quite an impressive résumé."

Every intelligent comment she might have offered flew from her head. "Thank you."

"Do you know that I knew Aaron Collins when he took over that little French restaurant in Washington Park? Here in Denver, way before he went to New York. He was green but he had so much talent, and he knew how to pick his staff. That alone commends your ability."

"He's tough, but I probably learned more about running a kitchen in two months with him than I had in my entire career to that point. He's not stingy with his knowledge."

"Not with people who will put it to good use. I'm looking forward to the meal tonight."

Mitchell headed for his son across the room, but Kathy lingered, her expression openly curious. "How did you and Alex meet?"

So Alex hadn't confessed to his part in this. Interesting. Surely it wasn't to keep them from knowing about her image problems, because he had to expect that Mitchell would thoroughly vet her. Or maybe she just wanted to know what Rachel would say. This had the distinct feel of a personal interrogation.

She decided on a diplomatic answer. "He wrote something about the restaurant, and the rest kind of happened."

"As these things do."

Rachel had a feeling they weren't talking about the supper club anymore. Kathy might be quiet, but Rachel would bet not much slipped past her.

"I've known Alex since he was a boy," Kathy said. "He always does the right thing, even when it doesn't benefit him personally. I've always thought it was his best quality, but I worry sometimes that he's too trusting."

Kathy's words felt like a warning, but Rachel wasn't entirely sure what she was being warned against. Did she think Rachel was taking advantage of Alex? "You might be right. But Alex has an uncanny way of reading people, even the secrets they don't want to admit."

Kathy smiled. "That he does."

With his typical perceptiveness, Alex arrived to

rescue her. "Kathy, are you going to join us on the roof deck? I've opened a bottle of 2010 Brancaia that Bryan brought over. I seem to remember that was one of your favorites."

Kathy excused herself, and Alex winked at Rachel as he guided the woman away. Slowly, the small group moved upstairs, leaving Rachel alone. Not two minutes later, Dina appeared. "When do you want them seated? Right now Alex and Bryan are playing bartender."

Rachel glanced at her watch. "Twenty minutes."

"Done. Time to go impress." Dina gave Rachel an encouraging smile and then climbed back up the stairs.

Rachel watched her go. Alex was lucky to have a sister like her. She'd always wished she'd had someone else around to talk to; now that she was older, she saw even more clearly what she was missing by not having a sibling. If things between her and Alex worked out . . .

Food. Tonight was about the food. There was a time when she wouldn't have had to keep emphasizing that point so strenuously.

At twenty minutes on the dot, Dina returned for the crudo, which Rachel had arranged on ceramic spoons on a serving tray. Each one was a miniature piece of modern art, topped with shaved fennel and baby arugula. "How's the mood up there?" Rachel asked.

"High anticipation, I'd say. Mr. Shaw has

been talking about how he's been looking for a restaurant to put on the ground floor of the new building. It's pretty clear what he's thinking."

"No pressure or anything." Rachel smiled despite the distinct twist in her stomach and helped load the tray that Dina would use to carry the seven small appetizer plates upstairs. "Give me a heads-up when you think they're ready for the next one."

"Sure thing." Dina swept the tray off the counter. "I'll let you know what they say."

As soon as Dina pushed through the door to the roof deck, another not-so-distant rumble of thunder sounded. Rachel circled the kitchen island to the wall of windows and peered out. What had been a typical covering of gray—which in the tradition of Denver summers could be rain or not—now had turned into a threatening, roiling mass of charcoal thunderclouds. Maybe they should consider moving the party back inside. She'd have Dina suggest it to Alex when she brought up the next course.

That would be the roasted kale topped with caramelized sweet onions and the tomato confit. She quickly checked on the stuffed trout, which had gone into the oven a few minutes before. She'd have to speed up service a little to make sure it went out while it was still hot. Recalculating in her head, she began thin-slicing the beef for the carpaccio. She was waiting for

Dina to return with a decision from Alex when a crack of lightning lit up the sky outside the windows, followed immediately by a bone-shaking boom of thunder. As if it had split open the clouds, a torrent of rain poured down with the roar of a raging waterfall.

Overhead, chairs scraped across the decking and footsteps thumped as the guests ran for cover. Immediately, the door flew open to reveal Dina leading the charge inside.

With a pop of bulbs and a winding hum of appliances, the power went out.

"No! Not now." Rachel checked the fish. Ten minutes on the timer. Not even close to being done. She couldn't count on it coming up to temperature as it rested, even with the residual heat in the oven. If she served it now, she'd potentially be serving raw fish and stuffing—not only unappetizing in this preparation but dangerous.

The guests thudded down the stairs in the near darkness, drawing her attention to the worst part of her situation: her investor and the rest of the guests were now nearly soaked to the skin.

Alex strode toward the bathroom. "I'll get some towels."

To her horror, Mitchell sidled up to the island, his wet hair plastered to his head, water droplets on his glasses. "At least I won't need to take a shower when I get home."

Rachel let out a relieved breath. "That's looking on the bright side."

He gestured toward the oven. "Was it finished?"

"Not even close."

"Did you have a Plan B?"

Rachel surveyed the kitchen. "I do now. Or I will in about five minutes." Alex returned with the towels and handed them to the guests. Somehow, being drenched only made him sexier. Yeah, she was a goner. "Do you have flashlights or lanterns and a lighter?"

Alex went to a cabinet and rummaged around, coming up with a battery-operated camping lantern and a butane lighter. "Will these do?"

"Perfect." Rachel switched on the lantern and set it on the counter to light her workspace. Mitchell watched in interest as she cranked on the cooktop knob and lit it with the long-tipped lighter. "I can't use the oven because the thermostat is electronic, but the cooktop is gas. Only the igniter is electric."

"What can I do?" Mitchell asked over the heavy drum of rain.

Rachel was about to send him to sit down and relax, but he looked genuinely eager to help. "Can you grab that stack of plates there and set the dining table? Alex, we'll need flatware too. I think it's all upstairs on the deck."

"This calls for rain gear."

"Thanks." She smiled up at him, then impulsively

pulled him back for a quick kiss. Surprise lit his eyes, but she could tell he was pleased. Why not? The evening was already off the rails. There seemed to be no point in keeping up pretenses.

She grabbed the lantern and held it with one hand while she pulled out the pan of stuffed trout, then inserted a metal cake tester from her kit. It came out cold. Not even close to the required 130 degrees. What now?

Guests had begun to gather around the island, either from curiosity or because it was the only circle of light in the room. When Alex returned with a handful of flatware, dripping water off his rain slicker, she called, "Hey, Alex. I don't suppose you have more pans?"

"No. But I know someone who probably does." He set the flatware on the countertop and then disappeared out the front door.

"What are you going to do?" Nadine asked.

"Pan-fried trout followed by pan-fried quail."

"It's like being on *Chopped*," Lydia said. " 'Make it work,' you know?"

Rachel laughed. "That's *Project Runway*, but close enough. We'll have food one way or another."

A few minutes later, Alex walked in the door, proudly carrying a stack of cast iron and stainless-steel pans. They were ancient, their outsides blackened and discolored from decades of use. "Mrs. Tajikian to the rescue. I thought she was going to make me sign over my firstborn as collateral before I took them." He set them on the cooktop grates and stepped back. "What can I do?"

"You can scrape all the stuffing out of the fish into that pot." She nodded toward a saucier already heating in the corner and put down five pans, one for each free burner.

"Is this the most impromptu change you've ever had to make?" Kathy asked.

Rachel lit the burners. "Not exactly. I was closing sous-chef at a restaurant in Manhattan during Restaurant Week. The opening sous had been responsible for ordering all the product, plus some extra, but someone had made a mistake estimating the number of covers, and by nine o'clock we had nothing left from the event menu. My chef and I ended up improvising a special 'late-night menu' based on what we still had in the walk-in. I was sure that everyone would balk at the idea of chicken liver crostini, but they were such a hit, they ended up being a permanent addition to our menu."

Lydia wrinkled her nose, clearly not an adventurous eater. Rachel pushed a little bowl and a paper-towel-wrapped packet of fresh thyme across the island. "Can you do me a favor and stem the thyme? If you hold it by the end, you can slide your fingernails down it and the leaves will come right off."

Lydia looked doubtful, but she did as Rachel asked, and before long she actually seemed to be enjoying it. Freed from formality, people began asking her questions about the jobs she'd held, why she liked to cook, what she cooked for herself at home. She answered them as she worked, heating the stuffing in a pot while she pan-fried the trout in butter. Alex set a nonalcoholic cocktail on the counter beside her, for which she threw him a grateful smile.

When the trout was done, she gave Alex and Dina quick plating instructions and then went to work getting the butterflied quail into the next set of pans. She half-expected the guests to take their plates to the table, but instead they remained around the island while she cooked, some seated, some leaning against the counter. They dug into their fish with enthusiasm, murmuring compliments before they returned to the conversation, which had shifted to Bryan's climbing career.

When the quail were cooked to a perfect medium rare, she halved each bird and arranged the pieces on a platter with a bowl of quince preserves. She had Dina bring that to the table with the cheese course and another loaf of Melody's wonderful crusty bread. The group followed the lantern's light to the table, the conversation pausing only long enough for guests to serve themselves and take a bite or two with a satisfied sigh.

"Rachel, Dina." Alex gestured them over to the table. Only then did Rachel notice that Mitchell had set the table with two extra places.

"I didn't cook enough for all of us," she whispered in Alex's ear.

He shook his head. "Don't be ridiculous. There's plenty. Sit. Enjoy."

Reluctantly, she slid into the seat beside Alex, but she refused to take a portion until everyone else had been served. As they worked their way through the food—much more than it looked, when it was served family style—Mitchell and Kathy began talking about their early years of marriage, how they'd struggled to get by, how many times they'd lost it all and started over. It felt like it was meant to be a lesson for them, but especially for Rachel. That not every ending was actually an ending, but the chance for a new beginning.

Alex stretched his arm across the back of her chair, stroking her shoulder absently while he talked, but Rachel remained quiet, her mind spinning. If that was true, what was the new beginning for her? Was it Alex, who had begun to show her what she was missing with her singular focus on work? Or was she being given a second chance for a restaurant, to prove herself worthy of all the confidence Louise had shown in her so many years ago?

And what if she were forced to choose?

When the conversation passed Lydia's way, it turned out the supermodel had a business degree and was going back to school for her master's in social work. Rachel felt a pang of guilt over her unkind judgment of both Lydia and Bryan. Maybe neither of them was as shallow as she had assumed.

The group lingered over coffee—made in a big French press with water boiled in a pot on the cooktop—and peach gingerbread with balsamic syrup, savoring every last bite of the sweet and spicy cake. Dina and Rachel were clearing the plates from the table when the power clicked back on with a glare of light and the buzz of electronics. Outside, they watched the chain reaction of lights go on as power was restored to downtown Denver. The guests blinked and stretched as if they'd been released from a spell.

"Just in time," Alex cracked. "I know none of you wanted to walk down fourteen flights of stairs."

The group laughed and began gathering jackets and handbags. The Shaws were the last to leave. When Mitchell shook Rachel's hand, he held it for a moment. "It was good getting to know you tonight, Rachel. Thanks for a very pleasant evening."

"Thanks for coming." Rachel smiled as Alex closed the door behind them.

"He liked you," Alex said. "I can tell. He's very particular about who he does business with."

"That's good, then." She went into Alex's arms like it was the most natural thing in the world, feeling inexplicably satisfied with the evening. Sure, her intricately planned, expertly timed meal had gone far off course, but it hardly seemed to matter.

"You're not disappointed?"

"Not at all." Her eyes closed as his lips neared hers.

"Uh, Alex?" Dina's voice rang from the stairwell. "You better come look."

The kiss was aborted before it ever began. Alex dropped his chin to his chest with a sigh. Rachel swatted him on the arm with a laugh. "Go on. I'll start cleaning up down here."

Reluctantly, he let her go and headed up the stairs to see what disaster had befallen his roof deck in the storm, while Rachel got to work on the kitchen. She had loaded all the dishes into the dishwasher when Alex came back with a trash bag in hand, its contents stretching and straining the plastic.

"Uh-oh. What happened?"

"You've heard about upsetting the apple cart? This is what happens when you upset the bar cart."

Rachel peeked into the bag and cringed at the broken bottles. "Did you lose much?"

"Quite a bit." He set the bag on the kitchen floor and reached for her. "Listen—"

Once more, Dina was on his heels. Did the girl have a sixth sense for these things or what? Alex dropped his hand. "I've been meaning to ask you. I don't know how long we'll be gone. Less than a week, I imagine. Could you come water the plants and feed the cat? Just until I get back?"

"You're trusting me with a key to your place? What if I decide to throw a wild party while you're gone?"

"I'm willing to risk it." He pulled his key ring from his pocket and removed a key, then set it on the countertop. "I'll feed him tomorrow before we go, so you don't need to come until Monday."

"Done. I'll treat it like my own home."

"I rather like the sound of that," Alex said, his low tone raising goose bumps on her skin. He moved close enough to murmur in her ear. "I wish I didn't have to go."

"But you will. Because you're a good brother, and it's the right thing to do." Rachel squeezed his arm and then went back to her cleaning.

With any luck, Mitchell had been impressed despite the change of plans and would be willing to invest in her. She'd miss the supper club, though, and cooking here in Alex's place. Somehow it seemed far longer than a month, far more than just two events, probably because of the significance it had taken on in her life. It had been a reason to keep moving forward. And it had been a reason to see Alex. Soon, his obligation, if he'd ever truly had one, would be over.

She packed her things and put Alex's key in her pocket. Everything was sparkling and pristine again, the borrowed pans scrubbed out and piled on the counter to be returned to Mrs. Tajikian. She waited on one of the counter stools until Dina and Alex came back, their arms laden with dishes and wet linens.

"I should get going now. I know you guys have to be on the road early."

"You don't have to leave," Alex said.

Rachel shook her head. "It's okay. I'm beat. We'll see each other when you get back."

"Let me carry your things down for you, then." Alex took the nearly empty cooler and one of the crates and opened the door for her. They rode down the elevator in silence, neither of them sure what small talk was appropriate in this situation. He had to be feeling the uncertainty in their relationship as much as she was. He had called her his girlfriend, but what had they really done that didn't relate to the supper club? Without it, did they have anything in common?

In the wet parking lot, Alex helped load her things and then pulled her close, his warmth seeping through the cold damp of the night.

"I'll call you as soon as I get back. We can do dinner or a movie or something."

"I'd like that. Thank you for all of this, Alex. Whether Mitchell wants to invest or not, I think it was something I needed."

"You're welcome." He kissed her softly, without a hint of desperation. Without a hint of good-bye.

Yet something about it made her heart ache, plied her with an urgency she didn't understand. She squeezed him tight and kissed him one more time. "Safe travels, Alex. I love you."

Before he could respond, she got in her car and drove away.

Alex stood in the parking lot long after Rachel's taillights disappeared, stunned by her words. Only when the soft patter of rain once more turned to bigger drops did he rouse himself enough to walk back to his building's lobby.

She loved him.

True, he'd said something to that effect earlier, but it had simply slipped out. When she'd pretended not to hear it, he figured he'd pass it off as a casual statement until the time was right.

There was nothing casual in the way Rachel had said it. There was nothing casual about the way he felt about her. And if only she'd stayed around long enough for his brain to process the words, he might have been able to express those feelings.

Dina took one look at him when he walked

back into his condo and said, "Oh no. What did you do?"

"What? I just walked through the door."

She studied him closely, hands on her hips. "You've got this guilty, worried look. You didn't do something stupid like break up with Rachel, did you?"

"No. I didn't. Why would I?"

"What gives, then?" Dina plopped herself on one of the counter stools and folded her hands in her lap, waiting.

"I'm not going to talk to you about my relationship with Rachel."

"So it *does* have to do with Rachel. Wait. She's not mad that you're going back to LA with me, is she?"

"Not at all. She understands this is a big deal to you." He put an arm around Dina's shoulder. "You don't actually think I'd make you do this alone, do you?"

Dina shrugged off his arm. "Nice try, Alex. You're not going to get me off topic."

Alex sighed. Might as well tell her, because she'd never let up until he did. "She said she loves me."

"And you said . . ."

"I didn't say anything. I was still trying to get my mouth to catch up with my brain when she drove away."

Dina smacked him on the back of the head.

"Idiot. Call her and tell her you love her, right now. Unless you don't love her, in which case I'm going to call you a liar because it's so obvious you're crazy about her."

"That's not something you say over the phone, Dina."

"Then drive to her house and sweep her off her feet with your declaration of undying love. Just be back here by the time we have to leave in the morning."

"I'm going to pretend you didn't say that."

"Whatever." Dina rolled her eyes and hopped off the stool. "I'm going to take a shower."

Alex watched her go, as puzzled by his sister as he'd ever been. He no longer understood a thing about her. Or maybe he never had. They hadn't been raised together in the usual sense, and when he had seen her, she was too busy being what their parents expected of her. Maybe he didn't truly know her because she didn't truly know herself.

He saw that same tendency in Rachel.

Except Rachel had let her guard down with him. She'd even unpacked her past, knowing that he'd read between the lines, understand how everything that had gone before had shaped her. With all her paranoia over being analyzed, she had decided to trust him.

She loved him.

As much as he wanted to linger over that

thought, he'd been somewhat derelict in his work this week, so he sat down at his desk and booted up his laptop. No sooner did he put his fingers to the keyboard than his cell phone rang. He snatched it up, hoping it was Rachel, but it was an unfamiliar local number on the screen.

"I'm so sorry to bother you on a Saturday night," the female voice rushed out when he answered.

"Who is this?"

"Oh, sorry. It's Beatrice Donlin. At *Altitude* magazine?"

He blinked. *Altitude* was a local publication that focused on the healthy Denver lifestyle—alternative health, fitness, and work-life balance. Bea had been one of the first editors to give him regular work when he dove into his writing career, partly because of his friendship with Bryan, who had been featured on the cover a few months earlier.

But why was she calling him tonight?

"It's okay. What can I do for you, Bea?"

"I've got an emergency. We go to print on Monday and I had to pull my feature article from the wellness section. A fact-checker noticed it had been partially lifted from the author's previous work for *Men's Health*."

Alex winced. Everything got passed through plagiarism software before being manually fact-checked, but some authors were better than others at beating the automated system. "And you need a replacement?"

"You know I wouldn't ask if I had any other choice. You're the only writer I know who can turn it on at such short notice. Unless of course we're small potatoes to you now—"

"Relax, Bea, you don't have to lay it on that thick. I can write something. What topic and how long?"

"Fifteen hundred to two thousand. And write anything you want, as long as it has to do with holistic wellness."

"Gotcha. I'll have it to you tomorrow."

Relief poured through his phone's speaker. "I owe you big time."

An idea pinged in the corner of his imagination. "How big?"

"What did you have in mind?"

"I have a chef friend with image problems and a new endeavor that could use some positive press."

"Ah, Rachel Bishop. I saw your Instagram. Are you two . . . ?"

"Yeah, kind of."

"Consider it done. Get me something I can use by tomorrow and I'll feature her in the local life section anytime after the August issue."

"Deal. Watch your e-mail." Alex hung up the phone, satisfied with the trade. Quickly, he jotted a note on the legal pad beside him so he'd

402

remember to follow up well before their press deadline. Of course, this all hinged on Rachel's agreement and his ability to turn out this article on time. Bea thought she was doing him a favor by giving him free rein, but on such a short deadline, a specific topic would have been much more useful.

Brainstorm time. He scrawled a few ideas for topics that could fit into the section's "balanced life" feel. No surprise that once again Rachel's influence crept from his subconscious.

Dina poked her head into his bedroom. "I'm going to bed now. Are you working?"

"Last-minute assignment. I'm bailing out a friend. You're probably going to have to take the first shift driving tomorrow so I can sleep. This is going to take me all night."

"You know, you don't have to come. I can probably fit most of my stuff in my car, and what I can't, I'll leave behind." Her tone was tough, but he detected a hint of vulnerability in her eyes.

"No, I want to go. I haven't seen you much lately. A road trip will be fun."

She smiled. "Okay, then. Good night."

Alex stared at the door long after Dina left. This would be good. Necessary. As much as he hated to leave Rachel, he was as responsible for Dina's situation as his parents because he hadn't stopped to ask her what she wanted to do. At least now he could begin to make it up to her.

But first, the magazine piece. One of the topics stood out more than the others, so he began his outline in a new document on his laptop. By the time he'd converted the bullet points to coherent paragraphs and done a quick editing pass, it was almost four o'clock. Blearily, he opened an e-mail to Bea, attached the article with his bio and head shot, and clicked Send.

He was about to shut down his computer when he noticed an e-mail that had come in while he was working. It was from his agent, subject line: *Re: Proposal.*

Alex,

Love this. It's not what I expected from you, but it's compelling and well-written. I want to make sure your editor has a solid feel for the book, so can you expand the sample chapters a little more?

The stuff with the chef is GOLD!

Christine

Alex rubbed his eyes wearily. He could easily add a few thousand words to his proposal when he got back. He added a reminder to the bottom of his legal pad and tossed the pen onto the table before stumbling to his bed. He barely managed to strip off his clothes before he climbed beneath the covers and fell asleep with the light on.

Chapter Thirty-One

Melody had been called in to work for a big catering job and Ana was out of town on business until tomorrow, so Rachel didn't even have the benefit of a breakfast download the next morning with her best friends to sort through her impulsive actions.

Had she actually told Alex she loved him . . . and then fled before he could respond?

Yes, she had. But she didn't regret it. She hadn't said it to elicit a reaction or gauge his feelings or force an intimacy that wasn't there. They weren't children anymore, obsessing over who said what first. She loved him. She could no longer deny that, not to herself and not to him. She'd already told him more difficult truths than her feelings for him.

Without anything in particular to do or anyone to do it with, she turned to her default: cooking. Melody might be the baker, but Rachel could turn out a respectable artisan-style *boule* when she put her mind to it. While her dough rose, she began simmering a stock from the leftover trout scraps. They might still be suffering through the hottest part of the summer, but a chowder was exactly the sort of comfort she needed right now.

And yet when she sat down at the table, alone

with an absolutely delicious bowl of soup and a hunk of crusty bread, she could only think about how much she missed Alex, how much better this would taste if he were sitting across from her.

She caved. She took out her phone and texted him. How's the drive? Where are you?

She tried not to stare at the phone beside her bowl, hoping for an immediate reply, but she still jumped a foot off her chair when it rang. She snatched it up. "Hi."

"Hey, you. We just checked into a motel in Moab, Utah. We got kind of a late start so we didn't make it as far as we'd hoped. We're going to try to drive straight through tomorrow."

"I'm jealous. I've always loved road trips. And all that greasy food from roadside diners."

"I think you're the type to plan your entire route around where to eat. Am I right?"

Rachel laughed, unexpectedly flushed by the warmth in his teasing words. "You're right. I am. Which is why I am such a fun person to road-trip with."

"You should have come. I'm already spending all my time thinking of you."

A smile crept onto her face. "I miss you too. Come back soon."

"As soon as I can."

Rachel hung up, enveloped in a glow of happiness. She was done for, no doubt about it. The mere sound of his voice filled her with longing. Who would have ever thought the man she'd pegged as her worst enemy and the architect of her career destruction would become such a central part of her life? She'd like to pretend she wouldn't be counting the days until he returned, but that would be a lie.

For once, she didn't have any plans. If Mitchell Shaw didn't bite, they would hold more supper clubs, but she wouldn't plan a menu until she knew for sure. In fact, she might simply combine the best of the two previous events. Instead, she stayed up late watching Netflix shows she'd added to her list. She slept hard and soundly, waking to midmorning light in her bedroom. If she planned it right, she could quickly feed Sunshine and then grab an early lunch at one of her favorite haunts on the way home.

An hour later, she rode the elevator up to Alex's fifteenth-floor apartment, the action simultaneously nerve-racking and oddly natural. The nerves took over when she let herself in with the spare key.

His place was as pristine as always, except for the bag of dry cat food on the counter next to several tins of pâté and a watering can. Of course Alex had thought of everything. Rachel wandered into the living room and rattled the cat's ceramic dish in its holder. "Sunshine! Here kitty! I'm going to feed you now."

Nothing. Not a jingle of a collar or a meow

to be heard. Rachel realized why when she saw the snap-off collar dangling from a branch of the rubber tree by the windows. What in the world? She'd never even seen the cat break into a run, let alone do anything to indicate he was capable of climbing four feet into the air and hanging from the branch of a houseplant.

Rachel stood there for a long moment, unsure what to do. The collars were meant to prevent strangling, but what if Sunshine was hurt? It wasn't like she was snooping if she was looking for the cat, right? What if she left and there really was something wrong? Dina would be devastated, and Rachel would never forgive herself.

She peered under the sofas, but there was barely enough space for the fat tabby to fit, so she wasn't surprised to find the spaces devoid of anything but a handful of dust bunnies. The windowsill, the back of the entertainment cabinet, and the bathroom likewise bore no sign of the cat.

She hovered outside the half-closed door to Alex's bedroom, uncertain. Entering felt like a violation of his private space, especially when she'd never been invited in. But there simply wasn't any other place for the cat to hide.

Rachel pushed the door open gingerly. "Sunshine? You in here, kitty?" She jingled the collar and heard a rustle from somewhere in the room.

Her eyes swept over the space. King-size bed with a contemporary headboard, the mattress draped in simple, minimalist linens. A wall of mirrored tile. Heavy wool curtains drawn back to showcase the stunning view. It managed to be sophisticated and sexy without seeming like it was trying too hard. Exactly like its occupant.

She inhaled deeply, momentarily distracted by Alex's familiar scent, a faint mixture of cologne and soap and cotton. Another rustle drew her attention to the desk, where Alex's laptop sat, a spinning cube on his screen saver bouncing around the edges like a ball in a pinball machine. Beneath the table, wedged between the wall and the leg amid a tangle of cords, was a big ball of orange-striped fur.

Lazy gold eyes followed her movements as she bent down beside the desk. "Are you hungry?"

"Mrow." The cat blinked. She could have sworn he would have shrugged were he capable of the movement.

"I've never heard of a cat who wasn't hungry, especially one as fat as you. Besides, we need to get your collar back on. If you got out without it, I'd be in big trouble." Sunshine looked unlikely to make a run for it, but still. When jingling the collar and coaxing him out with a mouse toy on a string didn't even earn the twitch of a muscle, she decided she had no choice but to go in after him.

"Come on, kitty. Make this easy for both of us." She got down on her knees and crawled beneath the desk. The minute she got one hand under the cat's rib cage, he dug his claws into the rug, sticking himself to the floor like industrial-strength Velcro. "Okay, fine. If you don't want to come out, just stay put."

She managed to somehow wiggle her hands into the space behind the table leg and get the collar back on, already regretting the whole fiasco. This cat wasn't going anywhere while she was here. Definitely not a flight risk.

Slowly, she scooted backward from beneath the desk and straightened—only to whack her head on the table's edge.

"Ow." She probed the back of her skull for the knot that was no doubt forming and unfolded herself to a kneeling position.

And found herself staring directly at Alex's computer screen, an e-mail open on the desktop. Rachel turned away, not wanting to snoop in his private matters, but the word *chef* caught her eye. What was this?

Despite her better inclinations, she read the e-mail once, then again. The return address was from a literary agency.

Was this about the book he'd been writing? Was she the chef?

A sick feeling crawled into her middle and took up residence there, growing heavier with each heartbeat. Surely he wouldn't do that to her. He knew how she felt about the negative publicity she'd already received. That's why she was in this mess in the first place.

Her eyes fell on the notepad next to the laptop, the sick feeling growing to a crushing weight. The page was filled with Alex's careful script, cryptic but all too understandable.

> Rachel feature—check Sept/Oct issue
> Perfectionism → addictions →
>   workaholism?
> Work success = self-worth = surrogate for
>   meaningful relationships
> Food = intimacy?
> Need to expand proposal by 8/15.

Rachel stood there, her limbs locked in horror, unable to even draw in a full breath. Surely she was reading this wrong. The wording was so cold and clinical, like he was trying to take her apart piece by piece, understand her moving parts like a machine. Was Alex researching the effects of her stepfather's abuse? Was he trying to fix her?

Her eyes drifted back to the e-mail, not wanting to believe the more-likely scenario.

She wasn't his girlfriend. She was his subject.

Rachel stumbled away from the desk, her lungs tight and her head throbbing. This couldn't be true. She had to be misunderstanding. She took her phone from her back pocket, returned to the computer, and snapped a photo of both the notepad and the e-mail. It was a complete invasion of his privacy, but she didn't care. The idea that he had been picking apart her psyche in order to write about it was far more of a violation than her accidental snooping.

She was halfway to the elevator when she realized she hadn't fed the cat, the stupid cat that had started this whole discovery. She darted back into the condo, overfilled the food and water bowls with shaking hands, and left without giving the watering can a second look. Let his plants die. She was a decent human being who wouldn't let a pet suffer, but his trees didn't get the same consideration.

Rachel took the ride down the elevator to compose herself, even though her thoughts were spinning, mad and incoherent. For a second, she thought she might throw up, but that too she forced down into the cold vault of pragmatism she held in reserve, the place in which she'd dwelt since she was fifteen, the place she'd begun to crawl out of when she met Alex. At least there she could accept his betrayal without feeling its full impact.

There she could forget how much of a fool she had been by letting down her guard and falling in love with him.

• • •

Halfway back to her house, Rachel's phone beeped. She fished it out of her back pocket and held it up to see the message on the screen. Voice mail. She hadn't even heard it ring. She punched a button to play the message over speaker.

"Rachel, this is Mitchell Shaw. I'd like to speak with you at your convenience about the possibility of investing in your restaurant. If you'll put together a business proposal for me, we can meet to go over the details."

He left his number at the end of the message, as casually as if he were ordering a pizza. Rachel stared at the phone for a second before she realized she should really be staring at the road and jerked her eyes forward.

He wanted to invest. It had worked.

She would have her restaurant again.

Despite the betrayal, despite what she'd learned not ten minutes before, her first inclination was to dial Alex. The realization that she couldn't brought on equal measures of anger and shame.

How could she have been so stupid? This was why she didn't trust people. This was why she didn't let them see who she really was. As soon as you made yourself vulnerable, they turned on you, used you to get what they wanted. She'd trusted him completely, and once more she was left questioning what she had done to cause his betrayal, wondering what made her a target for liars and users.

Rachel drew the cold around her heart until the anger passed, engaged the methodical side that had made her a culinary success. She already had a business plan she'd been working on, but she'd have to tweak it a bit before she called Mitchell back. She was working through the changes in her head when she parked in front of her house, then realized she should probably ask Melody and Ana to come over and celebrate. She texted them with the invitation and then marched inside to start dinner.

She usually loved to cook for her friends, but tonight there was no joy in it, just mechanically executed steps. It would be perfect, of course. She could rely on experience and muscle memory to do this even if her heart wasn't in the process.

When Ana and Melody arrived together a few minutes past six, Rachel opened the door, calm at last. "Hey."

"Hey." Ana shrugged off her suit jacket and hung it on the hook by the door. "Something smells good."

Melody narrowed her eyes, not fooled for a moment. "What's wrong?"

Where to begin? Rachel gestured for them to follow her into the kitchen where the table had been set, a mixed green salad with a lemon-and-shallot vinaigrette holding court alongside the other crusty loaf of bread she'd baked yesterday. She'd garnished a dish of whipped butter with *fleur de sel* and sliced citrus into their water glasses.

Melody was starting to look worried. "Rachel? What's going on?"

"I made lamb cassoulet."

"For a quick dinner?" Ana asked. "That had to have taken you all afternoon."

"It did. We're celebrating."

Ana and Melody exchanged a look.

"Celebrating what?" Melody asked.

Rachel pulled out her phone and played the message for them while she moved the Dutch oven to a trivet on the table.

"That's amazing!" Melody exclaimed. "Are you excited? Why aren't you more excited?"

"I am. This is my excited face." She took a seat across from them and lifted the lid from the pot in a plume of steam.

Ana narrowed her eyes. "I don't believe you."

Rachel sighed. Wordlessly, she pulled up the photos on her phone and handed it over.

Ana's expression changed as she read the e-mail and notepad. "What is this?"

"I accidentally found it when I went over to Alex's to feed Dina's cat. I bumped the desk and his computer went off screen saver."

Ana handed the phone to Melody, who read it, her expression pained. "Oh, Rachel. Maybe it's not what it looks like?"

"How else do I take that? He's writing about me and he's using his psychology background to . . . I don't know, shrink me." Rachel took her phone back and set it by her plate.

"Have you actually read what he wrote?" Melody asked. "Have you talked to him about it? Maybe it's not what you think."

"He's in LA with Dina, helping her move her stuff back to Denver. This isn't something I can discuss over the phone." Rachel reached for the salad tongs and began serving them automatically.

Melody took the utensil from her. "Stop, Rachel. We should talk about this."

"What's there to talk about?"

"You love him. You've never gotten this involved with a man. Don't you think you should hear him out before you throw it all away?"

"Throw what away? According to him, I use food as a substitute for intimacy. My feelings are nothing more than misplaced gratitude over his help in getting my restaurant back. I can only imagine how he's going to spin this. 'Our food-obsessed culture is looking for a replacement for Mommy and Daddy's approval. We eat our feelings instead of dealing with our issues. Take this workaholic chef who is so desperate for love, she'll believe anything a man tells her.' " Rachel took a slice of bread and buttered it with savage strokes. "Even though I'm getting what I want, I feel completely manipulated. I can't even enjoy the victory."

Ana placed her hands flat on either side of her plate. "As far as I'm concerned, if he was really using you, you'd better be getting something out of it."

Reluctantly, Melody said, "Ana's right. Why are you letting him spoil this for you? This is what you've always wanted."

"Is it?" Rachel shook her head. "I don't know. As much as I hate the idea that he's been analyzing me, maybe he's right. Maybe it's not about cooking after all. Maybe it is a substitute for the things I haven't had. If I'm really honest, it's been about proving I could do it on my own. That I could take care of myself without anyone's help."

As she said the words, they pierced with the ring of truth. She'd always known it, but as long as she moved forward, she'd been able to ignore it. And somehow Alex had come in and smashed her certainty to bits. Made her realize how much she wanted to share her life with someone. How much she needed to trust. How ready she was to move on.

She had simply picked the wrong man.

Melody reached across the table and squeezed her hand hard. "We're in this with you, Rachel. No matter what you decide. Whether you forgive Alex or you don't. Whether you go into business with Mitchell Shaw or you don't. But you need to figure out what you want. What you really want."

Rachel looked into the earnest faces of her best friends. She reached out her left hand, and slowly, Ana took it. "I love you both. I don't know what I would do if you weren't here."

"You'd do exactly the same thing," Ana said. "Conquer everything you set your mind to."

"We love you, too, Rach." Melody smiled at her and squeezed her hand again before letting it go. "So, can we eat now? I'm starving and that looks really good."

Rachel gave a watery laugh and swiped at her eyes. "Who needs Saturday night for a supper club, right? We've got all we need right here on a Monday."

"I don't know," Ana said. "If we're all single again, we don't have anything better to do on Saturday night."

Despite herself, Rachel cracked a smile. "Maybe we should resurrect the supper club. My kitchen. We all invite a friend in the same boat. And we can all be pathetic together."

"Not pathetic," Ana said. "Independent. Determined. Willing to hold out for what we really want, whatever that is."

"Hear, hear." Melody raised her water glass and clinked it with Ana's. "To the Saturday Night Supper Club, version 2.0."

Rachel clinked her glass with her friends',

her heaviness ebbing a degree, though she had a feeling it would take a long time to disappear. She had been wrong about one thing. Thanks to the women sitting across from her, she had begun learning to trust long before Alex came along.

Chapter Thirty-Two

Alex could barely contain his anticipation when he crested the Continental Divide and began the downward descent into Denver on Thursday night. He'd texted Rachel several times and called once since he and Dina had left LA, but his messages had gone unanswered. She was probably busy putting together the proposal for Mitchell. He'd called Alex on Monday to tell him he'd made contact with Rachel for a possible partnership.

Alex couldn't wait to celebrate their victory.

When they finally left the steep downward slope of I-70 behind for the city streets, Alex pulled out his phone and dialed. Dina would go straight to his place with the bulk of her possessions, but he couldn't wait even that long to see Rachel.

The call went directly to voice mail. "Hey, it's me. I'm back in Denver. I hear we have something to celebrate. I can't wait to see you. I'm going to drop by your house on my way home to see if you're there."

The thought of seeing Rachel, having her in his arms, eased some of the weariness from his trip. There was still plenty to do: find a storage unit for Dina's things, break the news of her return to their parents, help her find a job. He'd have time—no doubt Rachel would dive into plans for her new restaurant with even more enthusiasm than she had shown for the supper club. He just hoped she left some room in her schedule for him.

When he pulled up in front of Rachel's house, the lower-floor windows glowed with light. A smile came to his face as he walked up the path and knocked on the front door. Inside he heard movement, but saw nothing through the stained-glass window. He knocked again.

This time the blur of motion resolved into a familiar shape. Chains rattled and locks scraped as the door opened.

He exhaled on a rush of pleasure. "Rachel." He moved forward, wanting nothing more than to have his arms around her and her lips under his. But her posture stiffened and she backed up half a step, putting the threshold between them. He froze in place. What was going on? Had something happened?

"How was the trip?" Rachel asked.

Alex thrust his hands in his jeans pockets, perplexed. "Good. Dina seems happy to be coming back. After seeing the dump she was living in, I really can't blame her."

"I'm glad. Tell her I said hello and welcome back."

He reached out to tuck a lock of stray hair

behind her ear, but she jerked her head away. "Don't."

"Rachel, I . . . What's going on?" She was acting like they were strangers, as if less than a week ago, she hadn't told him she loved him.

"I saw."

His eyebrows pulled together. "Saw what?"

"Your notes. The e-mail from your agent. It was an accident, but I still saw them."

Guilt immediately coursed through him even though he had nothing to feel guilty about. The only e-mail he could think of was the one from Christine asking for more chapters. He couldn't imagine what was so heinous about that. And the notes . . . What notes was she even talking about?

"I don't understand." He automatically moved closer, but she backed up another step. "What did I do?"

She shook her head, hurt and anger entwined in her expression. Tears glimmered in her eyes. "Are you or are you not writing about me?"

He froze. "Rachel, it's not what you think."

"It's a simple question. Are you writing about me? Did you use the things I told you for material in your book?"

His heart was somewhere on the floor, one wrong move from being ground beneath her heel. "I did, but not in the manner you're thinking. Rachel, before we met, I was stuck. I thought it was my guilt over what I accidentally did to your career that was holding me up, but I realized I was weary. Tired of my own cynicism. Meeting you changed everything. You inspired me."

He'd heard many things in her voice to this point—anger, hurt, affection—but when she laughed now, it was the first time he'd ever heard bitterness. "Do you really think you can feed me some line, make yourself out to be the tortured artist, and I'll just ignore what you did?"

"Rachel—"

"No. Now you listen. The first time you wrote about me and ruined my life, you claimed ignorance. You don't get to use the same excuse twice. I trusted you and you betrayed me."

The hurt and disappointment in her eyes were almost too much to bear. It made him want to grovel at her feet until she let him explain. But her walls were up again, locking him out. She'd made up her mind about him. Now she would never believe that he loved her, that he never meant to hurt her. In her eyes, he was exactly like her stepfather, using her insecurities to his advantage, making her heart the casualty of some twisted game.

Still, he couldn't give up without one last try. "Please, Rachel, I'm begging you. Just read the manuscript. You'll see what I intended. You'll see I'm not using you."

She held his gaze, a moment of longing surfacing before it disappeared again behind the hard mask. She wrapped her fingers around the edge of the door. "Good-bye, Alex. Tell Dina I hope she finds exactly what she's been searching for."

She shut the door in his face.

Alex stood there long after her shape disappeared beyond the stained-glass window, every bit of him sick and aching. He didn't know how it had gone so wrong so fast. He only knew that he loved her.

And he'd lost her.

Alex let himself into his condo and dropped his bag inside the front door. It looked exactly as he had left it, and yet somehow the knowledge he would never see Rachel here again made it feel empty.

Sometimes it sucked being in touch with his feelings. Were he not a writer, did he not have his psychology background, he could go pound back a few at a local bar and convince himself he was better off without her. Unfortunately, he couldn't lie to himself that easily.

The sound of running water from the bathroom indicated Dina had already made herself at home. The last thing he wanted to do was face his sister right now. Instead, he went into his bedroom with a sense of dread. Where his laptop had gone back to screen saver. Sure enough, the screen still held the e-mail from Christine, which ended with the damning words, *The stuff with the chef is GOLD!*

Right beside it was his notepad—his reminder to check on the feature he'd negotiated for Rachel at the top; ideas for the last-minute articles beneath it, some of which had stemmed from the things Rachel had told him.

Alex stared at the notepad for a long moment and then swept his arm in one furious stroke across the desk's surface, sending the contents crashing to the floor.

It always seemed to make people in TV shows feel better, but he felt just as miserable as before. And now he was staring at a mess he'd have to clean up.

Dina appeared in the doorway of his bedroom, wearing her pajamas and a shocked expression. "What happened?" She rushed to grab the laptop from where it swung in a slow arc, the plug's position in the port as precarious as a climber's grip in the pouring rain. A few more swings and it would be on the ground, possibly damaged, his files potentially unrecoverable.

"Leave it," he snapped. What did it matter? He couldn't publish the book as it was now. So much of it had been inspired by or centered around Rachel. He'd intended on letting her see it when the time was right, just like he'd intended to tell her that he loved her. He'd simply waited too long.

Dina ignored him and rescued the laptop, then swiveled to face him. "What happened? What did you do?"

"Why do you think I did something?"

She arched an eyebrow at him.

"It doesn't matter. She made it clear she doesn't want to hear my explanation and she never wants to see me again. It's over."

"I don't believe that."

Alex wiped a hand wearily over his face. "You know what? It's fine. It's not like I'm not busy. Now that you're back, we need to find you a job and a place to stay—"

Dina perched on the edge of his desk, bracing her hands on either side of her. "Listen, Alex, I appreciate you coming back to LA with me to get my stuff. And it's been really nice to have you around for the last few days. But you need to butt out."

He blinked at her. "What?"

"I don't need you to fix this for me. I don't need your help."

"How can you say that when I helped get you into this—"

"No. You didn't." Dina rose and moved to face him straight on. "I made my own decisions. Yes, you stood up for me to Mom and Dad, but you didn't force me to do anything. I know it's hard to believe since I'm your little sister, but I'm a grown woman. I can make my own decisions, and I can take responsibility for them when they don't work out."

Her expression twisted into one of sympathy that made her seem like the elder sibling. "I've been thinking a lot about what Rachel said. About not being afraid to take risks. And I realized that for all Mom and Dad did to try to make us succeed, they never taught us what to do when we failed. They demanded we fix our mistakes, but that's not the same thing."

She shrugged. "I'm not a mistake to be fixed, Alex. I don't want to be your project. And I'd venture to say neither does Rachel."

His sister's words were like a punch in the gut. Alex sank down on the edge of his bed, barely noticing when Dina slipped out of the room. Was that what he had been doing this whole time? He'd thought that helping Rachel was the right thing to do, the honorable thing to do. Had he been treating her like a project instead of a person?

His eyes drifted back to the laptop and notepad, now glaring at him. He could certainly refuse to publish out of respect for her, even though she'd completely misunderstood the role she played in the essays. It would mean tossing away his best chance at a contract, but it might show her that she was far more important to him than any book deal.

And yet for the first time in years, he felt like

he had something worthwhile to say, all thanks to Rachel. She'd made him reevaluate his own cynicism, see his surroundings in a purer way.

She'd helped him to stop looking at the world as something that existed only to be fixed, corrected, perfected.

Mitchell's words, which now felt so long ago, came back to him. *"Whatever decision you make, be sure you're doing it because it's what God would have you do, not simply because it's most comfortable."* Right now, it felt easier to bail on the book and beg Rachel to take him back. He loved her.

And yet he wanted the world to get a glimpse of her heart, the ways that simple, pure, uncomplicated gestures could change everything for a person.

He pulled out his phone and dialed Bryan. "Any chance I can borrow the cabin in Breck for a week or so?"

It was technically Mitchell and Kathy's cabin, but Bryan was the only one who used it these days. Calling it a cabin underrepresented what it actually was—a sizable house in log cabin style, complete with sauna and hot tub, at the base of the Breckenridge ski area.

"Sure," Bryan said finally. "No one's going to be up there until the slopes open. But why? I figured you'd be spending all your time with Rachel now that you're back."

"She's not speaking to me. Likely permanently."

"What did you do?"

"Why does everyone immediately think I did something?"

"Didn't you?"

Alex ignored the question. "Can I come by and get the keys?"

"If you do it tonight. I'm driving to Pueblo early tomorrow to teach a climbing clinic."

Alex had intended to wait until the morning, but there was no reason to delay. He packed up his laptop, his notebooks, and a hard copy of his proposal, then swapped out the dirty clothes in his roller bag for clean ones. Then he strode out into the living room, where Dina had made herself comfortable on his sofa.

He tossed her his house keys. "I'm going to Breckenridge for a few days. Make yourself at home. Take my room while I'm gone, even. When I get there, I'll text you the cabin's phone number just in case."

"You're leaving? I just got here."

He smiled even though he knew it held little humor. "I'm doing what you asked, Dina. I'm butting out. I'll come back if you need me, but in the meantime, I have work to do."

He bent to give her a hug good-bye, then let himself out of his apartment, sure for once of his direction. Yet he found himself driving not to Bryan's but Rachel's place. He parked across the street, staring at the now-dark windows while he debated the wisdom of his actions. Then he yanked the envelope containing the printout from his bag, marched up the steps, and left it leaning against her door. There. No one could say he hadn't tried.

Even if he feared it wasn't nearly enough.

Chapter Thirty-Three

Rachel's light mood the next morning lasted only as long as it took for the memories of Alex's betrayal to return. With it came the grief and humiliation that felt at once fresh and sharp and all too familiar.

When would she learn? She'd thought her stepfather was what he seemed, a loving parent who only had her best interests at heart. She'd thought Dan and Maurice were trustworthy partners who shared her vision.

She'd thought Alex actually loved her.

He'd probably call her bad experiences with men pathological, something she sought out and repeated unconsciously over and over again. Wasn't that what shrinks did? Helped you figure out why you made bad choices based on your personal variety of trauma? For all she knew, he'd smelled it on her, picked her out as a target.

Seemed like no matter how well you thought you'd recovered, everyone was always going to recognize you as a victim.

It was fury that swallowed the pain and pushed her out of bed. No. She wasn't a victim. She wasn't going to curl up and die because her boyfriend turned out to be a user. Hadn't she always said the personal didn't matter? She was a chef. A brilliant, ambitious chef. All her guests cared about was amazing food, and all Mitchell Shaw cared about was getting bodies through the door. She might be naive, but she wasn't stupid.

She'd been avoiding returning the investor's call, but she wasn't going to do that any longer. Time to move forward to the next phase of her life. Time to pick up the phone.

After breakfast.

Rachel marched to the kitchen and put on a pot of coffee, then rummaged through the refrigerator. Eggs. That was all there was. Classic French omelet for breakfast, then. She whipped the eggs in a bowl, then headed for the front porch to pick some herbs from her window boxes. The chervil hadn't been looking good lately, but the tarragon, chives, and parsley were exploding from their containers.

When she opened her front door, however, a manila envelope tipped over the threshold. It bore a single word in a familiar masculine script—*Rachel*.

The sourness in her stomach threatened to rise. She tucked the envelope beneath her arm and picked the herbs for her omelet, then marched back inside. She tossed the envelope on the end of the dining table without opening it and got to work on her breakfast.

And yet that manila packet called her like a beacon, catching her eye wherever she moved in the kitchen. She poured herself a cup of coffee and barely managed to avoid picking it up as she walked by. She brought her plate to the table and sat to eat, all the while pointedly ignoring it. On her way back to the sink with her empty plate, she couldn't resist her morbid curiosity any longer, so she snatched it up and brought it with her to the corner of the sofa beneath her reading lamp.

Her heart thudded heavily against her rib cage as she picked open the clasp and slid out fifty or so typed pages on bright-white computer paper, a title printed in bold lettering across the front page:

Life from Scratch: Essays on Food, Love, and Identity

Rachel turned over the title page and began the first essay, simultaneously gripped with curiosity and dread. But as she read, her careful guard began to slip. When she'd reviewed the sample of Alex's first book, she'd thought he was talented: his intelligence shone through each word and clever turn of phrase. But it had been like he was performing, showing how adroitly he could twist the English language, showcasing biting humor and a sharp mind. That was certainly part of Alex's personality, as much as the need to fix injustice had made him write the opinion piece that started this whole debacle. If she were honest, she'd been afraid to find herself on the opposite end of that caustic wit.

But this book was different. This was like having Alex beside her, telling a quiet story to her over a cup of tea. An intimate reflection, a small peek into the bits that his cheerful, witty exterior concealed. He talked about childhood trips to the Russian market with his mother, how it had felt like a mysterious entrée into a clandestine world, where Americanized women only spoke the mother tongue and bought packages covered in unreadable Cyrillic. About how meals had been a way to connect to the old country, a heritage he might never fully understand because he had known only the plenty of a middle-class American upbringing, never a day of Soviet scarcity.

He spoke of his dismay and loss when an unnamed friend had pointed out his mother's recipes from home were every bit as much propaganda as her faded copy of *Book of Tasty and Healthy Food*, which showed elaborate dishes few ordinary Russian citizens had been able to afford. Yet he'd eventually realized it was a hallmark of resilience, how imagination and hope for something better had actually led to that something better. Those fraudulent recipes represented a dream come true.

Rachel turned the page, her throat tight.

Alex touched on why he entertained, why he kept the samovar on the kitchen counter, even though it was ungainly and out of place in the contemporary space. It was a reminder, he wrote, that prosperity demanded more hospitality, not less.

And then she came to the last essay in the batch, which held a paragraph that stilled her in her tracks.

It's always just been a room, but it comes to life in her capable presence, slowly, unconsciously. Her innate skill with food is still not as great as her capacity for affection, but one fuels the other. She has every reason to withdraw and become bitter, stingy, and yet she maintains a generosity of spirit that says each and every guest is worthy of her best, worthy of care, worthy of love. As with other performers, perhaps it's not the skill that makes the cook great, but the essential nature of her character.

She read it once, and then again. It took a third time before she could accept this essay might be about her. The ink blurred and the paper warped beneath the steady drip of tears as she struggled to make sense of this vision of her. She'd been sure he would take the pieces of herself that she'd exposed—her insecurities, her failures, her driving need for perfection—and reveal them on the page in stark relief to her outward successes. She'd been terrified to see him highlight her brokenness, the fractured pieces that, while mended, still fit together imperfectly.

This was her in his book, undoubtedly, but somehow he had portrayed those broken pieces as her strength, as proof of what more she could offer. Rather than feel exposed, she felt . . .

Seen.

He understood why she did what she did, maybe better than she. He was still laying her bare before the world, but his view of her . . . it wasn't one she was ashamed for everyone to see.

She'd been so quick to think the worst of him. She hadn't even given him the chance to explain. That made her as bad as all the strangers who had condemned her on social media without bothering to learn the truth, passing what they saw through their own damaged filters. Projecting every awful thought they had about themselves on someone else, just so they didn't have to face the pain.

Was that why she insisted on focusing so heavily on her failures? Because even as she tried to prove otherwise, deep down she felt it was no more than she deserved?

She'd prayed for a father, and she got a man who crushed her spirit.

She'd thanked God for her restaurant, and it was ripped away.

She'd taken a chance on loving Alex, and he'd revealed himself to be a fraud.

Somewhere along the way, she'd begun to think that when she asked for something good, God would repay her with some pale counterfeit. She'd dared to want something different for her life, dared to rebel against the mold that had been cast for her by her parents. Didn't she somehow think that if she did anything to attract attention to her success, she'd be punished for it?

"If God had wanted you to be anything other than who and what you are, He would have made you that way."

No, she'd pulled back, only allowing herself to be grateful for the small things she could afford to lose, lest God glimpse her true joys and take those away too.

But she'd been wrong. As scarring as her relationship with her stepfather had been, it had propelled her out into the wider world, helped her find the thing that truly brought her joy. Losing her restaurant had led Alex to her door, which had given her a new focus and a second chance to do what she was made to do. All this time she thought she was slipping beneath God's notice, and instead He'd guided her to right where He wanted her to be.

"Nothing's wasted. Not with God. Sometimes you just need to have faith that He's got what's next."

She folded her hands in her lap and opened her heart heavenward, a tentative prayer taking shape, halting and slightly uncomfortable. *What's next, then? What do You want for me?*

Some part of her had hoped for a dramatic, unmistakable answer, but in its place, she received a still, small conviction.

It was time to stop hiding beneath hurt and fear and take a step forward in faith.

She picked up her phone and replayed Mitchell's message. With a deep breath, she punched Call and listened as it dialed him back. She fully expected to get voice mail or his secretary, but Mitchell Shaw answered on the second ring.

She stumbled over the greeting. "Uh, hi. This is Rachel Bishop returning your call."

Mitchell didn't seem to notice her awkwardness. "Rachel! I'm glad to hear from you. I thought perhaps you'd changed your mind. I'm very interested in hearing about your vision for a new restaurant. The way you improvised in the power failure shows the kind of flexibility I want in a business partner."

"Thank you. I wanted to make sure that I had a solid business plan for you before I called you back." It was mostly true. She'd been tweaking the plan all week, even if she'd not been able to make herself pick up the phone.

"I'm over at the Seventeenth Street building this morning, but I can slip out for a bit about eleven. Any chance that would work for you?"

Rachel had been expecting him to suggest a time next week or even next month, and it took a second to get her mouth up to speed. "Of course. There's a restaurant in the station that serves an impeccable espresso, on the hotel side—"

"I know it," he said immediately. "Eleven o'clock then. I'm looking forward to it."

"Me too. Thank you."

Rachel hung up, still stunned. She'd never expected this to happen so quickly. She breathed slowly until the jitters in her stomach subsided and she felt solid again. She'd suggested The English Department because it was the closest to home turf she had right now, and being comfortable was an essential part of any negotiation. Make no mistake: this would be a negotiation.

She rummaged through her closet until she found the most business-appropriate outfit she owned: a pair of black slacks and a blue button-down, which she paired with her favorite silver hoop earrings. She twisted her hair into a neat knot at the nape of her neck, like she would wear it in her restaurant. A serious look. One that showed she meant business. Mitchell was ready to invest; all she had to do was convince him she was a risk worth taking.

Alex had called this "chef hair." She cut off the memory of how he had slowly removed the pins from her hair one by one, combing his fingers through it the night he kissed her for the first time. That would never happen again. There were a lot of things involving him that would never happen again.

And yet he had been right about her, then and now—about how she hid behind the trappings of her profession, afraid to let anyone see the real her. She pulled the pins out and let her hair tumble down around her shoulders.

She put on enough makeup to look finished, then printed out a copy of the business plan and the menu she had completed last night and placed them carefully in a presentation folder.

It was still only ten o'clock, but she was too jittery to wait around for an hour, so she packed a serious-looking tote bag and headed to her car. At least she could stake out the place, get something to drink, calm her nerves.

She managed to snag a metered spot across the street from the Shaw Building, a block off Union Station. This time she paid attention to her surroundings, the people who dotted the sidewalk. If all went well, this would be her new neighborhood. In the morning, it was businessmen taking late breakfasts or early lunches, mothers with babies in strollers, Korean tourists thumbing through their Hangul guidebooks. It was a side of the city she rarely experienced. She was far more familiar with its flip side: the partiers, theatergoers, and transients that dotted the streets when the sun went down.

How strange to think how one-sided her view of the city had been. How odd to realize the variety that existed outside the windowless walls of a kitchen.

She made it a point to wander past the empty retail spaces on the bottom floor of the Shaw Building, letting herself imagine one of those huge spaces as her own blank canvas. Thousands of people walking by every day, thousands of people who would see her name above the door.

This was the break she hadn't known she'd been waiting for.

Rachel made her way down the street to Union Station and into the restaurant, where she marched to the counter and ordered an Americano. Then she took her glass to a table by the window, where she could observe the passersby. No wonder Alex loved this place as much as she did. It was world-class people-watching, a playground for someone who made his living off observing the outside world.

The thought of Alex brought with it a bittersweet pang of longing that so fully enveloped her, she didn't notice Mitchell Shaw arrive until he was standing in front of her.

She blinked dumbly at him and he gave her a patient smile. "May I join you, or are you waiting for someone else?"

A self-conscious laugh slipped from her lips. "Of course. Sorry. I was just thinking how different downtown looks in the morning."

He seated himself across from her. "Too many years locked in a windowless kitchen?"

"Something like that."

"Then we'll make sure you have windows in your new one. There's nothing that says the kitchen has to be located in the back." He spread his hands wide. "But this is your show. Tell me what you're thinking."

Rachel turned the presentation folder toward him and flipped it open. "If you know Paisley, which you likely do, you've got a good idea of my culinary point of view. My tasting menus have consistently sold out, so this time I'm proposing a menu composed almost entirely of small plates."

"Plenty of restaurants are using that concept already."

"Plenty of restaurants don't have me as a chef." Rachel smiled, but she held his eye so he didn't think she was kidding. This was not the time for false humility. "I would make everything available à la carte, as well as within thematically arranged tasting menus."

He flipped the menu card over and his eyebrows rose. "That's interesting. Familiar, but still a unique hook. There's no one doing it quite this way in Denver. I see you've got one menu that's completely comprised of unusual dishes."

"Since we'd be sourcing our meat and vegetables locally from organic farmers, I'd take a nose-to-tail, root-to-stem approach. Special tasting menus are a good way to do that, giving adventurous eaters a story to tell while not alienating more timid guests. The clientele who will eat pork jowl and offal are not necessarily the same as those who want scallops and hanger steak. There should be something for both groups."

He began skimming the business plan. "I'll want to take this with me and look over the numbers, but it seems to be in line with what I had in mind."

"If I may ask, what *did* you have in mind?"

"Lower floor of my Seventeenth Street building, prime location. You'll have visibility from the street, potential to build out the space to your specifications." He smiled. "Including the kitchen on the window side. It would be a novel take on the exhibition kitchen idea. I contribute the space and the build-out; you contribute the rest."

"In return for what?"

"Fifty percent."

"Gross?"

"Net."

Rachel carefully let out a breath. It was generous. Rent on that space would easily be in the six figures per year. If he took his cut from profit and not receipts, and she had reduced overhead from not having a traditional lease, she could see a return on her investment in months, not years.

She reined in her excitement. "I want full creative and administrative control. Menu, staff, seating hours."

He shook his head. "I'm sorry. That's not possible."

"Why not?"

"You'll have input, but I still reserve the right to make a final decision. That space would command nearly $175,000 in lease income. You'll be making back your investment long before I do. Should you make any decisions that hurt the restaurant, I'd be the one taking the hit. Remember, I'm not the only one affected here. My shareholders, my tenants, even the foundations I support rely on me to make wise business decisions. And if you'll excuse my bluntness, you have somewhat of a flawed track record here in Denver."

Rachel's thoughts spun while she processed Mitchell's words. What he was asking wasn't unreasonable. He was putting up a big investment between lost income and out-of-pocket construction costs. Besides, this wasn't a quiet opening in some revitalized neighborhood. This would be a high-profile return to Denver's food scene. She would be in the same class as the other award-winning chefs with their own places in Union Station and Larimer Square. A destination for travelers and locals alike.

And yet, this conversation felt all too familiar. This was how her relationship with Dan and Maurice had begun, reasonable caution against potential risk. She'd had to compromise little by little, until the restaurant barely resembled her initial vision. She'd been afraid to stand up to them, afraid that they would pull their support and Paisley would go under. Afraid that without their help, she would reveal herself to be a failure. If she were completely truthful, she'd lost her restaurant long before they'd bought her out.

"Rachel?"

She folded her hands atop the table and let her gaze roam around the restaurant. "Every time I come here, I think, 'If I had it to do over again, I might have a place like this.' It's on trend and yet it has a sense of place in the community. I like that it's accessible to everyone for the cost of a pastry." She pulled her eyes back to the man across from her. "Admittedly, it will cost you fifteen bucks, but that's a low-enough entry fee to a beautiful spot in a historical landmark."

Mitchell's brow furrowed. "What are you saying?"

Rachel swiveled her menu toward herself and looked it over like it was the first time. It was excellent, both technically and creatively. But she had no more connection to it than she did to any of the dishes she'd created in other people's restaurants. She was confining herself to what would appeal to the Denver foodies and their expectations for high-end dining. In some ways, Alex's Russian dinner was a better meal than her own. Truly good food had to do more than fill the stomach. It should touch the heart, tug on memory.

The realization flew in the face of everything on which she had staked her career.

Ana's words came back to her: *Independent. Determined. Willing to hold out for what we really want, whatever that is.*"

And now, what she really wanted was a chance to do things her way. It would be on a smaller scale. It would probably be regarded by her fellow chefs as a big step down, a cautionary tale of what poor judgment could bring. But she couldn't go on indefinitely, too afraid to try.

Rachel took a deep breath. "I'm honored by your confidence in me. It's a generous offer. It's better than what I thought I could command after what happened at Paisley. But ultimately, I think I need the freedom to explore what kind of chef I want to be." She looked him in the eye, thought she saw a spark of growing respect there. "I might succeed or I might fail spectacularly. But I've let other people tell me who I am and what I should be for far too long."

Mitchell nodded slowly. "I'll admit I'm a little disappointed. I was there on Paisley's opening night, while we were still under construction on the building, and I told Kathy I was going to steal the chef for our flagship restaurant."

Rachel stared at him. "You didn't come to the supper club as a favor to Alex?"

"I came because it was a chance to see what kind of person you are away from the restaurant. I like to know who I'm doing business with. Talent only counts for so much if it's not matched by character." Mitchell chuckled. "Plus, Alex is like a son to me. I wanted to see this woman he was so taken with."

She rose and held out her hand. "I'm sorry to have wasted your time, Mr. Shaw."

He rose as well, but instead of shaking her hand, he took it in both of his. "You didn't waste anything, Rachel. I'll be watching to see what you do next."

He strode away without a backward glance, and Rachel lowered herself to her chair on shaking legs. She'd just turned down the offer of a lifetime.

And she didn't regret it.

As the adrenaline seeped from her body, a

weary, helpless laugh welled up in its place. Mitchell had known about her long before the supper club existed. All that striving and worrying and determination to make something happen, and it would have come about on its own one way or another. She might as well not have done the supper club at all.

She would never have gotten to know Alex and gotten her heart broken.

Wouldn't have broken his in the process.

And yet God had used him to help open her eyes, help her see that maybe she wasn't just a name above the door of a restaurant, that she had something to offer just by being herself. Yes, he should have talked to her earlier, told her what he was doing, but earlier she might not have been ready to hear it. Maybe she'd needed to first let go of one dream to embrace another.

Before she could embrace him.

She pulled out her cell phone and, heedless of the restaurant full of people, dialed. It went to voice mail on the first ring.

"Alex, it's Rachel. I read your manuscript." She swallowed and reordered her thoughts. "I need to see you. I wasn't fair to you. Call me, please? That is, if you can forgive me?"

She set her phone down in the center of the table where she'd be sure to see it ring. Then she went to the counter and ordered another coffee, daring to dream about what might come next.

Chapter Thirty-Four

"Johnny, pull the gratin out of the oven, will you?"

Rachel threw the question over her shoulder as she ran her knife through the pile of walnuts on her cutting board. She scooped up the pieces and transferred them to the salad bowl.

Melody appeared at Rachel's elbow. "What can I do?"

"Slice up that beautiful *miche* you brought and put it on the table with the butter?"

Melody immediately pulled a serrated bread knife off the magnetic strip while Rachel finished tossing the salad.

"Wait, the soup. Behind you . . ." Rachel wove around Johnny, grabbed two towels, and lifted the enameled cast iron pot from the range top. This kitchen wasn't designed for more than one cook, and yet somehow the inefficiency didn't bother her. No one was watching or judging here. No one was anxious to get out and on with their evening. Tonight there was no agenda beyond food and conversation.

She placed the pot on a trivet in the center of the table and called, "Dinner's on, everyone!"

Slowly, guests made their way from the living room, cocktails and glasses of wine in hand.

Chairs scraped the wood floor while they seated themselves. Rachel remained standing at the head of the table.

"Welcome to the Saturday Night Supper Club, take two. It might be a little less fancy than the first version, but what we lack in refinement, we make up for in volume."

The guests laughed, sending knowing looks at the crowd of dishes at the center of the table. No plated meals, she had decided. No fancy design or rare ingredients. Just good hearty food and plenty of it, served family style like the staff dinners she had loved. Appropriately, half of the guests were friends and coworkers with some connection to Paisley: Melody, Ana, Camille, and Johnny. The rest were newcomers to her table: Johnny's roommate, Regan, a medical student who kept as odd hours as the cook; Camille's friend Vanessa, who was a hairstylist at a downtown salon; and Melody's bakery coworker, Hugo. It was a friendly, outgoing group that had found commonalities from the moment they walked in the door.

And yet Rachel couldn't help but feel one conspicuous absence. It had been eight days, and Alex hadn't returned her call. After she'd moped around for four of those with her phone glued to her hand like a permanent appendage, Ana had taken her by the shoulders and demanded that she pull herself together.

"Find something to do, Rachel," she had said. "If he's going to call, he's going to call. But I swear if you're that anxious to talk on the phone, I'm going to put you at the reception desk at my office and make you field the incoming calls. While wearing a business suit."

Melody had shushed Ana, but the silly threat had been enough to snap Rachel from her melancholy, even though she feared Alex's silence was an answer she didn't want to hear. She'd asked Alex to call her back if he could forgive her. He hadn't. Seemed like a pretty clear answer.

"So, Rachel, why do I think you've got something important to tell us?" Camille leaned forward hopefully, her eyes sparkling.

"I do," Rachel said slowly, "but it's probably not what you think."

Melody and Ana looked at her in puzzlement. She'd told them that she'd turned down Mitchell Shaw's offer, but even they didn't know about her most recent conclusions. Now that it was time, jitters danced in her stomach. It was one thing to make a decision privately, another to say it aloud and make it true.

"I was recently approached by an investor who wanted to open a restaurant with me near Union Station—" Johnny and Camille grinned in anticipation—"but I turned him down."

"What?" Johnny asked.

"I have decided that I want to go a different direction for my next restaurant." She took a breath. "In the meantime, I have applied to CU Denver for the winter semester and I'm going to be teaching at a culinary school in the fall."

Ana and Melody looked as stunned as Camille and Johnny.

Camille voiced what they were all no doubt thinking. "Why?"

"I always felt like I missed my chance by not going to college. I want to better understand all the disciplines I've been missing—marketing, accounting, economics—so when I do open my restaurant, I have all the tools I need to be successful. I won't need to take a partner to fill in the gaps. And as for the teaching . . . I wouldn't have the life I have now if it weren't for cooking. I like the idea of passing my knowledge on."

"I can't say I'm not disappointed," Camille said. "Johnny and I were kind of hoping when we walked away from Paisley, we'd be going back to work for you."

Before, those words would have spiked guilt in Rachel, but not now. She could only follow the path before her and trust God would send her the right people to join her at the right time. She had no doubt He would be there beside her. "I know you'll find the perfect place. And if you two need a recommendation, you know where to find me. For what it's worth."

She seated herself and held out her hand. "What are you waiting for? Dig in."

The lids came off dishes; bread was passed; wine was poured. Vanessa turned out to be an enthusiastic home cook, and she peppered Rachel with questions about the meal: ingredients, timing, technique. Rachel didn't mind. She'd done the same thing in her days as a food runner, until they put a knife in her hand to shut her up.

Down the table, Camille and Melody were debating the respective merits of the music scenes in Austin, Nashville, and New Orleans, while Regan and Ana were talking about Manila. It turned out Regan had been an Air Force kid who spent his early years in the Philippines while his dad was stationed at Clark Air Base.

Rachel smiled and took the bread board as it was passed to her, warmed by the experience of strangers becoming friends over a table full of food. Wasn't that what she'd always wanted, both as a child and at her restaurant? To be part of the warmth, the particular intimacy that only came from sitting down and sharing a meal with people who were important to her?

A knock rattled her front door. She excused herself and rose to answer it. When she opened it, she blinked in disbelief.

"Alex? What are you doing here?"

He was dressed as always in jeans and a T-shirt, a week's worth of growth covering his face. He looked more rugged than usual but every bit as handsome. She couldn't quell the leap of her heart at his unexpected presence.

"I got your message." He looked past her at a sudden spill of laughter. "Are you having a party?"

"Saturday Night Supper Club, part two." She stepped out onto the porch and closed the door behind her, her heart thumping a drumbeat. When she crossed her arms over her chest, it was as much a barrier against him as the night's chill. "I had begun to think you weren't speaking to me."

"No! I was in Breckenridge and I forgot my phone charger. I didn't even think to check my messages until I got home—" He broke off as if he realized that wasn't really what mattered anyway. "I'm sorry. I never meant for you to think I was angry with you."

"What were you doing in Breckenridge?"

"Working. Finishing my proposal." He grimaced. "Rachel, it's not what you think. I know I should have told you what I was writing before I sent it to Christine, made sure you were okay with it. I truly never meant to hurt you or betray your trust—"

As much as she was enjoying seeing him flustered, he looked so miserable she couldn't let him continue to think the worst. She stepped forward and stilled his words with a finger to his lips. "I read it."

"And?"

"It was beautiful." Even now, she had to fight the prick of tears. "I never imagined when you were writing about me, it would be something like that."

"Then why did you turn down Mitchell? I almost didn't believe him when he told me. That was your dream."

"I realized that I've spent so many years trying to prove I could be successful, I never stopped to wonder what I should be successful at. I figured if I calculated my risks, played the odds, executed everything perfectly, no one would know I felt like a fraud.

"But your words that night, your essay—they made me realize I'm not going to be happy trying to be something I'm not. God made me this way for a reason, and it's time to embrace it. See what else He has in mind for me."

He captured her hand. "Does that mean I haven't ruined everything between us?"

She stepped closer and looked up into his face, so filled with hope. "Not if you can forgive me. I said I trusted you and then immediately thought the worst of you when you've done nothing but support me. I'm sorry."

He threaded his hand through her hair and tilted her head back so he could look into her eyes. "I love you, Rachel Bishop. I have for longer than you realize. And whatever we do from this point on, I want to do it together."

He kissed her gently, a whisper of a promise, a hint of tomorrows to come. She had trusted him with the scared, uncomfortable parts of herself and he'd held her heart carefully, seeing her whole where she thought she was broken, strong where she thought she was weak. He didn't complete her any more than success or acclaim did, but he'd given her the gift of seeing herself as God did, as someone who was worthy of love.

She stepped back and swiped away the sudden swell of tears. "Do you want to join us for dinner?"

"Do you have to ask?"

Rachel laughed as she took his hand and pushed the door open, her heart suddenly light. She led him into the kitchen, and the conversation immediately stopped.

"Everyone, I'd like you to meet Alex."

Ana and Melody looked at her as if to confirm it was okay to welcome him in. Rachel gave a quick nod, and the guests reshuffled themselves at the table to make room for an extra chair next to Rachel. She retrieved a plate and cutlery from the kitchen, set his place carefully, and then settled beside him.

Beneath the table, he reached for her hand and gave it a squeeze.

The group had already moved on to a heated discussion about what kind of restaurant Rachel should open, but she didn't object, too filled with gratitude to spoil their fun. Besides, if she'd learned one thing, it was that their guess about the future was at least as accurate as hers.

For now, she had a man she adored, loyal friends, and a sense of contentment she hadn't felt since those long-ago Sundays filled with love and powdered-sugar donuts. And that was enough.

A Note from the Author

It was this food nerd/writer's dream come true to set a book in the middle of Denver's thriving food scene—Rachel's restaurant and the supper club would feel right at home in the Mile High City. While Denver's real neighborhoods and landmarks set the backdrop for this story, all the restaurants mentioned are works of fiction. However, with so many inspiring chefs and restaurants in the city, I couldn't help but take my cue from real places.

Rachel's restaurant, Paisley, has no exact correlation in the real world, but I did borrow its Larimer Square location from Jennifer Jasinski's excellent Mediterranean restaurant, Rioja. If you're curious about the interior design, I loosely based the description off another of my favorites, Lon Symensma's ChoLon Bistro on Sixteenth and Blake.

Rhino Crash, the funky bar and food truck pod in the River North neighborhood, is a near-double for the quirky Finn's Manor, home to some of the city's best food trucks.

The girls' breakfast joint in the Ballpark neighborhood is an unabashed reference to the original location of Snooze, a retro-styled breakfast-brunch-cocktail spot that has now expanded to multiple locations in Colorado, Arizona, California, and Texas.

Lastly, The English Department was an excuse to pay homage to my very favorite spot in the city: Alex Seidel's Mercantile Dining & Provision at Union Station. If Rachel waxed a bit too eloquent when she visited, it's only because of my own barely restrained foodie glee.

About the Author

Carla Laureano is the RITA® Award–winning author of contemporary inspirational romance and Celtic fantasy (as C. E. Laureano). A graduate of Pepperdine University, she worked as a sales and marketing executive for nearly a decade before leaving corporate life behind to write fiction full-time. She currently lives in Denver with her husband and two sons, where she writes during the day and cooks things at night. Visit Carla online at www.carlalaureano.com.

Discussion Questions

1. Rachel's memories, good and bad, tend to be associated with food. What are your best and worst memories that are tied to food? Do you think they endure longer because of the association?

2. Alex criticizes the fact that public figures are treated as if their lives exist for public consumption. Do you feel that the media oversteps its boundaries, or is it merely a hazard that creatives and celebrities should expect to shoulder as the price of success? How would you feel if you were attempting to live in a similar spotlight?

3. Rachel rejects the idea of being a spokesperson for women in the food service industry and resents having to put her personal life on display, citing the fact that men aren't required to talk about anything but their cooking. Do you think women who reach the highest levels of their professions are obligated to speak out? Is that an unfair burden? Why or why not?

4. Alex struggles with freedom in his faith journey, wishing for a rule book. Do you relate to that feeling? Why or why not?

5. A single misrepresented comment of

Rachel's goes viral, leading to the shattering of her career. What do you think that says about social media in particular and society in general? What responsibility do we as Christians have to investigate the truth and temper our response to what we hear and read?

6. Because of her difficult family background and feelings of betrayal, Rachel looks for alternative families in both her kitchen staff and her best friends. What does that say about our innate need for belonging? Is our biological family different from our chosen one? Contrast the way her colleagues react to her crisis versus how her friends react.

7. Alex possesses a deep need to fix things and take responsibility for his actions. How is this a good thing? How might it also be problematic?

8. Both Alex and Rachel have experienced the weight of not living up to their families' expectations. How are their reactions similar? How are they different, and why?

9. Rachel hides behind her title and the trappings of her profession. Why do you think this is? How does she change over the course of the book?

10. Alex tells Rachel that he's learned "all the hustle in the world won't get me anywhere if it's not [God's] will." Later, Rachel has

a similar realization about her work and striving over her career prospects. What does this say about the tension between hard work or diligence and faith? What have your personal experiences taught you about this balance?

11. Rachel misunderstands the meaning of the e-mail and notes she sees in Alex's home and jumps to the worst conclusion. How is this similar to what happened to her on social media? What does this say about our natural tendencies as humans?

12. Near the story's end, Rachel prays for direction, hoping for "a dramatic, unmistakable answer," but receives only "a still, small conviction." Was it enough for her? How do you discern God's guidance—and what form does it usually take?

13. How does the evolution of the supper club format mirror Rachel's own personal journey? How is this a significant change from the beginning of the book?

| Books are produced in the United States using U.S.-based materials | Books are printed using a revolutionary new process called THINKtech™ that lowers energy usage by 70% and increases overall quality | Books are durable and flexible because of smythe-sewing | Paper is sourced using environmentally responsible foresting methods and the paper is acid-free |

Center Point Large Print
600 Brooks Road / PO Box 1
Thorndike, ME 04986-0001 USA

(207) 568-3717

US & Canada:
1 800 929-9108
www.centerpointlargeprint.com